A SONG
WITH
TEETH

A SONG WITH TEETH

A Los Nefilim Novel

T. FROHOCK

HARPER Voyager
An Imprint of HarperCollinsPublishers

A SONG WITH TEETH. Copyright © 2021 by Teresa Frohock. All rights reserved. Printed in the United States of America. No part of this book may be used or reproduced in any manner whatsoever without written permission except in the case of brief quotations embodied in critical articles and reviews. For information, address Harper-Collins Publishers, 195 Broadway, New York, NY 10007.

HarperCollins books may be purchased for educational, business, or sales promotional use. For information, please email the Special Markets Department at SPsales@harpercollins.com.

Harper Voyager and design are trademarks of HarperCollins Publishers LLC.

FIRST EDITION

Designed by Paula Russell Szafranski

Frame on title page © Shutterstock

Library of Congress Cataloging-in-Publication Data has been applied for.

ISBN 978-0-06-282577-3

21 22 23 24 25   LSC   10 9 8 7 6 5 4 3 2 1

For Glinda Harrison

constant reader, constant friend

AUTHOR'S NOTE

A quick note on the spellings used: the accepted spelling of the word is *Nephilim*. However, in Spanish the *ph* sound is replaced by the *f*, hence *Los Nefilim*.

This novel is primarily told from the points of view of my Spanish characters, so whenever I need to use the generic term *Nephilim* to indicate the species of Nephilim as a whole, I use the spelling *nefilim* (the lowercase *n* is intentional for plural *nefilim* as well as the singular *nefil*).

I also needed a way in which to distinguish the various nationalities of nefilim within the Inner Guard. Whenever you see capitalization—Los Nefilim, Die Nephilim, or Les Néphilim—I am referring to the Inner Guard's different divisions—the Spanish, German, and French, respectively.

While each of the Los Nefilim novellas and the novels can be read as stand-alone works, several characters and themes do recur. Likewise, those keeping up with the series might enjoy a mild refresher, as well.

The novellas (*In Midnight's Silence*, *Without Light or Guide*, and *The Second Death*) all served as an introduction into the world of Los Nefilim, as well as forming the basis for discovering the Key—the song that will enable the nefilim to open the realms as the angels do. The novels, which began with *Where Oblivion Lives*, concern Diago's actual composition of the Key. Somewhat like an opera in three parts, the story follows the crucial points that lead our heroes to the next act of the movement.

I understand that people might not remember the terminology from one story to another. With that in mind, I included a glossary in the back of this novel.

To remedy any memory gaps the reader might have, I'm also including a very brief, spoiler-free synopsis of the events from previous episodes. Again, to be clear: each of the novellas and novels can be read as stand-alone works.

However, I always imagined Los Nefilim as a serial, much like the old *Shadow* radio serials. In keeping with that tone, here is the story so far . . .

1931 (The *Los Nefilim* omnibus contains the novellas
In Midnight's Silence, Without Light or Guide, **and**
The Second Death)

Diago Alvarez, a rarity among the nefilim in that his mother was an angel and his father was a daimon-born nefil, discovers that he has a six-year-old son named Rafael. Having never officially joined Los Nefilim—the Spanish Inner Guard—Diago has always lived as a rogue. He maintains a superficial connection to Los Nefilim through his husband, Miquel de Torrellas, who is Guillermo Ramírez's second-in-command.

Rafael's presence changes Diago's priorities. The only way

he can protect his son from his daimonic kin is by joining Los Nefilim. Diago swears an oath to Guillermo Ramírez, the king of Los Nefilim, who wants Diago to try and compose the Key—the song that will enable the nefilim to open the realms as the angels do.

1932 (*Where Oblivion Lives*)

Now a member of Los Nefilim, Diago leaves Spain in order to solve the mystery of his missing violin, which torments his dreams. It's his first official mission as a member of the Inner Guard, and he succeeds in both solving the mystery and confronting his PTSD from the Great War. During the course of these events, Guillermo discovers traitors within his own ranks that are working for his brother, Jordi Abelló, who has returned to undermine Guillermo's right to command Los Nefilim. At the end of 1932, Diago and Guillermo work together and finally compose the first notes to the Key.

1939 (*Carved from Stone and Dream*)

Guillermo's forces have lost the war, and in a desperate attempt to escape, Los Nefilim flees to France. Diago is with Guillermo when a coded notebook is stolen. Together, they follow the traitor into the caverns beneath the Pyrenees only to find that Guillermo's brother, Jordi, is running a covert site that engages in medical experiments. For subjects, he is using the members of Los Nefilim that his soldiers find in the French concentration camps, including Diago's husband, Miquel, and his son, Rafael. Jordi has also uncovered one of the Grigori, a group of angels that committed such vile crimes against the mortals, they were cast out of the angelic realms. Jordi wears the Grigori's tear in a signet and has sworn himself to the fallen angels. Guillermo and Diago manage to recover the notebook and rescue Miquel and Rafael. It is Rafael who discovers the next movement of the Key.

Now the year is 1943. The Germans have invaded France and Los Nefilim have been ordered to lead the resistance. Our story begins in France . . .

PROLOGUE

Inner Guard Division: **Los Nefilim**
Don Guillermo Ramírez, Capitán General
Servicio de Investigación Militar
17 June 1940
SIM Report No. 708399

To the Honorable General Jonathan Lauer,
United States Nephilim:

I file this report in the name of Madame
Sabine Rousseau, Capitaine Général, Les
Néphilim. She asked that I inform the
American division of the Inner Guard
regarding the situation in France. Madame
Rousseau likewise requested that I extend
her gratitude to the United States Inner
Guard for persuading the mortals to
sell weapons to the French and British

governments during their ongoing conflict
with the Germans.

A pity this same munificence wasn't offered
to save Spain, but like you, I understand
the difficulty of influencing mortal
decisions. Unfortunately, the very world war
you hoped to avoid is now at our doorstep.

As you probably already know, the German
forces led by the rogue nefil, Jordi Abelló,
and Queen Ilsa Jaeger of Die Nephilim,
have conquered France in forty-six days.
The attack was an unprecedented success
primarily due to the drug Pervitin.

Based on Abelló's experiments during the
Spanish Civil War, the mortal generals dosed
themselves and their soldiers with this form
of methamphetamine to create an army of
berserkers. Utilizing Pervitin in the field,
the German soldiers were able to remain
awake for days at a time. The speed of
their attack allowed their panzer units to
raze France at great cost to the French and
British armies.

Nor did Abelló and Jaeger limit their
Pervitin experiments to mortals. The drug
gives a nefil the strength of an angel.
According to my second-in-command, General
Miquel de Torrellas—who was an unwilling
subject in those tests—such medically

augmented power comes at a terrible price,
both physical and mental.

In spite of the consequences, Abelló and
Jaeger found volunteers and medicated four
of their oldest nefilim with the drug: Irma
Koch, Gustav Frank, Hermine Bothe, and Ernst
Zweigelt. Bothe went insane and destroyed
herself. Frank and Koch died of heart
attacks within a month of one another. I
dispatched a team of assassins, and as of 5
June 1940, Zweigelt is no longer a threat.

We will watch for them.

The severity of the side effects appears
to have made an impression on Abelló and
Jaeger. They have abandoned further measures
to enhance their nefilim's songs, whether
through choice or due to a lack of willing
participants, we don't know.

The Nazis currently control northern France
and the western coast; Vichy France is
merely a puppet government with the elderly
mortal, Marshal Philippe Pétain, as its
figurehead and another mortal, Pierre Laval,
pulling the strings for their Nazi masters.

While not as aggressive as the Germans, the
Vichy government is rounding up members of
the Jewish, Roma, and Sinti populations for
deportation. Spanish Republicans, who had

taken refuge in France, are likewise placed on ghost trains and sent to concentration camps in the east.

As I indicated earlier, Madame Rousseau and her angelic consort, Cyrille, have accompanied the French government to London. Please forward any replies to this missive to Madame Rousseau's attention in care of General Elizabeth Cromwell, Special Operations Executive, British Division of the Nephilim, in London.

Rousseau continues to advise Charles de Gaulle, the leader of Free France. We received a transmission on the wireless this afternoon that both Rousseau and de Gaulle landed safely in London. It is our hope that Churchill will give de Gaulle time on the BBC to rally the French.

Los Nefilim has established a temporary base in the Free Zone, close to the Pyrenees, so that we can assist refugees fleeing the Nazi regime's policies. Members of Los Nefilim escort the evacuees over the Pyrenees into Andorra. My people can go no farther, because the Spanish nefilim remain under the command of Abelló's lieutenant, Benito Espina.

Communiqués with nefilim in Poland and Russia indicate the daimon-born nefilim are taking advantage of the angel-born nefilim's disarray. Our intelligence suggests the distinct possibility of the nefilim's war opening on another front.

Los Nefilim stands in a unique position, because we have a member who is half-angel, half-daimon. I authorized Diago Alvarez to initiate contact with his daimon-born kin; he now serves as a double agent under the code name Dragonfly, and he reports directly to me. Should anything happen to me, or to my council, let this letter serve as exoneration of his interactions with the daimon-born while under my direction.

We remain in touch with London via wireless and coded letters. Rousseau and her British counterparts are kept up-to-date with any intelligence we are able to send, and she will forward those missives to you as she sees fit.

This is not our first guerrilla war. We played this game in Spain to drive the French from our territories during the Peninsula War. We'll use the same measures to push the Germans back across the Rhine.

It's merely a matter of time.

And time is nothing to the nefilim.

[1]

VICHY, FRANCE

Diago sat at the café's rear table, his back against the wall. He wasn't hungry; not for food. Regardless, he made sure to eat, pretending to linger over his lunch and a book. He'd read the same paragraph five times and still couldn't recall the meaning of the words. Nonetheless, he finally turned the page with his left hand so that no one would notice the missing pinkie on his right.

As he did, he kept his ear attuned to the radio on the counter, which played Radio Paris and its Nazi-approved propaganda. The reliability of the café's signal was the primary reason Diago had chosen the restaurant.

He gave the room another glance. Other than the waiter attending the tables, no one seemed to notice him—a well-dressed man dining alone on a hot summer evening. His clothing was neither too ostentatious nor too modest, and in shades of blue that were popular among the mortals.

His only jewelry was the wedding band on his left hand, and a large signet on his right. The setting of the latter contained a crimson jewel threaded with silver streaks.

Another nefil would recognize the gem as an angel's tear, yet he couldn't bring himself to part with it. The very item that might give him away could also augment the magic within his song to save his life. Besides, wearing the ring allowed his husband peace of mind. *And Miquel has too many worries as it is.*

Only during this war had Diago come to fully appreciate his husband's concern for the lives under his care. As a rogue, Diago had been responsible for no one but himself. Now that he was a member of Los Nefilim, he oversaw three lines of spies in occupied France—one of which he feared was compromised.

His Parisian contact, who went by the code name Nightingale, was supposed to relay a message over Radio Paris this afternoon: Mozart's Requiem in D minor meant their line of spies was compromised; an original composition indicated they were safe.

Diago checked his watch. It was almost time for the Nightingale's program.

Remembering his meal, he took another bite of pasta, barely tasting it. He chewed and swallowed with mechanical precision.

His stomach clenched around the food. *Stress . . . it's only the stress of waiting.* Once he knew his people were safe, he'd be fine.

Maintaining his posture, he kept his discomfort from showing on his face. That was a trick his abusive family had taught him when he was a child. Never let anyone see your pain. Under their violence, he'd learned to remain in a state of constant vigilance, hyperaware of the moods of the people around him and his surroundings.

One would almost think they'd trained me to be a spy. The thought twisted one corner of his mouth into a wry smile. How poetic that he'd managed to turn those very skills against his kin.

The announcer's voice purred through the speakers and introduced the next program. Diago forced another bite of food down his throat.

A moment of static and then the Nightingale, whose real name was Nico Bianchi, spoke in French of the upcoming entertainment. Diago's practiced ear caught the faint Italian lilt still lurking within Nico's accent, but he doubted the mortals did.

Without much ado, Nico directed his string quartet to play an original composition. Diago's stomach cramps eased. His people were safe. At least for one more day. He took two more bites of his meal but made no move to leave. Nico composed elegant arrangements, and Diago wanted to enjoy the music.

As he listened, he noted a subtle change insert itself under the main melody. The violinist faltered as if unsure of the notes before him.

And then the music segued from an original composition to become Mozart's Requiem.

A door slammed within the studio. The cello squawked as the bow raked the strings. An instrument cried out as it dropped to the floor.

A few diners turned to look at the radio as if suddenly noticing its presence. The speakers hissed with static.

Dead air. Diago's throat tightened. Someone had cut the transmission. They were compromised. *Fuck, fuck, and fuck.*

Without missing a beat, the waiter reached over and twisted the dial, shutting it off. The other diners returned to their meals, hesitantly at first, but soon the murmur of conversations resumed amid the clatter of silverware.

Diago's fingers spasmed around his fork. He forced himself to swallow. Bite by bite, he cleaned his plate, closed his book, and took his leave of the café.

Bright sunlight mocked the dark news he'd just received. He turned left and started walking.

The cell of spies they'd code named the Machiavelli line was lost. One nefil and at least eight mortals were now at the Gestapo's mercy.

And how many, in turn, will they implicate? Could he trust the information coming from his other two cells? Or were they, too, giving him disinformation at the Nazis' direction?

Christ . . . Christ. All our work gone as quickly as the compositions had changed. Diago forced himself to stroll until he reached a vacant alley. Stepping into the shadows, he leaned over and vomited his meal to the stones.

Closing his eyes, he took several deep breaths until his nausea passed. Then he drew his handkerchief from his pocket and wiped the sweat from his brow.

Nico, Jesus Christ. We've got to get to Nico. If Jordi Abelló found his former lover in the hands of the Gestapo . . .

Diago shut down the thought before it could take legs and run. Nico knew the risks. He'd asked for the assignment.

To prove himself to Los Nefilim. And no one understood that desire more than Diago. Even so, he'd tried to talk Nico into an easier role, but the Italian had been adamant. *And now it is too late.*

Diago folded his handkerchief and tucked it back into his pocket. Holding his head high, he stepped to the alley's mouth and looked both ways. No one was on the street.

Unobserved, he continued on his way, doing the only thing he knew to do: put one foot in front of the other and keep going. *Just keep going.*

He had a train to catch and an appointment to keep.

Later that afternoon, he left a village train station and hurried down a deserted lane. By evening, he reached the dilapidated cottage where he'd left his gear.

He crept through the door. A shadow moved. He froze. His pulse hammered in his ears. Slowly, so as not to be conspicuous, Diago drew his pistol and aimed it at the shadow.

"Ya, ya, ya," murmured a familiar voice in Spanish. "It's me, Papá."

Rafael stepped from the gloom and held up his hand. He wore a signet similar to Diago's; except the angel's tear within his band was the carmine-colored stone bequeathed to him by Candela, his angelic mother.

While he had Diago's green eyes, he favored Miquel with his black curls and his dark skin. *Fault the angels for their intentions, but their knowledge of genetics is impeccable.* Candela could have passed for Miquel's sister, and the choice she made in her mortal form showed on his son.

In October he would turn eighteen, but his gaze already seemed far older as it flickered to his father's pistol.

Diago tried to ignore the trembling in his hand. *How*

close did I come to shooting my son? "What are you doing here?" The question snapped from his lips sharper than he'd intended.

Rafael didn't flinch. Diago felt bad nonetheless. *He wouldn't be here without cause.*

"The Shepherd sent me."

Code names, dozens of code names. They rattled in his head, except this one he knew without having to search too deep: Guillermo. "And?"

"He needs you back at the farm."

Diago exhaled and holstered his gun. The farm was Guillermo's main base of operations, situated between Tarerach and Perpignan. Diago wasn't due to return for another week. *Something is up.*

Guillermo wouldn't have sent Rafael on a whim, not with the Germans looking for workers his son's age. He might easily be picked up by the Nazis and shipped to any number of factories. *Or to the Russian front.*

They all knew the danger.

Diago paused beside Rafael and kissed his son's cheeks. "I've got one more stop."

Rafael shook his head. "The Shepherd says now. Rousseau is coming with de Gaulle. The Allies have a plan, and we've got to prepare. He wants you to begin work on the Key again."

The Key—the song that could enable the nefilim to shift the realms as the angels did—was almost complete. With it, Los Nefilim might be able to turn the course of the war.

Maybe.

Nothing was certain at this point. For one thing, they had yet to compose the arrangement's final movement, although Guillermo, Diago, Miquel, Rafael, and Guillermo's daughter, Ysabel, had all worked on the composition at some point. Diago didn't hold a lot of hope of them unlocking the chords. Even if they did, so much depended on the calculation of the right glyphs activated by the proper vocal shifts. *And with only one angel to assist us, we'll need to supplant the vocalizations with instruments.*

For another, they still weren't sure it would work anyway.

With their own survival in such a state of flux, and the Key being such a long shot, the song was often secondary to more pressing concerns. For Guillermo to shift the composition to a major priority meant he intended to leave nothing about this invasion to chance.

"I hope he doesn't intend to rely entirely on the Key?"

Rafael shook his head. "No. He just wants every angle covered. Ysa is going on a special mission to retrieve information from his grimoires."

The news should have brought Diago hope; instead, he felt nothing but more terror. Once the Allied forces touched French shores, the fighting would begin in earnest.

Still, what is better? This secretive deadly war of wits, or enemies in plain sight? He no longer knew the answers. His body moved of its own accord, marching forward, always forward.

Diago found his bag and changed clothes. Gone was the urbane gentleman and his fine suit. Now he resembled his son, with his rough shirt and trousers. He hoisted his old service bag over his shoulder. "I've one stop to make."

"Where?"

"The less you know—"

"The less they can drag from my lips. I know. I know.

Maybe I could speak to your contact in your name?" He was eager to step into his father's role as a spy.

He's still so young, he thinks this is a game. Diago glanced across the sunny field and then back to his son. *Or does he?*

The faint scars on Rafael's cheek were barely visible in the ruined cottage's soft light. Like Miquel, Rafael bore the mark of the Grigori they'd fought in the Pyrenees at the end of the Spanish Civil War.

The demented angels known as Grigori were feared by the daimon- and angel-born alike for their ability to possess nefilim and mortals. Cast out of the angelic realms for their crimes, their wings torn from their bodies, they were buried deep beneath the stones of the earth.

Except Jordi Abelló uncovered one in 1939. A vile creature that almost destroyed Miquel and Rafael.

Surviving an encounter with a Grigori was considered a badge of honor. Unlike Miquel, who wished his wartime scars would fade, Rafael wore his disfigurement like a medal. He was a capable youth and good in a fight. Already he'd made a name for himself in the maquisards, the rural guerrilla bands of French youths, who fled into the hills rather than be dragged to Germany's factories.

No. He doesn't think this is a game. But if he is seen too close to my spies . . . It wasn't that Diago feared his son would make a fatal error, he simply feared for his son. *And I've not been able to protect him, no matter how I've tried. These wars have stolen his innocence.*

"Papá?"

"The Machiavelli line has fallen. When our cells are captured, we ask them to try and hold out under torture for at least forty-eight hours. If they can do so, it gives us time to warn others and secure any supplies we have. We can't waste a moment. We don't know who will break or when. This is a message I have to deliver." He had to own his failures and make the others understand the danger. "Keep your distance from me just in case."

Rafael frowned. "In case of what?"

"We don't know who betrayed the Machiavelli line, or whether they've implicated me."

"I won't let anything happen to you, Papá. I promise."

Diago turned toward the bright day. He pretended the burning in his eyes was caused by the sun, but he knew in his heart it was pride. "I don't deserve you."

Rafael grinned and bumped shoulders with Diago. "I love you, too."

Using the uncanny speed of the nefilim, Diago hurried through the encroaching darkness. He made his stop at an outlying farm, where he passed the information about the fallen Machiavelli line to the inhabitants. He was barely inside the cottage before he was out again. His message to the mortal occupants was simple: *The Gestapo knows about you. Destroy evidence, move the ammunition, and flee.*

When he left them, he walked south, taking a back road until he could slip into the forest unobserved. He felt his son's presence as Rafael followed him.

Several kilometers from the farm, Diago finally deemed it safe enough for them to travel together. They met on a hill that overlooked the trestles. A train of cattle cars snaked along the rails.

Although he and Rafael were almost a quarter of a kilometer from the tracks, Diago tasted the despair of the train's occupants. Their misery floated upward, leaving the bitter scent of anxiety rank on the air. Diago's tongue flicked between his lips, and he tasted their panic, tangy and sweet. A pleasurable warmth spread across his chest and down into his stomach.

The physical response, caused by his daimonic nature, was purely involuntary. Touching the angel's tear of his signet, he called on his angelic nature and squelched his daimonic desire to feed on the prisoners' terror. To imbibe initiated a craving that demanded ever-increasing dosages, stripping him of his humanity each time he indulged.

Miquel had taught him control. With empathy and understanding, Diago's husband gave him the tools to resist his daimonic passions.

Diago glanced at Rafael, who wrinkled his nose as if he smelled something bad, but otherwise showed no sign of his daimonic ancestry. Rafael was only a quarter daimon— his mother had been an angel, and Diago was merely half-daimon himself.

None of that mattered to their kin. Diago's father, Alvaro, wanted Rafael and Diago to serve the daimons. That demand was as intense now as it had been when Rafael was a child. *And a good thing that it is.*

Diago had exploited Alvaro's greed to gain a toehold in the Scorpion Court's ranks. Not that they trusted him. Diago had switched sides before, with disastrous results. It was a dangerous waltz and one misstep could bring them all down.

"Ghost train." Rafael's whisper pulled Diago from his thoughts.

Probably leaving the concentration camp at La Vernet for Drancy. "I'm sorry for them."

"Why can't we help them?" The righteous anger in his son's voice ripped Diago's heart. If Rafael had his way, they'd raise their voices in defiance.

And we would die like flies. "We're too few." The Spanish Civil War had decimated the ranks of Los Nefilim, and Rousseau's Néphilim, who had never fully recuperated from the Great War, were now scattered due to Germany's invasion. He didn't need to reiterate these facts to Rafael. *Just cool his hot head so he doesn't do anything rash.* "We'll help them more by putting a definitive end to this war, and that takes time."

"They don't have time."

"Patience." Diago's murmur was almost drowned out by the train's distant horn. "Rousseau is coming with de Gaulle. We must move with care."

Rafael began to walk again. "Then we should get going."

Before following his son, Diago turned north one last time and looked toward the horizon, where Paris lay. He wondered if Nico survived, and if he did, what secrets would he tell?

"Papá?"

Diago tore his gaze from the dark skyline and caught up to his son. He put one foot in front of the other, moving forward. Always forward.

[2]

FRESNES PRISON

Someone was screaming. The long wail rolled through the prison's cellar, turning into an ululation, piercing the frigid air.

Nico sat on the floor of his cell and tuned out the mortal's pain, not from callous disregard, but because he had other worries. He focused on his hand. Three fingers were broken and if he didn't set them soon, he risked being maimed.

Unlike mortals, who took months to heal, a nefil's body rejuvenated at an accelerated rate. New threads of bone cells were shaped within days or weeks to form blood clots around a fracture. If the cells reached bone splinters, the result was the creation of new bone structures. Untended, the growths had the potential to leave a nefil deformed, or dead.

The older the nefil, the faster the healing. At only two hundred years in this incarnation, Nico was barely an adult by the nefilim's standards. But his youth didn't mitigate his danger.

He gingerly tested the middle finger of his left hand. The proximal phalanx was crooked and didn't move with the flexibility of a recent break. In normal circumstances, a broken finger—*or two or three*—wasn't a problem. *Except losing consciousness cost me time.* He had no idea how long he'd been out.

His last session with his interrogators had been one of the most brutal since his arrival several months ago. When he'd kept to his lies, the Gestapo major shrieked his questions at Nico before going icy calm. His last clear memory was seeing the white-hot poker as the major jerked it from the coals.

It's like they're losing patience with me. If he held even the slightest masochistic tendencies from his days with Jordi Abelló, the Gestapo had beaten him free of them. *But I deserve this.* He'd helped Jordi create this monster during the Spanish war. *Now karma is here and it's a motherfucker dressed in swastikas.*

Beneath his shirt, his flesh writhed and struggled to heal around the blisters on his back, spiking his nerves with constant flashes of pain. The healing was almost as bad as the initial injury.

Nico bit his lower lip and shuddered through another wave of agony. When it passed, he forced his attention back to his fingers.

I'll break them again if necessary. He tore a strip of cloth from the tail of his shirt and draped it across his lap. With a shaking hand, he touched the swollen finger. *Begin with the middle, then the ring finger, then the pinkie. But first, the middle.*

Rolling the sleeve of his jacket into a gag, Nico stuffed

it in his mouth and bit down hard. He might never play a guitar again, not with his left hand on the frets.

Doesn't matter. I can learn other ways to play, other instruments. Diago plays the piano with nine fingers . . . this is nothing. He closed his eyes and jerked the bone into place. As he did, his back struck the wall behind him.

Blisters exploded from the contact. He screamed behind his gag. A sob racked his throat. His body flushed with heat. A wave of nausea rolled through his stomach. Shadows blurred his vision. *Don't pass out, don't pass out . . .*

The nausea gradually receded and the room brightened again. He looked down. The finger was still crooked, but not as bad. *It's better.*

Before he could think too much about the pain, he moved to the ring finger, and finally managed to set the pinkie without losing consciousness. He had nothing to serve as a splint, so he bound them together with the strip of his shirt.

Nico relaxed his jaws and let the jacket fall to his thighs. If he lived through this, even Miquel would have to admit Nico's silence came at a price.

Not that he expected any such admission from the older nefil. Miquel held on to his grudge over the events during the winter of '39 and probably would for the next five incarnations. Nothing Nico did seemed to appease him.

So fuck him, just fuck him. At least I'll be able to look him in the eye.

Outside the cell, the other prisoner's screams faded to silence. *Dead or unconscious?* Nico wondered vaguely. *Was he a member of my group?*

Maybe. Anything was possible. Nico only hoped that Diago had heard Mozart's Requiem before the Gestapo stormed the radio studio.

The memory still troubled him. The Machiavelli line had gone down like a house of cards. Nico never imagined the ring of spies to be impregnable, but the speed at which it crumbled had almost taken him off guard. *Who betrayed us? Mortals or nefilim?*

He had to assume it was a mortal. *A nefil would have paid more attention to the compositions.* But his captors hadn't.

Sheer impulse had caused him to grab the sheet music he'd designed to disguise the Requiem that day. *Impulse or premonition? Or maybe just good luck.*

While good fortune might explain bringing the Requiem, it was Diago's research and attention to detail that gave Nico his edge. Diago had passed along photographs of undercover Gestapo agents, which helped Nico recognize the man smoking a cigarette by the studio's entrance.

That was when Nico knew his luck had run out. He snapped to a decision on a moment's notice. To leave without entering the studio might draw the Gestapo to him before he could alert Diago. He'd chosen to carry on; warn Los Nefilim if he could. Besides, the agent's presence didn't necessarily mean the Gestapo were there for him.

Nico had a thousand reasons for what he did, and he was satisfied with all of them. Diago would be proud.

Inside the radio station, Nico had faced another choice: Should he give his quartet the unmodified original composition, the full Requiem, or the modified sheet music that began with an original composition and then segued into the Requiem? The answer came sooner than he expected.

He glanced up when the studio door opened and his musicians filed inside. Standing just outside was the Gestapo agent, who led the station manager into an adjacent office.

Nico gave his quartet the modified composition. He pretended nothing was wrong and began his program on cue.

The agent entered the studio just as Nico guided the musicians into the Requiem. *Was Diago listening?* Nico had no way to know. *But for once in my life, I did the right thing.*

That knowledge had carried him through the torture. When he did talk, he gave the Nazis prepared lies; facts honeyed with just enough truth to make them stick. They, in turn, kept him clinging to life.

Who was it that told me nefilim were notoriously hard to kill? Jordi? Maybe Jordi. Maybe Benito. They both derived so much pleasure from another's pain.

It hadn't always been that way. Not for Jordi, anyway. When Nico had first met him, Jordi was a caring lover. But as he accrued power, his true nature revealed itself.

I thought he'd be a better person without the drugs. Instead, he'd grown more callous by the day, and Nico started to look for a way out of the relationship. But he was in too deep, and Jordi's enemies were suddenly his enemies.

Strangely enough, it was Jordi's brother, Guillermo, who gave Nico a shot at redemption—one he never expected to receive. Being a member of Los Nefilim offered him a slim prospect of safety from Jordi's revenge.

At least, it had. He shuttled the thought aside. If the Gestapo intended to give him to Jordi, he'd already be on his way. *I've got enough trouble without conjuring more.*

More than anything, Guillermo's act had given Nico a chance to make amends. Unfortunately, only Diago seemed to appreciate Nico's efforts. *And that is because Diago knows about mistakes . . . how one bad decision easily leads to another and another and suddenly the pit is too deep to escape.*

The sharp rap of boots marching down the hall jerked him from his thoughts. The footsteps stopped suddenly at his door.

Nico dragged himself upright and got to his feet.

The bolt turned.

A spasm of terror almost drove him back to his knees.

Was this how Miquel felt in that lonely cell? Fear of the unknown eating his soul? Nico sniffed and tasted blood in the back of his throat. *No, I don't wonder that he still hates me.*

Nico never forgot the first time he saw Miquel. He was on his feet and thinking. *He never buckled under the pressure. He never begged.*

Nico straightened his back. *Nor will I.*

The door swung open.

Nico's gaze flickered first to the German's eyes. He searched the officer's gaze for the reflection of light that indicated a nefil. The man's irises were leaden, the color of cold. *Mortal.*

Still dangerous, though. He wore the Waffen-SS's gray uniform; the black collar carried the insignia of SS-Obergruppenführer. With a curt gesture, he waved at Nico's jacket. "Bring your things."

My things. He almost laughed at that. All he had were the clothes on his back and the jacket. He struggled into the coat, pulling it on as quickly as he dared. Even taking care, he felt more blisters rupture across his back.

A thin line of anger lanced his pain. The rage kept him on his feet.

The officer nodded to two subordinates. The soldiers entered the cell and grabbed Nico's arms, hauling him forward. He offered them no resistance. The pain would come soon enough. He didn't need to antagonize them into making it worse.

Instead of turning toward the interrogation cells, however, they forced him toward the gate at the end of the corridor. Hope burst through his chest and warmed his chilled bones.

I'm leaving. They're done with me. At the very least, they were moving him to one of the upper-level cells. *Had Diago found me? He said Los Nefilim never forget one of their own. Has he sent someone to the rescue?*

Nico allowed himself to dream. He'd even be glad to see Miquel right now. *And I'll tell him I'm sorry, and he'll know I mean it. This time, he will know I mean it—he'll see it in my hand and my back and my eyes.*

Then the reality of his situation settled around him again. There wouldn't be a last-minute rescue, and escape was impossible at this point. While Nico still might sing his way to survival at some point, Fresnes was not the place. Too many obstacles lay between him and freedom. The starvation and torture had taken a toll; he was physically too weak to control the mortals' minds for a sustained period. He needed to bide his time.

Let them think I'm beaten. If the opportunity came to escape, he needed the element of surprise. He shuffled between his guards like an old man. For once, he didn't have to work very hard to fake a restrained pace.

They continued down the corridor, pausing at each gate. Odd. They weren't moving in the direction of the upper cells. It seemed they were leaving the prison.

Nico's anxiety crept upward with each step, his previous optimism long forgotten. *What now? Firing squad?*

He didn't expect the pretense of a trial, but knowing the Germans, he'd anticipated some formality—a paper, an officious mortal with dead eyes to pronounce judgment, *something.* Still, they were definitely leaving the building. He was almost relieved.

Diago promised to watch for him. *If they send you into your next incarnation, know that I will watch for you, as a comrade.*

Not as a friend. Not yet. But as a comrade. Nico wondered what it would be like to have someone who cared enough to watch for him—to have close friendships like the nefilim in Guillermo's division.

Maybe in our next incarnation, we can begin as friends. In his next incarnation, he wouldn't be seduced by Jordi's sweet lies. He'd know who his real friends were.

The guards took him to the train yard.

They're sending me to the camps. He should have been relieved it wasn't the firing squad. He wasn't. He'd been privy to Los Nefilim's intelligence on the subject of the concentration camps.

The mortals had even sent people into Auschwitz to report on the conditions and possibly organize an escape. A Polish resistance fighter allowed himself to be arrested and what he found was so horrific, his first message from the camp was simple: *Bomb Auschwitz.*

Nico gritted his teeth and consoled himself. *I've been given another day. Use it.* He surreptitiously glanced at the others, trying to formulate some type of plan.

Prisoners stood in lines and faced the tracks. Jews, Roma and Sinti, resistance fighters, and the poor souls who had the bad luck of being in the wrong place at the wrong time, were organized into groups.

The Jews were identifiable by the yellow stars they wore and were kept separate from the others. As much as he pitied those interned simply for their race, he couldn't afford to draw attention to himself by defending them. He had his own secrets to keep.

If the Germans find I'm homosexual, my fate will be no better. So far, his captors didn't know. Nico intended to keep it that way.

His guards maneuvered him toward a diverse group of men. They shoved him between two mortals at the back of the line and left him there.

The prisoners around him appeared as beaten and ragged as him. He didn't recognize either of the mortals flanking him, but that meant nothing. Fresnes was huge and overcrowded. They might have been in adjoining cells at some point over the last few months and not known it.

The men didn't speak. They didn't dare.

The yard crawled with both French and German soldiers that guarded the lanes between the tracks and the buildings. Nico immediately discounted an escape attempt.

The doors of the cattle car nearest Nico's group opened to reveal dozens of men already inside. They didn't leave the car. Instead, the guards herded Nico's group toward the open door.

As they neared the car's dim maw, the lines broke and turned into a seething mass of bodies. Nico felt himself swept forward.

He scrambled inside and managed to work his way beneath a window opposite the door. A cold breeze touched his upturned face. He put his back against the wall and held his spot as more bodies were crammed around him. The car was filled until no one could sit. They stood together packed tight.

The doors slammed shut.

In the dimness, they waited. Someone coughed.

The man beside Nico murmured, "Do you know where they're taking—?"

Nico shook his head.

The man fell silent.

It was hours before the train finally moved. By the time it did, four men had already died, propped up by the living bodies around them.

The train's floor rattled beneath their feet. Nico wasn't tall enough to see through the window, but the cold breeze mitigated the smell of so many bodies pressed together. They'd been given buckets for their waste, but no chance to empty them, let alone room to use them properly. His cell at Fresnes had begun to look like a luxury suite.

Nico lost all track of time. Eventually the train braked for another stop, but this one felt different somehow.

Instinctively, he looked up. Flurries of snow drifted through the window.

The engine hissed. Someone on the other side of the car muttered to the man beside him. The comment was murmured from ear to ear in tones of fear: *Guards with attack dogs.*

A shudder of anxiety ran the through the men.

Nico straightened. "Can you see where we are?"

The mortal in front of him whispered the message back to the man by the doors.

Nico didn't have to wait long for the reply.

"Mauthausen."

Mauthausen. Jesus. Extermination through labor.

The doors suddenly opened. A blast of frigid air blew into the car.

Guards shouted: "Dalli, Dalli!"

No one needed an interpretation. All the prisoners knew enough German to understand they were to move and move fast. The men spilled through the doorway to land on the frozen ground. Guards with truncheons speeded them along with blows.

Nico stepped over a mortal. Whether the man was dead or unconscious, he had no way to know and no time to find out.

The guards took vicious glee in the confusion, shoving the prisoners to the side of a road. Nico narrowly missed taking a club to his face. He bobbed right and landed hard, skidding on the loose gravel. Regaining his balance, he got his feet under him and ducked into the writhing mass of men.

The doors to the Jewish cars weren't opened. The passengers inside jostled and pressed their faces to the few barred windows. They begged for water. They were ignored.

Soldiers, aided by snarling Alsatians, forced Nico's group farther from the train. A hard hand grasped his arm and jerked him into place.

Nico barely resisted lashing out. The German was young, barely nineteen. He screamed in Nico's face ordering him to remain still.

Instinctively, Nico knew what to do. He lowered his gaze in submission and bowed his head. *Grit your teeth and pretend it's Jordi.*

He managed to present the soldier with enough submissiveness to avoid further abuse. He held himself still until the mortal shifted his attention to the next man. Then he wiped the German's spit from his face.

The prisoner beside him coughed, a wet, racking sound that lurched up from his lungs. Nico didn't need a stethoscope to diagnose the condition. *Pneumonia. He won't live a day in this place.*

Somehow, they all remained standing as the Germans counted them. And counted. And counted again.

Nico grew numb from the cold. The sound of the soldiers' voices faded and the world suddenly turned surreal, as if he lived through a dream.

The man beside him collapsed. Before Nico could assist him, the young Nazi returned and shot the man in the back of the head.

Shifting his gaze forward, Nico felt the small thread of anger return to his chest. His rage brought the world back in stark relief.

Now he understood Miquel's fury. *I'm going to survive this. I'm going to survive just to make these bastards pay.* His teeth chattered from the cold. Hate kept him on his feet.

After a fourth count, the train belched a thick cloud of steam and crept away from the station, as if ashamed of its purpose. The passengers' cries became a memory carried by the wind.

Snow fell from somber clouds. Nico thought again of the SS-Obergruppenführer's frigid eyes.

Suddenly the guards began shouting. "Move! Move!"

The prisoners were forced to run. Nico made sure to mimic the mortals' shambling, stumbling gaits, careful not to go too quick—so they wouldn't realize he wasn't mortal—nor too sluggish—so he wouldn't be beaten. Given his hunger and exhaustion, parodying the mortals wasn't difficult.

The dogs snarled and snapped at the prisoners' ankles. In stark comparison to the strange centipede of men clambering through their streets, the villagers went about their daily business as if nothing unusual transpired. They studiously avoided making eye contact with the prisoners.

Nico tried to catch even one person's eye and failed. *How can they pretend this is normal unless they see it every day?*

As the group of men reached the edge of the town, a cluster of children threw rocks at them. "They'll work you to your bones, then up the chimney you'll go!"

Nico glared at a boy. The child looked away. He didn't leave the group, but he threw no more stones.

At least they can *feel shame.* Nico turned his attention back to the road. He had to be careful not to fall. Anyone that did was shot. Nico counted six deaths before he stopped counting.

Soon enough it was all he could do to keep running.

The Mauthausen camp loomed in the distance, growing closer with every step. The bracketed rooflines flanking the stone gates conjured images of pagodas.

If pagodas were surrounded with skeletons. Nico's eyes narrowed. Men with swollen ankles and sunken cheeks paused in their work. They weren't some daimonic nightmare but actual mortals starved to the brink of death. A few called out questions, but their voices faded before he caught their words.

He barely had time to acknowledge their presence before his group was driven through the gate. They were herded into an area between the showers and the fortress wall, where they finally halted. Once more, the Germans forced them into lines.

Four men in striped clothing entered the area and began to count them. *Kapos.* Nico had heard about them, too. He noted the green or black triangles on their uniforms. *Criminals, but they all seem to be German.*

Another man passed in front of the shower room's door and spoke to someone in Spanish. The answer came back—also in Spanish.

And where there are Spanish mortals, there might be Spanish nefilim. Either way, he'd find safety in numbers. Hope once more touched his heart with a delicate finger.

Suddenly the men around him began undressing. One of the kapos rapped his truncheon against his palm.

Something happened, some order was given, and he'd missed it. He immediately began to strip. The kapo's eyes shifted to another.

He barely finished when someone shouted, "Achtung!"

The kapos removed their hats and snapped to attention.

Two officers walked toward the group of prisoners. Nico recognized them from photographs he'd seen during a meeting with Guillermo's staff.

The first officer, SS-Obersturmführer Heinrich Eisenhöfer, was in charge the expropriation of the prisoners' belongings. According to Guillermo's sources, Eisenhöfer inspected incoming prisoners to get first pick of any valuables.

He's out of luck with this group. Anything of value that Nico had possessed disappeared after his internment in Fresnes. He assumed the rest of the men in his group were as poor.

Nonetheless, Eisenhöfer strode before the prisoners, examining the belongings at their feet. He took his time.

Nico turned his attention to the second man. His rank was lower, but that made him no less dangerous. *Anton Streitwieser, Third Schutzhaftlagerführer.* He was tasked with maintaining order in the routine running of the camp. An Alsatian with a savage grin sat at his feet.

After a nod from Eisenhöfer, Streitwieser began to speak. He told them the rules of the camp and promised the crematorium's chimney was their only exit.

Now they all understood the children's taunts. The prisoner beside Nico began to cry. Tears rolled down his cheeks, but he made no sound.

Streitwieser motioned to one of the kapos. The man consulted a clipboard and called out three numbers.

At first nothing happened. Nico could almost hear the men weighing their options. Finally, three prisoners broke the lines to shuffle forward. One of them was the weeping man beside Nico. He was less than five paces away.

"These are the queers transferred from Natzweiler-Struthof," the kapo announced to Eisenhöfer.

The wind shifted. Heavy black smoke churned from the chimney. Ashes mixed with the snow. The world turned black-and-white. Not even the color of Nico's song could save him, because his throat swelled shut with fear.

Not my number. They didn't call my number, because they don't know. And he damn well intended to keep it that way.

Streitwieser snapped his fingers. "This is what we do to queers in Mauthausen." The bitch's hackles rose. A growl rippled across her lips. Streitwieser gestured at the weeping prisoner close to Nico and asked, "Where's the beggar?"

The prisoners' confusion over the question was short-lived. The Alsatian leapt at the weeping man. Her jaws snapped at his flesh and broke his bones. His screams echoed between the buildings.

The attack went on for minutes—it went on forever.

With another snap of his fingers, Streitwieser summoned the bitch. She broke off her assault and trotted to him.

Nico looked down at the gore around his feet. The man on the ground wasn't dead. Not yet, but death wasn't far.

Beside the dying prisoner, the second man's eyes were glassy with shock; he stood in his comrade's gore and yet somehow kept staring straight ahead. The third prisoner shuddered beneath the falling snow, his chattering teeth loud in the sudden quiet.

Eisenhöfer signaled for the kapos to carry on. He walked back to the command area. Streitwieser slipped a piece of meat to the Alsatian and followed.

Next to the showers, a shadow stirred . . . man-shaped, but faceless. In spite of the Waffen-SS uniform, no cries of *Achtung!* followed him as he peeled away from the wall. He wore a long wool coat trimmed in fur. A whipcord tail lifted the hem and then disappeared as he advanced on the line of naked, shivering men.

Nico frowned. A chill that had nothing to do with the cold suddenly washed over him. *Daimon-born.*

Los Nefilim had intelligence that indicated the daimon-born were staying close to the camps, feeding on the prisoners' misery. *And now we know those reports are true.*

Unlike the neatly shorn guards, the nefil's dark hair

touched his collar. As he stepped into the light, his craggy features became clear: a heavy brow and an aristocratic nose over a well-shaped mouth.

Nico shifted his gaze, hoping the other nefil hadn't noticed his eyes, but he was too late. The daimon-born nefil assessed him with black eyes that swallowed the light and gave back nothing but shadows.

Nico's dry throat clicked. Goose pimples wafted over his exposed flesh. He gave up any pretense at subterfuge. One look in those eyes told him the nefil was old. *No, Diago is old. This one is ancient.*

Ashes continued to flutter from the sky. The other nefil parted his lips; his tongue flickered into the air and then withdrew behind teeth that were long—*too long and sharp, so very sharp.*

The nefil sang a guttural note that sounded almost like a chant. The kapo turned away; his eyes glazed.

Ignoring everyone but Nico, the daimon-born nefil approached. His gaze roved up and down Nico's body. "Spanier?"

Spaniard? He wants to know if I'm Spanish. But was that good or bad? If he told the truth and said he was Italian, then the Spaniards in the shower rooms might overhear. *They'll remember the Italians fought against them during the Spanish Civil War. I'll lose any advantage I might have to find more nefilim.*

Nico nodded. "Jawohl, Spanier." He glanced at the shower room door and noticed that one of the prisoners watched him carefully. *Good. They heard.*

The nefil lifted one gloved hand and never lost his smile. "Come."

Nico looked to the kapos. He begged them with his eyes: *Keep me here, keep me with the others, please.*

One of the kapos mistook Nico's plea for confusion and gestured to a translator, who said in Spanish, "He wants you to go with him."

Nico bent to gather his clothes.

"Leave them." The daimon-born nefil took off his fine, heavy coat and wrapped it around Nico's shoulders, surprising both him and the guards.

Guiding him back to the main entrance, the nefil indicated a black car. The chauffer held the door. By his uniform, Nico saw that he was another camp inmate. His eyes indicated that he, like the ancient nefil, was daimon-born.

But he is like me . . . afraid. Nico ducked into the backseat.

The ancient nefil glided in next to him. The chauffer shut the door and took the front seat.

When the car had moved beyond Mauthausen's gates, the ancient nefil spoke. "I know you speak German. What is your name?"

"Nicolas." He curled his bare toes against the warmth of the floorboard.

The nefil made the name a question and probed for more information. "Nicolas . . . ?"

Nico hesitated. He couldn't say Bianchi. Too many dangerous people knew him by that name.

"Ruiseñor," he blurted. The name meant nightingale in Spanish. At least this way, if his life was lost, Diago might find the alias and know what became of him. "Nicolas Ruiseñor."

The nefil smiled with his too-long teeth, as if amused. "You may address me as Herr Teufel."

Sir Devil. He wondered if Herr Teufel was counting on him getting the joke.

Nico stared at the back of the chauffer's head. "Why me?" The coat slipped from his shoulder.

Teufel adjusted the garment and fastened the top button. "I have a job for you, Nicolas Ruiseñor."

"And if I say no?"

"I didn't say you had a choice." Teufel grinned with his long, long teeth and placed the pink triangle assigned to homosexuals on Nico's thigh.

The blood drained from his face. He felt it happen. His pulse thundered through his veins, and he wondered how much fear his heart could stand before it stopped beating. And then he recalled Jordi . . . or maybe it was Benito . . . saying that nefilim were notoriously hard to kill.

[3]

THE FARM

Ysabel perched on the edge of her chair and watched Guillermo move the oil lamp closer to the parchment. He bent his head and squinted at the grimoire's page.

It was all she could do not to point out the beginning of the glyph to her father. "Do you need a magnifying glass?"

Guillermo's gaze snapped up. "There is nothing wrong with my eyes."

Except they are bloodshot from so much reading in the dark. She kept the thought to herself. The farmhouse had a generator, but they used it only in emergencies. Stealth was their objective in the so-called Free Zone.

She forced what she hoped was an innocent expression to her face. "I didn't say you needed glasses."

"Good. Because I don't."

"It's a tiny mark, and I had difficulty finding it."

He gave a low murmur that was more like a growl. "Yes, but I put it there, so I know exactly what I'm looking for."

She leaned back and snapped, "Fine."

The retort won her a concerned look from her father, and she immediately regretted her tone. It wasn't his fault her patience was short this evening.

The trip home from Toulouse had been long and exhausting. She'd endured delay after delay only to find herself sharing the bench on the last train home with a member of the Milice. The policeman's hands kept creeping to her thigh, his wedding ring glinting on his finger, as he tried to engage her in conversation. She'd finally popped him with a hard sigil so he'd sleep. She hoped he missed his stop.

Guillermo's fingernail traced the faint curl of ink that indicated the first loop of the ward. "I found it. See? I'm not going blind."

"Stop teasing. I'm worried about you." And that was no lie. Losing Spain to his brother's Nationalists had been a hard blow to her father's pride. *And to mine.* "You need to rest."

"I'll rest when the war is over."

"Any news regarding when the Allies will attempt their crossing?"

"Spring at the soonest, summer at the latest," he mumbled as he followed the twist of ink across the parchment.

In order to reinforce the Atlantic Wall, Die Nephilim had placed deadly sigils along the French coast to repel an invasion. Los Nefilim's job was to find a way to get the Allied forces past those wards without alerting Die Nephilim.

And the maritime song hidden beneath the grimoire's sigils would do the trick. It was a complex arrangement designed to manufacture a supernatural weather system that worked on two levels.

The first series of glyphs would interfere with the vibrations of protective wards, such as the ones used by Die Nephilim. The second wave of sigils created a veil of mist, which enabled the attackers to see clearly, while keeping the approaching fleet hidden from the enemy's view.

Like the mortal governments, the various divisions of the Inner Guard jealously secured their secrets. The glyphs and chords of Los Nefilim's maritime song were so guarded, Guillermo had hidden the pages of the composition in five separate grimoires. To further confound discovery, he placed each of the grimoires in a different library—first in Spain, and when Spain fell to Jordi's Nationalists, within French universities.

As a final deterrent, each of the five pages was guarded by violent sigils. Only Guillermo and Ysabel possessed the tonal range that would unlock those glyphs to reveal the composition hidden beneath the text.

Culling the pages from the grimoires while navigating the Nazis' and Milice's tortuous obstacles had been daunting enough. Dodging both daimon- and angel-born nefilim, who were also interested in acquiring the song, had turned the assignment into a dangerous game of cat and mouse.

But we're almost done. Leaning forward again, Ysa watched her father hum a low note.

Flashes of light sparkled across the gold lettering. The wards protecting the page fell away. Musical chords emerged across the parchment—the sound of a fog that moved like a veil.

The tension left her shoulders. "Four down. One to go."

Guillermo lit a cigar and peered at the page through the smoke. "The last page is the most difficult."

They'd agreed he would tell her where each one was hidden as she brought them in. That way if she was captured, she couldn't reveal the whereabouts of the other pages.

She leaned forward expectantly. "What am I looking for next?"

He watched her carefully. "We need *Le Livre d'Or*."

"*The Book of Gold*."

"Tear out Psalm 60."

She didn't write down the information. She would remember. "And where is it?"

"Bibliothèque Sainte-Geneviève."

"Why there?"

"Rousseau advised me it would be safe from the daimonborn."

She thought about the location, and it made sense. The library had been designed with exposed iron arches. Over the years, members of Les Néphilim had reinforced the lacy patterns with subtle glyphs that magnified the effect of iron on the daimon-born nefilim. Even Rafael walked blocks out of his way to avoid the library.

One thing troubled her, though. "Saint-Geneviève might deter the daimon-born, but what about the angel-born?"

The lamp's glow set Guillermo's irises alight with sparks of supernatural fire. "They'll see the warning wards."

"You've cursed it?"

"They'll lose a finger if they're lucky, their hand if they're not. My curse will follow them into their next incarnation. They will not know a day's peace." He flicked the ashes of his cigar into the ashtray and the firelight sent orange and red streaks through the Throne's tear in his signet.

As a king of the Inner Guard, her father's song carried the authority of the Thrones themselves. Ysabel didn't pity the nefil that crossed him. *They'll get what they earn.* "I can pretend to be a student."

Guillermo shook his head. "They've taken women out of most of the universities. Your cover story is that you're helping your invalid father with his research."

Her lip quirked upward in a smile. "You're not an invalid."

"I feel like one some days." He turned his head as if ashamed of the admission. "You'll have to request the grimoire from the librarian. Suero will give you his name."

Her father's secretary knew precisely how to cut through the Nazis' bureaucratic snarls. "When do I leave?"

"In the morning if you like. Suero has new papers for you. I want you to be very careful. We lost Nico in Paris."

"Any word on his whereabouts?"

Guillermo shook his head. "No. By the time we finally got someone into Fresnes, he'd been transferred, or shot. We're not giving up, though. Not until I have proof of his death."

Ysa had no doubt. He left none of his nefilim behind if he could avoid it, and his loyalty to them cemented their devotion to him.

Even those like Nico, who swore their allegiance to the Inner Guard under duress, often wound up being some of Los Nefilim's most faithful soldiers. Ysa hoped that she would one day command the same respect when she became queen.

But that day is long in the future. For now, she simply wanted to learn as much as she could from her father.

Guillermo opened a drawer and withdrew a bottle of orujo and two shot glasses. "I don't want to lose anyone else, especially you. If I had another nefil whose voice could unlock those wards, I'd send them in heartbeat. I'd go myself if I could."

She accepted the glass he offered her. "I doubt you would make it far. Things are happening faster than the news can travel. I overheard a pair of soldiers talking about Korosten." West of Kiev, the city of Korosten held a major railway node that supported the Ukraine. "They said the Nazis were forced to retreat."

Guillermo held the bottle suspended over the glass. That piece of good news won his rapt attention.

"Interesting." He poured them both a round and then raised his glass. "Salut."

"Salut." She threw back the shot. The warmth of the alcohol seeped into her chest.

He leaned against the desk and looked down at her. "Tell me more."

"There are rumors that the Soviets have pushed the Germans back across the Polish border. Whether that's true or not, I don't know. But I can tell you this: the rank and file here in France are nervous. I can see it in the soldiers' eyes at the checkpoints."

She kept talking as her father poured them another round. "The Germans and the Milice are suspicious of men, especially anyone not clearly attached to a wife or mother, because the maquisards are becoming bolder. Women, on the other hand, are questioned less. The Nazis don't believe we're capable of thinking strategically. I say let's keep using their misogyny against them." She lifted her glass. "Salut."

"Salut." He drained the shot. "I remember when you were but seven or eight and you kept playing that spy game . . . do you remember that?"

She smiled as she recalled facing down her father and demanding that he train her to be a spy. "I remember."

"And you remember I said that if you wanted to be a good member of Los Nefilim, then you had to learn to follow orders? Do you remember that?"

"Yes, Papá."

"Then I order you to come home safe to us. Because if I lose you, I'll lose my heart."

She was surprised to see him blink away a tear. *Or maybe he is just exhausted.* The circles under his eyes looked blacker in the office's near-dark. "You need to rest," she said again, more gently than the first time.

He ignored the statement and took her hands in his. "I know you've spent a few days at each of the universities."

"I wanted to look at several grimoires so no one would guess which one I defaced."

"And that was smart. But not in Paris. You get in, get that psalm, and get on the first train home. Understand?"

She didn't argue. "I will."

He kissed her cheeks and released her. "See your mother before you leave."

"You know I will."

"And come back to us."

She blew him a kiss. "You know I will." As she closed the

door, she glimpsed him one last time as he poured himself another shot. *He's working too hard.*

But it wouldn't be for much longer. All she needed was one more grimoire, and then she would be here to help him. They'd finish this war together.

[4]

THE FARM

Diago glared at the composition on the piano's music stand. He picked up his pencil and set it down again. The Key's complex series of notes mocked him. *It's not the arrangement of chords but something simple, something basic, something that is right before my eyes and I cannot see—*

Someone closed a door in the farmhouse, interrupting his train of thought. Voices from the kitchen floated toward the music room as the other nefilim went about their daily activities.

Sound. Too much sound, intruding on the quiet he so desperately needed.

Christ, don't they realize I'm trying to work? In his anxiety, he snapped the pencil in half.

"I can't do this." He had to go upstairs to Guillermo's office and simply tell him the truth: *I can't compose the Key. Not under pressure. Not like this.*

The music room door opened, and Rafael poked his head inside. "Do you want some lunch, Papá?"

"What I want," he said with exaggerated care as he placed the broken pencil on the stand, "is some goddamn quiet."

Rafael considered the statement. "Lunch would be easier. Take a break, come back to it fresh."

"No time."

"Maybe Juanita could help?"

To her credit, Guillermo's wife had spent weeks with him, but in the end, they realized the collaboration wasn't working.

"She is an angel." With three sets of vocal cords that allowed for complex tones. "And nefilim don't have the same range. Everything she composed would have worked beautifully for angels, but when the nefilim tried to sing her compositions . . ." He brushed the air with his fingers as if waving away a bad smell. "It was like taking an arrangement designed for a flute and playing it on a kazoo."

Rafael laughed.

"It's not funny." But his son's laughter eased the tension in Diago's chest. A smile crept to his lips in spite of himself.

Still chortling, Rafael came into the music room and closed the door. "If you're not hungry, let's take a walk. We can come back in twenty minutes. It'll still be here."

Diago glanced toward the terrace, where the snow hid the broken stones. The flagstones were one of the many cosmetic repairs the nefilim neglected due to the war.

They'd found the three-story farmhouse abandoned shortly after the Germans drove them from northern Paris. Whoever owned the property had vacated the area long ago. Guillermo's secretary, Suero, found the appropriate papers; money they could scarcely afford to lose changed hands; and the titles were transferred into one of Guillermo's many aliases.

The house itself had been a wreck when they first occupied it. Wallpaper peeled from the plaster, the floor tiles buckled, and the stairs were barely usable. They'd repaired the interior defects, and then the barns, where they hid their petrol and guns.

Furniture had been scavenged from trash heaps, or they'd simply made what they needed themselves. The upright piano had been a recent purchase.

And here I sit, squandering it. Diago touched an ivory key.

Rafael scooted onto the bench beside him just as he used to do when he was small. *He was barely six and marveled over every extravagance in our little house.*

The piano had been his favorite instrument until he learned the violin. Diago smiled at the memory as Rafael gently pressed the keys to cover the sound of their conversation.

He whispered, "Miquel sent me. He said you haven't checked for messages in a week."

Rafael meant messages from Diago's daimon-born cousin, the Condesa Christina Banderas. Diago kept his voice low. "I haven't been able to get away. Violeta is beginning to notice that I walk after each snowfall." Christina sent her sigils through the storms. "She tried to follow me the last time."

Rafael played a bagatelle. "Maybe we should tell her what's going on."

"No. Too many people know already." He pressed the keys and added a few notes of his own to his son's jaunty song. "Aren't you the Three Musketeers or something?" He recalled that when they were young, Ysabel, Rafael, and Violeta would run around their Spanish compound with sticks for swords and chicken feathers in their hats. They read Dumas together, passing the book around so that each could read their Musketeer's dialogue. "Can't you call her off?"

"She listens to Ysa, and Ysa is in Paris." Rafael ended the bagatelle and lowered the fallboard. "I'll walk with you. It'll give you some cover."

"Okay, you win. This time."

Rafael grinned. "You say that every time."

They left the music room and passed the kitchen on their way to the mudroom. The Corvo twins, Eva and Maria, were having lunch with Guillermo's secretary, Suero.

The Corvo sisters were old nefilim, who'd been with Guillermo's household since his firstborn life as Solomon. Through their rank and allegiance, they were part of Guillermo's household and his inner council. Eva had served as Rafael's governess, while Maria watched over Ysa. Now that the children were grown and no longer in need of bodyguards, the twins had settled into the task of monitoring Guillermo's supply of ammunition and guns.

Suero kept the details of Guillermo's day-to-day business in constant motion. A lesser nefil, he made a very complex job appear easy. He looked up from his soup and gestured to the chair next to him. "Want something, Diago?"

"Rafael has persuaded me to take a break. Maybe after our walk."

Maria rose and grabbed a metal lunch box from the counter. "Good, walk to the northern field. Violeta didn't come in for lunch."

Rafael intercepted the box. "I'll take it to her."

They went past the kitchen and into the mudroom for their boots and coats. Outside, the day was blindingly bright with sunshine and snow.

Heading in the direction of the northern field, they kept walking until they were out of sight of the house. Then they ducked into the dense pines that bordered the farm's outer edges.

Rafael dragged the heel of his boot across the snow and murmured a soft song. A breeze carried snow over their tracks.

"That's a very good trick," Diago said.

"I use it whenever I'm working with the maquisards. I have another one to confound any dogs that pick up our scent."

"War forces us to improvise."

"I wish we could be inspired without so much killing."

"I agree." The path turned steep, so they saved their breath for walking until they reached the summit.

From there, they took a circuitous route through the forest until they reached a ravine. One boulder jutted over a straight drop, forming a ledge. Thin cracks marred the stone's surface. Within the cracks, pools of ice and snow glittered like veins of pyrite.

Diago followed the lines and saw hints of indigo and lighter shades of blue threaded throughout. *Christina's song.* She *had* sent a message during the last storm. "Okay, stand back and keep watch. I'll be as quick as I can."

Diago waited until Rafael withdrew to the tree line before he eased onto the boulder and examined the labyrinthine fissures. He removed his glove and tapped the surface. A spark of green fire emerged from his fingertip and turned into a cyclone of scorpions. They writhed over the surface and took the form of a tarot card: the High Priestess.

Of course—Christina would consider herself no less. The figure's mouth moved and spoke with his cousin's voice. "Come to the manse at rue Émile Zola as soon as you can. I have urgent news."

A chill went through him. That was right into the scorpion's lair. *Is this a trick to lure me to my death? Do they suspect I'm working as a double agent?* He waited for more, but the figure didn't speak again. The scorpions faded under the sun and disappeared.

Rafael returned and squatted beside Diago. "Was there a message?"

Diago nodded.

"What does she want?"

"To meet with me. She wants me to come to her house. I have no idea why."

"Then it could be a trap."

Everything in war was a trap. "Maybe." He backed away from the stone and started walking toward the farm again. "I won't know until I go."

Rafael didn't argue, but Diago could tell he wasn't happy about the situation. "Is she really our cousin?"

Diago picked his way carefully through the wet pine needles. "She is a collateral relative, a cousin five or six times removed. *Cousin* is just less of a mouthful and close enough to the truth." He glanced at Rafael from the corner of his eye. "You don't usually like to talk about the daimon-born. Why this sudden curiosity?"

Rafael shrugged. "Ever since you've become involved with them again, you've started having bad dreams."

Diago kept his gaze on the ground. The resurgence of his childhood traumas was no secret to the small household. Even so, it wasn't a subject he was comfortable discussing, especially with his son.

"We suspected my contact with my family might cause some . . . issues." It was as if associating with his cousin had inadvertently unlocked the door to Diago's most caustic memories. With each visit, his childhood wounds opened in increasingly larger increments. In many ways the daimon-born still owned him. The handprints of their blows had faded from his flesh to become invisible tattoos inked into his psyche. "Juanita is helping me with it. Besides, I've always had bad dreams." He tried to sound nonchalant, to put his son at ease.

"Not like these," Rafael whispered, clearly not mollified. "I hear you in the night, walking. Sometimes I wake and find your protective sigils on my door."

Sometimes I forget he's no longer a child. "The movement soothes me. That's all."

"You once told me that not all of the daimon-born are evil."

Curious to see where Rafael intended to take the conversation, he conceded, "That's true."

"What about Christina? Where does she fall on the spectrum?"

"Christina . . ." *What can I say about her?* He shrugged. "Christina is . . . ambitious."

"Then she's not a good person?"

"Jesus, I don't know if she's good or bad. The daimon-born are like the angel-born and mortals. There is a lot of nuance in people . . ."

"You're prevaricating."

"Oh, what big words you've learned." He teased his son.

Rafael didn't smile back. "I'm serious, Papá. Don't change the subject."

"Okay." He'd once promised himself that he'd always be honest with his son. *And this is one of those times—uncomfortable though it may be.* "I can't tell you if she is good or bad, only my experience with her. She and I have encountered one another many times through the centuries. We've sometimes even helped one another. She has, on occasion, shown me compassion. That quality tends to mitigate her more ruthless schemes, and it's why I approached her when Guillermo gave me this assignment."

"And if she discovers you're spying on them?"

"She will look to her own interests. She is ambitious," he repeated. "She believes she should be Moloch's priestess."

"I still don't understand how Moloch survived. I know I was only six, but my song tore his flesh from his body. I saw it happen."

"Do you still have nightmares about that night?" Diago asked gently.

Rafael pressed his lips together as if he might hold back, and then he blurted, "I had one this morning."

"Do you want to talk about it?"

Rafael shrugged. "I dreamed the whole scene all over again. It was the day you found out about me, and I was so happy. I didn't have to live in the orphanage anymore, because you promised to let me live with you."

Diago recalled the shock of finding that he'd fathered a child with the angel Candela. Rafael's birth was the product of a deal with the devil. Moloch, who used his daimonic skills to create weapons of mass destruction, had offered the angels the blueprint of a bomb that would stop all wars. In exchange, he wanted Diago's child.

And the angels complied, because they're merciless bastards, who will stop at nothing to get what they want. Candela's assignment had been simple: seduce Diago and, once she gave birth, to hand the child over to Moloch. But somewhere along the line, the angel fell in love with her son, and she refused to part with him. When her kin closed in on her, she'd hidden Rafael in an orphanage and died the second death rather than disclose his location.

Except to her brother, Prieto. Diago realized his son had stopped talking. "What happened in your dream after we found one another?"

"The angel Prieto put us on the train and ordered you to give me to Moloch."

So far, Rafael's dream held to the facts. Candela's brother, Prieto, found a way to give Diago a chance to save Rafael.

Diago encouraged his son to go on.

Rafael didn't need much prompting. "While we were on the train, you and Miquel decided to make a golem that looked like me. You carried the golem to Moloch and tricked him into taking it, and he gave you the blueprint for the bomb. But as you were running away, Moloch realized he'd been deceived. He sent his vampires after you, and they caught you, and beat you, but you wouldn't give up that bomb . . ."

Because Prieto said he would kill Miquel if I didn't make the exchange. Diago didn't speak, though.

Caught up in the telling of his dream, Rafael's breath quickened. "And I heard you scream . . . and I knew I had to save you, because I had waited so long for you to come, and I remember I had a little mirrored box in my hands."

The casket was an angelic gift from Prieto. It was made of mirrored panels, and the lid had a triptych etched in the glass: a woman dancing on the first panel; on the second, she and Diago standing face-to-face; and on the third, the figure of a child, representing Rafael.

"I held up the box and ran down the stairs as fast as I could. When I got to the sewer, I saw you on the ground between two vampires. They'd beaten you and broken your arm and bit off your finger . . ."

Diago automatically clenched his right hand into a fist, feeling the phantom pain of the vampire's venom rush up his arm again.

Rafael didn't seem to notice. He stopped walking, lost within the dream. "And I held up the box and sang . . . I sang for the memory of my mamá and for you and for Miquel, and the mirrored box shattered and a thousand golden snakes spun through the air."

Rafael's chest rose and fell as if he were running, or even standing in that sewer again, singing for their lives.

Diago didn't like the glazed look in his son's eyes. "And all those things happened," he whispered.

"Except in my nightmare, the snakes didn't tear into Moloch's body. In my nightmare, he brushed them aside and laughed at me. He grabbed my throat, and when I screamed, he turned into mist and rushed into my mouth and suddenly he was me."

Jesus.

"Could the dream be a prophecy?"

Diago faced the fear in his son's eyes and didn't lie to him.

"Maybe." He certainly hoped not. "I don't know. Prophecies are fickle. I don't put much stock in them. Given our circumstances and the stress you're under, it could just as easily be anxiety."

"Did Moloch force himself on Alvaro like that?"

Not *my grandfather* or *your father* but *Alvaro*. Rafael didn't even see himself as related to the daimon-born. *And that is definitely for the best.*

Diago took his son's arm and started walking again. "No. Alvaro allowed Moloch to possess his body. He *let* him inside. It's a . . . benign possession."

Rafael considered the explanation. "The same way Jordi allowed the Grigori to possess him in 1939?"

"It's a similar process. The difference is that the Grigori's spirit never left his own corporeal body. He simply needed a physical link to Jordi in order to infect him with his commands."

"And the Grigori's tear in Jordi's signet was that physical link." Rafael kicked a pine cone.

"Exactly. When Guillermo shattered the tear within the signet, he broke the connection, and freed Jordi from the Grigori's influence."

Rafael considered the scenario. "Alvaro wears Moloch's signet. If the stone is damaged, will that break Moloch's hold on Alvaro?"

"No. The ring is simply a symbol to the daimons. It doesn't function like the signets of the Inner Guard's kings and queens. Moloch is a god, not an angel. He doesn't require a superficial link. His soul essentially cohabitates with Alvaro's soul in a single body."

As they walked, Rafael seemed to leave the nightmare

behind, and Diago felt some small sense of relief at that. "And having Moloch within him works to Alvaro's benefit, because the other nefilim see him as a god."

Diago patted his son's shoulder. "Now you've got it."

"What does Moloch do when the nefil's body begins to age? I mean, we're long-lived, but we're not immortal."

"That's why the position of high priest is so important. When Alvaro's body eventually dies, the high priest becomes Moloch's next host."

"So Christina doesn't just want to become high priestess . . . she wants to be a goddess."

"Now you understand."

They reached the edge of the forest, emerging close to the northern field.

Rafael paused to hide their tracks once again.

Diago caught movement in the distance and nodded.

A woman walked at the edge of the field. Diago recognized Violeta, the head of their guard unit. The young nefil had the same black hair as Diago, but where his skin was olive, hers carried the lighter coloring of a Catalonian. She'd been spared her mother's long face and stern features, but then again, Violeta was only in her firstborn life . . . she had plenty of time to develop the distrust and rage her mother had worn straight to the grave.

Rafael followed Diago's gaze. "I'm going to deliver her lunch and stay with her for a while. She's always morose while Ysa is gone."

"It's because she loves Ysa."

"Yeah, but Ysa's heart belongs to Los Nefilim. Violeta has a hard time with that."

"I know you'll help them work it out."

"That's what friends do." Rafael touched the tip of his cap. "I'll be in later."

Diago lifted his hand and walked back to the house. He put one foot in front of the other, each step heavier than the last. He needed to see Guillermo and Miquel. They had to make plans for a trip into Perpignan.

[5]

BIBLIOTHÈQUE SAINTE-GENEVIÈVE

Ysabel sat on the edge of the rooming house's bed and tied her shoes. Her packed suitcase waited by the door. *A quick trip to the library, get the psalm, back here to retrieve the suitcase, and then catch the next train.*

"Let's hope it goes that easy," she whispered. It was the closest thing she had to a prayer. She retrieved a pair of glasses from the nightstand and traced two small glyphs over each lens. Humming a soft chord, she activated the sigils.

And now the test. At the blotchy mirror by the door, she adjusted the ugly black frames on her face. The sigils were designed to magnify her eyes and change the color of her irises from light brown to blue. Instead, the wards made her eyes seem green.

I've got to work on that. Regardless, it wasn't a bad disguise.

Her suit was conservative but fashionable—Parisians

might forget a face, but they never forgot a bad outfit. Violeta had suggested the skirt, which was neither too long nor too short and was pleated to give her a full range of movement.

My Violeta always has her eye on clothing that works well in a fight. Which, when Ysa thought about it, wasn't necessarily a bad thing from a tactical viewpoint.

The dull brown coat made her auburn hair seem more vibrant, so she pulled her curls into a low bun and covered her head with a cheap cloche hat. Her shoes were sensible with low heels, in case she had to run. Other than her watch, she wore no jewelry.

This is it. She checked the time. The library should be open, and most of the students would be in class this early in the morning. It was time to meet the librarian, Pierre Fronteau.

Although Los Nefilim still had a few safe houses left in Paris, Ysa avoided them. Her father had lost enough people, and she wanted no one to be able to trace her movements back to their nefilim.

She opened the door and listened. Quiet. Most of the house's occupants had left for the day.

Grabbing her satchel from its hook, she slipped out of her room and down the stairs. The mortal landlady, Madam Tillet, was busy in the kitchen.

Ysa waited until the woman disappeared into the pantry. Moving quickly, she sneaked past the kitchen and outside.

The overcast sky kissed the air with a light mist. Hopefully, the weather would keep people inside.

The library was only a few blocks away, so she decided to walk. She disdained public transport unless it was absolutely necessary, because there were simply too many ways to be trapped. Too, on her feet she could run with the speed of the nefilim and lose any mortal in Paris's winding alleys.

She wasn't as fast as Rafael, but she could hold her own. *No one is as fast as Rafael.* The thought of her friend usually brought a smile to her lips, but not today. Rafael had become withdrawn lately—not unfriendly, but they'd drifted apart.

Five years ago, she'd forbidden him to spy on the traitor Carlos Vela, at the end of the Spanish Civil War. Instead, he disobeyed her, wound up in a portal realm with a Grigori, and almost died at Jordi's hand.

It was an experience that left scars on Rafael far deeper than the ones he wore on his face. Although he claimed he didn't harbor resentment over his punishment for violating her order, Ysa sensed subtle changes to their relationship.

He kept her at an emotional arm's length, as if he no longer trusted her with his secret thoughts. *And I don't know how to reach him anymore.*

According to the nefilim's hierarchies, Rafael was her subordinate; within her heart, he was still her little brother. The balance between their interactions often required finesse, and Ysa was the first to admit, she sometimes blundered in that regard.

Maybe once she returned to the farm, she'd liberate that bottle of orujo from her father's desk and talk to Rafael. Better yet, she might just listen.

But first she had to get home.

She turned the corner and saw the library's entrance. Retrieving her card from her bag, she hurried up the stairs and into the lobby.

The line for students was short. She joined the queue as three young women passed her on their way out of the library.

The clerk checked the cards of the two men in front of her and then hers. With a smile, he motioned for her to proceed.

A few meters away, two German soldiers in Wehrmacht green stood by one of the many busts lining the corridor. They carried German-to-French phrase books, consulting them frequently as they read the plaques.

Soldiers from the front, probably enjoying a week's leave. Each of them looked up at the click of her heels and then almost immediately discounted her huddled form as unworthy of romantic pursuit, which was perfectly fine with her.

Even on her best days, she wasn't what the mortals would call a classic beauty. Her power, according to her mother, came from the confidence in her stride and the directness of her gaze—two distinct qualities she sought to downplay in her undercover role.

Lifting her head slightly, she scanned the corridor. The rest of the mortals were a mix of men and women, all moving to and from the library's main reading room.

A secretary walked toward the staff's wing. The soldiers watched the woman's slender calves and enjoyed a lewd exchange in German.

Ysa rolled her eyes. *Christ, do they ever think of anything else?*

Too bad the Inner Guard wasn't interested in the thoughts of randy soldiers. Ysa could have filled their dossiers for days.

Falling into step behind the secretary, Ysa passed the decorative iron railings by the stairs. She stopped at Pierre Fronteau's door and knocked.

"Come in!" called a voice that was quite tuneful for that of a mortal.

She turned the knob and entered. "Good morning, monsieur. My name is Francine Proulx. I believe I am expected?"

Fronteau, a dignified man with compassionate eyes and a receding hairline, looked up from a tattered book he'd been transcribing. His smile faltered, but he quickly pasted it back into place. "Good morning, Mademoiselle Proulx. I didn't expect you so early."

Ysa picked at the flap of her satchel. "I hope to be quick, monsieur. I'd like to be back with my poor papá as soon as possible."

His fingers fluttered against his tie before he reached for his log. "Please sign in for me."

She leaned forward and wrote her alias neatly on the numbered line.

Fronteau stood and adjusted his demeanor as one would a hat, leaving aside his nervous smile for a more professional deportment. "Your father's letter said that he required *Le Livre d'Or*." He retrieved the key from his desk.

"Correct, monsieur."

"Your father is very old?"

Centuries, over five hundred to be exact. "Yes. He finds travel very difficult these days."

A minor tic jerked the corner of his mouth just before Fronteau bowed his head. "I see. You are a good daughter to help him, then."

"You are kind."

"If you'll wait in the reading room, I'll bring the book to you shortly."

"Thank you, monsieur." She left and went to the main reading room, an open chamber with high domed windows.

Exposed iron arches displayed lacelike patterns that were incorporated into the ceiling's design. Ysa detected Les Néphilim's glyphs twisting around the metal's artistic flourishes.

Several meters of shelving that held thousands of books occupied the center of the room. A low rail, with a gate near a librarian's desk, surrounded the unit.

Reading tables with elegant lights were placed throughout the room. The scent of old leather and oiled wood filled her senses. She loved the smell of libraries.

The shared spaces at the tables were occupied by a few students. All seemed to be mortal, but that didn't mean she had nothing to fear.

One young man looked up from his text and smiled at her. She noted his swastika armband and pretended not to see his greeting. Brushing past his table, she aimed herself toward a spot near a maintenance exit at the back of the room.

She took a seat as far from the main entrance as possible, but one that gave her a full view of the door. That way she could easily see potential adversaries before they saw her, giving her the chance to slip away unnoticed if the need arose.

From her position, she had two available escape routes. The shortest was through the maintenance exit behind her, which she knew from her study of the building's floor plans led to the basement and then to an outside door. If that was blocked, she intended a bold run to the upper level and through a staff door. From there, she could use the employees' stairwell to return to the main level in order to reach another exit.

The room was cool in the best of circumstances, but with the war and oil shortages, most buildings had little or no heat. Sainte-Geneviève was no exception. Ysabel, like the other students, left her coat on.

Movement by the door caught her eye. Monsieur Fronteau entered and approached her table with the grimoire. The book was smaller than she'd anticipated. Even with the wooden cover, the entire manuscript could easily fit in her coat pocket.

He placed it on the table. "Return the book to me in my office when you're finished."

"Of course," she whispered.

He turned and walked away.

She briefly considered stealing the entire book, but quickly discarded the idea. Monsieur Fronteau might not miss a few pages, but he'd certainly notice if the book itself disappeared.

Don't get sloppy now. So far, everything had gone to plan. *Don't jinx it.* She turned the brittle pages to Psalm 60.

Psalm 60 wasn't there.

"No," she whispered. Heart pounding, she went through the leaves. It was gone. *Oh no . . . no, no, fuck no, this isn't happening.* But it was.

No mortal could remove those pages without damaging her father's wards, and she saw no indication of mortal tampering. *Nefil, then, but who?* She returned to the section where the psalm should have been, tilting the book so that she could see the binding's broken threads.

The sound waves of a nefil's song twitched between the leaves. The light within the gunmetal-gray vibrations indicated the nefil was angel-born.

She ran her fingernail over the leaf. Rusty splatters dotted the page. *Not enough blood to indicate the loss of a hand, but Papá's curse probably took a finger or two.*

Only members of Los Nefilim knew of the grimoires and the sigils they held. Even fewer knew the exact location of *The Book of Gold.*

A traitor, then. Whoever had stolen the page possessed a strong will, or was desperate enough to spend hours singing their way past multiple wards.

Loud voices echoed outside the reading room. Ysa looked up. The words were indistinct, but the authoritative tone with which they were delivered was unmistakable. *Police.*

It was time to go. She could always circle back later and question Fronteau about the missing page.

Rejecting her earlier plan to leave the book in the library, she stuffed the grimoire into her satchel. *I need to examine it to find the vandal.*

Using the distance between them to her advantage, she stood and walked toward the maintenance exit. The shelving unit in the center of the room shielded her movements from the main entrance.

Barely a meter separated her from freedom when the maintenance door opened. A soldier entered the reading room. He cradled an assault rifle.

Definitely not *on leave.* Ysa registered the weapon with a practiced eye. It was a MP40. If the soldier possessed a full cartridge, he'd have roughly thirty-two rounds of nine-millimeter Parabellums. The submachine gun could easily take down a target over three hundred meters away. Even if he was a poor shot, a spray of bullets would eliminate her and any mortals that got in the way within seconds.

Fuck, fuck, fucker. Her mouth went dry, but she didn't panic. To run now would be the end of her. She swerved toward another shelf closer to the stairs leading to the upper level and pretended to examine the spines.

Boots struck the metal walkway overhead as another soldier cut off her second plan of escape.

Okay. When all routes are closed, Diago says wait for the right moment. Knowing the precise time for flight or fight could easily mean the difference between life or death.

Her papers were forged, but so far she'd passed multiple checkpoints with them. It was time to bluff and hope they didn't decide to search her satchel.

The soldier by the maintenance exit cleared his throat. "Fräulein." He nodded in the direction of the table she'd vacated.

She squinted at him through her glasses and replied in French. "What?"

He gestured with the muzzle of his gun. The meaning was clear. She was to return to the table.

With no other choice, she sat and tucked the satchel against the table's leg.

Three men were at the reading room's entrance, conferring with Fronteau and another librarian. The tallest of the three wore the black uniform of an SS officer. Every line of the coat was sharp enough to cut and the boots were polished to a mirrored shine.

They don't send officers out for routine checks. As she observed the group, the man glanced her way. Detaching himself from the others, he strolled in her direction.

Shit. The grace of his movements gave him away. He was a nefil. *Oh shit, shit, shit, and bitter shit.*

At the entrance, the shortest of the trio broke the silence with German-accented French. "Everyone remain seated. We only want to see your papers."

More soldiers entered and began moving among the students. All of them wore the green uniforms and black collars of the SS, and by their movements alone she guessed that most were nefilim.

Someone came loaded for war. She switched her gaze back to the tall nefil, who was almost to her table. Another hot wash of fear burst through her gut as she recognized him.

Jordi Abelló. Until now, she had only seen pictures of her uncle. Nothing prepared her for his physical presence.

In contrast to her father's coarser features, Jordi possessed both the refinement and grace that his brother lacked. Her father looked like a soldier, Jordi a king. His nose was less prominent than Guillermo's and his cheekbones more pronounced, giving his features a rapacious cast.

Our eyes are shaped the same. The realization surprised her. She had always kept the idea of their blood relationship so distant in her mind that she never expected to share features with him.

He allowed his aura to flare outward. The magnificent cape of fire sparked around his body in a savage nimbus of orange and red, quelled at times by deep golden hues. While the display remained invisible to the mortals in the room, Jordi's blazing aura brought tears to Ysa's eyes.

He's like a peacock, flashing his plumage in an attempt to cower me. She hated to admit it was working. *Then put a stop to it.* It was time to summon her own confidence. Straightening her back, she met his gaze.

He stopped in front of her table. Centuries of knowledge churned in those bright irises.

He is old and he is dangerous. She would have to move with care.

He held out his hand. "Fräulein. Your papers."

So he intends to play the game to the end. Fine. She reached into her coat and withdrew the documents.

Ysabel noticed that the ring finger and the first section of the middle finger on his right hand were missing. Then she saw the ring on his index finger. The signet was similar to the one her father wore, except instead of Los Nefilim's sigils, this ring contained the SS Totenkopfring design: a skull, sun sigils, and a swastika.

That's Queen Jaeger's signet. She had lent the ancient symbols to the Nazis through Die Nephilim's ties to the mortal Himmler. The gesture was intended to be a clear sign to other divisions of the Inner Guard that she endorsed Hitler's rule.

Is she dead? But when? Where? Such news should have spread like wildfire among the nefilim. *Unless Jordi is keeping her absence quiet for some reason.*

Regardless of the circumstances, he'd obviously claimed kingship of Die Nephilim. Which meant that whatever edge her father once had over his brother was gone. *If they fight now, they fight as equals.*

Jordi scanned the page with a faint smile playing on his lips.

"Francine Proulx," he murmured. "I see your father in your face." With a careless gesture, he tossed her papers to the desk. "Fräulein Ramírez."

Ysa unglued her tongue from the roof of her mouth. "You've mistaken me for someone else, monsieur. My name is—"

"Ysabel. Ysabel Ramírez, daughter of my brother, Guillermo Ramírez." He pointed to the documents on the desk. "The only correct information is your age: nineteen."

Twenty in May. To argue with him would prove his point. She ignored his statement and stuck to her alias. "—Francine Proulx."

"Don't toy with me. I know my kin." He jerked the glasses from her face and tossed them to the floor. "Those are a terrible disguise."

"I thought the sigils were a nice touch."

His eyes widened slightly at her riposte. She'd caught him off guard with her humor.

To her surprise, he chuckled—a genuine sound that brought a grin to one mortal's face, because surely a man who laughed couldn't possibly be a threat. Ysabel knew better.

Jordi's charm and charisma were part of what made him so dangerous. His easy manner caused people to lower their guard. She wasn't fooled. Her uncle was probably one of the most ruthless nefilim—ruthless *beings*—alive.

"I am pleased to finally meet you, my niece." He didn't offer his hand. "You're under arrest. Come with me."

She pushed away from the table and stood, leaving her satchel on the floor by her feet. With a little bluster and luck, she might distract him from the bag. The last thing she wanted was for him to find the grimoire.

Lifting her hand, she allowed her own aura to snap around her body. She kept her voice low so that her words remained between them and no one else. "And if I choose not to go?"

He stepped close and lowered his head until his lips were

beside her ear. "Then all these mortals will see us fight. And I will have to kill them. Their lives rest in your hands. Choose."

"Fine," she snapped. "I'll go. But my father—"

"Is impotent."

Rage flushed her cheeks and set her heart on fire. *We'll just fucking see about that.*

He grabbed her arm and pulled her along.

Good. He didn't see the satchel.

"Fräulein!" It was the soldier who'd directed her to sit. He hurried to them, carrying the satchel by its strap. "Your bag."

Great. Fucking great. Which meant it wasn't. She thought of Diago's training. When all else fails, lie. "That's not my bag."

The soldier opened his mouth, but Jordi didn't give him time to speak. He released Ysa and jerked the satchel from the man's grip. After a quick look inside, he met Ysa's gaze again. "Thief."

"That's *not* my bag."

"A thief *and* a liar." Jordi snapped the bag shut. "Take her outside."

The soldier moved close and gestured to the door.

Feeling the mortals' eyes on her, she allowed him to escort her to the exit. She doubted Jordi intended to kill her outright, not when using her as a hostage would further his game *and* torment her softhearted father.

Her papá wanted to negotiate with his brother, find a way to end the wars, and Jordi would use that desire against him. Of that Ysa had no doubt.

However, the knowledge of their dealings helped her. Miquel had taught her to understand her adversaries. *Know what they want, learn how to dangle it before their eyes so you can lead them to their destruction.*

That was simple. She and Jordi wanted the same thing—to one day rule Los Nefilim. The crucial difference between them was that she remained perfectly willing to wait for her father to transfer his kingship to her in his own time, while Jordi intended to take what he thought was his by destroying his brother.

By that same token, he'll see me as a threat to his rule. Unless I can lead him in a different direction. One that might save her father's life. *But first, I must save my own.*

[6]

CHÂTEAU DE L'ENTREPRENANTE
FONTAINEBLEAU

Outside the library, three cars were parked along the curb. The sidewalk and street were cordoned. Ysa thought about running but quickly discounted the idea. She doubted she would get far. *No, don't risk it.*

She shifted mental gears and analyzed the scene. Her mind raced with the implications of this many soldiers turning up all at once. The raid was planned to the last detail.

Somehow Jordi knew I was here. Did he have the missing psalm? She immediately discounted the idea. The colors of the nefil's song in the grimoire's margins were all wrong to be Jordi. Besides, why would Jordi steal the psalm when he could simply order the library to turn over the entire book?

No. Someone had betrayed her. *But who?*

The soldier led her to the middle car. A woman wearing the uniform of an SS-Oberaufseherin stood by the rear door of a sedan. Sergeant's stripes decorated her sleeves. She was nefil.

Ysa wasn't surprised.

The woman opened the door and Ysa got inside, where another woman already waited. She, too, was a nefil, and like the matron outside the car, she wore a dark green uniform with the SS insignia sewn on her black collar. Her age was indeterminable and difficult for Ysa to assess.

The nefilim's physical bodies didn't age as rapidly as those of mortals. Instead, a nefil's maturity was reflected in their eyes. Yet Ysa didn't try to look too deeply at the other woman—in these circumstances, to do so would be considered an act of aggression.

Outside, the matron finished her conversation and got in beside Ysa. Sandwiched between the two nefilim, Ysa made herself as small as possible and tried to quell her runaway pulse.

Fear amplified both sight and sound. The creak of the leather seats as they all settled into place popped as loud as gunshots. Stale cigarette smoke on one of the women vied with eye-watering levels of perfume on the other. The driver, an older nefil with watery brown eyes, glanced into the rearview mirror before returning his attention to the street.

Taking deep breaths, Ysa relaxed her hands until she no longer made fists. She wished they'd just get going. The waiting was debilitating.

Jordi paused to speak with the two policemen before he walked toward the lead car. A smartly dressed young driver held the rear passenger door open for him.

A tall blond nefil with a scarred face joined Jordi. He, too, wore the black uniform of an SS officer.

Ysa recognized him: Erich Heines. He was Ilsa Jaeger's second-in-command. Or, if her suspicion was right, maybe he was now Jordi's second-in-command.

If Jaeger was dead, Heines's presence would reassure the legitimacy of Jordi's ascendancy to the ranking members of Die Nephilim. That bit of authority denoted less contention among the troops. It signified more immediate control for Jordi.

It meant he was even more dangerous.

Heines reached into Jordi's car. When he stood again, Ysa saw that he held her satchel. He snapped his heels and saluted, then he shut the door and turned toward Ysa's car. His expression belied no emotion as he opened the passenger door and got in beside the driver.

He didn't turn, nor did he speak.

This wasn't a good development. Heines's presence indicated she would be questioned. While the different divisions of the Inner Guard sometimes deviated in methodologies, important prisoners were usually interrogated by the second-in-command. Miquel served in that role for her father; she had no reason to believe that Heines's responsibilities would differ.

And what did I think was going to happen? Jordi would ask me about the grimoire over a nice dinner? She bit the inside of her cheek.

Another excruciating minute passed before the cars finally pulled from the curb. Ysa felt strangely relieved, if only for a moment.

As much as she wanted to let herself go numb, Diago had taught her not to give in to her terror. *Fear can induce lethargy . . . it is the body shutting down, the heart giving up. Keep thinking, keep watching, no matter how painful your circumstances. Your survival depends on your ability to read your captors.*

Ysa immediately disregarded Heines, who was a known factor. Careful not to be too obvious, she glanced down at the shoes of the woman on her left. Unlike Jordi's polished boots, the toes of the nefil's loafers were scuffed and well worn. The woman's hand twitched in her lap. Her fingernails were ragged and chewed. A bright red line of blood half-mooned one cuticle. It was fresh wound.

A nail-biter. Either she wasn't comfortable with Ysa's arrest or she was nervous by nature. It wasn't a good sign. Ysa's father had taught her a jumpy nefil made mistakes.

She shifted her attention to the sergeant on her right. If it was possible to remain at parade ease for an entire car ride, this woman intended to do it. She was a professional soldier—her nails were immaculate, her shoes shined as bright as Jordi's boots.

Ysa didn't need a second look into her eyes to know that, like Jordi, she was a killer. The woman would be careful but efficient. She was an older nefil, in both years and experience. Not someone to trifle with.

Likewise, the driver was a soldier, a member of the Inner Guard. His gaze took in not just the road, but the sidewalks and the crowds on the streets. Every eight seconds, he gave the rearview mirror a glance to see if anyone followed.

Ysa was immediately reminded of Suero, who often served as the family's driver. He gave their route the same attention and care as this nefil.

The nervous woman on Ysa's left might be duped at some point, but first she'd have to be separated from the others.

The driver and the sergeant were both seasoned nefilim, probably in their second- or third-born lives.

And Heines. He was a nefil to be feared. During the Great War, Miquel and Heines had met on the battlefield. *At Amiens? Was it at the Battle of Amiens?*

When her father was deep in his cups, he'd told her how Miquel's small unit had held their position against Heines's greater numbers and superior firepower. Some nefilim called their encounter a stalemate, but others said that even Heines conceded Miquel's prowess during that fight. They'd emerged with a deep respect for one another.

But that had been over twenty-five years ago. *And Heines respects Miquel, not me.*

The streets began to fly by faster than her thoughts. They were leaving Paris.

She glimpsed her face in the rearview mirror. Her fear marked her with splotchy white marks on her cheeks. Already her body betrayed her by showing emotions she needed to keep hidden.

Taking a measured breath, she concentrated on relaxing her facial muscles. For the last five years, she'd practiced in the mirror at home until she could mimic the calm she saw her father exude. Even under duress, he managed a manner that was both engaged yet slightly distant in tone.

When she opened her eyes again, she noted that her color had evened. Just thinking of her father soothed her. *Make him proud.*

They left the city behind, traveling south. An hour later, they reached the Fontainebleau Forest. Winter had stripped the trees bare. A light dusting of snow covered the ground.

A chill went through Ysabel when she saw the first sigils.

To a mortal's eyes, the sharp-edged notes glittered like icicles in the trees, but the glyphs were deadly to the nefilim. The bands of light hummed around the trunks and glinted with barbed spikes.

The lead car turned right onto a service road and halted before iron gates. The drive was flanked by guardhouses at the base of twin pillars, which had once been decorated with Les Néphilim's crest and the name of the estate: Château de l'Entreprenante. The property had served as Queen Sabine Rousseau's main base of operations.

Similar to her father's former town of Santuari in Catalonia, Château de l'Entreprenante also functioned as a sanctuary for Les Néphilim. While Santuari had undergone Guernica's fate when Jordi ordered the town bombed, Château de l'Entreprenante suffered a less devasting but equally humiliating defeat. Jordi had apparently taken over the estate and renamed it Schloss des Ewigen Reiches.

Castle of the Eternal Realm, indeed. Ysa glared at Les Néphilim's plaques, which were gouged and scarred with powerful wards. Die Nephilim's sigils—the sun rune represented as twin lightning bolts, or SS, and the Totenkopf—were now seared into the pillars. Twin banners in the familiar black and red hung on either side of the iron gates, their swastikas prominently displayed for any passersby to see.

A soldier left the guardhouse beside the gate and approached the lead car. The same deadly glyphs that Ysa had seen in the forest writhed over the metal gates.

The guard conferred briefly with the driver of Jordi's car before gesturing to two other soldiers. The nefilim neutralized the wards with their song and then opened the gates.

Their small convoy started rolling again.

The grounds were familiar to Ysa. She had accompanied her father to the estate many times, and Rousseau had taken her hiking on those occasions.

A small thread of hope twisted inside her. If she could escape her captors, she could hide in the forest, maybe even find her way around the terrible wards.

The woman on Ysa's left shifted restlessly in her seat. Like the sergeant, Ysa remained perfectly still and focused on their destination.

The château loomed into view. It was a palace with twin towers, one on either end of the structure. Across the main entrance, Les Néphilim's great seals had been replaced with Die Nephilim's runes. Nazi banners hung from the windows and fluttered gently against the bricks.

The drive encircled the château. Jordi's car stopped at the front steps. Ysabel's car continued to the rear of the house.

She knew exactly where they were going. At the base of one of the towers was a set of stairs that led underground to Les Néphilim's gaol.

Her pulse throbbed in her ears. A quick check in the rear-view mirror assured her that her face remained calm, and she took what little pride she could in that.

When the car stopped, the other nefilim exited. Ysa slid across the seat and stepped between the two women. To her relief, her knees didn't buckle and her steps were steady.

They escorted her to the stairs and down into the château's basement. From there, they turned left and followed a short hall, then down another set of stairs.

The chauffer unlocked a door. The windowless room contained two chairs and a desk. The women escorted her inside and made her strip. Ysa didn't let herself think. She moved when they said move and stood still when ordered. They searched her body and each seam of her clothing before they finally allowed her to dress again.

The nervous woman took her coat. The sergeant cuffed Ysa's hands behind her back. A bolt of fear shot through her chest as the metal snapped around her wrists. The woman led her to the chair in front of the desk and forced her to sit.

They weren't gone long before Heines entered the room and sat at the desk. He carried her satchel and a file.

And now it begins. In the back of her mind, she heard Miquel's voice as clearly as if he spoke in her ear.

You'll be scared, but that's okay. We all get scared. Keep your wits about you for as long as you can. Joke with them, ask for a smoke, just don't blink. If they want to skin your mother and castrate your father, you'll be good with it, because if you say 'stop,' or 'no,' or 'please,' that counts as a blink, and when they see you blink, they'll know they have your weak spot. That's how they make you talk. So your job is to tell them lies, and if they hit you, thank them and ask for another, smile through your tears, and never, never let them see you blink.

Ysa met Heines's gaze over the desk.

Flipping through the grimoire's leaves, he stopped at the torn section. "Where is it?"

She blinked. "What?"

"The psalm, fräulein. Where is Psalm 60?"

"I don't know."

He slammed both palms on the desk. Ripping open the file, he removed a photograph and held it up for her to see. It was a picture of the grimoire's missing psalm. "I want to know who you're working with."

She met Heines's gaze evenly. "I have no idea what you're talking about." And that was the truth.

Heines rose and stalked to her chair, forcing her to look up. "We received this photograph two weeks ago. A nefil promised to tell us where to find the psalm in exchange for a favor from Herr Abelló."

Only someone who knew the worth of that psalm to Los Nefilim would work so hard to tear it from the grimoire. To the best of her knowledge, Jordi had no idea what kind of song Psalm 60 hid. *So why would the blackmailer approach Jordi and not my father? What could they hope to gain from Jordi?*

Those were questions she had no way to answer in her current predictment. All she knew for certain was that Jordi and Heines had taken two weeks to find the psalm's location. *Just my rotten luck to be there when they showed up.*

Or had it been a trap? She recalled Monsieur Fronteau's nervousness when she'd requested the book. Suero had made arrangements with him two days ago. That gave Jordi plenty of time to arrange his little greeting party. *And I walked right into it.*

Heines confirmed her suspicions. "We tracked the psalm to *The Book of Gold* at Sainte-Geneviève, and then contacted the librarian to let us know if anyone requested it. We were ready for you."

"I thought you were there for a security check."

He slapped her.

She licked the blood from her lip. "Apparently I was misinformed."

He raised his hand again.

She glared with fire in her eyes. "You'll do well to remember who I am."

His mouth twitched. He lowered his hand.

I'll take that as a blink. Time to lie and see where it leads. "Our interests might be joined, Herr Heines. My father was sent a similar photograph. He wanted me to see if the grimoire was intact."

Suspicion rimmed his eyes. "And what demands did the blackmailer make to your father?"

Oh fuck me; he would ask. "My father wouldn't tell me. He's grown paranoid and . . . addled." *That should make Jordi happy.* She lowered her head and looked away as if ashamed.

"Addled, you say." Heines perched on the edge of the desk and folded his arms. "How do you mean?"

She shook her head. "I've said too much."

Heines watched her for several moments. Twice he looked from the grimoire to the photograph, and then back to her. "Do you love your father, Ysabel?"

Ysa thought of the last time she'd seen him. *Do you remember that spy game you used to play?* The tenderness in his expression as he'd taken her hands in his. She'd give anything for five more minutes with him. Tears cascaded down her cheeks.

Heines retrieved the desk chair and sat directly in front of her. "You can help him, Ysabel. Tell me the truth. What do you mean when you say he is addled?"

She sniffled and began haltingly. "He doesn't remember what year it is. Sometimes he thinks we're still in Spain. His nefilim no longer trust his judgment. Worse, I suspect Diago is working with the daimon-born." *Precisely as he is supposed to be, but Heines doesn't need to know that.*

When she peeked at him through her lashes, she couldn't be sure, but she thought she noticed a flash of compassion in his gaze. *Miquel respects him as an adversary. That says something positive about Heines's character. Stay the course.* "Please, Herr Heines. I need to speak with my uncle."

Heines considered her request and finally nodded. "We'll see." He stood and left the room.

Ysa heard the lock click and then there was silence. *I've threaded the hook, now let's see if Jordi takes the bait.* If he did, then it would be the first verse in a very dangerous song.

Her arms grew numb and no matter how she shifted her position, her back ached. She had no idea how much time passed before the lock clicked again.

Instead of Jordi or Heines, a round nefil entered the room. He carried a black bag and wore a white coat. Without a word, he deposited his bag on the desk and opened it.

The sergeant entered and rolled Ysa's sleeve up. The doctor tied a rubber tube around her upper arm.

Ysa recalled Miquel talking about his time in Jordi's pocket realm, where Nico had performed experiments on the nefilim. *Is that what this is? An experiment of some kind?*

"There's been a mistake," she said.

The man didn't answer. He filled a syringe from a vial.

"Herr Heines has gone for my uncle." Ysa glared at the doctor, trying to summon the same rage that had stayed Heines's hand earlier. Nothing but fear rose to her voice. "What is that?"

The matron stood behind her chair and held her still. "Relax, fräulein. Everything will be over soon."

"What the hell does that mean? Where is my uncle?" Panic rippled around her questions. She swallowed hard. *Blinking. Shit and bitter shit. I'm blinking at them.* She bit her tongue to keep from crying out.

She felt a pinprick. Something hot entered her vein. She closed her eyes and waited.

The doctor and matron left her again. The door locked.

All Ysa heard was her heartbeat, loud in the sudden silence.

[7]

20 January 1944
RUE ÉMILE ZOLA, PERPIGNAN

Diago tugged the brim of his fedora low over his eyes and stepped into a pool of shadows. Although the rue Émile Zola was almost deserted, he didn't believe he moved unobserved.

Several meters away, a maid swept a doorstep on the opposite side of the street. Her busy strokes sent puffs of dust into the gutter. She kept looking up, nervously assessing the encroaching shadows as she went about her work.

The bitter scent of her anxiety wafted on the air, inciting the familiar warmth that spread across Diago's chest and down into his stomach. He fought the urge to approach her, knowing the presence of an unknown man on her street would only heighten her fear.

Touching the heavy silver ring he wore beneath his glove, Diago called on his angelic nature and squelched his daimonic desire for harm. He would wait a few minutes so as not to distress the woman even more.

Or was he just being a coward, using the maid as an excuse to put off his inevitable visit with Christina? *Probably a little of both*, he admitted to himself. Regardless, he'd wait for her to go inside before he continued.

Besides, the less he was seen, the better. Especially here.

Farther down the street, a pair of workers scraped away at German propaganda posters covered in graffiti. The print's faded colors and missing patches showed a French mother hugging her child while the father stood behind them in a worker's coveralls, factory equipment at his back.

Finís les mauvaís jours! proclaimed the poster. Papa gagne de l'argent en Allemagne!

Bad times are over! Papa makes money in Germany!

Someone had painted a red *V* over the poster—part of Radio London's campaign, which encouraged the French to defy their German occupiers. *V* for victory. In case there was any doubt as to the graffiti artist's intent, they'd added one last line: *Patience, de Gaulle will come!*

One of the workers drew Diago's attention. His movements were more measured than those of his companion, as if he intentionally stifled an intrinsic grace the mortal beside him couldn't possibly replicate.

He's nefil. Though whether the man was angel-born or daimon, Diago had no way of knowing from this distance. All he could see was the man's back and his clumsy attempts to mime the mortal's rough gestures.

The nefil could simply be a rogue, attached to neither side, and scrambling to make ends meet in the wartime economy. Or it was possible that Christina had stationed some of her daimon-born nefilim to guard her home.

Looking over the street with renewed interest, he focused

on the doorways and shadows, searching for more of his cousin's people. He saw none.

The maid finally tapped her broom against the stoop and went inside. The two men working on the poster had their backs to Diago's route. It was now or never.

He started walking again. Two doors down, a man and woman emerged from a building. The man wore a double-breasted coat and leather gloves; the woman's fur-lined coat was accessorized with a fashionable hat.

Only the rich managed to endure a war without privation. Their clothing inoculated them against the cold just as their money protected them from the food shortages faced by the less fortunate.

The couple strolled in Diago's direction.

He swore under his breath. To duck into a doorway would arouse suspicions. Nothing to do but continue as if he had every right to be on the street. With the brim of his hat already low over his eyes, he pretended to check his watch.

Humming a soft a tune, he used his right hand and touched the colors of the darkness that lived against buildings. He pinched a small amount between forefinger and thumb.

As he drew parallel with them, Diago lifted his hand. He twisted his wrist so that the dull sunlight caught the band of his watch, and then he tossed the darkness at the man's eye. The shadow took the shape of a scorpion and scuttled across his iris, obscuring his vision.

It was a daimonic trick, one that allowed Diago to cast a minor spell over the mortals to cloud their minds. With supernatural speed, he created a second scorpion for the woman and flicked it at her eye. The couple gripped one another a little more tightly and hurried on their way without acknowledging Diago's presence. They might remember seeing a man, but neither of them would be able to describe him with any clarity.

The workers down the street made no sign that they noticed either the couple or Diago. If the nefil was one of Christina's people, he was either exceptionally sloppy or damn good.

Diago went with the latter. It never hurt to be overcautious. Lengthening his stride, he passed the Hôtel Pams, easily distinguishable by the JOB logo on the lintel. Christina's manse was merely a few doors down.

He assessed her building for possible escape routes. On the ground level, two window bays were covered with grilles similar to those on the Pams. The thick bars prevented anyone from breaking into the mansion while serving the dual purpose of making a quick getaway next to impossible.

The second floor consisted of a long balcony. Wooden shutters covered the three doors that opened to the street. The drop to the pavement wasn't so high as to present a problem for a nefil.

If *I land properly.* An escape from that level gave him a better option . . . one he hoped he wouldn't need.

Following a narrow alley to the servants' entrance, Diago reached into the pocket of his threadbare coat and withdrew a tarot card—the High Priestess. The card served as insurance. Had Diago not been able to keep the appointment, the drawing incorporated sigils known only to the daimon-born nefilim. In this way, Christina and her retinue would recognize the messenger came from Diago.

Not that he ever intended to send anyone else into this scorpion's nest. He gave the door two sharp raps and mentally prepared himself for his role.

A daimon-born nefil opened the door. Thick-bodied and dressed in a pin-striped suit, he looked like a gangster from an American film and exuded the same arrogance.

Swell. Francisco. Christina had dragged him into her ranks from the port of Santander, where Francisco had been a dockworker. In better days, a goon like him would have hardly been worthy of her attention, but they'd all lost loyal nefilim during the Spanish Civil War. *Still, she scraped the bottom of the barrel for this one.*

Unintimidated by the bigger man's physique, Diago lifted the card.

Francisco grunted and snatched it from his hand. He made a great show of examining the sigils. Diago half expected his lips to move as he worked through the meaning of the glyphs.

Finally he looked up and grinned. Diago had time to notice that the brute was missing two more teeth since his last visit.

Probably walked into someone's fist.

"Wait here. I'll see if you're expected." Francisco started to close the door.

Diago's palm stopped it midswing. "My cousin needs a smarter doorman."

Francisco's grin disappeared. "Wait here."

Diago snatched a shadow and formed a ward in the blink of an eye. He tossed the scorpion at Francisco's face. The younger nefil shaped his protective glyph too slowly. He took the scorpion in his eye.

Unlike the soft shadow Diago had flung at the mortal couple, he created this one to sting. Francisco bellowed and clawed at his face.

Diago walked into the short hall and followed it to the main entryway. He almost ran into the Vizconde Edur Santxez, Christina's lover and second-in-command, who'd come to see what all the commotion was about.

Edur looked down the hall. "What the hell did you do to him?"

"I taught him to respect his elders." Diago removed his hat but not his coat.

Another large nefil in a suit barreled past them to go to his comrade's aid.

Edur's eyes narrowed, but he didn't admonish Diago. The daimon-born didn't abide weakness. Poking Francisco in the eye would be frowned upon; letting him get away with his intimidation tactics would make Diago look weak—not the kind of reputation he could afford with his family.

Edur obviously decided to let the incident go. "What took you so long to get here?"

"Your doorman."

"That's not what I meant and you know it."

"They're watching me closely. It was a week before I could slip away and check for messages." No lie there. "We're going to have to arrange a new place for Christina's sigils."

"That may not be necessary."

That doesn't sound good. Nonetheless, Diago held Edur's gaze and merely raised an eyebrow at the statement. "What do you mean?"

Edur lowered his voice. "Christina might believe in your

charade, but I'm still not entirely convinced that you've switched sides."

"Is that what this meeting is about?" Because if it was, Diago wanted to know now while the exit was relatively close at hand.

"No. Christina believes you. I'm merely expressing my suspicions."

To throw me off my game, or to keep me on my toes? It didn't matter. The message was loud and clear. Diago had a long way to go before he won their complete trust. "A little suspicion is healthy. Just remember: that blade cuts both ways."

Edur acknowledged the comment with a tilt of his head. He gestured to the entrance hall. A ruby cuff link the color of blood caught the light. "Please. We shouldn't keep the condesa waiting."

"Of course." Diago followed him past burnished wood panels and doors with frosted patterns etched on the glass.

From deep within the house, someone played a piano, striking the keys with more force than necessary. Diago recognized one of Nico's original compositions. It had been the last song the doomed nefil had played just before the Gestapo arrested him in the studio.

How could they possibly know that? Had there been a recording? Or have they somehow obtained the sheet music Nico used? And, as they usually were, all his questions were followed by the most damning one of all: *Did I somehow slip around my cousin and accidentally betray Nico?*

The answer could be six of one or a half dozen of the other. The daimon-born had infiltrated the Nazi regime just as the angel-born had done. Anything was possible.

Regardless of how they came by the composition, Diago reexperienced the same mix of terror and rage that had consumed him in the restaurant in July. *And if the pianist decides to segue into Mozart's Requiem, does that mean Christina has discovered I am a spy?*

His cousin would delight in a morbid joke such as that. A new level of anxiety ate into his stomach. From the corner of his eye, he saw Edur lick his lips. The other nefil's gaze softened with pleasure.

He's feeding on my uncertainty and fear. Diago mentally kicked himself. He should have known they would pull some stunt like this.

While the daimon-born usually satisfied themselves with the mortals' emotions, a nefil's panic was an elixir to them. It was the difference between grape juice and a fine wine: one satisfied a thirst, the other produced intoxication.

Diago clamped down on his emotions. As he'd done when he was a child, he imagined a wall around his heart. No one could see past it. No one could get in. He focused his mind by counting the stones of that wall backward . . . *501, 500, 499 . . .*

By the time Edur brought them into an immense room with a marble staircase, Diago had regained control of his fear. He continued his internal countdown as they climbed the stairs.

The music still grated his nerves, but not as violently. At least no longer to the point that Edur could feed.

Good. Let him starve.

At the second level, they ascended to the gallery that looked down over the hall. Nefilim moved among the rooms, boxing items and spreading white sheets over the furniture.

Pistol grips occasionally poked free of the servants' pockets, and Diago had no doubt they were all armed. Christina left nothing to chance.

The guns worried him less than the nefilim's activities. *And where is Christina off to, I wonder?* He didn't ask. The move might be the reason for her abrupt summons.

Edur halted before a pair of glass doors. Inside the room, Christina stood before a packing crate. A framed painting leaned against the wall.

She held a glass of wine in one hand and a cigarette in the other. Her hair, as dark and shiny as her cigarette holder, was fashionably styled and adorned with pearls. The forest-green tea dress accentuated her full figure, with the flared hem ending just above her high heels. Stockings, which must have cost a fortune due to the wartime shortages, covered her shapely legs.

The sitting room's elegant furniture was arrayed to showcase the grand piano and the handsome woman at the keyboard. She was none other than Christina's favorite bodyguard, Iria Mejia. Her short platinum-blond hair was combed back behind her ears. She wore a crepe and chiffon evening gown. The white skirt fluttered around her ankles as she pumped the pedals with bare feet.

Diago went to the piano and slammed the fallboard over the keys, barely missing Iria's fingers. He matched her glare for glare and spat the words in her face. "You play that tune to mock me, but you forget the Machiavelli line was a source of information to the daimon-born, as well. My loss is everyone's loss."

Iria opened her mouth to retort, but as she did, she glanced around Diago and then closed her lips.

Probably some sign from Christina. Before he could straighten, he felt his cousin's hand on his shoulder.

"Come, now, Diago," Christina's smoky voice purred behind him. "She was only having fun. Where is your sense of humor?"

"I left it in Spain." He turned to face his cousin.

She pursed her lips and stroked his cheek. "You look awful, and that suit hasn't been in style since the pronunciamento."

He took her hand and brushed his lips across her knuckles, but he didn't release her. "It's dangerous enough that you summoned me directly to your house, worse if I'm remembered by any mortals and word somehow travels back to Guillermo. The suit is part of the disguise. I can't stay long."

She tugged her hand free. "Does Guillermo suspect anything?"

"He's taken to keeping his plans from me. That's not a good sign." Lowering his voice, he hissed, "And if you, through an indiscretion, blow my cover, there will be consequences—in this incarnation and all to come."

She tapped the ashes from her cigarette into a tray and feigned indifference, but he could tell by the way her gaze slid from his that he had struck a chord. "I'm afraid I wasn't able to use a more discreet message. We've been summoned to Paris on an urgent matter."

Edur moved to the dry bar and poured himself a drink. "In the middle of winter, no less. Can you imagine anything more dreadful?"

Diago could have regaled Edur for hours with a litany of horrors viler than winter travel, but he'd already excited Christina's lover enough for one day. *Let him get his kicks somewhere else.* Turning back to his cousin, Diago asked, "What's going on?"

She answered by motioning to the painting. "It arrived this morning."

Diago looked down, first to the packing crate. The label indicated a route heavy with inspection stamps. From Poland through Italy, and then from a north Italian port to France. *Interesting. My cousin has a Polish admirer.*

He shifted his attention to the painting. At first, all he saw were the dark sounds of the dead—the frequencies of those mortals and nefilim who died violent deaths—writhing across the canvas in shades of black and gray.

How much blood was spilled to create this? He had no idea, nor did he want to know.

As he watched, the colors took shape and became a grotto submerged beneath a red fog. The figures took on the intense surrealistic tones of Goya's Black Paintings.

Shadowy faces with thick streams of black running from their eyes peered at a child, who walked a path set between braziers. No more than six years old, the boy was dwarfed by the hulking shapes around him. A single angel's wing, denoting an angelic mother, overshadowed the child's left shoulder and rose upward into the fog.

At first he thought the figure was a likeness of his son, but the boy's hair was straight, not curly. Rather than Rafael's dusky skin, this child's flesh was paler, olive-colored.

With a mild shock, Diago realized, *That's me.* He quickly shifted his attention to the other figures.

Standing beside one of the braziers was his father, Alvaro. His strong features bespoke a Berber lineage diluted by Visigoth blood, but there any similarities to a nefil ended. The artist had painted him in his new form, with his pupils and irises the color of smoke and nickel—white eyes, as if he had no eyes at all.

Swirling all around him were Moloch's colors of puce and gray. The daimon's wizened features were superimposed over Alvaro's face to signify the joining of their souls within Alvaro's body.

Sidling closer to Diago, Christina watched his face. "It's your Gloaming."

The Gloaming was the rite of passage for daimon-born children. At age six, they were brought before the Scorpion Court's Council of Nine, which was composed of elders chosen by the nine branches of the family. The Nine, as they were known, determined which nefilim were trained for the higher courts and which served as slaves to the daimon-born families.

Diago felt as if he'd been kicked in the stomach. "What is this? Another sick joke? I had no Gloaming," he snapped at her. His father had abandoned him, and she damn well knew it.

"You did have the ceremony," Christina whispered. "You just don't remember it."

Nor did he want to. *Although that might be this evening's horror show of a dream.* "It's odd that some nefil decided to send *you* a portrait of *my* Gloaming."

She puffed blue smoke at the painting. "It was sent by someone who calls himself Herr Teufel. Alvaro has asked me to transport the painting to Paris."

"Teufel?" He didn't have to feign his ignorance. The name meant nothing to him. "Do you think it's a code name?"

"I have no idea."

He searched her gaze for any sign of deception. She didn't look down and to the left as she normally did when she dodged the truth. No, she wasn't lying. In fact, she seemed to be examining him in precisely the same manner to see if he withheld information from her.

Her lip quirked to become a smile that wasn't quite a smile. "Alvaro has summoned the court to Paris. He intends to finally hold the vote for Moloch's high priest."

Diago tried not to sound hopeful. "Is Alvaro sick?"

"No. He is looking to the Scorpion Court's future." She took a long drag from her cigarette, that strange half smile teasing her lips.

She knows more. Before he could devise a question that might draw the information from her, Edur distracted him.

The vizconde poured himself another drink and examined Diago over the rim of the glass. "We have word from our agents in Toulouse that Guillermo's daughter is visting several university libraries. Do you know what she is after? Or why she has gone to Paris? Or why we had to hear this information from someone other than you?"

Time to obfuscate. "I didn't want to say anything until I had something concrete to pass along to you. I don't know what she is after. Not yet. But—"

Edur thumped his glass on the table. "Not yet, not yet, not yet! Christ, Diago, you've got nothing but excuses for us. Do you intend to find out?"

"I told you! Guillermo is keeping his plans from me. I have to move carefully. If he finds I've betrayed him again, the angel-born will judge me. They might very well give me the second death." The death from which no nefil could reincarnate. Diago didn't believe he was overplaying his hand. The threat was credible.

Edur didn't seem impressed with the explanation. "Your kin might do the same if you don't become useful to us."

The colors of the painting swirled violently as if picking up on the nefilim's sudden hostility. In the back of his mind, Diago heard an authoritative voice shout the word *Abomination!*

He flinched, knowing the denunciation was aimed at him. The memory was there and gone before he fully grasped why it terrified him so.

"Edur!" Christina admonished her lover. "Don't say such things."

Diago glared at the other nefil with a bravado designed to conceal his fear. "The only reason I'm here right now is because Christina told me to come. Do you believe I'd put myself in such jeopardy if I wasn't loyal to her?"

Christina came to his side and stroked his arm. "And I appreciate your service, cousin. You know I do. Forget the Ramírez girl for now." She tossed Edur a warning glare. "We have more important concerns. Jordi Abelló is in Paris. He's taken over Die Nephilim."

Diago's mouth dropped open. "What?"

She drifted past him and joined Edur at the bar. One bright-red-lacquered fingernail tapped the cigarette holder with three hard clicks. The ashes spilled into an art deco ashtray, which depicted two angels facing each other. The angels' heads had been removed and their wings broken. "It's true. He sent Jaeger into her next incarnation with a poisoned syringe. Now he wears her signet and has petitioned the Thrones for their blessing."

A pit of coldness settled in Diago's stomach. That was the worst possible news. With his murder of Ilsa Jaeger, Abelló commanded the power of Jaeger's signet. He could make his move against Guillermo any day now.

Christina continued. "Abelló has taken over Rousseau's former estate in the Fontainebleau Forest as his base of operations."

Fontainebleau . . . Paris's backyard. And Ysa? Has she avoided her uncle? Christ, he hoped so. *Keep them talking.* "Then we've got to do something. His lieutenant, Espina, rules Spain in Jordi's name. If Jordi takes France and Germany, our court will be forced to merge with another."

"That is a matter best left to the elders and ranking members of the court." Christina held out her hand to him. "I need you to concentrate on advancing my agenda. I want you to carry a message to Guillermo."

After a wary glance at Edur, Diago approached his cousin. She took his arm and walked him to the sitting room's door. "Tell him about Jordi. That will shift his eye from the Scorpion Court's gathering in Paris. He'll be so focused on his brother, he won't notice us. Make him believe the daimon-born insist that he remain king, and Rousseau must return to France to reclaim Les Néphilim. They both have their faults, but they abide by the treaties written in our blood and in our songs.

"Give him this message: Guillermo can rely on the daimon-born nefilim under my command to fight against his brother, just as we fought beside Los Nefilim during the Spanish Civil War. This time we will win."

"If I'm not to mention the Scorpion Court, how do I explain your little trip to Paris?"

"Reconnaissance. I'm going to personally coordinate a fifth column to assist the Allied invasion. Oh, don't look so surprised. We all know it's coming, it's merely a matter of where and when."

"What if I need to contact you again?"

"Send a postcard to the Théâtre de Rêves, thirteen rue de la Ville Neuve."

Theater of Dreams. He memorized the address.

Edur gestured to Iria. "Please see Monsieur Alvarez to the door."

Christina's words followed him into the hall. "I will watch for you."

The promise wasn't said with the same endearing tones that Diago shared with his angel-born comrades, but she offered him no malice, either.

"And I for you." Turning away from his cousin, he followed her bodyguard to the stairs.

At the first step, he paused and looked back. Christina walked to the painting and stood before it again. Her mouth tightened into a thin red line. Edur placed his hand on her shoulder in a protective gesture. As she leaned against him, Diago turned and followed Iria downstairs.

He couldn't deny a small jab of jealousy eating at his heart. Christina never had to pretend she was something different in order to be accepted by their family. Although Diago had found a place in Los Nefilim and love from his found family, they, too, had expectations for his behavior. No matter which side he chose, his loyalties would always be, to some degree, suspect.

Iria led him back the servants' hall, where Francisco had returned to his post. The brute glared at Diago from his good eye. The other was concealed beneath a bloodstained bandage.

As Diago neared, Francisco muttered under his breath, "Watch your back, asshole."

Diago lifted his hand and had the satisfaction of watching Francisco flinch. "I will." He pointed at his own face. "With both eyes."

Before Francisco's sluggish brain could form a retort, Diago stepped into the alley.

Cold air slapped his cheeks. He drew his collar against his neck as he reached the street and glanced both ways.

The workers were gone and so was the poster with its accompanying graffiti. Hurrying back the way he had come, Diago caught a tram. He found an empty seat and pushed his cold hands into his pockets.

Francisco might not be the smartest nefil Diago ever encountered, but his parting advice was something to take to heart. *Watch your back.* Los Nefilim's place in the world had suddenly become very precarious. *And there is nothing to do but keep moving forward.*

[8]

PERPIGNAN

Diago doubted Francisco or any of his goonish friends would follow him, but it didn't hurt to be safe. He left the tram several blocks from his destination and walked at a brisk pace.

Turning down one street and then another, he glimpsed a familiar figure, hanging back, but always just a half a block behind. It wasn't Francisco in his pin-striped suit. This man was dressed in coveralls and a stained coat. *One of the men covering the graffiti.*

Without making any outward sign that he noticed, Diago continued for another block before pausing in front of a to-bacconist shop. The window reflected the opposite side of the street. No one stood out to him as a nefil, and the mortals kept moving. Nor did anyone seem to pay particular attention to his presence.

Looking to his left, he noticed the man pausing to light a cigarette. He was half turned to face the opposite direction, so his features remained indistinct, but Diago had no question it was the same man he'd seen near his cousin's manse. His mortal companion was nowhere in sight.

One of Francisco's friends, maybe?

The skin of the nefil's face seemed incredibly flawless. The flesh shone with unnatural luminance.

A mask. Between the injuries suffered by survivors from both the Great War and the Spanish Civil War, a mask wasn't seen often, but neither was it completely unusual. The painted tin might cover a legitimate wound or merely be a disguise.

Somehow, he didn't think any of Francisco's friends would bother with a disguise. *No, that kind is like the Milice—they simply stomp down the street and knock heads. Subtlety isn't their forte.*

Diago entered the tobacconist's shop. Though he didn't smoke, he still enjoyed the smell of tobacco. Too, the warmth of the stove drove the iciness from his joints. He browsed the offerings under the proprietor's suspicious gaze and settled for two packs of cigarettes—one for Miquel and the other for Rafael.

Then he returned to the street and paused, pretending to count his coins. Instead, he surreptitiously surveyed the area. The strange nefil was gone.

Walking two more blocks, he took an alley that he knew ended in a dead end. The shadows worked in his favor. He stepped into a recessed doorway and drew the small knife he carried in his pocket, flicking the blade open with his thumbnail.

Patient as a cat, he waited.

The conversations of pedestrians filtered to him as the mortals hurried along on their errands. Somewhere nearby a horn honked. A woman laughed. The clop of a horse's hooves and the grind of steel wheels indicated a cart on its way to or from deliveries.

Two full minutes passed. Then Diago heard the sound he'd been waiting for: footsteps shuffling over the alley's rough cobblestones. The mingled scents of man-sweat and tobacco preceded the person. Underlying it all was a sour smell, the putrescent odor that accompanied a fetid wound.

The nefil passed the doorway. He became aware of Diago a second too late.

Diago launched himself out of the darkness and shoved the other nefil against the opposite wall. Pinning the taller man against the bricks with his forearm, he pushed his knife against the nefil's throat.

The man tensed but didn't resist. "I thought it was you," he whispered.

In spite of the mask covering the left side of his face, Diago instantly recognized him. Eyes that were once gunmetal-blue and hardened by war blurred beneath a drug-induced addiction. His hair had gone completely silver. A scraggly beard covered hollowed cheeks. The putrid smell seeped from beneath the mask.

"Carlos Vela." Diago muttered the name as he would a curse. "I thought you defected to Jordi's Nationalists. Either you're the bravest nefil alive, or the dumbest."

Carlos lifted his hands in surrender. His right hand was maimed—the thumb and three fingers were missing. A gangrenous odor seeped from beneath the stained wrappings.

His words rushed out in a ravaged whisper. "It's taken me weeks to locate you. I need to talk to Don Guillermo before the daimon-born find me."

What is wrong with his voice? "You betrayed Miquel to Jordi's forces, spied on Los Nefilim, and almost got my son murdered." He narrowed his eyes. "Tell me why I shouldn't kill you right now."

"Because I have something Guillermo needs."

"Switching sides again?"

"I'm a rogue and will stay one after this." Carlos reached up and removed his mask. The entire left side of his face was scarred with raw, scorched flesh. The wound seemed as inflamed as the day Guillermo filled a tunnel with the fire of the Thrones.

"For five years I've suffered with this injury. When Guillermo killed the Grigori, I was on the train platform. A single spark caught my cheek. My body can't heal it, and the morphine doesn't kill the pain anymore. I can't keep living like this. I have important information for Guillermo. But only if he heals me. I'm going to reach into my jacket."

"Slowly."

Carlos carefully withdrew a crumpled envelope and gave it to Diago. "Show him this. He'll want to talk to me. When he's ready to negotiate, tell him to send word to fourteen rue du Paradis. I'll meet him at the destination of his choice."

Keeping his hands up, Carlos moved sideways and backed toward the street. At the mouth of the alley, he turned and ran.

Diago stuffed the envelope in his pocket and followed. By the time he stepped onto the sidewalk, Carlos was gone.

[9]

20 January 1944

THE FARM

Diago checked his watch. *Damn it.* He didn't have time to follow Carlos. If he didn't join Miquel soon, his husband would assume the meeting with Christina went badly and be on his way to her mansion.

Right now, that's the last *thing I need.* With a final glance both ways, Diago followed the street until he reached a small café, the Golden Brûlée. Inside, a few workers finished their lunch and paid him no heed.

Pretending he had every right to be there, he opened the door and went into the kitchen. Bernardo Ibarra looked up from the grill. Big as a bear and twice as ugly, the nefil lifted his spatula in greeting and tilted his head toward a door at the back of the room.

That must be where Miquel is. Diago nodded a greeting and walked past the steaming pots to the alley door.

A farm truck occupied the space between the buildings.

While Diago met with Christina, Miquel had spent his day trading on the black market for goods, especially petrol.

Only five cans disguised as "cooking oil" were in the truck's bed. It was a thin haul.

And that won't do much for his mood.

Miquel shoved an empty crate against one of the cans. Curls as black as his eyes fell across his forehead. A long, jagged scar coiled from his cheekbone to the corner of his mouth—a souvenir from his own battle with the Grigori that Jordi had found in 1939.

Miquel checked his watch. "Another five minutes, and I would have come looking for you."

"That's why I hurried." He helped his husband secure a canvas tarp over the bed, further hiding the contents.

As they worked, Diago told him about the encounter with Carlos in a low murmur.

"Oh fuck." Miquel cinched a knot with a hard pull that belied his frustration. He stood there for a moment with his head bowed. When he looked up again, he offered an apologetic smile. "I'm sorry. I'm not angry with you."

"I know." His husband wasn't the type to shoot the messenger. Even so, Diago didn't relay the news about Jordi yet. *No sense in overwhelming him.*

"I can't go looking for Carlos now." He inclined his head toward the contraband in the truck.

Diago agreed. The idea was out of the question. They'd have a hard time making it back to the farm before the evening curfew as it was.

Miquel pocketed his work gloves. "Go ahead and get in. I forgot my hat." Without waiting for an answer, he returned to the restaurant.

Diago watched him go, knowing that he intended to give Bernardo instructions to watch Carlos. When the kitchen door shut behind his husband's back, Diago retreated to the cab. A bottle of beer and a sandwich wrapped in wax paper sat on the seat.

A surge of love lifted his spirits. Miquel's thoughtful little touches always took the edge off a bad day. He got inside and opened the beer first, because after a session with Christina, he needed a drink.

Miquel opened the truck door and climbed inside. He wore a flat cap that wasn't his. "Do you have the envelope?"

"Yes." Diago offered it to him and went back to his lunch.

Miquel examined the cheap stationery for sigils and then handed it back to Diago. "I told Bernardo to send someone to rue du Paradis and to bring Carlos to the farm." He pressed the clutch and turned the ignition. "Don't just drink. Eat something. You're too thin again."

Diago returned the envelope to his pocket and took up his sandwich. "So you're going to wine me and dine me and whatever comes next?"

"We'll definitely get to whatever comes next when we get home." Miquel waggled his eyebrows but his grin seemed forced.

Something is bothering him. Diago picked at the sandwich in order to please his husband.

Shifting the truck into gear, Miquel eased onto the main street, sparing Diago a glance as he did. "How did it go with Christina?"

"Worse than with Carlos." He relayed the information Christina had given him during their meeting.

With a frown, Miquel guided the truck onto a backstreet

in order to avoid the main thoroughfare and any potential checkpoints. "So Jordi has killed Queen Jaeger and wears her signet." He exhaled a frustrated sigh. "Shit. That's bad."

That was the understatement of the day. "I'm worried about Ysa."

"She's a smart nefil. Probably on her way home now."

He's saying it like he's trying to convince himself she's fine. Then again, she might even be at the farm by the time they got back. "Did you find out anything about Nico?"

Miquel took another side street that meandered through a bleak neighborhood. "Yeah. I don't know how to soften the blow, but my Lyon connection informed me that Bianchi and four other resistance fighters were put on a ghost train and sent to Mauthausen."

"Mauthausen," Diago repeated numbly. *Poor Nico.* Mauthausen was extermination through labor. *Unless Jordi finds him first.* "When?"

"They think he was transferred out in late November."

"Jesus." Diago wondered if he was even still alive. "Do we have anyone that can get in?"

"To Mauthausen?"

"Yes!"

"No! What are you even thinking?"

He didn't know himself. *We have so many other things to worry about . . .* "Guillermo made me Nico's handler from the day he took his oath to Los Nefilim. That means he's my responsibility."

"You're taking that responsibility over and beyond your duty. You're his handler, not his savior."

"It just seems wrong to abandon him now that we know where he is. Especially considering what's he's done for us."

"What? What has he done for us?

Diago wasn't sure if Miquel was serious. "He organized resistance efforts at Radio Paris, in the Nazis' own damn studio."

"That was his fucking job."

"And when he was caught, he kept his mouth shut."

"How do you know?"

"We're still here."

"The Milice is probably waiting to make their move."

"Mr. Sunshine."

Miquel shot him a sour look. "I'd be surprised if anyone could stay silent under the Gestapo's tender mercies."

"Mortals have. And Nico has much more to lose."

"You're still protecting him."

"I'm being realistic."

"Ya, ya, ya, he's been playing you like a violin ever since you showed him empathy in the Pyrenees. He's done nothing but try to drive a wedge between us."

"He has done nothing but try to win your trust." *Not that he's making any headway. Maybe that's why I became his champion.* Diago related to being alone and under constant suspicion.

"He'll never have it."

"Fine, I'll find some way to get to Austria and take care of the matter."

Miquel stopped at an intersection. "Absolutely not."

"I wasn't asking your permission." He glared out the window.

Miquel shoved the truck into gear and pulled away from the stop. He didn't speak again until they'd left the city far behind. "Guillermo might have made you Nico's handler, but he won't let you go to Austria. Not into one of the camps."

"I promised—"

"No!" Miquel struck the steering wheel with the palm of his hand. "You make promises like you're still a rogue, like you can come and go at will, and you cannot. Not anymore. Not into the camps. No." He turned the truck onto the road toward Tarerach. "No more promises, Diago. Nico is on his own. You've done all you can for him. If he really wants to die, all he has to do is spit on a Nazi, or walk into the fence."

"We talk about dying like it's so easy, but when we're actually faced with the prospect, we cling to life with the same tenacity as mortals." Diago stared out the window, the bottle of beer forgotten in his hand.

Miquel lit a cigarette. "I'm sorry." He exhaled blue smoke at the windshield. "You think I'm being overprotective, but that's not it. I swear to you—"

"Nico helped save your life."

"And Nico followed Jordi's orders to give me the drugs in the first place. Wasn't that Nico, too? I think it was."

"Five years ago . . ."

"Five years is nothing to the nefilim." Miquel took another sharp drag from the cigarette. "Nico wanted out of his relationship with Jordi . . . he would have used any one of us as the means."

"He saved Rafael. He could have left with him, but he insisted on going back for you."

"Why? Why do you think he did that? Out of love?" Miquel scoffed. "Rafael was fourteen. What good is a fourteen-year-old in a fight?"

"He held his own, if I remember correctly."

"But Nico didn't know that. He wanted a soldier, someone who could get him out of the country."

"And he stayed, and he joined Los Nefilim—"

"Under duress."

"He did a good job, Miquel. He didn't have to stay in Paris—"

"No, but he did, because if Jordi came to France, where would he go? To Paris. The city is fucking crawling with Germans."

The twisting road corkscrewed dangerously. The truck's bed slewed left. Miquel clamped the cigarette between his lips and downshifted, barely guiding the vehicle through the curve without going into a skid.

He's going too fast. Driving like he was angry, because he was. Diago remembered the beer and finished it, tossing the bottle into a sack. He rewrapped the sandwich. "You taught me to see the good in others."

"I didn't teach you to be a fool."

A flash of rage suffused Diago's chest. *There is no reasoning with him today.* It was time to shift the argument from the symptom to the disease. "This has nothing to do with Nico. This is about you and your fear that something will happen to me."

Miquel cranked his window down a few centimeters, letting a blast of cold air into the cab that did nothing to extinguish the heat between them. He shoved his cigarette out the crack and barked a harsh laugh. "My what?"

"You're afraid. All the time. I know it, because it's how I used to be." And if today was any indication, how he still could be.

Gripping the wheel in both hands, Miquel pretended to concentrate on the road, but Diago could see his words had hit home. The muscle just under his husband's cheek jumped as his jaw worked.

Diago pressed his advantage. "You're afraid of losing me, and it affects your judgment."

The road passed under them and Miquel did not speak for a long time. Almost a full kilometer later, he whispered, "Is that so wrong? To love you?" He glanced at Diago, his eyes glassy in the late afternoon light. "To be afraid of losing what we have?"

Diago reached across the seat and touched his husband's thigh. "No. It's not wrong to be afraid. Fear is good. But someone very wise taught me that letting my fear control my decisions is not." He gave Miquel's leg a gentle squeeze and then let go.

"Someone wise," Miquel murmured.

"I think it was you."

"I don't feel very wise anymore."

"That's okay. Because I believe in you."

Miquel wiped his eyes on his sleeve and sniffled. He glanced at the speedometer and brought the truck to a more reasonable speed. "I need you more than Nico ever will. Do you understand?"

"I'm not leaving you."

"Okay, that's a promise you can make, and I'm holding you to it."

Diago smiled at his husband. "You do that."

The sky glowed red with the sunset by the time they reached the first of the nefilim's sigils. The glyphs spun in the dying light and hid the road to Guillermo's farm from prying mortal eyes.

Miquel turned the truck onto a lane that was little more than a dirt path. They bumped along the rutted road and meandered through a copse of trees. On the other side of the grove, they reached another clearing.

The main house lay straight ahead with two buildings flanking it—one on either side. The manor housed Guillermo, his family, and personal staff, while an adjacent dorm belonged to those within his guard. The barn was set in a wide field, away from the main house.

As Miquel turned the truck for the barn, Violeta emerged from the dorm.

Miquel rolled down his window. "Any word on Ysa?"

She shook her head. "Not yet. We're expecting her any day now."

Any day now had become their mantra. Christina's news about Jordi and Ysa's prolonged absence gave Diago a bad feeling he couldn't shake. *She should have been home two days ago.* Either she was lying low or had become ensnared by the Gestapo. No one wanted to think it was the latter.

Guillermo had been tense as a bear ever since his daughter had left for her assignment. Today's news wasn't going to alleviate his concerns.

As the truck neared the barn, Rafael emerged and pushed the wide doors open. Miquel drove inside and cut the engine.

Rafael opened Diago's door. "How are you?" he whispered.

Diago knew Rafael was still worried about his interactions with Christina. "I'm fine. You'll be relieved to know they're leaving."

The news actually brought a smile to his son's lips. "If you wake up tonight because of bad dreams, come get me. Okay?"

"I will."

Rafael raised his voice so that Miquel could hear. "Don Guillermo wants to see you both. We received a package today."

During the war, even the most mundane comments held double meaning. In one village, the arrival of new Bibles meant incoming refugees; in another, a shipment of grapes indicated the Allied planes were dropping a load of hand grenades; nonsense phrases had become the language of covert operations. For Los Nefilim, a package referred to a refugee that needed to be "shipped" over the Pyrenees into Andorra.

"Where did it come from?" Diago got out of the truck.

Rafael shrugged. "We don't know."

Diago exchanged a worried glance with Miquel, who tossed the truck's keys to Violeta. "We got five cans of petrol today. It's not doctored, so put it with the good stuff. Get them hidden before you do your rounds."

The teenagers nodded and went to work.

Diago followed his husband out of the barn. They didn't speak as they walked to the villa. Neither of them relished having to give Guillermo the news about his brother.

[10]

20 January 1944

THE FARM

Miquel and Diago were met at the door by Suero. The younger nefil held an oil lamp to light their way. "Don Guillermo is waiting for you in his office."

They hung their coats and followed him through the kitchen and into the house. The lamp's flame sent their shadows fluttering over the walls.

The home's aesthetics were austere compared to the villa Guillermo had owned in Catalonia. A few items of art hung from the walls, but little else in terms of decoration. Juanita purchased pieces that would quickly bring them cash in their times of need.

Sigils glittered on each riser of the main stairwell, carrying the vibrations of their treads up to the second floor. At the landing, they followed a short balcony to the office door. Suero knocked twice and entered.

Guillermo sat at a large desk. He lifted his shaggy head

from the report he'd been reading. More lamps glowed on the desk and tables, softening features made craggy by hunger and worry. "What news?"

"All bad," Diago said as Suero left them.

Guillermo didn't seem surprised.

Even in the semidarkness of the room, he sees the truth in our eyes. Without waiting for an invitation to continue, Diago recounted his meeting with Christina.

His friend seemed to age another hundred years. "Shit and bitter shit."

Miquel tried to mitigate the damage. "Surely the Thrones will not stand for Jordi murdering a queen of the Inner Guard."

"We can't depend on them," Guillermo murmured and shook his head. "Time does not move for them as it does us. If Jordi is tried, it will be by the remaining kings and queens of the Inner Guard, and that is only if we win this war. If he wins, it's my head on the block."

Miquel straddled the chair in front of Guillermo's desk. "Don't lose hope. We've been through worse than this."

Guillermo chuckled and shook his head. "I'm hard-pressed to remember just when."

Miquel nudged Diago. "Tell him the rest."

Diago winced. The news about Carlos would be like salt in a wound, so he gave it to Guillermo fast. "I saw Carlos Vela today. He followed me into an alley."

The big nefil grunted. "That wasn't the smartest thing he could do."

"He's half mad with pain, and there is something wrong with his voice. He could barely speak above a whisper."

Diago quickly described the encounter. Withdrawing the envelope, he placed it on the desk. "He sent this. We checked it and found no sigils."

Miquel lit a cigarette. "I told Bernardo to bring Carlos in for questioning. He said he'd find him and have him here as soon as he could."

Guillermo nodded as he examined the envelope carefully before reaching for his letter opener. Tearing the seal, he removed the note and a photograph. A moment passed, and then he read aloud: "'Don Guillermo, Forgive me. The Thrones' fire never leaves me. I do not wish to suffer like this for all my incarnations. Herr Teufel forced me to extract Psalm 60 from *The Book of Gold*. I can tell you where to find it in exchange for your power to heal me. Carlos.'"

Diago exchanged a concerned look with Miquel. "Ysa . . ."

Guillermo lifted his head, and to Diago's surprise, he didn't appear alarmed. Instead, he used a magnifying glass to examine the photograph by the lamp's light. "It looks authentic. That could very well explain why Ysa isn't home."

Diago was the first to get over his shock. "I don't understand."

"She doesn't know Carlos stole the psalm. Didn't he say that it took him weeks to find us?"

Diago nodded.

"And it's probably true. Which means he was in Paris while Ysa was still in one of the other four universities acquiring the other pages."

Miquel picked up the thread. "Then she gets to Sainte-Geneviève and the book is gone."

Guillermo sighed and passed the letter to Miquel.

"Knowing my daughter's tenacity, she's now working at Sainte-Geneviève in the rare manuscripts division still trying to track down *The Book of Gold*."

Perhaps it was his interview with his cousin, but Diago still didn't feel reassured. "Wouldn't she have contacted you to let you know what's going on?"

"Not unless she had something to report. We keep our communiqués brief, or avoid them altogether if we can. Less chance they'll be intercepted. We know where she's staying, and she checked in with her landlady on time. I'll have Suero ring the rooming house tomorrow to call her back to the farm. Meanwhile, I want to know how Carlos knew where to find that psalm."

"That's easy." Miquel looked up from the note. "We moved the grimoires into France in late 1938 as a safety measure. Carlos was a member in good standing with Los Nefilim at that time. He was one of my capitanes. I put him in charge of relocating them."

"Then he turned traitor and screwed us to the wall." Leaning back in his chair, Guillermo rubbed his eyes. "Fucker. I'll kill him."

Diago had an uncomfortable thought. "Carlos was working for Jordi by the end of the war. Do you think he told Jordi about the grimoires?"

Guillermo's stare swung to Miquel. "Well?"

"Probably not." He flicked the edge of the paper with his fingernail. "If he had, Jordi would already be in possession of all the grimoires. He wouldn't waste an opportunity like that."

Diago took the seat beside his husband. "So Carlos sat

on the information, waiting for when it would do him the most good?"

Miquel concurred. "That would be my guess. Carlos is shrewd. His knowledge of those grimoires was like money in the bank. He'd save it for just the right price."

Guillermo drew a cigar from the box on his desk and snipped the head. "Second question: How did Carlos and Herr Teufel know that we're looking for the grimoires, specifically *The Book of Gold?*"

Diago didn't need to give the question much thought. "Daimon-born agents have been watching Ysa's movements. Edur wanted to know why she was visiting university libraries, but I managed to put him off. He must have been testing me, because it's apparent he already knew the answer."

"Maybe not." Guillermo met Diago's gaze. "He might have simply wanted confirmation they were on the right track. The most likely scenario is that Edur and Christina's agents picked up on Ysa's movements and passed that information to Alvaro, who alerted Teufel, and then Carlos connected the dots." He took a long draw from his cigar and then pointed at Diago. "Third question: Any idea who the devil might be?"

"It's an alias for another member of the Scorpion Court. I don't believe Christina knows his name, but if Alvaro is feeding Teufel information, then he is someone with rank. And now they have Psalm 60."

Guillermo watched the smoke from his cigar curl toward the ceiling. "They won't crack the sigils. I've designed those glyphs to burn the document if the daimon-born tamper with it. The only nefilim who can unlock its secrets are Ysa and me." He fell silent for a few moments and then asked, "What about the painting? Any clues to Teufel's identity there?"

"He didn't use the colors of his song; otherwise, I might have some inkling as to who he is. Instead, he painted with the dark sounds of the dead and dying. The shipping label indicated that the point of origin was Poland."

Miquel tossed Carlos's note back to the desk. "The Germans have a lot of concentration camps in the east. Do you think Teufel is hanging around the camps?"

"I'm almost certain of it," Diago answered. "But that doesn't explain how he came into contact with Carlos. Unless Carlos was interned in that area."

Guillermo smoked and considered the explanation. "It's something to think about. Miquel?"

"I'll get someone on it first thing in the morning."

"All right. Juanita has our package in the basement. She doesn't think he's going to last the night. Miquel, go down and see what you can get out of him. Diago, you stay. I want you to refresh my memory about rogues."

As Miquel rose, he brushed his fingers over the back of Diago's hand. "Sure. I'll see what I can find out from him."

The touch was discreet—their version of a light kiss.

They'd cultivated the hidden signal primarily for mortals, who didn't accept their relationship. Guillermo never minded their displays of affection, but given the war and the Nazi regime's extreme hatred of homosexuals, they made covert gestures a habit.

Diago hoped that if they lived long enough, the world would reach a point where they could live openly. *But that day is not today, and to slip in public risks a death sentence.*

Guillermo waited until Miquel's footsteps receded on the stairs. "Carlos claims to be a rogue now. Isn't that what he told you?"

"Yes."

Guillermo ran his thumb over his lighter and considered the situation. "Don't rogues have some sort of tribunal for nefilim that draw the ire of the Inner Guard?"

"It has more to do with rogues that draw mortal attention to our existence as nefilim." Mortals, for the most part, were unaware of the supernatural creatures in their midst. Far outnumbered, the nefilim remained inconspicuous as a matter of self-preservation. They'd learned hard lessons about mortal fear and aggression during the Inquisition and similar purges.

The Inner Guard required its members to move through the world discreetly. The rogues, lacking the military discipline and intensive networks of the Inner Guard, maintained their own code of invisibility.

Guillermo relit his cigar. "What happens if they're found guilty of interfering in mortal affairs?"

"Then a council of the oldest rogues is called and judgment is passed. But that is a rare event."

"Has it ever happened?"

"Once that I know of. Rasputin was judged, and when he refused to abide the council's decision, we sent him into his next incarnation."

"I remember that. It got . . . messy."

"Mortals were involved. They complicated things."

Guillermo clicked the lid of his lighter. "And someone like Carlos?"

"Is no Rasputin. The rogues would consider this a matter

for the Inner Guard and its tribunals, especially since Carlos was once a member of Los Nefilim."

"Good. That makes me more comfortable about taking care of Carlos myself. I don't want to damage Los Nefilim's relationship with the rogues." He puffed his cigar. "Last question: All this time, Alvaro has gone without a high priest. Why now? Is Alvaro sick or dying?"

"I asked Christina that same question, and she indicated that Alvaro was looking to the Scorpion Court's future."

"That could mean anything. Or nothing."

"I would guess the former. My father has long desired to fulfill Moloch's dream of retaking the mortal realm for the daimons. With the German death camps, Jaeger and Jordi have performed a human sacrifice of mammoth proportions, feeding Moloch's power."

Guillermo exhaled sharply and picked up the note again. "I've been afraid of that."

"Can we stop the Scorpion Court from meeting?"

"No. Alvaro is perfectly within his rights to gather his court and choose Moloch's next priest. The Inner Guard can't interfere."

"Not even with Christina's admission that she wants to distract your attention from the meeting? Wouldn't that alone indicate they might be acting on more nefarious plans?"

Guillermo shook his head. "It's too circumstantial. I need direct evidence to move against a legal gathering."

"But the psalm—"

"The psalm is a secret. In order to use it as a reason to disrupt Alvaro's court, I'd have to divulge its contents to the other divisions of the Inner Guard. That I will not do, especially with my brother as a rival king."

"Nothing but bad news."

"Not your fault." He lifted his head and finally offered Diago a weary smile. "Go to bed. We'll deal with all this in the morning. There is nothing more we can do tonight."

Diago hesitated. With Miquel occupied elsewhere, he could broach the subject of Nico's rescue without further agitating his husband. Diago only felt a little guilty about going over his husband's head, and quickly absolved himself. *If he wasn't such an ass about it, I would have said something while he was here.*

"There is one more thing," he blurted before he could change his mind.

Guillermo peered at him through the cigar smoke. "What's going on?"

"I'm sure Miquel is going to put this in his report to you tomorrow—"

"Then you might want to let him."

"I could, but it concerns Nico."

"Are you going to drag me into a fight between you and Miquel?" Guillermo's furrowed brow reflected his displeasure.

"No," Diago said, raising his hands in a gesture for peace. "Your word is final. But I know we need every nefil we can muster—"

"Where is he, Diago?"

"Mauthausen."

Guillermo crushed his cigar in the ashtray. "Shit."

"Yeah. We need to get him out."

"I've got no one to send."

"Send me."

"No." Guillermo pointed one blunt finger in Diago's direction. "I need you."

"So Nico is expendable?" Diago regretted the question the moment it left his mouth.

Guillermo's eyes smoldered. "No one is expendable."

Damn it. I walked right over the line. "I'm sorry. I shouldn't have said that."

"Damn right you shouldn't have."

"It's just . . . I feel responsible for him."

"I understand." Guillermo sighed and rocked back in his chair. "But part of my job is to know my nefilim's strengths and weaknesses. Nico lived with Jordi through some of my brother's worst abuse. He is a survivor. And he's had you to guide him. We'll get to him, Diago. I promise you. He just has to hold out until we can."

Diago didn't try to hide his disappointment. "I told him I would watch out for him. I promised."

"And you have. That's the part you're not seeing. You *have* watched over him, like I take care of all my nefilim. It's just that sometimes there is only so much we can do with the limited resources at hand. That's not your fault, or mine. Understand?"

"I do."

He looked at Diago as if he weren't quite sure he believed him. Finally he said, "Go and get some rest. We're going to have a busy day tomorrow."

"Sure." Diago rose and turned toward the door. "Oh, and we never had this conversation. You know, in case Miquel asks."

"That sounds like a plan to me. If you see Suero, tell him I need him."

"I will." Diago left the office and headed downstairs.

He found Suero in the kitchen, nursing a cup of tea. "How are you?"

The answer was in the dark circles under Suero's eyes. He avoided Diago's question with a question. "He needs me, doesn't he?"

"He does." Diago patted Suero's shoulder as he passed.

As the younger nefil left, Diago proceeded deeper into the kitchen. The boiserie at the back of the pantry was carved with sigils for concealment. With a low hum, Diago sang the counter-notes to neutralize the wards. The panel became a door that opened to reveal a set of rough stairs, leading down to the servants' quarters.

The faint illumination rising from the basement's depths gave his daimonic vision enough light to see. He descended the winding steps to a narrow hall.

Two rooms, each with four beds apiece, flanked the corridor. Whenever refugees fleeing the Nazis were sent Guillermo's way, he kept them here until they were able to make the perilous trip over the Pyrenees and into Andorra.

Currently, the rooms were empty. The last group of "packages"—which had included a Canadian airman and three OSS operatives—had been led over the mountains by Guillermo's nefilim last week. From there, they would enter Spain and then Portugal before returning to England.

At the end of the corridor was the clinic. The small room gave Juanita a place to tend to sick nefilim or mortals, whichever the case might be.

The soft glow of lamplight fluttered beneath the threshold. Suddenly someone cried out with an animalistic sound, a series of short yips, high-pitched and filled with pain and fear.

[11]

THE FARM

Diago threw open the door. The man's cries immediately ceased.

Juanita sat on a chair beside the bed. She bent over the patient and softly began a death song to ease the nefil's transition from this incarnation to another.

Miquel perched on a stool opposite her and shifted his position uneasily. Diago knew it was because his husband still hated infirmaries, even small units like the one they were forced to keep. The rooms reminded him too much of lost battles, fallen comrades, and needles filled with experimental drugs.

Given his experiences at the end of the Spanish Civil War, no one blamed him. Diago pretended not to see Miquel touch his chest, an unconscious gesture that communicated his discomfort louder than any words.

Picking his way around a table and a cart, Diago stopped

at the foot of the bed. He bowed his head and waited respectfully until Juanita finished her song.

She traced a sigil over the dead nefil's forehead and blessed his journey. "May you find peace and a gentle transition from this incarnation into your next."

"We will watch for you." Diago and Miquel murmured the nefilim's promise together.

Juanita tied off the saline drip and removed the needle from the patient's arm. "I'm sorry we couldn't ease his suffering."

When she moved back, Diago got his first good look at the man. His cheekbones were sharp and high, and his arms were bare sticks with knobs for elbows. His rounded belly testified to the fluid buildup associated with starvation.

Diago looked over the emaciated form. "Christ. How did he even live long enough to get here?"

Juanita shook her head. "I have no idea. He claimed to know you."

"I don't recognize him."

"He had two sets of identity papers, but when I asked him his name, he said it was Petre." She met Diago's gaze. "Of course, that name wasn't on either set of papers."

"Petre," Diago murmured. "Could you tell his ethnicity?"

"He was daimon-born," Juanita said. "A rogue."

Diago raised an eyebrow. That wasn't exactly what he'd meant, but then again, he considered the source. Because she was an angel, Juanita's mind didn't immediately rotate toward mortal connections.

"I meant his country of origin."

"Ah." Juanita shook her head. "He was delirious and used several languages, sometimes mashing them all together."

Miquel added helpfully, "He predominantly used Polish and Russian."

Diago peered more closely at the dead nefil. A small scar curved from the corner of his eye to touch his cheek.

And he used to wear stage makeup to hide it. The face and name snapped into place. "Petre Balan," Diago said with confidence. "We met with three other daimon-born rogues at the Moika Palace in Saint Petersburg to judge Rasputin." How odd that Guillermo would ask about Rasputin's trial and suddenly Petre was here.

Miquel turned the blanket down to reveal a large sequence of numbers tattooed on Petre's chest. "I haven't seen a tattoo like this before."

The numerals were distinctive due to their size and placement in the center of Petre's chest.

Diago recognized the technique. "It's an early form of tattooing they employed at Auschwitz. The Germans used a metal stamp with needles about a centimeter long. It punched the entire sequence of numbers into the flesh in one blow. Then they rubbed ink into the open wound."

"Jesus Christ." Miquel lifted his hand as if he intended to touch his chest again and caught himself before he could complete the gesture.

"You don't see it often. The process was quickly abandoned. The camps were filling fast and the process took too much time. Most of the people with these tattoos are dead."

Juanita reached down and gently extracted an amulet from the corpse's fingers. "He said this was only for you to open. No one else." She passed the necklace to Diago.

He held it up to the light. The pendant was a dented white

oval with no decoration; the chain was black with tarnish. He didn't recognize the piece. *Why would Petre want me to have this?*

Miquel touched the pendant. "Let me check it for wards before you open it."

"Aren't you being a bit overprotective?" He bit down on *again* before the word could tag the end of the question.

Unlike Guillermo, Juanita never had any difficulty stepping into a disagreement between them. "It's not a bad idea, Diago. The daimon-born make no secret of wanting to sow distrust among us. It could be a trap."

"From a rogue?" Diago tangled the chain around his fingers and didn't relinquish the necklace to his husband.

Miquel gave the pendant a gentle tug. "Why not? They'd use someone you know and trust—someone who isn't blatantly connected to one of the daimonic courts." Warming to the topic, he outlined his case. "The locket might carry a spell. If it does, and I trip it, then no one in Los Nefilim can say you augmented it with your song."

And with me playing double agent, I don't need to give anyone ammunition. "Okay." Diago opened his fingers. "You win."

"It's not about winning," Miquel retorted.

Something in his smile said otherwise, but Diago let it go. He'd learned long ago that sustaining a relationship meant picking his battles, and this simply wasn't a hill he wanted to die on.

His husband carried the locket to one of the lamps and tilted it first one way and then the other.

Resisting the urge to follow him, Diago turned to Juanita. "Did Petre have anything else with him?"

"Very little." She gestured to a table that contained the nefil's clothing and a rucksack. "A pair of underwear and two pairs of socks. His identity papers and a few reichsmarks."

"The latch is stuck," Miquel murmured.

Diago barely heard him. "May I?" He gestured to the rucksack and clothing.

"Of course." She followed him to the table. "What are you looking for?"

Running a finger along a seam, he felt for any telltale lumps. "Rogues carry their possessions with them. It would be strange if Petre carried no mementos at all, so I'm looking for hidden inseams or pockets." He lifted the shirt and then the pants, checking the hems and lining.

He found nothing. *Strange. Surely he'd accumulated something on his journey from Poland.*

Behind them, Miquel formed a protective sigil and sang it life. Pearlescent colors of pale blue and pink and ivory floated between him and the pendant. He shaped the ward until the lines of his song were bright and strong.

Diago turned to look.

Miquel pried at the locket's catch.

"What are you doing?" Diago stepped toward his husband.

"Checking it."

"I think that's going a bit too far."

Juanita caught Diago's arm. "Let him."

"Did it occur to either of you that someone might say Miquel is covering for me?"

Juanita was quick to resolve that complication. "Not with me as a witness." She nodded to Miquel.

To his credit, he didn't smirk over the victory. All business, he opened the locket. A folded piece of paper fell to the table. He unfolded the fragment and scowled. Moving closer to the lamp, he lifted the scrap. As he did, the lamp's wick sputtered and sent up a column of smoke that struck Miquel's eye.

He cried out and dropped the paper.

Damn it. Diago hurried to his husband's side. "Are you all right?"

"The lamp flared and I caught smoke in my eye. It's nothing."

Diago hoped that was all. "Petre said the locket was for me. It's possible he placed a ward on the note to stop anyone else from seeing the message."

Miquel didn't seem worried. "My protection sigil should have deflected that kind of spell."

"Maybe. Or it could be that your glyph simply blunted the damage. Come and sit so I can take a proper look."

"It's okay," Miquel protested verbally but allowed himself to be steered to the chair Juanita had used. "It stung for a moment, but I'm fine now. Get the note. There was writing on it."

Juanita examined it. "There is nothing here." She held it up.

Even from where he was standing, Diago could see the paper was blank. He grabbed a penlight from one of the trays and gently pushed Miquel's head back. "Look up." He shone the narrow beam in his husband's eye.

Juanita creased the paper along its fold and inserted it back into the locket. "Do you see anything?"

Diago shook his head. "No, but I want you to look." The fact that Miquel was the only one who'd seen writing on the paper bothered him.

She accepted the light and examined Miquel's iris and pupil. "Everything seems fine." She frowned suddenly and tilted her head.

Diago forced himself to stay back. "What?"

She took her time and spoke to Miquel. "Look up at the ceiling . . . now left, right. Hmmm." She flicked the switch and straightened. "I thought I saw something that looked like a shadow, but it must have been the angle of the light. I can't find any trace of a ward."

Diago sighed with relief. "Thank you."

Miquel went to the sink and splashed his face with the cool water. "There." He toweled himself dry and blinked a couple of times. "I'm okay."

Though the eye remained bloodshot, the tearing had stopped. Dropping the towel beside the basin, he picked up the locket and gave it to Diago. "It's been a long day. Let's go upstairs."

"Go ahead." Juanita drew the blanket over Petre's face. Turning to the metal tray beside the bed, she began to put items away. "I'm going to stay here and clean up."

Diago followed his husband, gripping the locket in his fist. *Why would Petre go to such lengths to bring me something so worthless?* He'd obviously been in terrible pain at the end. Between his starvation and agony, he must have suffered delusions.

Surely that had to be it. Yet even as Diago rationalized the incident, the thought that he'd missed something important nagged him all the way upstairs.

[12]

CHÂTEAU DE L'ENTREPRENANTE

FONTAINEBLEAU

Ysabel tried to open her eyes. One had swelled shut, the other took in the blurred room.

Something awakened her. *The key in the lock?*

Such a small sound, but one that had come to strike primal fear in her heart. *First the key, and then the questions.*

Sometimes it was Heines, who'd overcome his reluctance to strike her; sometimes it was the doctor . . . *Jimenez* . . . Dr. Jimenez with his nasty shots. On rare occasions, the sergeant entered with them, but her visits were brief, perfunctory, and she rarely spoke.

Ysa saw no rhyme or reason to their comings and goings, but Miquel had warned her about that, too. However, knowing how the system worked and actually living it were two different things.

The questions blurred together with her answers, but she

kept her lies close enough to the truth so they were easy to remember. Occasionally she blinked. Sometimes she cried. Pain was no one's friend.

A door shut somewhere in the distance. *That was it. That was the sound she'd heard.*

Her arms were numb. She couldn't feel her hands. She pushed her heels against the floor and tried to sit up straight. A shock of pain wrung an involuntary cry from her lips. Her damp panties and skirt stuck to her skin. *Christ. Did I piss myself again? Or is it blood?*

Approaching footsteps silenced her chattering thoughts. The key turned in the lock.

Her mouth was suddenly dry with her fear. *Steady. Hold steady.* She steeled herself for another round of questioning.

She heard the door open, but she didn't twist to see who was there. *They'll make their presence known soon enough.*

The scent of cologne preceded the man. It was a subtle musk, slightly masked by cigarette smoke.

Definitely not Heines. He smells of spearmint gum and a floral aftershave.

A pair of polished boots drifted into her line of vision. *Jordi.* She raised her gaze and met his eyes.

She couldn't read his expression.

He held a blanket in his hands.

My shroud? Unsure what she should say or do, she remained silent. *This is his song. Let him sing the first verse.*

The brush of fingertips against her wrists caused her to start with surprise. The cuffs were unlocked. Ysabel moved her arms for the first time in days.

She reeled forward from the pain, but caught her scream before it could crash the silence.

Jordi enveloped her in the blanket. He wrapped the wool tight around her body and gently lifted her, as if she were a child.

He carried her into the hall. As he turned toward the stairs, Ysa glimpsed the sergeant pocketing the cuffs and then trailing several paces behind them.

At the end of the corridor, two soldiers snapped their heels together and saluted. Then one of the men opened the door.

A set of stairs led upward to the next level. Once there, they passed through another door, another hall, at the end of which was an elevator, where two more soldiers awaited. Like the previous pair, they bolted to attention at the sight of Jordi. One man opened the elevator's gate.

Jordi stepped inside and the matron followed. Gears churned and the car began its ascent. Ysa closed her eyes and rested her cheek against Jordi's chest.

His arms tightened around her.

The elevator stopped. A liveried servant met them.

Heat kissed Ysa's cheeks and brought color to her face. She tried to mark the route, attempted to note the statuary and the delicately shaded lamps, but her vision blurred until the world became nothing more than shades of gold and pale green, outlined in shadows that passed from gray to black.

The sharp clack of heels snapping together brought her from the precipice of sleep. Jordi carried her past a pair of armed sentries and into a room.

Where the bright corridor had blinded her, the bedroom soothed her sore eyes. Gray light filtered through the heavy drapes. Ysa had no idea whether it was early morning or late afternoon.

Or maybe it's just a gray day. She allowed her listless

gaze to take in her surroundings. A canopied bed big enough for four took up the center of the chamber. A dressing table and wardrobe were stationed along two different walls.

Jordi placed her on her feet but he didn't release her. "These women will see to you."

One of the nurses took her hand. The other hovered nearby, waiting to take Jordi's place. He hesitated for just a moment before releasing her. Then he was gone.

The nurses helped her out of her filthy clothes and bathed her. She remained submissive as they dressed her wounds, massaged the feeling back into her sore joints with healing songs, and then pulled a silk gown over her head.

The sergeant stood in one corner, monitoring the entire process. Ysa kept her gaze on the floor.

Wait, Diago had said. *You'll know the time.*

And the time was not now.

Comfortable for the first time in days, she let them ease her into the bed. The sergeant finally left the room, only to return moments later with Dr. Jimenez.

Fuck, fuck, fucker. She gritted her teeth and forced herself to remain limp as Jimenez took her pulse and gave her a cursory examination. Then he reached into his poison bag and withdrew a syringe. She barely felt the pinprick of the needle, but its effects were immediate.

The world faded away. When she woke again, it was night. *But which night? The night Jordi brought me here, or have I slept through a day and night?* She had no idea. Time had become fluid, moving with no end, no beginning.

All she knew for certain was that the house was still. She felt the silence around her, soft like snow.

Only one nurse remained. She slumped in her chair, an

open book in her lap. Beside her, the lamp gave off quiet light in the quiet room.

Sitting up, Ysa touched her bruised cheek. The swelling in her eye seemed to have diminished. At least she could see out of it. Her shoulders and joints still ached and probably would for a couple more days.

A glass of water sat on the bedside table. Ysa lifted it to her lips and sipped, forcing herself to drink slowly. The last thing she needed was to be sick.

Is this the moment that Diago told me to watch for? No way to know unless she moved. Easing her legs over the side of the mattress, she found a pair of slippers on the small round rug. They fit her perfectly.

The nurse didn't stir.

A silk robe was draped across the foot of the bed. She pulled it on and fastened the tie.

If they were smart, they'd burned the suit she'd worn during her interrogation. She certainly didn't want it back.

Opening the wardrobe to search for outdoor clothing might awaken the nurse. She decided to investigate first.

The woman gave a soft snore and shifted slightly in her chair before falling deeper into her slumber.

Ysabel tiptoed to the door and turned the latch, wincing at the click. To her surprise it was unlocked. A single lamp lit the corridor. The sentries were gone. *This is too easy.*

Pulling the bedroom door closed behind her, she knelt on the floor and looked for traps in the form of sigils. Nothing. Nor did she see any threads that indicated a more mundane type of wire trap.

None of this made sense. Her father would never allow a captive to roam freely in his house.

Rising again, she stood too fast and experienced a mild episode of vertigo. *Jimenez's shots.*

That explained the lack of security. They expected the medication to bind her to dreams. Obviously, Jimenez underdosed her, undoubtedly thinking her exhaustion would do the drug's work. *That probably means they're experiencing supply issues.* With most narcotics being funneled to the front, it made sense for him to conserve stock.

Happy news for me. Ysabel proceeded down the hall. If she was stopped, she would feign confusion and simply plead a visit to the lavatory.

She encountered no one and reached the stairs without incident. At the landing, she looked upward to the next level. Dark shadows moved along the walls.

A discordant melody thrummed down the marble steps—a piano, yes, she was sure of it, a piano, groaning beneath hard hands on the keys. The notes pulsed with the intensity of distant bombs.

Someone laughed a lonely, mirthless laugh. The sound rippled across Ysa's flesh and left her disconcerted.

Keeping her back close to the wall, she descended to the main floor. The great entry hall spread out before her and retained its French opulence. The high ceilings were still painted in Rousseau's favorite colors of pale gold and gray. Otherwise, any reference to Les Néphilim had been scoured from the chamber.

The Inner Guard's celestial banner now joined Nazi emblems on the walls. Die Nephilim's runes marked the walls in great plaques made of crimson and black.

Another wave of dizziness caused her to hesitate by the

balustrade. She waited for the episode to pass—*hoped* it would pass.

Down here, the discordant piano and mad laughter were faint, almost nonexistent. Outside a nearby window, flecks of white fluttered through the night. It was snowing.

That wasn't good. The silk gown afforded her no protection from the cold; her slippers would be equally ineffective. *No wonder they haven't bothered with guards.* If the drugs didn't keep her in her room, the weather would prevent her from going outside.

For now that was true. *I need to see what my options are and then make a decision.* If she had to risk a run into the night, she would.

Leaving the steps, she hurried across the open space of the entry hall, a plan formulating in her mind as she did. She needed a weapon, no matter how small. The kitchen would have knives.

Prowling through the corridors, she left barely a shadow as she reached the state-of-the-art kitchen. A massive refrigerator hummed against one wall, every surface gleamed, and to Ysa's frustration, every drawer was locked.

Shit. It was a problem, but a minor one. Her father had taught her to pick locks when she was five. The difficulty before her was which drawer to choose.

Her father loved to cook when he had time. She recalled him in their kitchen in Santuari, humming as he taught her the art of fine cuisine. *And like his forge, he kept his tools organized where he could reach them quickly.*

The sharpest knives would be at the butcher's block. She found the heavy table near the range.

A flash of light through a window caught her eye. She ducked and froze. The light disappeared.

Ysa remained still and counted. At fifty, she rose and crept toward the back door. Another wash of light flooded the yard.

Spotlight on the roof. No sentries moved on the grounds. *That I can see.*

With a sigh of relief, she returned to the butcher's block, which had a single drawer secured by a hasp and padlock. She examined the lock. It was a simple thing that could be easily opened, but she needed a couple of hairpins or paper clips. She had neither.

And how long can I creep around before the nurse wakes or someone stumbles on me? Time was against her.

Searching for an office risked discovery. Kneeling on the floor, she pressed her forehead against the drawer and resisted the urge to smash her fist on the table. Frustration would get her nowhere. Anger tightened the vocal cords and ruined a nefil's song.

Take a moment. She remembered her father beside her, calming her when she grew impatient with herself. He always brought himself to her level so that they were equals. She felt his presence as keenly as if he were there, kneeling beside her, talking her through her doubts.

Take a moment and calm yourself, he would say. *Most problems require finesse, not a hammer.*

She even smelled the combination of scents that always followed him: the hot Catalonian sun in his hair, smoke from his forge mixed with his cologne, and the thick Cuban cigars of which he was so fond. His hair, grown shaggy from lack of attention, framed those golden eyes so like her own.

She closed her eyes and when she opened them again, she saw his shadow next to her. He placed his large hand on her shoulder and whispered, *Sometimes, all you have is your song.*

The searchlight swept the yard and illuminated the kitchen. No one squatted next to her. She was alone. *I'm hallucinating.*

That wasn't good. *What the fuck is Jimenez putting in those shots?* She had to get a grip. Focus.

Her father's encouragement echoed in her mind. *Sometimes, all you have is your song.*

She lifted her head. The lock's tumblers moved on pressure and the right vibrations could trip the mechanisms.

With trembling fingers, she lifted the padlock and hummed a hard note. Before the vibrations of her voice disappeared, she shaped a sigil designed to push the cylinders and sent it into the keyhole.

Soft clicks rattled through the metal, springing the lock. She quickly opened the drawer and was relieved to find an assortment of knives. After she chose a small blade that she could easily conceal, she returned the lock to its hasp.

The light illuminated the kitchen's back door again. A heavy coat hung on a peg and a pair of wooden shoes were placed neatly on the mat.

Staying low, so that if there were any sentries they wouldn't glance in and see movement, she lifted the coat from the peg and wrapped it around her body. It was two sizes too big. She cinched the waist. The shoes were also too large, but she found rags that helped cushion her feet. Blisters were a small price to pay for freedom.

Squatting by the door, she checked the latch for sigils and found none.

Fine. Let Jordi's overconfidence be my key to getting out of here. Ysa slipped outside and quickly pulled the door shut.

The cold took her breath away. She might as well be naked from the waist down, for all the protection the silk gave her.

The searchlight swept the perimeter once more. She flattened herself against the wall. One section of open yard lay between her and the woods. Still no sentries.

The light made another sweep. The moment it passed, she ran toward the forest. The clumsy shoes hampered her speed. Nonetheless, she made it into the first line of trees by the time the light crossed the area in front of the kitchen again.

Crouching low, she remained perfectly still until the beam circled past. Then she tucked the knife into the coat's sash and moved as fast as she dared.

The snow fell harder, which was good. It would cover her tracks.

Remembering the barbed sigils she'd seen on her ride in, she moved carefully. The wards would be almost invisible in the night.

This was one of those times she envied Rafael's daimonic night vision. As if summoned by her thoughts, she felt him beside her. Her little brother, her dark rose.

She heard his voice in her head, and he said, *It's all right, Ysa. I'm here. I'll help you see.*

"You're not," she whispered back. "You're not here." Yet she definitely sensed him there, moving beside her. He wore his heaviest coat and his curls mingled with the wool of his shearling hat. The muzzle of his rifle poked over his shoulder and a band of ammunition rode on his hip.

Christ, he looks so real. She forced herself to pick up her pace and pinched her wrist. When she looked again, Rafael was gone.

A quick glance over her shoulder told her the searchlight no longer swept the yard. It had halted in front of the kitchen door.

Someone shouted.

Ysa ran. Boulders loomed from the darkness, some as high as her waist. She dodged them, but the wooden shoes rendered her footing treacherous.

The trees, shorn of their leaves, let the snow fall between their trunks. No animal stirred, not even an owl.

Then, from behind her, she heard another shout—this one louder, closer. Dogs barked in the distance, obviously roused by their handlers.

Gasping in the icy air, she paused beside a boulder and listened until she thought her ears would bleed. Another voice called out, this one with urgency, followed by a third and a fourth. The dogs grew excited.

They'd discovered her trail.

Ysa pushed away from the boulder and started moving again. Her panic lent her speed.

She slid down a steep incline. The gown ripped and rode up over her hip. The stinging on her thigh was nothing compared to the pain she'd already endured. She regained her feet and ran.

Shadows flitted among the tree trunks. Nefilim, old ones, moving fast, but none veered to stop her.

Ysa zigzagged through the forest, keeping to the deeper patches of darkness, hoping the pale material of her gown would be taken for the falling snow.

Footsteps crunched behind her. She ducked behind a large rock and drew her knife.

Four nefilim ran past her hiding spot. Waiting, she counted to sixty. She stood and turned.

A tall figure blocked her path.

Jordi.

He offered his hand. "Come home, Ysa."

She held the knife close to her side. *Hold it close*, she heard Diago say. *But keep your stance loose. With a blade you must be quick. Strike for the arteries.*

Which meant she had to get closer to him. *Too close.* He was older, faster, stronger.

The snow blurred between them and instead of white flakes, she saw wards: clefs and quavers, beamed notes, ghost notes, caesuras, glissandi and portamenti, all floating white around her.

"Ysabel?" Jordi took a step toward her. "Are you all right?"

Lifting the knife, she impaled a bass clef and shaped it into an icy spear. With her contralto, she charged the glyph and forced it toward Jordi.

He effortlessly raised a shield of fire. Ysa's spear melted in the heat, but not before it stopped mere centimeters from his heart.

His eyes widened and his mouth twitched.

I surprised him.

He smiled. "You should have been my daughter."

The wistfulness in his voice sounded heartfelt, but she didn't trust him. *He's trying to lure me into a sense of security.* She wasn't having it. They were several days and too many beatings from forming a loving relationship.

Taking a step closer, he tried to reason with her. "You'll

never make it past the barrier. Why do you think the other nefilim ran past you? To keep you safe. One wrong move and those sigils will cut you in half. How will I explain to my brother that I murdered his daughter? I cannot have it."

She retreated, raising the knife. "Then let me go home."

"Don't be a child. You know this is war. You were trained to be a queen. Act like one."

The admonishment struck her like a slap. The ghostly notes continued to fly between them and yet he made no move to restrain her.

Then she saw Miquel. He stood just beyond Jordi. Flakes of snow caught in his black hair and his eyes were almost invisible in the night, but his voice was clear. *Don't trust him, but don't be a fool. Save yourself until we can find you.*

She blinked the mirage away in time to see a concussive sigil aimed at her. With a sharp cry, she formed a protective ward but her sore arms failed her and she couldn't raise it in time.

Jordi's glyph slammed against her, hard enough to knock her out of her wooden shoes. Her head struck something, whether a rock, a tree, or the ground, she didn't know. But the world went black and the silence came down . . . quiet, like the falling of snow.

[13]

THE FARM

Diago reclined on their settee and snuggled deeper beneath his quilt. Their third-floor rooms usually retained the heat of the day a little longer than the lower levels, but today's overcast skies robbed them of that extra layer of warmth.

Their small stove pushed back feebly against the cold. Diago didn't dare add more coal. He worried they might not have enough to get through the winter.

Holding the locket by its chain, he watched his husband undress. "How do you feel?"

Unbothered by the chill, Miquel tossed his shirt over the back of a chair. "I feel fine." He came to the divan and gently extracted the amulet's chain from Diago's fingers. Turning to one side, he placed the locket on their night table. "Look." He lifted his hair from his forehead. "See? It's not even bloodshot anymore."

Diago had to admit, his husband's eye had cleared. "I'll take your word for it."

"That's because I'm an honest guy." Miquel kissed him gently. "Now, what did I promise you this afternoon?"

Diago thought back to their ride home. "To wine me and dine me and whatever comes next." Noting how the shadows played over Miquel's torso, Diago traced a pattern across the dark skin of his husband's abdomen. *He looks so chiseled, but his flesh is soft . . . tender.* Diago hooked a finger in Miquel's waistband before releasing him with a sigh. "But a bottle of beer and a cold sandwich are poor substitutes for wining and dining."

"There *is* a war going on, comrade."

Caught up in their game, Diago allowed the day's tension to fade. "Excuses, excuses."

A wicked light gleamed in Miquel's eyes as he straightened. "I see you're going to play hard to get." He went to the wardrobe and bent over to withdraw his bag.

Muscles rippled beneath the curves of his shoulders as he sought whatever prize lay within. His pants were loose and exposed the dimple at the small of his back—a ticklish spot that sent shivers over him whenever Diago found it with his tongue.

Miquel glanced over his shoulder and seemed pleased that he had his husband's undivided attention. "While I was meeting contacts in Perpignan this afternoon, I took the liberty to acquire something nice for us." He returned to the divan with a bottle, a corkscrew, and a wineglass. "Hold this for me."

Diago pushed himself upright on the seat and accepted the empty glass. "Is that—"

"Château Margaux." Miquel poured. "Say you love me."

"I love you," Diago murmured as the deep red liquid filled the glass. He swirled the wine gently and inhaled the aroma. The vintage was perfumed with an earthy scent accompanied by subtle hints of violets and oak.

"You don't need this." Miquel peeled the quilt away from Diago's body and sat beside him on the settee. "It's about to get very warm."

"Is it, now?"

Miquel watched him hold the glass of wine with a smile. "Are you going to sniff it or drink it?"

"It should breathe."

With his fingertip, Miquel traced a seductive line along Diago's throat. "Don't make me wait."

Barely able to breathe himself, Diago lifted the glass to his lips and allowed himself a single sip. The sweetness flowed over his palate and filled his mouth. He closed his eyes and relished the luxurious flavor.

Warmth spread through his chest. The wine resurrected the memory of their days in Santuari. In Catalonia, they had spent their evenings outdoors in the lingering heat of a setting sun. Their music flowed between them, binding them more closely with every chord.

Diago opened his eyes and noted Miquel held no glass of his own. "Aren't you going to have some?"

"I'd rather taste it on your lips." Without waiting for a response, he bestowed the gentlest of kisses on Diago's mouth before withdrawing. He licked his upper lip and pretended to evaluate the flavor. "Hmm, sweet, not overly so. There is just a hint of acidity, but I can't tell if that is you or the wine. Have some more."

"Are you trying to get me drunk?"

Miquel brushed his thumb across Diago's mouth. "Hush and play the game."

More intoxicated by Miquel's presence than the wine, Diago obeyed. With a smile, his husband leaned close.

It was game that lasted deep into the night.

Abomination!

Diago woke. His heart raced; he couldn't move. The word faded from his brain—the echo of some violent incident from his past.

The room was bathed in darkness, though he detected pinpricks of gray around the blackout curtain. They were in the gloaming just before dawn.

I'm home. In bed. Safe.

He didn't remember the dream, only the terror that shook him to his core. His mind usually protected him by blocking out the most traumatic episodes of his early life, unless some event triggered a memory.

Yesterday's visit to Christina was most likely the cause of this morning's disturbance. Reaching out for something solid, he felt Miquel beside him. He recalled their lovemaking, and his fear backed away in the face of his husband's love. His heart rate gradually returned to normal.

Miquel snored softly. The lines of his face, which lent his countenance an authoritative cast when he was awake, had softened. He smelled of cigarettes and wine and their sex—a heady mixture that filled Diago's senses.

Feeling calmer, he smoothed a black curl from Miquel's forehead, wishing all their nights could be so decadent.

Miquel's eyes opened. He gripped Diago's wrist.

Unprepared for the sudden movement, Diago instinctively jerked backward. "Miquel?"

His husband's dark eyes swiveled frantically, as if trying to take in the entire room at once. It could be a nightmare, but if it was, it was something new. Diago was as used to his husband's bad dreams as he was his own. Miquel tended to thrash and cry out. He never experienced this sudden stillness, nor the rapt horror with which he observed his surroundings.

Treat it like a nightmare. "Miquel." He kept his voice even and calm. "You're having a bad dream. I need you to wake up."

"Something went wrong," he whispered in an agitated mix of Italian and Castilian.

The hair on Diago's arm went straight up. The inflection sounded just like Nico's.

"Miquel?"

"Miquel is here! With me. He doesn't want me in his mind. He fought me. This was the only way." His eyes went wider still and he sat up, gripping Diago's shoulders. "Petre was supposed to say the locket was for you. Why would Miquel open it?"

"You *wanted* to open it."

"No. Goddamn it. It's me. Nico! What did Miquel do?"

Diago gaped at his husband. *But this isn't my husband, it's Nico. The smoke in his eye . . . it wasn't from the lamp—*

Miquel's muscles locked in terror. "Herr Teufel is coming for me—" He shook his head. When he met Diago's gaze, his eyes were clear. He said in Catalonian, "What the hell is happening to me?"

Before Diago could answer, Miquel switched to Italian again. ". . . wants me to wake. I'm too late . . ." Miquel blinked. His gaze became unfocused again, and his breath puffed in short bursts. Diago felt his husband's pulse accelerate. His voice went up two octaves with Nico's terrified cry. "Pietà, pietà!"

The room's gray light grew brighter. The gloaming passed to become the dawn. Miquel's body slumped on the mattress. He panted in short ragged breaths.

"Miquel?"

His husband's eyes narrowed. "What in the fucking hell just happened to me?"

Before Diago could respond, the floorboards outside their room creaked. A soft tap came at the door. "Papá? Miquel? Are you all right?" It was Rafael.

He sounded groggy, as if he was still half-asleep. *He probably thinks I've had a nightmare.* Unwilling to leave Miquel's side, Diago called softly, "We're fine. What time is it?"

"Five or so. I think."

"Go back to bed. Everything is fine." The deceit rolled out his mouth with the ease of a thousand parental lies.

"Okay." But the shadow beneath their door hesitated as if Rafael detected Diago's guile.

Miquel started to speak, but Diago pressed his fingers over his husband's lips. He watched the threshold until Rafael finally moved away, his footsteps retreating to his room.

When he was sure their son was gone, Diago lowered his hand from Miquel's mouth. "Tell me what you remember."

Miquel rolled away and found his cigarettes on the night

table. Kicking against the mattress, he pushed his back against the headboard and didn't speak until he'd filled his lungs with nicotine three times. "I had a nightmare." Miquel picked at the sheet with two fingers as if plucking a guitar string.

"Tell me."

He sighed and smoothed the sheet. "I was . . . in a square. And it was cold. So cold. I was naked." He frowned and stared at the door without truly seeing it. His gaze seemed to be turned inward, concentrating on the images in his mind's eye. "No. I wore an undershirt, but it was in shreds."

"What kind of square?"

"It was in a compound . . . there were barracks in three neat rows. I can't see to the end of the lanes, but somehow I know that there were fifteen buildings, five in each row . . . there were watchtowers, one in the center of the square." He shuddered. "It's a camp, a prison."

Mauthausen, maybe? Diago didn't ask. He didn't want to influence Miquel's memory of the dream. "What happened?"

"I'm facing row upon row of men." He stopped and closed his eyes. "They're little more than skeletons . . . hungry and cold. I'm cold. My hands are lashed behind my back. There is a rope around my neck and I'm standing on a stool. Christ, it's awful, and the cold . . . it is in my bones." His breathing quickened. "There is a small orchestra of prisoners playing violins and accordions. They're playing 'J'attendrai.'" He paused and shook his head as if confused by the selection.

It was a song Rina Ketty recorded in 1938 and had remained popular throughout the war. People reinterpreted the melancholy lyrics of one lover awaiting the arrival of another as every person's longing for the end of war.

Diago couldn't imagine what the music meant in the dream. "Keep going."

"Someone walks up to me." Miquel's dark eyes glittered. "He kicks the stool from beneath my feet, and when he looks up, he wears your face."

"And then?"

"I died. I was dead. There was nothing. No sound. And then I heard someone speak in Italian, but it was me, but it wasn't me."

"Okay." Except it wasn't okay. "Go back to last night. When you opened the locket. What did you see on the paper?"

"A sigil, but Juanita said it was blank."

Writing that appeared and disappeared. It made no sense, unless . . .

Diago got out of bed and grabbed the locket. He snatched Miquel's matches and went to a lamp. As the wick gained luminance, Diago removed the scrap from the pendant and held it over the flame. Moments passed and then faint brown lines emerged on the paper.

It was a sigil.

"I can't believe it," Diago whispered.

"What?" Miquel slid out of bed and joined him.

"Is this what you saw?" He held up the note.

Miquel nodded. "How did you . . ." He glanced at the lamp and then understanding dawned. "Invisible writing?"

Diago sniffed the paper. "Onion juice, if I'm not mistaken."

"You rarely are." Miquel put out his cigarette. "But what kind of sigil is that?"

The pieces fell together and suddenly he understood exactly what had happened to Miquel. "Do you remember at the beginning of the war, we experimented with astral projection?" They'd hoped that instead of relying on mortal means to communicate, their angel-born spies might relay secrets through one another's dreams. "We abandoned the project because of its unpredictability."

Miquel shrugged. "So?"

"Nico excelled at it."

Miquel became very still. "I dreamed of Nico," he whispered. "Before I dreamed of the square, Nico and I were in a café. It was the same one where you two used to meet when we lived in Paris. You know, that shabby little place on the corner—"

"I remember it."

"Nico wanted to talk to you and I told him no. I told him to go away and not come back. He kissed me, and then the dream switched—"

"To the square and the hanging?"

"Yes. How did you know?"

"Nico had to simulate your death so that his consciousness could take over your body. Don't you see? His sigil was meant for me—"

"Wait. Wait. Go back to the part where he killed me."

"It was the only way to make you lose control, so he made you think that you died in the dream. With your consciousness out of the way, his spirit could then reach me with your voice."

"I'll strangle him." Miquel grabbed his pants.

"*Think*, Miquel. Nico is with Herr Teufel. The daimonborn are going to the camps to feed on the prisoners' misery, and somehow, Teufel has taken Nico. If he's keeping Nico close to him—"

"Oh, no, I see where your mind is going with this."

Diago gathered his scattered clothing and dressed quickly. "We've got a spy embedded right next to Herr Teufel. We need to see Juanita and Guillermo."

Someone knocked at the door.

Diago answered and found Suero there.

"Oh, good, you're dressed," the young nefil said. "Don Guillermo wants both of you to come to his office." Without another word, he turned and went to the stairs.

Miquel grabbed Diago's arm and drew him back into their bedroom, though he didn't shut the door. Keeping his voice to a whisper, he said, "Will Nico be able to speak through me anytime?"

"No. He can only communicate with you through your dreams."

Miquel nodded and brushed his lips against Diago's cheek. "Okay. Let's go down and talk to Guillermo and Juanita. We'll see if we can use this to our advantage."

"I've got to speak to Rafael. I just want to let him know what's going on. I'll be right behind you."

Miquel left him, and Diago hurried to his son's bedroom. He knocked twice and opened the door.

An easel stood near one of the room's two windows, the beginning lines of a sketch already shading the canvas. It was a portrait of Ysabel and Violeta, drawn from one of their favorite photographs. They sat on a hillside together; Violeta leaned against Ysa, who had her arms protectively around her friend as she stared off into the distance.

Toward Spain, Diago recalled. They were both looking

toward home. He knew because he had taken the snapshot for them.

Though Rafael hadn't been present when the photo was taken, he'd managed to give both the women the same longing Diago had sensed in them that day. They'd left Catalonia as children and now they were determined to reclaim their home.

Rafael looked up from pulling on his boots. "Do you like it?"

Diago nodded. "It's very good. You've captured their souls."

Rafael made a face. "It needs a lot more work." He stood and grabbed his sweater. "Did you have a nightmare?"

"Not me. It was Miquel." Diago noticed a small box beside his son's bed. A shard of glass was cushioned by a piece of velvet. It was the only remaining image from the glass box Prieto had given Diago—the same casket Rafael had held in his fight against Moloch when he was six.

The edges were jagged and a crack touched one corner, but the image was untouched. It was the silhouette of a woman poised to dance, her arms raised over her head, her face turned upward as if looking at the sky. She was dressed in rags that rose behind her and gave her the illusion of wings. Around her throat was a small serpent with golden scales.

"Hello? Papá?" Rafael waved his palm in front of Diago's face. "Is Miquel okay?"

Startled by the gesture, Diago focused on his son. "Yes. He's fine." He quickly explained the situation.

Rafael frowned, clearly uncomfortable with the development. "Do you think that means we'll have some answers soon?"

"I hope so." Diago's gaze was drawn back to Candela's image.

His mind conjured the hard scent of tin—*and carnations, she kept carnations by the bed*—and he recalled Candela lazily tracing the scars on his chest. The golden snake slid from her hair to coil over his heart, cool like water, soft like silk. The serpent had watched him with ruby eyes, but Diago had barely been aware of anything other than Candela's voice, murmuring the name she would call her song. *Rafael.*

And that was all she had left her son: her angel's tear and a shard of glass.

Noting the direction of Diago's gaze, Rafael wrapped the shard in velvet and placed it in the little box. "I'm sorry." He gently closed the lid. "I know the memory of what she did brings you pain."

"That doesn't change the fact that she was your mother and you love her."

He cradled the box. "Sometimes I don't know how I feel about her. She put you under a spell so she could become pregnant, knowing that whatever child was born would be given to Moloch in exchange for the blueprints of a bomb. I wasn't conceived in love. It was an act of deception. But at the same time, I love her, because she did try to protect me. And sleeping with her image beside my bed tends to keep the nightmares at bay. It's confusing."

"We can't always control our emotions, especially about family. It's okay to love her *and* question her motives. You can do both without disrespecting her memory." He couldn't believe he actually stood there defending his rapist. *Talk about confusing.*

At the same time, he refused to discount his son's feelings.

"If we look at the positive side of things, she gave me you, and I've never regretted having you in my life."

"Hey!" Miquel called up the stairs, startling them both. "Diago! Are you coming?"

Ignoring his husband, Diago nodded at the box in his son's hands. "I've made my peace with Candela. There is no need for you to hide her presence."

Miquel shouted again. "Diago!"

"He's getting grumpy, I'd better go. We'll talk more later if you want."

Rafael grinned. "I'll be down in a few minutes."

Diago quickly left his son and approached the stairs. "Yes! I'm here!"

"Good, because Bernardo is on his way with a package."

Diago hurried down the stairs. Carlos Vela had gotten his wish. He had an audience with Don Guillermo.

Diago reached the second-floor landing to find Miquel leaning on the banister. "Everything okay up there?"

"Everything is fine."

"Then let's go. Guillermo is waiting for us."

They went down the hall and found the door ajar. Miquel gave the frame two raps and went inside.

Juanita was already there, drawing the drapes. "Let some light in here, corazón."

Guillermo rubbed his eyes and rocked back in his chair. Diago wondered if he'd been to bed at all.

"Knock, knock." Suero brought in a serving tray and set it on a side table. A coffee urn, cups, and some of Eva's croissants caught everyone's attention. "Breakfast."

No one waited for a second invitation. They helped themselves and retreated to various points in the office.

Miquel carried his to an easy chair by the bookcase and took a sip from his cup. "Chicory." He grimaced.

"Mmm," Guillermo grumbled as he winced at the taste. "Nothing like a cup of ersatz coffee first thing in the morning to turn the stomach." He added some saccharine tablets before addressing Suero. "Have you been able to reach Ysa's rooming house?"

"Not yet, Don Guillermo. The phone lines are down this morning. I'll keep trying throughout the day."

"Thank you. You don't need to stay for this."

The lesser nefil bowed his head and retreated, closing the door behind him.

Guillermo ate his croissant in three bites and then cradled his mug. "Okay, Miquel gave us the highlights. Let's see if I understand this: Petre Balan brought a pendant that held a disappearing sigil; Miquel opened it, took a mysterious hit to the eye, and then this morning was possessed by Nico's astral projection . . . what the fuck is going on?"

Juanita glanced at Diago from her place behind Guillermo. "Diago, would you mind explaining?" She mouthed the words, *No sleep.*

Diago nodded and took the chair closest to Guillermo's desk. "Do you remember at the beginning of the war, we experimented with astral projection in the hopes that the process would enable our spies to communicate with one another?"

Guillermo's bleary gaze cleared with understanding. "Right. I remember now. You and Juanita and Nico were working on some way to eliminate communiqués that could be intercepted by the enemy."

"Exactly. The method we finally developed entailed drawing a sigil with invisible ink—we used either onion or lemon juice on a piece of paper. The ward was designed to link two nefilim through their dreams. Then we'd find a discreet way to deliver the note. The person who received the paper would hold it over a flame, the heat of which would reveal the glyph, and activate the link."

"Okay, I'm with you now." Guillermo lifted the lid of his cigar box and drew one out. "And you think that Petre delivered such a message to you last night."

"From Nico. Except Miquel opened it and held the paper over the flame. So instead of me, Nico connected with Miquel's dreams this morning."

Guillermo chuckled at Miquel over his cigar.

Miquel scowled at him. "This isn't funny."

The big nefil struggled to compose himself. "I'm sorry. You're right. It's not funny. Maybe a little poetic . . ."

Miquel's glare intensified.

Guillermo stood and cleared his throat. "Okay. I'm sure Miquel formed a protective ward before he opened that locket, so riddle me this: How did Nico's ward skirt it?"

Diago answered the question. "It wasn't an attack, so Miquel's shield didn't react. Nico's spell bounced around Miquel's ward and went directly into his subconscious. That's why neither Juanita nor I saw any reflection of a sigil when we examined his eye."

Guillermo paced up and down the room once before stopping in front of one of the windows. He stared into the distance.

He's looking for the plume of dust that will announce Bernardo's arrival.

Guillermo finally lit his cigar but he didn't return his lighter to his pocket. "The astral projection experiments failed, because the nefilim can't sustain the link for long periods of time. We also found it difficult to untangle real events from the dreamers' projections or opinions."

Juanita refilled her cup. "Nico was actually quite good at it."

Guillermo flicked the lid of his lighter with three measured clicks before he turned to face Miquel. "Last night, Diago informed me that you found Nico had been transferred to Mauthausen. Is that true?"

Diago pretended not to see his husband's sharp side-eye.

"According my sources, yes." Miquel's voice was tight.

Nibbling his croissant, Diago avoided looking in his husband's direction. If his tone was any indication, he was unhappy that piece of information leaked. *And the truth is, I shouldn't have done it.* That meant he'd have to apologize. *Later.*

Guillermo clicked his lighter. "The Gestapo took Nico in July of last year?"

"Fifteen July," Diago concurred.

"Six months," Guillermo murmured and then switched his attention to Miquel. "Do you know when he was sent to Mauthausen?"

"My sources say late last November. Why?"

"I'm considering the time span and Nazi techniques. Do you believe it's possible that either the Nazis or the daimonborn have turned Nico? Maybe they're using him to get to us?"

Miquel shrugged. "Anything is possible."

Guillermo gave his lighter two more clicks. "Diago?"

"If you're asking for an opinion based on what I heard this morning, I'd have to say no. His voice went up two octaves when he thought he'd been discovered by this Herr Teufel. He was terrified."

Guillermo returned to his desk and sat. "Will he try to make contact again tonight?"

Diago couldn't discount the possibility. "If he can, he will."

Guillermo jabbed his cigar in Miquel's direction. "If he does, you talk to him. Understand? Interrogate him like one of your sources. Got it?"

Miquel didn't look happy, but he nodded.

Juanita glanced out the window. "Bernardo is here."

"Maybe our friend Carlos can reveal the identity of this Herr Teufel." Guillermo crushed his cigar in an ashtray. "Let's go see what he has for us."

Trouble, Diago thought as he followed Guillermo and Miquel down the stairs. Carlos Vela was nothing but trouble.

They reached the yard just as Bernardo shut off the truck's engine. The first thing Diago noticed was that Bernardo was alone. The lack of other nefilim to guard the prisoner meant Carlos came willingly, which Diago didn't doubt. He wanted to be brought to Guillermo. He just couldn't be seen as being *too* willing. Desperation made a poor negotiating partner.

Guillermo met Bernardo at the cab. "You brought him in alone?"

Bernardo slammed the truck's door hard enough to rattle

the window in the frame. "He's not going to give anyone problems anymore."

Diago's stomach did a slow flip. This didn't bode well at all.

Bernardo went to the truck's bed and lowered the gate. The body was concealed under several empty crates and a tarp, but it didn't take long for Bernardo and Miquel to uncover the corpse.

Juanita immediately waved them down. "Let me up there."

Guillermo stood back. His face was white with rage. "What the fuck happened?"

"We went to the address Diago gave us and this is what we found." He gestured at the corpse.

Diago climbed onto the truck and squatted opposite Juanita. Carlos was an ugly nefil in life; death did him no favors. The side of his face that had been scorched by the Thrones' fire was black. The other half was pulled into a permanent snarl of agony.

Juanita stood and looked over the truck's side. "Miquel, can you get my bag? And find me a couple of nefilim to carry the body. We'll need to do an autopsy."

He raised one hand in acknowledgment and returned to the house.

Guillermo's thumb stroked his lighter. He turned to Bernardo. "Did you find anything other than a corpse?"

"He had negatives hidden beneath a floorboard." He withdrew an envelope from his coat. "They appear to be multiple photographs of the psalm."

Diago opened the collar of Carlos's shirt. Someone had crushed the nefil's larynx. It was a common gesture, used by both the angel- and the daimon-born nefilim, symbolic of silencing an enemy's song. A ruby cuff link had been mashed into the wound.

Reaching down, Diago pulled the cuff link free. "Edur wore a pair exactly like this yesterday."

Juanita frowned. "What is Edur's connection to Carlos?"

"Morphine," Diago whispered. As he thought back over his interaction with the dead nefil, the facts suddenly became clear. "I had too many other things on my mind when I cornered Carlos in that alley." Looking up, he met Guillermo's gaze. "It didn't hit me then."

The big nefil looked as if he might leap onto the truck's bed and yank the answers from Diago's skull. "What?"

"Carlos told me the morphine didn't help his pain anymore. The *morphine*. Morphine is almost impossible to find. Where do you think Carlos was getting his supply?" He didn't wait for an answer as he recalled his cousin's teasing smile. "Christina."

Guillermo growled the question. "As payment for his services to the daimon-born?"

"That would be my guess. But now Christina has been ordered to Paris. Carlos is about to lose his drug supply, so he reaches out to you."

The big nefil glared at the corpse. "But why would Edur kill Carlos?"

"Edur might have commited the act, but the order came from Christina. She is tying up loose ends. Carlos is a complication because he is angel-born. Once she's left the vicinity, she can't control him anymore." Diago fingered the cuff link and wondered if Edur was saving the other one for him.

"Christ, if Carlos wasn't already dead, I'd kill him." Guillermo flicked the lid of his lighter and stared into the distance. "And then we have the mysterious Herr Teufel. Who the hell is he and how does he figure into all this?"

It was a good question. One Diago couldn't begin to answer.

[14]

CHÂTEAU DE L'ENTREPRENANTE
FONTAINEBLEAU

Ysa awoke in bed. *But not my bed.* She took in the room and struggled to remember where she was . . . how she'd gotten here. *Jordi.* He'd come into the interrogation room and brought her upstairs . . . *and last night, I tried to escape.*

Sitting up, Ysa threw back the covers. The room swayed around her. She fought down her vertigo and nausea. *I made it out of the house and into the forest.* Or had she dreamed it? Her feet were clean and her gown was as fresh as if she'd just pulled it from a drawer.

The back of her head hurt. She reached up and gingerly felt the lump on her scalp. Jordi had thrown a sigil and then everything went black.

That explained the nausea and the vertigo. *I've got a concussion. Easy does it, then.*

She found a pair of slippers on the little rug beside her

bed. *Not the same ones as last night.* These were pink, the others had been white. She slid her feet into them.

The nurse's chair was vacant, the book on the floor.

She was alone.

Taking her time, she stood and steadied herself before going to the nurse's chair. She lowered herself to the seat and retrieved the worn book. It was a collection of short stories by Virginia Woolf, open to "A Haunted House."

A drop of blood marred the *o* in the title.

Someone knocked at her door. Ysa's head jerked up. Her fingers clenched. The page ripped. Without understanding her sudden fear, she shoved the book into the night table's drawer.

The room spun again. *Shit. Be careful.*

Another knock, this one louder, more impatient.

"Wait a moment." Her robe was at the foot of the bed. With careful steps, she made her way there and hurried to pull the dressing gown around her.

Show no weakness. She straightened her back but didn't move away from the bedpost. "Come in."

A maid entered with a breakfast tray, which she placed on a table beside the hearth. "Good morning, fräulein. Herr Abelló regrets he cannot join you for breakfast due to an early meeting. He does require your presence at lunch, which will be served at one."

Ysabel didn't answer.

The maid didn't seem to need a response. She drew the heavy drapes away from the window and smiled. "Herr Abelló hopes you enjoy your view. He instructed me to remind you that all actions have consequences."

Ysa barely heard her. Outside the window, the snow

flurried among the branches of a large oak. Hanging from a limb like a forgotten angel was the nurse, her white hat crooked on her bent head.

Such a shame. Her only crime was to fall asleep. Still, the nurse was the enemy. *She chose her side.*

The wind fluttered through the branches, sending a shower of sparkling flakes across the woman's body.

Gripping the heavy bedpost, Ysa swallowed hard against another bout of vertigo.

The maid's smile turned into a grin.

The vertigo. She mistakes the vertigo for guilt. "I envy my uncle. His nefilim must be great in number if he can afford to murder them so wantonly."

For a precious second, the maid froze; her grin morphed into a grimace. "Ma'am?"

"Move my breakfast there." Ysa pointed to the table in front of the window. "I want to enjoy the view."

With furtive glances at Ysa, the maid hurried to obey. She poured a cup of tea and then went to the door. "Will there be anything else?"

Ysa remained by the bedpost. "Convey to my uncle that I will gladly join him for lunch. We have much to discuss."

The maid curtsied. "Ma'am."

She waited until the door closed before she sagged against the post. Her knees were weak.

When was the last time I ate? She couldn't recall. For now, she needed to get some food into her body. *Give myself some time to heal.*

She went back to the night table and retrieved the nurse's book. Maybe the stories would relax her.

The area in front of the window was cold, but Ysa didn't

mind. She touched the lump on the back of her head again and, to her relief, it felt smaller. Hopefully, as the concussion healed, the nausea and vertigo would go away, too.

She opened the tray. Ham and eggs were arranged on the plate along with toast and butter. A jar of marmalade sat to one side.

Her mouth watered at the sight of it. They were probably hoping she would devour the meal without thinking. Ysa forced herself to nibble each item one at a time, cleansing her palate with water before moving to the next. The marmalade left a bitter aftertaste on her tongue.

Having found the sedative, she pushed the jar aside and buttered her toast. Opening the book, she found a bookplate pasted to the endpapers. THIS BOOK BELONGS TO and then in a delicate spiral of handwriting was the name *Greta*.

Lifting her teacup to the corpse outside her window, Ysa murmured, "Bon appétit, Greta." She turned to the short story, "A Haunted House," and began to read as she ate.

Rather than entertain her, Woolf's prose left her unsettled. The idea of doors shutting and knocking like the pulse of a heart mired in her head and made her think of the château coming to life with unclean intent.

She glanced at her empty plate. It was too clean, but she'd been famished. After stirring her knife through the marmalade, she smeared some among the toast's crumbs. *There, they'll think I ate the drug and that I'm down for the day.* She couldn't wait to surprise them.

Rising carefully, she tested one step and then two. The light-headedness wasn't as difficult to manage. In all probability, the concussion was mild and hunger had been the biggest instigator of her vertigo. *I hope, anyway.*

She went to her dressing table and returned the book to a drawer. The mirror showed her the yellowish bruise over her eye was rapidly fading. Heines's ring had sliced the eyebrow open, leaving a gash behind. A cut beside her lip looked deep enough to leave a small crescent scar.

Lowering the robe, she assessed her other injuries. Black and purple flowers bloomed all over her upper body. Some were edged in green or yellow, and she remembered each blow imprinted on her flesh.

"I'm still alive," she whispered to herself. *I have one more day.*

A silver-handled brush and matching comb lay side by side. She picked up the comb and worked it through her curls, dislodging the occasional pine needle as she did. Opening a drawer, she found an old cold cream jar filled with hairpins. With a smile, she used a few in her hair. *Never know when one of these might come in handy.*

She didn't bother with powder. Let Jordi see his goons' handiwork in bright, living color.

The wardrobe revealed a selection of stylish dresses. She chose one she liked and put it on. Though she much preferred pants, the full skirt didn't hinder her movements, so she resigned herself to Jordi's attempt to feminize her.

A quick check told her that her footwear selection was consigned entirely to heels. *How to hobble a woman without chains*, she thought as she chose a pair of pumps that matched her dress. Of course, most men didn't seem to realize that those spiked heels made a wicked weapon in the right hands.

Ysa had the right hands.

Now to see what awaits outside my door. She wondered if they'd locked her in, or if there were guards.

Opening the door, she found no sentries in the corridor. *Interesting.* Jordi still didn't believe that she needed to be watched.

Her room was in the château's east wing. If she remembered correctly, the library would be on the opposite wing. She doubted Jordi would place *The Book of Gold* in such an obvious spot, but one never knew.

In no particular hurry, she strolled down the hall and peeked over the balustrade. Downstairs, the lobby bustled with activity. No one got in or out without being observed by a quartet of soldiers. Ysa assumed others were stationed elsewhere below.

From her visits with her father, she knew the other doors on this level led to various suites. Though some, like Ysa's room, were reserved for guests, others were used for meetings. Since the maid indicated Jordi would be in a conference until lunch, Ysa didn't risk opening doors at random.

Stumbling on her uncle might make him angry, and the last thing she wanted was to find herself back in the cellar. The fact that Jordi hadn't returned her to the cell after her attempted escape told her that he wanted her free, too. For what reason, she had no idea.

Besides, conference rooms were better investigated at night. *Who knows what secrets they might yield?* A misplaced note or scraps in a wastepaper basket might reveal some tactic or plan. She made a mental note to steal an electric torch.

Ambling across the landing, she strolled into the west wing. Opposite the library was a bedroom Ysa knew well. It was the one she always requested.

She resisted the urge to peep inside her old guest room and stepped into the library. Floor-to-ceiling bookshelves occupied the walls. Except some sections were now noticeably empty. She drifted closer to the units. It took her several passes to realize the French titles had been removed, as if some malignant librarian had pulled them from the collection.

All that remained were books in German. *Where had the Virginia Woolf collection come from? Had Greta the nurse claimed it during the purge?* Ysa decided to keep it hidden.

She soon concluded that she'd been right: Jordi hadn't placed *The Book of Gold* in the library. He probably kept it close to him. *In his room.* Not that it mattered. The important part had been torn out.

A clock ticked comfortably in one corner. It was only eleven. She had plenty of time. Ysa selected a slim book at random as a prop. Reading wasn't on her agenda.

Overstuffed chairs with ornate tables were scattered throughout the library. In spite of the size of the room, it was easy to carve out a niche of one's own. Ysa had passed many a comfortable evening in the chair by the door.

Strategically placed so that it was invisible to anyone passing outside, the spot had enabled her to eavesdrop on more than one conversation when she was a child. *But now I've set aside my childish things.*

Happy the chair was still tucked in its special spot, she kicked off her shoes and settled herself on the cushion. Angling her head just so enabled her to see into the corridor. She made sure of her position and then curled her feet beneath her.

Almost an hour passed before her stealth paid off. The sound of voices grew closer, although it was apparent the men were trying to be quiet.

Jimenez, he of the needles and long sleeps. Though she'd only heard him speak a few times, she recognized the lilt of his words. When Diago became angry, he slipped into seseo with that same slight lisp, which changed the *z* sound of his words to *s*.

Jimenez was probably Andalusian, too. Unlike Diago, who was fluent in several dialects, Jimenez spoke German with a heavy Spanish accent.

Ysa tilted her head and her suspicions were confirmed. The rotund doctor's figure lumbered into the west wing.

The very memory of his clammy hands made her skin crawl. She resisted the urge to rub her arm. Though her chair wasn't in plain view, movement might draw his attention.

He stopped in front of the door to her old guest room and unlocked the door.

Her lip curled with disgust. *I'll never sleep in there again.*

Jimenez gestured to someone who remained outside Ysa's line of vision. "Quickly, Herr Strzyga!"

"I thought we were going upstairs to see Herr Abelló." The other voice was polished and the man spoke with an Eastern European inflection to his German.

"*Quiet*," Jimenez hissed like a cat with its tail on fire. "He's not there. He's in a meeting in another part of the château."

Strzyga placed his black bag on the credenza beside Jimenez's door. "I'm not slinking into your den."

Ysabel finally got a glimpse of him. His long black hair touched the collar of his uniform. Like Jordi, he wore the black of an SS officer. Dark glasses covered his eyes.

In profile, he reminded her of the paintings she'd seen of Vlad Dracula. *Great, Jimenez is doing business with Dracula, and given Jordi's proclivity toward experimentation, Frankenstein's nefil is probably in the attic awaiting his lightning bolt.*

Ysa heard the snap of a bag opening followed by the sharp click of vials placed on the credenza. She counted fourteen clicks.

"It's imperative that I speak to him." Strzyga kept his voice low, but Ysa detected an edge of frustration to his tone. "We've waited too long for a war like this, and our nefilim won't be reassured if the angel-born are led by an addict."

He's making a clear distinction between the angel-born and his nefilim. She squeezed the book between her palms. *He is daimon-born.* That explained the dark glasses inside the château.

What was Jimenez up to? Or perhaps the better question was: How could she use this knowledge to her advantage?

Her uncle's tremendous tolerance for drugs was no secret. Diago often suggested that the morphine Jordi took merely prevented withdrawal and did little to affect his judgment. From what she'd witnessed so far, she found she agreed.

The sound of Jimenez scurrying across the floor and the clink of vials told Ysa he was moving the morphine into his room. "I understand your frustration, Herr Strzyga. I just need a little more time to set up a meeting. It's just that the war—"

Strzyga cut Jimenez off. "Can you afford to open another front in this war?" The bag snapped shut. "Get me an interview with him. Or your last source of morphine in this city will dry up. And then how much favor will you find with him, Herr Doctor?"

"Give me another day, and I will be in touch. I swear it. Let me see you to the door."

Ysa held perfectly still until she was sure they were gone. Stretching her legs, she wiggled her toes and sighed with relief. Courts were hotbeds of intrigue, with courtiers always maneuvering for favor. *But conspiring with the daimon-born?*

It was all quite peculiar. Slipping her feet back into her shoes, she stood and returned the book to its shelf. The clock told her she still had an hour until lunch. *And according to Jimenez, Uncle Jordi is in a meeting elsewhere in the château.*

The corridor outside the library was clear. Ysa left and returned to the landing. From her few visits to the château, she knew Rousseau's private chambers were on the third floor. She was positive Jordi's pride wouldn't allow him to accept any accommodations other than those of the queen herself.

What could it hurt to take a look? She recalled the strange laughter she'd heard last night, but the daylight chased those ghosts away. Walking on tiptoe to keep her heels from clacking on the marble steps, she started up the stairs.

At the next landing, the corridor's lights were dimmed and the shadows grew deeper. Here, she felt as if she'd stepped back into the night. Although sigils twisted on every door in both wings, their fires smoldered rather than burned.

Except on the door at end of the hall. That glyph blazed with the Totenkopfring design on Jordi's signet. Sparks crackled around both the skull and the runes.

Ysabel eased closer. The hair on her body rose in response to the electricity in the air.

This wasn't the place to test her glyph-breaking skills. If she knew for a fact where he was and when he would return, she might have risked peeking inside his room.

But I can knock gently. It would give her an idea of the strength of his sigils.

She formed a small ward of her own and sent it forward, timid as a light peck upon the door. The deep auburn tones of her aura touched Jordi's glyphs and melded with them as one. She felt a mild jolt that tingled across her skin.

Then, to her surprise, Jordi's sigil blazed once before it dimmed. The door opened.

Make a note: Jimenez is a liar. "Uncle Jordi?" she called as she sidled another step closer. "May we speak?"

"Come in." His voice drifted into the hall, soft and melodic. Once more, she thought of her father. Except, where her father's voice awakened the memory of hearth fires holding back the night, Jordi's tonal frequencies brought to mind the colder drifts of space.

Even so, she didn't wait for a second invitation. She walked to the door and pushed it open. Although the suite occupied the area directly over hers, it was twice the size of her room. A huge bed dominated the wall near the fireplace.

At the opposite end of the room, beside the window, was a Rococo piano made of Brazilian rosewood. Three exquisitely carved legs held the body erect.

Though the music stand was sculpted in swirls that indicated angelic glyphs, the width and height of it matched the piano's broad dimensions. It was a beast of an instrument—large and imposing, gleaming in the morning light.

A manly piano for a manly-man. She noted the room's furnishings matched the piano in tone. The curtains around the bed were crimson velvet. Subtler reddish hues were entwined in the room's décor.

Red, the color of kings. Her father's contempt for such trappings had been drilled into her consciousness over the years until she, like him, found herself avoiding the color whenever possible.

Jordi showed no such restraint. He surrounded himself with powerful lines, from the gilded border on the wall's pale boiserie to the brocade adorning the thick carpets. His black writing desk was also trimmed with brash lines of gold-leaf.

That was where she finally found him—at the desk. His back was to her. He wore a voluminous robe that reminded her of Diago's favorite garment, which looked more like a houppelande with its long flowing sleeves. Jordi's robe wasn't as intricately embroidered as Diago's, but the two men favored fine silks padded for warmth.

And attire from the same century. She wondered if it was because it reminded them of their youth. Not that it mattered. She swore she would never allow herself to become entrapped by a period's styles.

Jordi continued to write. "I could have murdered you five times over since you've walked through my door."

"If you'd wanted to kill me, you would have done it by now. What boggles my mind is how you allow a hostage to wander through your house unattended. Aren't you the least curious as to why I'm not sleeping the sleep of the drugged in my room?"

His pen never wavered. "Because Jimenez is incompetent."

And a traitor to you. Her instinct told her now wasn't the time to make that accusation. "It wasn't so much his incompetence but my skill as a doctor."

"I am impressed."

Ysabel knew sarcasm when she heard it. "It sounds like you're humoring me."

"It doesn't matter if you're here through Jimenez's incompetence or your competence. I'm not afraid of children."

"Perhaps you should be."

"They warned me that you are a precocious child."

"I'm not a child." Her rebuttal sounded peevish to her own ears.

A note of amusement touched his voice. "But you are precocious." He signed off on a form and turned to another as he dipped his pen in the inkwell again. "I said we would have lunch together. A woman would have waited, a child has no patience."

"And a man would have immediately sought you out to parley. I'm not a child. I simply don't woman well some days."

His pen faltered and he put it down. Turning in his seat, he met her gaze. "What does that mean: you don't *woman well*?"

"Women are expected to be demure and quiet. We're to patiently await the attention of men. That is what it means to be a woman, and I've no use for masculine perceptions of femininity."

"Those are the expectations of mortals, not nefilim."

She arched her eyebrow at him. "Apparently not all the nefilim received that memo. Many of them take on mortal attitudes and allegiances." A pointed look in the direction of his immaculate black uniform on the headless mannequin was her only indication that Jordi also mimicked mortal pretensions.

He followed her gaze. "Perceptive, but also wrong. The double lightning bolt, the SS insignia, those were . . . repurposed by the mortals. In some cases, Queen Jaeger sent her nefilim to guide the mortals in their beliefs."

"You mean like Wiligut?" Karl Maria Wiligut, known as Himmler's Rasputin, claimed that he designed the death's head symbology of the SS. "Didn't he say he was the spiritual heir of the nefilim?"

Jordi's nod of appreciation, when it came, was barely perceptible but there nonetheless. "He was the progeny of a lesser nefil, probably eleventh or twelfth generation and angel-born. Far enough removed to have strong psychic abilities for a mortal, but according to our laws of consanguinity, a mortal nonetheless."

"Didn't he go mad?"

Jordi made a dismissive gesture with one hand. "A small sacrifice."

"I don't understand how you can be so callous."

"I'm not. We're giving the mortals the belief systems they need." He opened a casket on his desk and removed a gold wedding band from the box.

Ysabel's eyes narrowed. She recognized the sigils on the band. It was the ring Jordi had stolen from Miquel at the end of the Spanish Civil War. Though her father had fashioned a new one for Miquel, he still mourned the loss of his first wedding ring. *And now Jordi toys with it like a trophy.*

Jordi slipped the band onto his left ring finger and pretended to admire the sigils. "In Spain, for example, it was Christianity . . ." He paused and examined her more closely. "Are you old enough to remember the Spanish War?"

"I was twelve when it began."

"Then you probably recall that in Spain, the mortals revered Christianity. That particular religiosity was so entrenched, we merely manipulated their beliefs to benefit our politics. We made them afraid they were about to lose their precious religion to secularism; although the most influential rebels didn't care about religion—they simply wanted the power to control other people's beliefs. Once we were able to divide them on an ideological basis, we set them against one another on the military fields.

"Likewise, in Germany, we used the Armanists, Ariosophists, and those that dabble in the occult to achieve the same means. We saw the Germans' collective self-esteem had taken a terrific blow from the loss of the Great War. We simply rebuilt their sense of self-worth through the concept of racial superiority—propaganda they desperately wanted to believe—and in doing so, we gave their lives meaning. That is what gods do."

Ysabel felt as if she'd stepped into an abyss. She didn't know where to begin. "Wouldn't it be better if we taught them to love one another?"

Jordi chuckled. Whether it was her naivete that amused him or the thought of mortals living in harmony, she didn't know.

"Take the blinders off your eyes, child. The mortals are merely pale echoes of us. They want what we all want—power. Even in love, they look to dominate each other."

He stood and approached her. It was all she could do to remain still.

Taking her hands in his, he gazed deep into her eyes and

allowed the nimbus of his aura to expand. "But mortals will never have this."

Deep golden hues filled with umber and red smoldered all around him. The flames of his song struck the air and diminished his mortal form until he almost appeared as an angel in their truest manifestation of light and sound.

Her vertigo returned, weakening her knees even as she allowed her own aura to flow around her in self-defense. She kept her feet, but just barely. Crimson flames streaked with gold and orange flowered around her body. With the colors of her own song shielding her eyes, she saw deep into Jordi's core.

And his aura wasn't untainted. Sickly green threads twisted through his song. *The Grigori.* Jordi was still contaminated by the fallen angel he'd served during the Spanish Civil War. *Papá wasn't able to heal him completely and he still bears the Grigori's mark.*

Jordi's grip tightened. The bones in her wrists ached.

She forced herself to meet his gaze.

"Your aura is pure." He relaxed his hold on her but didn't let go. "Do you know why this is?" He didn't wait for an answer. Instead, he leaned close and whispered in her ear. "The Thrones themselves dictate the nefilim's genealogical lines. They mate nefilim and angels with meticulous attention to detail. You, my dear niece, are the culmination of centuries of planning. A grand success in the cosmic scheme."

His snaking rhetoric unsettled her. *He bends the meaning of our existence into something that it's not.* She sought a clear path through his tangled discourse. "That doesn't make us gods."

"To the mortals we are." His aura flared around him, and then gradually receded. He drew his soul close to his body and released her.

Ysa clutched the doorjamb to steady herself.

With his thumb, Jordi caressed Miquel's wedding band and returned to his seat. "Play for me."

Halos encircled the light fixtures. She flexed her hands and noted the faint bruises encircling her wrists. Needing a moment to get her breath, she stalled him. "Will we exchange songs?"

It was a reasonable request and a matter of professional etiquette that when one nefil played for another, they exchanged songs. To see the flash of another nefil's aura wasn't the same as hearing them sing. To play, to sing, this proved the nefil's ability to manifest either emotion or magic through the power of their voice.

"I want to see the type of nefil my softhearted brother has raised. Impress me."

"As a child, a woman, or a man?"

A smile tugged at his lips. "As you will."

Ysa went to the monstrous piano and sat on the padded bench. "Is there anything in particular that you'd like to hear? A rousing rendition of the 'Horst-Wessel-Lied'? Or would you prefer Wagner?"

"You have your father's sense of humor."

"I'm glad I could lighten the moment."

"I didn't say you were funny."

She directed a tight smile at him and raised her eyebrows. "Well?"

"Give me an original composition."

Something original. The long white keys were slender as

finger bones. She kicked off her heels and adjusted her feet over the pedals. A quick run through the scales allowed her to get a feel for the instrument and to think. Her mind kept wandering back to last night, and the hallucination of her father kneeling beside her on the kitchen floor.

As she thought of him, her fingers wandered to the lower notes, striking a pattern like the sound of his hammer on the anvil. The melody turned to smoke and fog as she fled into the night. Diago appeared as earthy chords cementing Juanita's more ethereal notes within the ice and cold. Rafael's leitmotif carried the pulse of his youth and courage, while Miquel's presence emerged with a militaristic beat. All around them, the snow swarmed in falling sigils, pale and blue against the night.

Her fingers momentarily faltered as she spun Jordi's theme across the keyboard. He rose from the night, at first as a monster, and then she recalled the tenderness in his voice. *You should have been my daughter.*

She repeated the chords of that last line with the longing she'd heard in his voice. *You should have been mine.*

When she finished the piece, she sat still as the notes faded.

In the ensuing silence, she became aware of a clock ticking softly in the background. She counted a hundred beats before Jordi finally spoke.

"It doesn't have an ending."

She turned to face him, unsure what to expect. Rather than the contempt she was sure would be there, she found only curiosity. "What do you mean?"

"You played the events of last night, but you didn't give it an ending."

She shrugged. "I don't know how it will end yet. Neither do you."

Withdrawing a handkerchief from his sleeve, he patted the sweat from his brow and winced.

The morphine. He's in withdrawal. She immediately thought of Strzyga and Jimenez conferring in the hall. *Maybe now is the time to tell him about them.* She opened her mouth, but he turned back to his work.

"I need to change before lunch. I'll meet you in the foyer. Then we will discuss *The Book of Gold* and your father." He pressed a button on his intercom. "Stultz, come escort Fräulein Ramírez downstairs."

A young soldier in uniform came to the doorway and snapped his heels as he gave Jordi a Sieg Heil salute. "Sir!" Then he bowed to Ysabel. "Fräulein, if you please."

She didn't please. Not at all. But she also knew she would gain nothing by antagonizing her uncle. For now, keeping him happy meant obeying him.

Besides, while her little adventure might not have seemed exciting on the surface, she'd gathered more information than she'd hoped. War, Miquel had taught her, was much more a measure of risk and strategy than the application of brute force. The objective was to gain intelligence about the enemy, analyze it, and then apply the information to gain leverage against the foe.

Ysa had accomplished the first part; now she needed time to think.

In the foyer, Ysa took a seat in an alcove and observed the château's visitors. Various officers, both nefilim and mortals, came and went on Reich business.

One mortal in particular caught her eye as he entered the building. He wore a patch over his left eye, and it was apparent that his right hand was a prosthesis. As he withdrew his identification, she noted that two fingers on his left hand were missing.

Due to the nature of his injuries, Ysabel instantly placed him: Claus von Stauffenberg. According to Los Nefilim's intelligence, Stauffenberg had ties to another mortal, Henning von Tresckow, a leading member of the German resistance. Thus far, they'd hatched no fewer than three plots to assassinate Hitler. All of which had failed. But mortals, like nefilim, could be exceptionally persistent.

As she had in the library, Ysa became very still. Wolves stalked their prey with less intensity than she watched the mortal at the door. *I wonder who he is here to see?*

The answer came sooner than she expected. Erich Heines strode into view and greeted Stauffenberg. Although she wasn't close enough to hear their discussion, it was clear by their smiles they knew one another well. Heines gestured toward the western wing and they moved off together.

Ysa tapped the arm of her chair thoughtfully and tucked that information alongside Jimenez's dealing with the daimon-born. With any luck, she might get the opportunity to talk to Heines alone.

One of the soldiers by the doors looked upstairs and snapped to attention. The others followed suit.

Jordi must be coming. She stood just as he reached the bottom of the staircase. Ysa noticed that Jimenez trailed behind her uncle.

The doctor smiled beneath his toothbrush mustache. The gesture was a limp affectation that brought to mind worms crawling through the night. Her imagination didn't have to stretch far to see him approach the daimon-born for drugs.

Jordi's physical discomfort appeared to be gone, though he showed no signs of being inebriated by the morphine. He offered her his arm and she took it. Stultz remained in the foyer, and Jimenez drifted off in a different direction.

Rather than take her to the large formal dining room as she expected, Jordi escorted her to an adjacent room with a small table set for two. He seated her in front of a dossier and then took his place at the head of the table.

As he poured the wine, he nodded to the file. "Why did you steal *The Book of Gold* from the library?"

Time to keep my story straight. In spite of the beatings and whatever drugs Jimenez gave her, she recalled the gist of her answers to Heines. "My father has become . . . confused. He seems to think that he has buried some secret in a grimoire somewhere in France. That's why I've been traveling to collect them for him."

Jordi didn't seem impressed with the answer. "If he is so addled, then why are you obeying him?"

"To save his life." She met her uncle's stare. "I traveled so he wouldn't go himself and get killed."

"Why haven't you simply taken over Los Nefilim?"

"He has moments of lucidity, and I've had a hard time convincing Miquel there is a problem." When he didn't contradict her, she congratulated herself on recalling a story told under duress.

Jordi nodded to the folder. "Go ahead. Tell me if you recognize the photograph."

It was the same picture Heines had shown her during her interrogation. "Yes, I remember. Heines mentioned a letter."

Jordi ignored the statement and tapped the photo. "It's a photograph of Psalm 60 from *The Book of Gold*. The same psalm that is missing from the book you stole from the library."

"But I didn't deface the book. I took no photograph, and I sent no letter."

"Carlos Vela sent the letter."

She recalled the aura she'd seen in *The Book of Gold*'s binding. *Carlos Vela. That son of a bitch.* "I remember him. He was one of Miquel's capitanes. He defected to your side sometime during the war."

That was why the aura was familiar to her. And now was the time to use that information to win Jordi's trust. "If you look closely at the grimoire's binding, you'll see Vela's aura. He vandalized that book. My father warded all his grimoires, and this one contained an especially nasty curse."

Jordi didn't appear convinced.

"Look . . . see this?" She pointed to a splash of dark pigmentation that discolored the lower part of the grimoire's page. "It's hard to tell from the photo, but given the way the spot has feathered into the paper, I'd bet my lunch that is Carlos's blood."

Jordi pursed his lips. Taking the picture from her hands, he tilted it. His expression cleared. "I think you're right."

"What kind of letter did he send you?"

"First he wanted to exchange the psalm for a healing, and when I showed no interest, he tried to blackmail me."

But he doesn't say how. Curious. Had Carlos threatened to bear witness about Jordi's interaction with the Grigori? That was certainly possible.

She returned the photograph to the folder and tsked. "Traitors are like unfaithful spouses: if they'll cheat *with* you, they'll eventually cheat *on* you. Why did he want you to heal him?"

"When your father flooded a tunnel with the fire of the Thrones, he created collateral damage in some of my nefilim. Several took their own lives. Others had to be put down."

Put down. Like they were dogs. Her stomach curdled at the thought. "You could have healed him." She nodded toward his signet.

"I will not be blackmailed by a traitor."

No. Not Jordi. Besides, a healing of that magnitude required the mingling of auras. Jordi wouldn't pollute himself by allowing Carlos's song to join with his. "Why didn't you . . . put him down?"

"That was my intention. Unfortunately, he disappeared."

"We have no idea where he is. If my father knew, he'd give Vela a death sentence."

Jordi observed her quietly for a few moments. Without breaking eye contact, he lifted the small bell beside his plate and rang for their lunch.

Once the first course had been served, he casually asked, "Are you really concerned about your father?"

She stirred her spoon through her soup. "Yes, I am. More so for the members of Los Nefilim. They deserve to be treated fairly."

"Perhaps we can come to some agreement—your father and me."

"Such as?"

"If he would be willing to step aside as the king of Los Nefilim, I would consider absorbing his people into Die Nephilim's ranks—with the exception of Miquel, of course. I'm sure we could find another division of the Inner Guard to take him. That would protect the nefilim in Guillermo's care, and give you time to nurse your father."

She didn't ask what he intended for Diago and Rafael; she didn't want to know. His intentions for them would make it harder for her to play this game. "Are you serious?"

He shook out his napkin and placed it in his lap. "Yes."

Sighing, she pretended to think about the offer. *Don't jump too fast.* When she thought she'd given her consideration enough time, she feigned defeat and nodded. "What do I need to do?"

Reaching out, he touched her chin and applied gentle pressure until she tilted her head to the left.

The bruises. He's gauging how much longer it will be before I've healed.

"Tomorrow morning, you may call him and invite him here."

That wasn't exactly what she had in mind. Once her father entered the château, he'd be at Jordi's mercy. *And Jordi will definitely want him to come alone.*

Something in her expression must have given away her anxiety, because he stroked her cheek and smiled. "I promise, we are only going to talk. What happens after that depends on your father, and whether or not you can convince him to see reason."

And if I don't play this game, he'll find another way to use me to draw Papá here. She had to maintain some measure of control so she could warn her father.

"Thank you," she whispered. "I'll do anything I can to make him safe." She forced a spoonful of soup between her lips.

"Excellent." Jordi lit a cigarette and watched her eat. "Bring him here, and we'll work this out, like a family should."

Oh, we will. She swallowed past the lump in her throat. *One way or another . . . we're going to work it out.*

For years Ysa had analyzed her father's face as he negotiated with friend and enemy alike, and now she maintained his studied expression, always nodding in just the right spots, never saying too much, or too little.

All the while Jordi explained how her father had cheated him of his birthright. It was an ancient resentment that began in their firstborn lives, but as she listened, Ysa realized her uncle truly felt he'd been wronged.

Jordi smoked and nursed his wine, barely touching his food. "I was known as Adonijah. I was the eldest son, so the right to rule the nefilim was mine. Unfortunately, your father's angelic mother maneuvered him into the kingship over me. She turned both David and Solomon against me. Because of her . . . meddling . . . Solomon ordered my death."

It is also somewhat more nuanced than that. From her father, she understood that David had passed the mantle of kingship to Solomon. Adonijah had initially objected, but Solomon quickly consolidated his power, forcing Adonijah to use intrigues in order to achieve his goals.

When Adonijah seemed on the cusp of success through a politically opportune marriage, Solomon ordered his brother's execution. The ugly event was made more tragic by Adonijah's cowardice. He ran into the temple and hugged the altar, begging Solomon for his life. Instead of mercy, Solomon sent Benaiah to murder Adonijah.

Jordi crushed his cigarette in his saucer and concluded, "It was a terrible affair."

She shook her head in sympathy. "I'm so sorry. I cannot even imagine how horrific that must have been for you. But we don't have to keep repeating the same mistakes from one incarnation to another." She stirred cream into her coffee. "For one thing, I think you've changed."

"How so?" He genuinely seemed interested in what she had to say.

"Last night, you said something that struck my heart."

"I did?"

"You said that I should have been your daughter. Did you mean that?"

He coughed a soft laugh. "I . . ."

"I just want you to know that I'm honored. And I'm sorry my father kept us apart. I would like to get to know you."

Suspicion darted into his gaze. "I see what you're doing. It's not going to work."

She gave him her most charming smile. "I don't expect you to believe me this soon, but I'm hoping that you and my father can find some way to reconcile. I know he is genuinely sorry for how he treated you in your firstborn lives."

"He's spoken to you about his?"

"He has."

Someone knocked at the door.

Go away, I'm working, go away.

"Come in," Jordi called.

A private entered the room and snapped to attention. "I have a message for you, sir."

At a signal from Jordi, the private came to his side and

whispered in his ear. Ysa feigned disinterest, but strained to hear.

Something about a supply disruption . . . She didn't catch the name of the town. *The maquisards must have damaged another bridge. Good for them.*

Jordi lifted a hand and nodded. "I'll be right there." He smiled apologetically as he stood. "I'm so sorry." He took her hand. "We'll continue this conversation at dinner. I'd like very much to hear your thoughts about a reconciliation. However, I'm afraid I must leave you. Reich business."

She started to stand, but he touched her shoulder.

"No, no. Sit and enjoy your coffee." He motioned for the private to leave, and then he bent down to whisper in her ear, "Last night, I saw myself in you. I meant what I said. I wish you were my daughter." Then he stood and left her alone.

That didn't mean he trusted her. *But he's given me an admission—a way into his thoughts.* She didn't kid herself. This was a game of manipulation, and he had far more experience than she. Winning his trust wouldn't be easy. *But at least now I know that it's possible.*

When she finished her meal, she left the dining room, intent on finding Heines and Stauffenberg. Heines wouldn't jeopardize himself to save her, but she might be able to get a message to her father through Stauffenberg.

The sergeant met her in the hall. The woman looked no friendlier than during the car ride to the estate, but her demeanor was merely professionalism. She snapped to attention and gestured toward the stairs. "I've been asked to escort you to your room, fräulein."

Don't argue. Compliance will eventually cause them to drop their guard. "Of course, Sergeant . . ." She allowed the sentence to dangle, hoping the nefil would fill in her name.

"Esser, fräulein."

"Of course, Sergeant Esser." Ysa nodded to the woman and proceeded to the stairs.

At the second-floor landing, Dr. Jimenez waited for her with his black bag. "Fräulein, I hope you enjoyed your lunch."

"I did. Thank you," she said as he passed him. She kept her pace sharp, hoping to leave him behind. Instead, she heard his soft tread on the runner. *Shit.*

Esser moved in lockstep with her.

Ysa reached her door and stopped on the threshold. She glared at Jimenez. "Why are you here?"

"It's time for your medicine."

"I don't want any medicine."

"I'm afraid that decision has been made for you."

She grabbed the doorknob and attempted to close the door. Esser's palm halted the door midswing.

Jimenez seemed completely unperturbed. "I can summon others, and this can get quite ugly, but you *will* have the shot. Herr Abelló has ordered it."

Why? Does he want me to be an addict, like him? She immediately discounted the idea. This was about control of both her movements and her body. *Jordi is making a point. He doesn't trust me and won't for some time.*

The smirk on Jimenez's face sent her back to her first hours in the château. She'd struggled against that first shot. *I blinked.*

A fight would be satisfying. At the very least it would give her a chance to inflict damage on the enemy. But she was outnumbered.

I blinked once. Don't blink again. Ysa released the door-knob and stood aside to allow Jimenez into her room.

As she did, she noticed the dark rings Jordi had left on her wrists looked less like bruises and more like manacles.

[15]

THE FARM

Later that evening, Miquel sat at the rickety desk in their bedroom and pecked the typewriter's keys with two fingers. The only thing he hated more than writing reports was having to type them. He'd give a crate of hand grenades for his own secretary.

Maybe I'll hire someone like Suero for these jobs after the war. If the war ever ended.

Night had fallen while he worked, forcing him to stop and light a lamp. He turned up the wick and saw the *e* wasn't firmly striking the paper.

"Goddamn it." He added a new typewriter to the list and muttered, "Why couldn't it have been *z*?" He'd have to fill them in by hand when he was done.

Diago came into the room and dropped a file beside the typewriter. "Your copy of Carlos's autopsy report."

"Oh, our friend Carlos." He opened the neatly typed

report and skimmed to the conclusion: *Asphyxia due to ligature strangulation.* "What kind of ligature?"

"Garrote. Based on how deep it cut into his neck, we're guessing they used a wire."

Miquel closed the file. "Your relatives are thugs."

"I was born to them. You *chose* to marry into the family."

"Touché," Miquel smiled and looked up at his husband. He took Diago's hand between his palms. "How are you holding up?"

"I'm okay. I'm glad Christina has gone to Paris. Guillermo won't be sending me there, so I've got a reprieve from that assignment." He reached over Miquel's shoulder and lowered the lamp's wick. "You're wasting oil."

Always conscious of every franc. Miquel didn't admonish him. Diago's frugality stemmed from his days as a rogue. *Except he splurges like a millionaire on Rafael and me.* "Let me finish this report and then I'll stop."

"Leave it. I'll type it for you in the morning. Consider it my penance for blabbing to Guillermo about Nico being at Mauthausen."

Miquel resisted the urge to admonish him again. *Let it go. I'd rather him care too much for someone else's welfare than not at all.* If only it was anyone but Nico. "I accept your apology and the offer. Just don't go over my head with Guillermo again."

"I won't."

They both knew he would. Diago's behavior was as predictable as the rising of the sun.

Miquel kissed his husband's palm. "Did Suero ever get in touch with Ysa's rooming house?"

"The lines are still down. Bernardo said he saw a crew working on them this morning. We're hoping everything will be operational by tomorrow. If they're not, Bernardo will try calling when he gets back to Perpignan."

"I'll relax when we finally hear her voice."

"Me, too. Maybe Nico can give us some useful information if you don't scare him off again."

Miquel raised his hands in surrender. "I'll be good. Is Juanita coming up?" He hoped Diago didn't hear the slight nervousness in his voice. He still wasn't entirely comfortable with the idea of reconnaissance through his dreams. *Especially with Nico.*

Diago went to the stove and added a couple of pieces of coal. "She's going to give us an hour and then come up. Hopefully by then you'll be asleep."

"I'm not sleepy."

"You will be."

"That sounds ominous."

Diago didn't smile.

"Is something wrong?"

Diago removed his coat and didn't immediately answer. *Not a good sign.* Whatever was bothering him ran deep. "Hey." Miquel went to his husband and took him in his arms. "Talk to me."

Diago's muscles tensed as if preparing himself for an argument. "Can you, please, try and show Nico a little empathy tonight? He risked his life to get a message to us."

Nico. Again. He simply wasn't going to let it go. *At least he's not planning to invade Mauthausen anymore.* Miquel caressed his husband's shoulder and kept his temper; he didn't want another fight like the one they'd had in the truck. "I've never heard you plead someone's case as you have his. I'm starting to get a little jealous."

Diago stepped out of the embrace. "I'm serious, Miquel."

Meet him halfway and be honest. "I know you're worried. And I'm trying. I really am. It's just that every time I think of him, I see him standing in my cell's door with that damn clipboard, asking me my name while knowing full well who I am. He played Jordi's game for so long, I have difficulty divorcing the two of them into separate individuals. So you tell me: How do I forgive him? How do I let all that pain go and trust him?"

"See him as he is and not as he was. Sort of like you did for me."

Miquel sighed. *Touché again, my love.* "I'll try. That's all I can promise right now."

"That's enough." The hard lines around Diago's mouth eased and he visibly relaxed. "Now take off your clothes."

Normally that was a command Miquel didn't argue with. Except he wasn't exactly in the mood for play. "I'm not sure I can rise to the occasion tonight."

Diago went to the wardrobe and retrieved his violin from its case. "We don't just get naked for sex."

"That's the best reason." Miquel gave his husband a wicked smile as he lifted his sweater over his head. He was gratified to see Diago smile back. "What are you planning?"

"One of the issues we faced when using astral projection was the inability to distinguish between the informant's conscious relay of information versus the unreliable subconscious imagery inherent to the dreamers. I think I've devised a way that will help you distinguish between the two."

Miquel marveled at his husband. *My world is all about battles and strength, but he understands metaphysics in ways that I can only guess.* "I understood about a third of that. But I trust you with my soul."

He unbuckled his pants and let them fall around his ankles. Stepping free of his garments, he spread his arms. "What do you need me to do?"

Diago guided him to the center of the room. "Just stand still."

He tucked the violin beneath his chin and drew the bow across the strings, leaving mournful notes shivering in the air. After a minor adjustment to the tension on the E-string, he tested the pitch again. His expression indicated he was satisfied with the sound. He began to play.

Entranced by his husband's poise, Miquel watched him. With hypnotic grace, Diago's fingers danced over the strings, leaving viridian streaks of light floating in his wake. Lost in the beauty of his husband's music, Miquel felt the day's anxiety fade from his neck and shoulders.

Using the bow like a wand, Diago reshaped the vibrations into sigils. He augmented the music with his voice, effortlessly vocalizing from the higher ranges to the low.

Relaxing beneath the resonance of his husband's music, Miquel gave in to the lethargy flowing over him. He closed his eyes and tilted his head back. A small gasp escaped him when the first of Diago's wards brushed his skin. The magic left mild shocks rippling across his body. The feeling was far from unpleasant.

He opened his eyes in time to see the glyphs shimmering against his flesh, a million points of light that were absorbed into his body. *Protective wards. He's shielding me.*

Lowering the bow, Diago brushed his finger across the back of Miquel's hand. The jade reverberations of his song were laced with lighter hues of blue and gray to form an intricate pattern.

This was a different glyph. It melted against Miquel's skin like warm wax. With a final mellow note, Diago charged the sigil.

The ward glowed softly, a tattoo of green and black loops highlighted with the paler tones of blue and gray.

Diago looked up at him. "How do you feel?"

Miquel opened his eyes. "Relaxed. Sleepy. What is this?" He indicated the glyph on the back of his hand.

Diago traced his thumb over the lines. "If you have any doubt as to whether you're actually talking to Nico's astral projection, or if you simply dream, look to your hand. I wound Nico's aura into the glyph so it will respond to his soul. When it flares, you're seeing Nico's astral projection."

"How could you do that without having him here?"

Diago put his violin back in its case. "I used the vibrations of the glyph he sent with Petre. I don't know how long it will last. I also shielded you with my wards. If something strikes out at you, I'll know, and we can wake you."

He's so clever. Miquel yawned. "I'm lucky to have you watching out for me. Lie down with me."

Diago followed him to the bed.

"Not like that," Miquel whispered. He tugged at Diago's shirt. "Take off your clothes. I want to feel your skin next to mine."

Diago didn't argue. He stripped and got into the bed next to his husband.

Beneath the covers, they warmed one another. Miquel closed his eyes and let sleep take him into a dream . . .

. . . and he instantly recognizes the cell. He is back in Jordi's black site. This is where Guillermo's brother held him while Nico shot him full of drugs.

Bricks stud the cell's floor, jutting upward in the concrete. The design is a labyrinth calculated to impede free movement. Walking requires great care lest he twist an ankle or knee.

All around him, angelic glyphs writhe on the walls and provide the only light. The razored sigils are rendered in sharp, high notes designed to slash the tongue and mouth should he sing a defensive glyph.

Of course it's what I would dream. Miquel's hand tingles. He looks down. The ward Diago drew there pulses softly, like a warning.

The cell door slams open. Heavy snowflakes drift across the threshold. Ashes mingle with the snow.

Suddenly the glyph flares to life.

This is it. Nico's dream-spell has begun.

When Miquel looks up again, Nico stands just beyond the door. His hair is shorn close to his skull and his cheeks are hollowed with hunger. His striped shirt has a pink triangle sewn beneath a number.

Miquel knows the meaning of the camps' badges. *They marked him as a homosexual.*

Pants, the legs of which are too long, are rolled over ankles encrusted with sores. The wooden shoes on his feet aren't the same size, yet Nico barely seems to notice.

On his wrist is a metal tag, secured with a wire. Stamped on the tag is a number. Miquel can only read a couple of the digits, but it seems to match the patch over the triangle.

Behind Nico are rows of men, standing at attention. They face one another across a lane between buildings.

In the distance, the camp's gates open. A prisoner marches ahead of a small orchestra. He pumps his baton in time with the charivari's lively march, bowing first to the left and then to the right. The grin pasted to his face is a rictus of terror.

Nico comes to the threshold of Miquel's cell, but he can't seem to cross. His face arrests Miquel's attention. Something has changed within him. His features seem harsher now. "You came."

"I came. Does anyone dream with you?"

Nico shakes his head with a barely perceivable movement. "Watch behind me, though."

The tattered orchestra precedes a tumbrel pulled by two prisoners. Ribbons and banners adorn the cart. Painted in large letters, the signs proclaim in German: *Hurrah! We're home again!*

Three men stand on the platform. Their chests are bare and black with bruises.

Miquel frowns at the scene. "What's happening?"

"The men escaped and were captured. They were made to enter the gates on their knees, and then tortured to find out who helped them. Now they will hang. This is my nightmare. Like that is yours." He gestures to the cell Miquel occupies. "Were you able to get Petre into Spain?"

Miquel shakes his head. "He died." He tries to soften his tone. It's obvious Nico cared for the nefil. "We will watch for him."

"He is lucky." Nico looks away.

The tumbrel draws closer. The music grows louder. They play "J'attendrai."

Now Miquel understands the terrible significance behind the song. It's played to mock the prisoners and their suffering.

The inmate leading the procession waltzes like a buffoon, slowing the motion of his baton to match "J'attendrai's" mournful beats. His face contorts and his terrible grin seems to grow out of proportion with his face.

The sigil on the back of Miquel's hand starts to fade. *It's Nico. Either he's losing himself in his own nightmare, or I'm getting lost in his.* Miquel snaps his focus to the interrogation. "You mentioned someone called Herr Teufel. Who is he?"

The ward on Miquel's hand flares to life again as Nico's gaze clears. "I don't know his real name. He lurks around the camps to find nefilim."

"And then he feeds." It isn't a question.

Nico nods. "And sends them out to do his bidding. He is ancient. Older than you."

Miquel doesn't doubt it. He has heard of the old ones, the ones who sleep. "What do you know about him?"

"He claims he is a member of the Scorpion Court. I don't see any reason to doubt him. He has been to Houska Castle. I overheard him in a phone conversation with Alvaro. Teufel said the sound waves from the mortals' shelling has weakened the glyphs."

Miquel knows of the castle. It was erected by the angelborn nefilim in the thirteenth century. The walls are designed with sigils embedded deep in the stone. The keep encircles one of the gateways between the daimonic and mortal realms.

And now, if Nico is right, it's a Red Zone of broken magic over one of the most dangerous portals between the realms.

Nico glances over his shoulder.

Something changes about the procession. A darker figure now leads the band. His face is no face. A thin tail sweeps the ground behind him.

Chills ripple across Miquel's naked body. His heart starts to race.

Nico whirls to face Miquel again. He speaks faster. "Teufel found Carlos at KL-Gusen after he took me from KL-Mauthausen. When the Scorpion Court's spies discovered that Ysabel was visiting various universities, they got suspicious. Teufel asked Carlos about it.

"Carlos guessed that Guillermo was trying to stop the war with the song you had him hide back in '38. He offered to steal the psalm from Sainte-Geneviève in exchange for a healing. Teufel let him go, and Carlos returned with the psalm, but Teufel couldn't heal him, so he sent him to Perpignan, where Christina Banderas keeps him supplied with morphine."

Teufel dangled that healing in front of Carlos, knowing damn well he couldn't cure him. Miquel lets the thought go. Carlos is beyond anyone's pity or rage at this point. "That psalm is useless to Teufel without the other sections."

Nico glances over his shoulder again, and then back to Miquel. "Teufel doesn't care. He just wants to prevent Guillermo from stopping the war."

Miquel doesn't need to ask why. *With this much killing, the daimon-born's power will grow until they, once more, control the mortal realm.* "Where are you now?"

"We're on our way to Paris. We should arrive at the

hotel adjacent to the Theater of Dreams tomorrow. Teufel claims to have a plan that will enable him to open the gate at Houska."

"Details?"

"All I know is that he is trying to get an audience with Jordi. He's made me his servant." He toys with the wire of his bracelet and murmurs, "He said my tears are sweet."

The last wrings Miquel's heart. *Diago's right. No matter what Nico did in the past, he is one of ours now, and no member of Los Nefilim should be used so roughly.*

His jaw tightens as another thought occurs to him. "You don't talk in your sleep, do you?"

"Do you think I would have survived Jordi if I did?"

"Fair point."

The trundle's wheels creak as the procession nears. The faceless leader whirls. Ashes spew in his wake.

Miquel's heart hammers in his chest. He felt this way once before. *Just before my heart stopped in '39.*

"He's coming, isn't he?" Nico's fear engulfs his face.

"Yes."

Nico's breathing quickens. He looks Miquel in the eye. "I'm sorry for how I treated you, Miquel. I truly am."

Miquel steps forward. It's like walking into a gale. He pushes against the invisible resistance of time and space, reaching out. His fingers brush against Nico's hand. He gives the other nefil the closest words to forgiveness that he can muster. "I believe you. Hold firm. We'll get you out if we can. Watch for us."

A wave of sound hits the barrier. It's the thunder of a bomb. Miquel is thrown backward, dimly aware of Nico's startled shriek.

By the time he regains his feet, the faceless Herr Teufel stands behind Nico, one hand wrapped around his throat. He lifts him and shakes him as a dog would a rag.

Nico sobs with terror. Teufel licks the tears from the nefil's face.

Miquel's pulse thumps in his ears—one part fear, one part rage. "Let him go!"

Teufel doesn't turn. His tail lashes out at Miquel like a whip.

Diago's wards flash in response. Scorpions shimmer across Miquel's flesh. They snap at Teufel, turning into a cyclone of light.

The devil's tail slices through the scorpions. From somewhere nearby, Miquel hears Diago cry out in pain. *But he's not here* . . .

The reek of burning flesh fills the dream.

Teufel's tail circles the air and makes another swipe at Miquel. He can't lift his arm in time. The tail strikes, hard like a blow . . . it's followed by another and another . . .

He hears Diago shout, ". . . up . . . wake . . ."

". . . up, Miquel!"

Miquel opened his eyes and neatly caught Diago's wrist as his husband prepared to slap him again. "I'm awake."

The room snapped into focus. Juanita stood beside the bed, her eyes still swirling in indigo and gold. A cobalt halo surrounded her head.

Something startled her . . . Just beyond Diago's shoulder, Miquel saw Rafael, a sigil already half formed by one hand.

And Diago . . . *my knight, shining in scorpions* . . .

Diago straddled him, the muscles in his forearm still

tensed as if he might pull free of Miquel's grip and slap him
again. A wide ugly burn sizzled on his chest in a diagonal
slash. Another marked his forearm.

*Both in the exact direction of Teufel's strike on the scor-
pion shield.* "What happened?

Diago finally began to relax. He rocked back on his heels.
"You tell us."

Miquel touched Diago's chest. "You're hurt." And he
would feel the pain when his adrenaline rush evaporated.

Juanita came to Diago's side and put her hand on his
shoulder. She took his arm and examined the scorched flesh.
"Let me see to you while Miquel talks."

Diago remained where he was for a moment, his palm
against Miquel's breast, just over his heart. "It's beating
too fast."

"I'm okay," Miquel assured him. He eased himself up,
forcing Diago to move.

Rafael brought Diago his robe and draped it across his
shoulders. "Come here and sit." He led his father to the settee and Juanita followed with her bag.

Miquel watched his husband with a worried gaze. "I
don't understand. Dreams shouldn't hurt us."

Rafael filled a basin from the pitcher on their washstand
and brought it to Juanita.

From the corridor, footsteps approached their room—
someone in a hurry. Guillermo flung the door wide. He still
wore the same clothes he'd worn yesterday; it was apparent
he hadn't been to bed.

He quickly surveyed the scene. The realization that everyone seemed to be all right registered with him and the flush
of urgency gradually left his cheeks.

But he came through that door primed for war. Miquel lifted his hand. "We're all fine." He gave Diago an uneasy glance. "I think."

"I'm okay," Diago assured them. "It looks worse than it feels."

Juanita reached into her bag and withdrew a jar. "Because those nerve endings haven't begun to heal yet."

Guillermo closed the door and came to the foot of the bed. "What happened?"

Miquel recounted the dream and then stated the obvious. "If the wards at Houska Castle are damaged, we've got to move nefilim into place to guard that gate."

Guillermo reached into his pocket and withdrew his lighter. He flicked the lid with nervous clips. "We don't have anyone to send. The Inner Guard is spread too thin from our own infighting."

Juanita bandaged Diago's chest to keep the ointment from his clothes. "Then I've got to inform the Messengers. Maybe a daimonic threat will move the different factions to a truce." But the doubt on her face contradicted the hope expressed by her words.

Miquel exchanged a glance with Guillermo. If Jordi found out that Juanita was gone, he might make his move against Los Nefilim. "Do you have to go?"

"Yes. This isn't a message to be relayed. I need to convey to them the urgency of the situation, and I can only do that with my presence."

Guillermo looked down at his lighter and then stuffed it back into his pocket. "When will you go?"

"Right now. I'll stop and let Eva and Maria know, and then I'll leave."

"Provisions?"

"I won't need any. I'm just going far enough into the mountains so no one can trace my departure point to the farm."

Miquel tried to imagine stepping between the realms with the ease of an angel. He recalled when his heart had stopped in '39 and Guillermo had escorted his spirit to the celestial river of fire.

I understand why the kings and queens fight so hard to maintain their sovereignty. Although he had no desire to rule, Miquel would have loved another chance to fly through the stars and touch the night skies.

Guillermo's voice brought him back to the cold bedroom. "How long will you be gone? Mortal time?"

"Three days, a week at the most." She paused beside him on her way out of the room. Reaching up, she stroked Guillermo's cheek. "Try to sleep. Promise me."

"I promise." He kissed her in a rare display of open affection.

Miquel and his small family looked away to give them a measure of privacy.

Juanita turned to them. "Watch for my Ysa. All of you. Don't let anything happen to her."

It was Rafael who spoke for them. "We won't, Doña."

Guillermo released her hands. "She'll be home before you." He kissed her again. When she left them, Guillermo turned back to the matter at hand. He gestured at Diago's chest. "Did Teufel do this?"

"No. What Miquel saw in his dream was an astral projection of Nico's soul, his song. Nico brought his fears with him, and those fears manifested in the form of the Nazis' hanging ritual and Teufel."

Guillermo frowned at him. "I'm not sure I follow. How did that manifestation strike out at you?"

Diago thought for a moment before he spoke. "In normal circumstances, a nightmare is the way our psyche deals with trauma; for example, Miquel dreamt of his cell in Jordi's pocket realm, because he associates that particular event with Nico.

"But that's not what's happening to Nico. Teufel has infected him with so much terror that the fear has become a part of him. He can't escape it, not even in sleep. His mind is feeding on itself. When Miquel reached out to him, he came close to actually touching Nico's soul by weakening Nico's protective barrier. Miquel intended to give Nico a gesture of comfort but remember that Nico also fears Miquel to a certain extent, and because of that fear, he instinctively lashed out."

Miquel opened his mouth to protest that he had never threatened Nico, but Diago cut him off before he could speak. "The threat you pose to him is implicit. You're his superior, and in that capacity, you maintain a measure of control over his life. He wants your approval, you withhold it, and that leaves him in a persistent state of anxiety."

Miquel closed his mouth. *Christ, I never thought of it like that.*

Diago turned back to Guillermo. "So in the dream, Nico's fear, in the form of Teufel, lashed out at Miquel, struck the protective sigils I'd placed around Miquel, and—"

"Here we are." Guillermo finished for him. "How can you be so damned sure it was Nico?"

Diago lifted his injured arm and pointed to his chest.

"I am daimon, too. A burn like this only comes from the angel-born."

And because of my own rage and pain, I inadvertently hurt both Nico and my husband. Feeling somewhat chastised, Miquel wanted Diago to know he understood the ramifications of his actions. "But Nico didn't know he was doing it. He genuinely thought it was Teufel who attacked him and me."

"Because in his mind it was," Diago murmured. "Teufel keeps him in that condition because a nefil's terror is nectar to the daimon-born."

"He's like a vampire," Rafael said.

"More of a psychic one, but yes, precisely like that."

Guillermo withdrew his lighter again. "Did you say that Teufel is trying to arrange a meeting with Jordi?"

Miquel nodded. "I can't be sure, but from the way Nico made it sound, it seems Jordi is resisting the idea of either a meeting or an alliance with Teufel."

Guillermo didn't seem surprised. "Jordi won't meet with the daimon-born. My brother is many things, but he is angel-born to his core. If Teufel wants a meeting, why doesn't he offer Jordi the psalm? Diago?"

"That would be like handing Jordi a weapon. No, the daimon-born will keep the psalm a secret until they feel they're in a position of power. Still, Teufel must have some hold over your brother that makes him believe he can force Jordi to do his bidding. What it is, I can't imagine."

"We need to get that psalm out of the Scorpion Court and find out what they're up to."

Miquel's heart ramped up again. He glanced at Diago. *He*

is the only person who can get close enough to gather that kind of intel. Or maybe he isn't.

Rafael edged into Guillermo's line of vision. "I'll go. I can get the psalm and the information."

"No." Diago's tone broached no argument. "We don't know Teufel's motives, but Christina is positioning herself for the title of high priestess. To her, you're a threat."

Rafael wasn't deterred. "Won't she think the same thing about you?"

Diago held firm. "No. My past betrayals exempt me from consideration."

Guillermo put an end to the discussion. "Your father knows the politics and the intrigues. This is something only he can do. But knowing that the daimon-born intend to move on that gate gives us a weapon. It's a violation of their treaties. That furnishes me with enough cause to put an end to their little get-together."

Miquel reached for his pants. "That's all fine, but our only proof is from a dream."

Guillermo didn't seem concerned. "If there is direct evidence to be had, Diago will get it. Where did Nico say they were staying?"

"In some hotel adjacent to the Theater of Dreams."

Diago stood and started to dress, as well. "I know where it is. Christina gave me the address: thirteen rue de la Ville Neuve."

"I'll see if Suero can get any information on the building. I'm certain the daimon-born will have escape routes that give them access to the sewers, or the metro."

"They'll have those passages heavily warded against the

angel-born." Diago tried to lift his undershirt over his head and hissed with pain.

Rafael helped him dress. "If we can disarm the traps, the angel-born will be able to pursue any escapees without fear."

Guillermo thumbed the lid of his lighter. "Could you defuse them?"

"Yes." Rafael's tone was all business. "And it's safer if I do the job. An angel-born nefil might accidentally trip a dark sound, or trigger a scorpion attack. Because I'm part daimon, the wards will respond to the daimonic vibrations in my aura without attacking."

Miquel glanced at Diago. "He's right. It's either him or Diago."

His husband evaluated their son carefully. Though he wasn't happy, he didn't seem averse to the plan. "But that's all you'll do. Nullify those wards and join up with the main force. That's the order. Understand?"

"I do," Rafael answered.

Though Diago didn't say it, the implication was clear: none of them wanted a repeat of when Rafael disobeyed orders to stand down. While Guillermo's formal reprimand over that incident had made an impression on Rafael, Miquel didn't underestimate his son's proclivity to find trouble.

Guillermo opened the door and stepped into the hall. "Go down and get some breakfast. Miquel, meet me in my office in an hour. We'll formalize the details."

"Will do."

Rafael followed Guillermo and paused at the threshold. "I'm going to make you proud."

"You already do," Diago whispered. "Every day."

Miquel winked at him. "Go on. You're good for this job."

Rafael grinned and went downstairs.

Miquel grabbed his jacket. "Do you think I'll dream of Nico again?"

Seeming more himself, Diago thought about the question. "Probably not. He delivered his message. Any other contact is an unnecessary risk."

Miquel heard a note of uncertainty in his husband's voice. "You're making that up, hoping you're right."

"I'm afraid so," Diago admitted.

It wasn't the answer Miquel wanted to hear. *Doesn't matter. Better armed and wary than taken by surprise.*

[16]

THE FARM

Guillermo returned to his office and picked up the phone. Silence. With a growl, he dropped the receiver back to the hook and sat at his desk.

Suero knocked and came in with a breakfast tray. "Good morning, Don Guillermo."

He wasn't sure it was. "You know, you're not a maid. I can go down and get coffee myself."

"I know." Suero pushed the tray onto a side table. "But you won't." He went to his desk and picked up a pad of paper and a pencil. "What's on today's agenda?"

"Phones?"

"Bernardo rode out to check this morning. He said the crews are finishing repairs and everything should be working by this afternoon."

"Is he still here?"

Suero nodded. "He is waiting until you get in touch with Ysa before he leaves."

"Where is he now?"

"Downstairs, having breakfast."

"Good." He poured himself a cup of ersatz coffee and added saccharine tablets. "Reports?"

Suero went to his desk and returned with three files. "These came in last night, along with an SOE agent and two Canadian airmen, all mortal."

"Anyone injured?"

"No."

"Then they can leave tonight. Tell Violeta to pick someone to lead them into Andorra."

Suero nodded and left him alone. With a sigh, Guillermo returned to his desk and read through the reports. Occasionally he lifted the phone to see if the service had been restored. The action had become a nervous habit.

Miquel knocked and stepped into the office. "You wanted to see me?"

"Come in. Where's Diago?"

"He's still downstairs with Rafael, going over his notes on the Key."

"Good. How's he doing?"

"He's holding up."

Guillermo stared at him. "Truth?"

"He's tired."

"We all are." Guillermo toyed with his lighter. He examined the sigils etched along the metal's flanks. Wisdom. *I don't feel very wise.* "This would be easier if we had support from Die Nephilim."

Miquel winced. "Are you going to talk to Jordi?"

It wasn't unreasonable. Regardless of how he ascended to

the position, Jordi *was* a king of the Inner Guard. *But there is more than one way to sing a song.*

"I was thinking of a different approach." Guillermo tapped the file at the top of the stack. "Sofia Corvo sent a message last night that corroborates Diago's information. It seems that Ulrich, the Messenger assigned as Jaeger's consort, was killed in a battle at the Russian front in December. Very soon afterward, Jaeger fell ill and died."

Miquel had no trouble putting the pieces together. "Jordi saw his opening with Ulrich's death and made his move."

Guillermo winked. "All before Jaeger was assigned another angelic protector to replace Ulrich."

Miquel lit a cigarette. "That explains why Jordi hasn't made a move against us. Without an angelic consort, he won't pit his nefilim against Juanita's power."

"And given the stress of the war on the angelic ranks, he won't receive a consort until after an armistice is reached."

"So we've got a sliver of time."

"Just a little. Now we need to widen the gap. In this same report, Sofia noted that Erich Heines has been meeting with Claus von Stauffenberg. He was severely injured in Tunisia and has been reassigned as a staff officer to the Ersatzheer." What the German mortals called their replacement army. *Training more young men to throw at the Russians.*

Miquel didn't seem impressed. "Stauffenberg being part of the German resistance doesn't necessarily mean Heines is working with them."

"Do you really believe Heines is behind Jordi's scorched-earth policy? Burn the dissenters and rule those left behind? He's already shown some queasiness at Jaeger's policies."

Miquel scoffed. "Why? Because he argued against the concentration camps at one time? He seems just fine with them now."

"Maybe." But Guillermo wasn't entirely convinced. While he was stuck at the farm, his spies were in the field, taking photographs, noting who attended important Nazi party events, catching the murmur of unrest sometimes heard at parties. It was from those photographs that Guillermo registered Heines's disgust in the pull of his lips, or how his gaze slid away from the lens. Jaeger's second-in-command now strictly avoided camp tours and steadily pulled from the limelight, as if he didn't want his image associated with the events unfolding around him.

Guillermo continued his argument. "Even a token objection from someone of his station would raise alarms with me. He has never seemed quite at ease with all their policies, but Heines is a soldier. He's sworn himself to the Inner Guard, and while I never doubted his loyalty to Jaeger, I wonder if he holds those same feelings for Jordi, especially considering this information." He tapped Sofia's report about Ulrich's death and Jaeger's subsequent demise. "What if Heines suspects foul play regarding Jaeger's death? You're my second, what would you do if Jordi pulled the same maneuver in Los Nefilim?"

"I'd cut his throat—but I'm Spanish."

Guillermo laughed in spite of the seriousness of the issue. "Pretend you're German."

Miquel considered the idea. "It's not unrealistic to think that Heines is working to undermine Jordi through the mortals. That particular methodology gives him time to make adjustments, calculate whether the risk is worth the outcome.

At the same time, expecting him to help us is a long shot into the dark."

Guillermo agreed. "It's not something I would broach under normal circumstances, but Alvaro gathering the daimon-born in Paris gives us an opening with Heines."

"How so?"

"We can appeal to his higher nature; the call of the Inner Guard over the more secular positioning of divisional territories. We're here to prevent the daimon-born from taking back the mortal realm. In this matter, we must set aside our political differences so that we can join together and answer our oaths to the Thrones."

Miquel put out his cigarette. "What are you suggesting we do?"

"I want you to talk to Heines—one commander to another. You have a rapport with him from the Great War. Use it. Feel him out and see if he can be swayed, and if he can, pull him to our side."

"How do you know he won't arrest me on the spot?"

"Because you'll be wearing the uniform of a Spanish general with the accompanying sidearm. If he makes a move against you, shoot him." Guillermo tossed the folder to the edge of the desk. "Sofia made a list of his favorite cabarets."

Miquel scanned the names. "A jazz fan."

Guillermo drew a cigar from the box. "What do you think?"

"Jazz is fine."

"About the meeting, Miquel."

"I don't mind feeling Heines out, or shooting him, for that matter. What happens if I run into a problem?"

"You're old and you're fast. Take care of it however you

see fit. Negotiate with him, or not. I'll leave it up to you, and I'll back your decisions." For Guillermo to give one of his nefilim a promise like that was the ultimate sign of trust. *And there aren't many I trust like Miquel.*

Miquel snapped the folder shut. "Okay. When do you need me to go?"

"I want you to leave in the morning. I'll have Suero radio our Parisian contacts today. I'm hoping they can get us blueprints of this Theater of Dreams and the hotel. We have a uniform that should fit Rafael, too. We'll get him into the city as your driver. While you're working Heines, Rafael can make contact with our nefilim and take care of the theater's wards."

"Anything else?"

"Yeah, get your asses back to me safely. I need you both. Diago needs you more."

"I'm on it."

"Good. Send Diago up when you get a chance."

Miquel lifted the file in farewell and headed down the hall.

Guillermo lit his cigar and watched him go. He wished he had the luxury to gauge the risk of a maneuver before moving forward with a plan. *Nothing to do but keep going.* He needed the psalm, or the Key, but more than anything, he wanted his daughter safe at home.

"Where are you, sweetheart?" He touched the phone and closed his eyes.

[17]

THE FARM

In the music room, Diago packed his notes on the Key into an accordion file. He placed it on a table and spoke to Rafael in a near-whisper. "Take it and hide it. If something happens and I don't come back, I want you to finish it."

"You're coming back," Rafael said, but no longer with the same insistence he had used as a child.

If war taught his son anything, it was how quickly a life could be extinguished and for such little cause. Diago didn't contradict him, though. He wanted to believe he was coming back, too.

But in case I don't, my son needs to know the truth about me. He closed the doors and drew the curtains to give them privacy. Taking his son's hand, he led him to the couch. He had to do this quick before he lost his nerve. "We need to talk."

"You're coming back, Papá."

"Then you can say, *I told you so*. Until then, there are some things you must know."

"What kind of things?"

"About me, about my firstborn life," he blurted before he could change his mind. Twisting his wedding band on his finger, he hesitated, suddenly unsure if this was the right time, or the right place. *If not now, when? Rafael is a man. He deserves to know the truth from my mouth.* "When we escaped Spain, you were too young to hear this. Or I was too much of a coward to explain . . ."

He bowed his head and looked down at his hands. *I'm doing this badly.* Using the relaxation techniques Miquel had taught him over the years, he centered himself before he continued. "But there is no excuse for me not to tell you now. If I die, people will recall whatever portions of my life might have touched them. Some will remember only half-truths. I want you to know what happened."

There, that sounds better. He glanced at Rafael to gauge his expression. The compassion in his son's eyes almost broke him.

"You don't need to do this to yourself, Papá. I've heard Miquel and Don Guillermo reminisce."

Diago shook his head. "Those are their memories. You deserve mine."

Rafael took Diago's hands in his own. "I'm listening."

Gathering his courage, Diago met his son's gaze. "In my firstborn life, as Asaph, I made many mistakes, primarily because I allowed my daimonic kin to manipulate my feelings. They knew how to incite my fear and make it grow. They twisted my hurt into rage. And I allowed them to do so because I thought that if I did what they asked, then they would love me.

"So when my father told me to seduce Benaiah in order to work my way into Solomon's inner court, I did. Only no one expected me to fall in love with Benaiah, least of all me. Nor did they anticipate that Solomon and I would become friends.

"And the more time I spent with Benaiah and Solomon, the more my kin demanded that I choose a side. *Their side.* When I refused, they twisted Solomon's heart against my relationship with Benaiah, so much so that Solomon and I quarreled. I was furious, because I saw Solomon's intolerance as a betrayal of our friendship. We said things to one another . . . . terrible words we could never take back . . . and when I glimpsed myself through the veil of his prejudices, I was ashamed of the man I saw. I used our argument as my rationale to break with him, but I wasn't done with him.

"I wanted Solomon to feel my humiliation and powerlessness, so I stole his signet and gave it to the daimon Ashmedai, who imprisoned him in the daimonic realms. I thought with Solomon out of the way, I'd be able to live freely with Benaiah. But my guilt tormented me until I confessed my crime to him. And in the end, I lost everything—my family, my lover, my friend."

His eyes burned but he couldn't stop, and in a rush of words, he told the rest. "In my next incarnation, I managed to evade my family and my friends. I swore I would spare myself any pain by loving no one. I died miserable and afraid. In my third-born life, I eluded my family and found my friends, but we were never close in that incarnation. In my fourth-born life, we resumed our friendship and I died to save them. I thought that surely, *surely* that sacrifice would wipe away my sins.

"It was only at my death in that incarnation that I realized Solomon had already forgiven me—Solomon who became Guillaume who became Guillermo—and that Benaiah still loved me . . . my Benaiah, who became Michel, who became Miquel.

"And in this incarnation, my daimonic family tried again to bring me into their fold. I escaped them, only to be found by Miquel. He treated my rationales with tough love and didn't let me sink into despair. It was he who taught me to love again, and now that I have experienced that love and Guillermo's friendship again, I never want to jeopardize either relationship for any reason.

"Guillermo and Miquel think I don't remember, but I do. I simply choose not to wallow in that grief. My incarnations have changed me from the arrogant young nefil of my first-born life. I've learned humility, and more importantly, how to give love as well as receive it. Those are my weapons now, and I want them to be yours, too." He stroked a tear from his son's cheek. "I want you to understand why it was so important that I forgive your mother. Why it's so urgent that you don't turn your heart to hate others."

Before he could continue, Rafael leaned forward and engulfed him in a hug. "I love you, Papá. And I will remember. I will remember for you."

A flash of pain reminded Diago of the wound on his chest, but he didn't pull away. He held tight the boy who was now a man and whispered in his ear, "But beware, Rafael. The very love that nourishes us can destroy us, too. When we become afraid that affection will be taken from us, or if it turns to jealousy, or as a way to dominate another, then love becomes poison."

Rafael sniffled and nodded against Diago's shoulder. "I understand."

Diago pulled back and pressed his forehead against Rafael's. "I love you, too."

A light knock came to the door. Rafael wiped his eyes and went to answer. It was Miquel.

"Hey." Miquel glanced from Rafael to Diago with a quizzical eyebrow raised. "Is everything all right?"

Rafael answered for them both. "We're fine."

Miquel gently cuffed Rafael's curls. "Time to get a haircut, my friend. You're going to be a driver for a Spanish general."

Diago felt relieved. "He's going with you?"

Miquel nodded. "He is. Guillermo wants to see you."

Diago rose and slipped by them. Strangely enough, his heart felt lighter, and rather than trigger bad memories, his confession left him cleansed.

[18]

THE FARM

Guillermo picked up the handset again. The pleasant buzz of a dial tone touched his ear. "Ah, you sweet thing."

He rang the operator and gave her the number for Ysabel's rooming house. A few clicks later, he heard the phone ring in Paris. He counted, ten, then fifteen, then twenty rings . . . *come on, come on* . . . before finally hanging up.

A quick look at the clock told him it was midmorning. *They're probably all out. I'll check in again later.*

Suero came into the office. "Phone lines are up." He went to the phone on his desk. "I'll ring the boardinghouse."

"I just did. No answer. We'll try again later."

The sound of the phone ringing startled them both.

Suero answered the extension on his desk. "Hello?" His eyes widened and he grinned. He mouthed, *Ysa.* "Yes. He's right here, hold on."

Guillermo thought his heart would burst from relief. He lifted the handset. "Hello?"

"Papá? Did I wake you?"

"Are you kidding? I've been up." *Where the fuck are you?* But he didn't ask. For all he knew, the lines were under surveillance. *If she's in trouble, she'll give the code.* "How is my songbird this morning?"

"A bluebird full of happiness."

Shit. She's in trouble. He motioned for Suero to pick up the other line and to take notes. The young nefil didn't hesitate.

Guillermo forced himself to be jovial. "Are you having a good time?"

"Oh, Paris is lovely. I went to the library, but the book I wanted had been defaced. Can you imagine?"

He glared at the photograph of Psalm 60 on his desk. *Fucking Carlos . . .* "It takes all kinds, sweetheart."

"You'll never guess who I ran into at the library."

Guillermo's coffee soured in his stomach. "Who?"

"Uncle Jordi!"

Uncle Jordi. In the library. And I wonder what he was looking for? Psalm 60? Did Carlos send Jordi a photograph, as well? Guillermo pinched the bridge of his nose.

All of it made sense. Carlos sending those photos to anyone he thought might have the power to heal him, Jordi going to the library to retrieve the book himself, and the sheer bad luck of Ysa being there when he arrived.

Guillermo closed his eyes. The only song that mattered now was Ysa.

"Papá? Are you there?"

Guillermo's voice locked on him. He tried to summon a

clever riposte, but the world started spinning and he couldn't seem to set it straight.

"Papá?"

"I'm here . . ." He sounded hoarse, unsure of himself. Suero threw him a sharp look. *Get it together.*

"Oh, Papá, are you having one of your spells?" Her voice grew muffled. "He usually only becomes addled when he's tired. He must not have slept well last night."

Addled? Who the fuck is addled? "I'm here," he said more clearly. "So how is Uncle Jordi?"

"He is a god among men." She sounded far too cheerful to be his daughter, but there was something else—her words seemed to slur together, too hard and too fast.

Is she drugged? If she was, she maintained her focus on the situation.

Ysa's false cheer prattled in his ear. "He bought me some beautiful new dresses. One is in my favorite color: red."

She hates dresses, and she hates red. She might as well be tapping an SOS in Morse code against the receiver with her fingernail. "I see. So when are you coming home?"

"Well, that's why I'm calling. Uncle Jordi wants to talk to you."

In spite of his best efforts, his tone turned deadly. "Put him on the phone."

"Now, Papá, you know you don't hear well."

He suddenly realized the clues weren't in what she was saying but in how she was treating him . . . like an old befuddled mortal.

Does she remember that I'm the younger brother? Deciding to play along to see what she would do, he muttered, "Say again, dear?"

She enunciated carefully. "Uncle Jordi thinks we can all sit down and come to an agreement like a family. He is now staying at Rousseau's old estate at Fontainebleau, and he has offered you safe conduct to visit us here."

Like a family. "An agreement about what?"

"About our inheritance."

Give him Los Nefilim, or what? He kills my daughter?

"And how do you feel about this . . . meeting?"

Her tone shifted as quickly as his. She no longer sounded like the cheerful debutante. Whatever assistance she needed, required him. "I think it's something we must do—together."

"Let Uncle Jordi send you home first."

"That won't happen."

He hadn't believed it would, but it had been worth a shot. "It will take me a few days to get away." *And set up an escape plan.*

The false brightness returned to her voice. "Can you be here the day after tomorrow?"

Jesus. That didn't give him a lot of time. *But we've moved on tighter timetables.* "I can be there."

"Excellent! Be sure to get plenty of rest so you don't take one of those spells that leaves you so befuddled. Will you do that for me?"

"Of course."

"I love you, Papá."

"I love you, too."

She rang off and he sat there for a moment, glaring at the phone.

"Don Guillermo?" Suero placed his handset on the hook.

Guillermo did the same. "Get me Miquel and Violeta. I want to know how many people they can spare. I need blondes, fair skin, with the kind of faces the Germans put on posters. We'll use members of Les Néphilim, as well, but they must be fluent in German. Understand?"

"On my way." He hurried from the room and almost crashed into Diago, who sidestepped just in time to avoid a collision.

Guillermo looked past him. "Are you alone?"

"Miquel said you wanted to see me." He came inside and shut the door.

"Ysabel just called."

"She's all right?"

Guillermo hated to quash the relief on Diago's face. "She's thinking on her feet."

"Well, she is your daughter. Where is she?"

Guillermo relayed the conversation. "Jordi is using her as a hostage to get me into Fontainebleau. To put him off his guard, she has somehow managed to convince him that I'm addled, half-deaf, and nearsighted."

"Won't Jordi be surprised to find out otherwise? Are you going?"

"Of course I'm going."

"Are you sure that's smart?"

Walking to the window, Guillermo looked down at the yard. Suero and Bernardo strode toward the dorm, their heads bent toward one another. Four nefilim were busy repairing a fence in the distance. Three others had brought a stolen staff car with Spanish plates to the front yard. Two men washed the vehicle while a woman checked the engine.

They all trusted his judgment and depended on him. *Then don't let them down.*

"I don't know what is wise anymore," he murmured.

Glimpsing Diago's reflection, he saw his friend's concern. "I'm going to save my daughter, not just because she is Los Nefilim's future. But because she is my life."

Diago tilted his head in acknowledgment of the sentiment. "I understand. I'd do no less for my own child. But in the past, you've talked about reaching an accord with Jordi to stop the wars. Will you parley with him this time?"

"I don't know. I'm not negotiating at full strength with Ysa in danger. But maybe if we see one another—Jordi and me—look into one another's eyes . . . we might remember bonds other than jealousy and hate. Maybe this is what we need. I'm going to have to play it by ear, but I also intend to set up a rescue for Ysa. That way if something does happen to me, she'll be able to take over Los Nefilim."

"Tell me what you need me to do."

"Keep to our plan. Get into the Theater of Dreams. Your job is to gather enough intelligence for us to justify a raid. Get the psalm if you can. Determine its location if you can't. I'll back your judgment. If you get the opportunity to neutralize the threat, do it. Something tells me that if we cut off the head, the snake will die."

Diago grimaced. "The head of that snake is my father. While we haven't actually seen eye to eye on anything, I'm not sure I'm ready to engage in patricide."

Guillermo shook his head. "I wouldn't ask you to do that. It's Teufel who is the main threat. Leave your father for the Inner Guard's tribunal."

Diago seemed relieved by the order. "I'm going to say goodbye to my family and go. My cover story is that I was seen at Christina's manse and denounced as a traitor to Los Nefilim. I'm going to them as if I'm on the run from you."

His hand hovered over the location of the burn on his chest. "This morning's incident can be used to back up my claims. I was cornered and fought back; barely escaped with my life."

"I'll put out the word among our people to give the story credibility if they hear it." He hoped the daimon-born hadn't destroyed the psalm, but he had to move forward as if they had. "When you're finished, don't hang around. Go straight to one of our safe houses. They'll get you out of the city."

"When will you be at Fontainebleau?"

"Day after tomorrow."

"Christ, this is going to be tight."

"Just like old times. No room for fucking up. I will watch for you, Diago."

"And I for you." He bowed his head and then slipped away.

Guillermo turned back to the phone. *Okay, Jordi, I'm coming and we'll finish this—like a family.*

[19]

THE THEATER OF DREAMS

Diago's expertise as a rogue helped him maneuver between checkpoints and avoid both nefilim and Nazis on his way to Paris. Before he'd left the farm, he'd given Miquel his wedding band to hold for him. The only jewelry he wore was the signet with Prieto's tear. He could justify that ring's existence to his relatives, who had no issue with using the angel-born's gifts against them.

Last night, he'd slept rough. The wound on his chest had seeped through his undershirt and the one on his arm was a constant misery. Rather than diminish the pain, the mending flesh aggravated his discomfort.

Although his first day and night on the road were harsh, the dawn had brought him luck. He'd managed to hop an empty boxcar as a train slowed for a crossing. The long kilometers passed beneath the clacking wheels. When the train finally crawled through an industrial yard on Paris's outskirts, Diago stepped from the car.

234 ■ T. FROHOCK

He stumbled before he got his feet under him. Once he regained his balance, he walked as if he had every right to be there. *That's the trick. Always* look *like you belong and no one will question you.*

Someone had left a lunch box on a stack of railroad ties. Diago picked it up as he passed. He walked to the storage shed and sheltered beneath an open stall.

Tugging his coat more tightly around him, he hid in the shadows and assessed the yard. The loading docks were busy. Men bustled around the cargo. A supervisor with a clipboard checked off items with a stubby pencil.

Diago opened the lunch box. It contained a thermos of thin soup and a dried apple. Guilt pinched his gut.

I'm stealing from mortals who can ill afford to lose their food. Although his stomach protested the ill-gotten meal, Diago forced himself to wolf it all down. He needed his energy.

From where he squatted, he noted a tear in the chain-link fence surrounding the yard. The gap was small, but then again, so was he.

The mortals on the loading dock were gathering around a crate. Whatever was inside must have been heavy, because they worked like ants to secure it to a boom pole.

If he intended to go, he needed to leave now, while they were distracted. Crouching low, he duckwalked to the rip in the fence, and then stooped through. His coat snagged on a wire. He heard it tear, but it wasn't enough to stop him.

Jerking free, he ran to an alley between two stout buildings. A quick glance back told him no one had noticed the breach.

Or the escape. He gave himself another moment and then

started walking. Keeping to the alleys, he skirted the main avenues and worked his way deeper into the city. Walking briskly, he followed the boulevard de Bonne Nouvelle until he reached the rue de la Ville Neuve—a narrow street that was more like an alley.

Diago hesitated at the street's entrance with his heart leapfrogging in his chest. *This is it.* Up until now, he hadn't allowed himself to think too clearly about how he might be received by his daimon-born kin.

Edur's line of questioning in Perpignan meant they already suspected him of treachery. He reached in his pocket and fingered the ruby cuff link the vizconde had left embedded in Carlos's throat. If Diago didn't want to find himself in the same condition, he needed to keep them on the defensive.

Gathering his courage, he stepped onto the street. The first business he passed was the Café des Coulisses. In spite of his fear, he smiled at the clever name. *The Backstage Café.*

The location was perfect. Once he secured the evidence Guillermo needed, Diago simply had to get inside the café and give the cashier the code. The information would then be passed along to a member of Les Néphilim, and from them, back to Guillermo.

The theater was only a few doors down from the café. The blinds were drawn across the ticket box and the doors were shuttered. The entire establishment gave off the feeling of abandonment. If only it was truly vacant.

But Diago knew otherwise. The feeling of emptiness was merely a ruse for the mortals. All along the shutters and doors, daimonic sigils curled in the shadows. The glyphs scuttled like roaches over the theater's façade.

He proceeded beyond the ticket booth to an ornate black

door that sat somewhat crooked in its frame. The number overhead matched the one Christina had given him.

Diago rapped on the door.

Francisco answered. The giant nefil looked dapper as ever in his pin-striped suit. The patch over his eye made him seem more ominous. "You!" He spat the word like a curse.

Diago slipped around him and into the corridor. "I need to see my father."

Francisco's meaty palm landed on his shoulder. "I'm going to fucking twist your goddamned head off if you don't stop."

Diago lifted his hand as if he held a scorpion.

Francisco flinched and released him.

Straightening his jacket, Diago started walking again. The corridor was dark. The single bulb hanging overhead sent yellow light over the faded green wallpaper and scuffed floor. The daimon-born had invested no time or money in this portion of the theater, which meant they didn't intend to stay for long.

A set of stairs loomed ahead. On the right was a padded door. *That probably leads to the theater.* "Where's Alvaro?"

The theater door opened. Christina stepped into the hallway and almost walked into him. She wore a simple day dress, yet she gave the garment an air of careless glamour. Her lipstick was the color of fresh blood.

She halted and stared at him as if she couldn't believe her eyes.

Maybe she can't. He cleared his throat. "There's been a problem."

Getting her wits about her, she closed the door and glared at Francisco. "Get on the street."

The monstrous nefil treated Diago to a final glare and retreated outside.

Christina waited until he was gone before she spoke. "I thought you were going to send a postcard. What the hell are you doing here?"

"Circumstances have changed. I'm no longer with Los Nefilim."

She looked at him as if noticing his rumpled clothing for the first time. "What? What's happened?"

"My little excursion to your house was noticed. Then on the way home I was accosted by Carlos Vela."

Her eyes narrowed at the name.

"Carlos had a picture of one of Guillermo's grimoires and tried to blackmail him with it. So Guillermo sent his nefilim to bring Carlos in, except Carlos was found with this jammed into his throat." He withdrew the ruby cuff link and showed it to her.

She tried to snatch it from his palm.

He was quicker. Closing his fingers around the cuff link, he returned it to his pocket. "They found out that you were giving Carlos his morphine. Guillermo thinks you have his grimoire, and that I've been covering for you. I barely escaped with my life."

"And Rafael?"

"He chose Los Nefilim over his father."

"That apple didn't fall far from the tree."

Her claws are out today. "I need to see Alvaro."

"Why?"

"I want to join the daimon-born."

"Why can't you just be a rogue again?"

"Because Guillermo has declared me a spy and put a price

on my head." He pushed his sleeve up so she could see the injury on his forearm. "I have a matching one on my chest. Want to see it?"

"No." She wrinkled her nose and turned her head. "How do I know that's not self-inflicted?"

"Touch it."

She placed her fingertip against the wound's outer edge, and then jerked her hand back against her chest. A thin curl of smoke drifted from her fingertip.

"I need protection." He lowered his sleeve. "Please, Christina. I need my family."

She studied him. "Do you sincerely believe Alvaro will take you back?"

"Of course he will. Because my cousin will speak for me."

She arched an eyebrow at him and folded her arms. "Oh, really? And what makes you so sure that I'm going to put my head on the block for you?"

"Because I helped you escape the Sun King's court during l'affaire des poisons."

She scowled at him. He was sure it wasn't because she didn't remember the incident, but because she did.

Having befriended the king's mistress, a certain Marquise de Montespan, Christina found herself entangled with the infamous Catherine Deshayes, known more commonly as La Voisin. When Montespan was implicated in l'affaire des poisons, Christina was imprisoned with the other ladies of Montespan's court.

Montespan herself was never tried. Being Louis's courtesan came with a few perks, the most important being that the king had no desire to appear the fool. A lengthy trial for Montespan promised to be precisely the kind of fiasco Louis wanted to avoid. So rather than the burning court, Montespan found her way into a convent.

Using his own considerable influence within the court, Diago helped Christina avoid a hearing of her own. As soon as he was able, he facilitated his cousin's escape to Barcelona. They never again spoke of his assistance to her, but Diago pocketed that event like a valuable coin.

And now it's time to spend it. "You're alive today because of me."

"You give yourself a lot of credit."

"*Deserved* credit. I saved your life. All I'm asking is that you pay me back."

"And then we're even. Forever."

"Forever."

"Follow me." She opened the theater's door and led him into the shuttered lobby.

Though the carpet was faded and frayed, this area seemed to be in better condition than the corridor they'd just left. The wallpaper had been pinned in several places, and the chandeliers were in need of a good dusting, but otherwise they could open the doors for a performance at any time. Two sets of stairs on each side of the wide room led upward to the balconies.

From the direction of the theater doors came the muted strains of a cello playing "J'attendrai."

Christina pointed toward the lavatory. "Clean yourself up."

The imperiousness of the command made her sound as if she'd already assumed the mantle of high priestess. *And my best course of action at this point is to obey.*

He went into the men's room and scrubbed the worst of the road dirt from his face and hands. As he washed, the instrument's mournful wail floated through the vents to serenade him.

Diago listened with the practiced ear of a teacher. The musician seemed competent. It was obvious the person understood both technique and style—the accents landed in all the right places, the chords were precise—but the cellist's execution seemed to lack spirit and emotion, which left the interpretation flat.

The cellist suddenly stopped playing. Silence prevailed for five beats. Then the piece began again.

Diago finished washing and toweled himself dry. When he emerged, he was somewhat less disheveled than when he arrived. "How do I look?"

She opened the theater door and whispered, "Like a ruffian."

"*That* is part of my charm." Diago adjusted his collar and stepped inside.

The entrance brought them to the center aisle. The house lights were up. Other nefilim were scattered throughout the seats. All of them most likely armed with pistols or knives and songs that killed.

Diago guessed that roughly twenty of the daimon-born were present for the rehearsal. Probably a fraction of their forces, but far more than he could take on alone.

The cellist was the only person on the stage. He was a young nefil, fourteen, maybe fifteen, with black hair that fell into his eyes as he sawed the bow back and forth over the strings. Sweat stains darkened the armpits of his shirt and his collar had come undone. His forearms trembled as he began "J'attendrai" from the beginning.

The painting Herr Teufel sent to Christina stood on an

easel just behind the cellist. The dark sounds of grief churned across the canvas with every chord.

Near the orchestra pit, a lone figure stood at attention. He wore the striped uniform of a camp prisoner. A metal bracelet encircled one wrist. The wooden shoes on his feet didn't seem to be the same size.

His glassy eyes were surrounded by dark circles that gave him the look of a cadaver. When his gaze noted Diago, his body gave a little jerk of recognition.

Diago frowned. He recalled Miquel's description of Nico from his nightmare. *Could it be?*

As he drew closer, he saw only the faintest resemblance to the nefil he'd once known. *He's like Petre.* Starved and not just from lack of food.

And didn't Miquel mention "J'attendrai" from the nightmare, as well? The camp orchestra had played the song as the prisoners were taken to the gallows. *What had Nico said to Miquel?* Something about Teufel hanging around the camps to feed. *He says my tears are sweet.*

Diago noted the blood streaking the cello's neck. The determination in the youth's eyes said that he didn't care how much of his blood spilled, he'd play until he learned to wring every ounce of emotion from Nico.

This wasn't a rehearsal. The daimon-born were waiting to feed. *Oh, Nico. I'm so sorry.*

But if Nico was here, then that meant the mysterious Herr Teufel was likewise nearby. Diago scanned the audience. Sure enough, seated front-row center were two men.

Their proximity to Nico didn't necessarily signify either of them were Teufel. *But the devil is close.*

Christina led Diago toward the pair, and he immediately

recognized his father by his posture. Alvaro sat straight, his palm on a knobbed walking stick. His only attire was a song of scorpions, a glistening coat of blue and black that rustled around his nude body, revealing his withered penis and thin legs.

At Alvaro's right sat another nefil. The man wore an SS uniform. His long hair touched the unbuttoned collar of his shirt. The unfashionable hairstyle and his languid pose made his attire seem more a mockery than an attempt to assimilate.

It's a costume to him, because he enjoys ridiculing mortal pretensions. Diago recognized him: Alessandro Strzyga. He was Alvaro's first cousin, though they were more like brothers in affections.

When he makes a point, he has a habit of rapping his palm on the table to punctuate each word. And that hand had a disquieting tendency to strike out hard and sharp.

If Diago had to guess, he'd put his money on Alessandro as Herr Teufel. It was a hunch. Guillermo would demand proof. *Then get it for him.*

Alessandro looked right through Diago, as if he weren't there. The elder nefil's disrespect was the equivalent of a slap.

Diago pretended not to notice.

Alvaro lowered his dark glasses and examined Diago with eyes the color of smoke and nickel. He lifted the walking stick and gave the floor two sharp raps.

On the stage, the nefil's bow halted midsweep.

Christina broke the sudden silence. She curtsied to Alvaro and, as a sign of respect, tilted her head toward Alessandro as she rose. "I beg your pardon, my lord. Diago has come with an urgent request."

Alvaro held out the hand that bore a heavy signet. He didn't appear happy to see Diago.

Not a good sign for me. Diago stepped forward and knelt before his father. He kissed the puce and gray stone set within the ring's band.

Alvaro pulled his hand away as if something nasty had touched him. "Why are you here?"

Christina spoke for him. "Diago has been assisting me. He has spied on Los Nefilim from within, and his work has been above reproach."

Alvaro kept his stare locked on Diago. "I'll ask again: Why are you here?" Christina started to answer, but Alvaro lifted his hand. "My son has a voice. Let him speak."

Diago licked his lips. "Guillermo found out I was spying on him. I barely escaped with my life. I need sanctuary."

Alessandro finally looked down at Diago. "Kill him, and when the Inner Guard comes to our door, give them his head."

Diago locked gazes with his father, but he didn't beg for his life. He'd be damned if he'd give Alessandro the pleasure.

From somewhere nearby, Diago heard the snap of metal. Someone had just inserted a round into the chamber of a gun. His heart picked up speed. *I've died before, I'll die again.* He mentally prepared himself to search out a new incarnation.

"Kill him," Alessandro whispered.

"No." Alvaro's glare hardened. "This time we do things my way." He pointed at Diago. "If I allow you to stay, I want Rafael as a member of this court."

Diago had expected such a condition. "I understand. Give me the time necessary to bring him to our cause."

"Is this an oath I hear?"

"It is a plea for your forbearance while I do what needs to be done."

Alvaro laughed. "Oh, you have become a master of useless words." With uncanny speed, he lifted his walking stick and snapped it against the side of Diago's head.

The blow was hard enough to knock Diago to the sticky floor. Blood filled his mouth but the cut inside his cheek seemed superficial. The bruise forming on the side of his face was a more substantial injury.

Still, coming from his father, it was a mere tap. *He's testing me to see if I'll lash out.* Diago spat blood to the concrete.

Not a nefil moved in the auditorium. It was like they held their collective breath, waiting for the play's climactic scene.

Alvaro settled back in his seat. "Get up."

Diago stood and faced his father.

Alvaro examined Diago with a calculating gaze. "We found something that belongs to Guillermo. A document that seems to be very important to him according to Carlos Vela. Do you know anything about a psalm?"

Time to mix the truth with lies. "The only one I know of is Psalm 60 from *The Book of Gold*. Beneath Guillermo's protective wards, there is a song for a weapon. His daughter, Ysabel, can unlock those wards, and she is nearby, at Jordi's estate in Fontainebleau."

Alvaro's eyebrows shot up in surprise. "Well, well. Something of value has finally rolled through your mouth."

Alessandro turned his gaze to Diago. "He's lying. I was there recently and didn't see her."

Diago regarded the old nefil. "Would you even know

her?" He turned back to his father. "Are you working with the angel-born now?"

A faint smile touched Alvaro's mouth. "We're supplying Jordi with morphine. That's all."

The cunning on his father's face said otherwise. "I know Ysabel. She grew up around me. She trusts me."

Alessandro scoffed. "You betrayed her father. Why would she trust you?"

"She can't possibly know I've been forced out of Los Nefilim, because she was in Paris when I was accused of being a spy. I've been around her since she was an infant. She'll trust me. I'll even convince her to sing Guillermo's protective glyphs away from the page. Then we'll know the details of the secret weapon behind Guillermo's plan. The trick will be getting into the estate and back out again."

Alvaro tapped the head of his walking stick with one restless finger. "Play for me."

He wants to measure the worth of my song. Diago glanced at Nico. *And he wants to feed on Nico's despair.* "I have no instrument."

Alvaro gestured to the young nefil with the cello. "Gael will loan you his."

The youth stood and bowed his head.

To refuse would indicate weakness. He had no choice other than to hurt Nico or admit his desire to return to the Scorpion Court was a ruse.

Diago ascended the stage on numb legs. *Forgive me, Nico. Please forgive me for what I'm about to do.*

Gael handed Diago his bow and the instrument. His stiff posture and abrupt movements conveyed resentment over lending his instrument to a stranger, but it was merely a performance for the nefilim in the audience. Unlike the others, Diago was close enough to see Gael's relief at being dismissed from his endless lesson.

Diago waited until the youth left the stage before taking the seat. He ran through the scales to get a feel for the cello, making minor adjustments as he did. When he felt sure of the strings' response, he launched into "J'attendrai."

He recalled Miquel's description of Nico's nightmare. Closing his eyes, he imagined the camp's gates opening. The sound of a tumbrel's wheels clattering along to the beat of a drum; the wail of violins. He conjured the figure of the bandleader grinning and bobbing as he weaved among the horrified prisoners.

He felt their humiliation and turned it into chords. Wringing the descant from the cello's throat, note by note, he re-created the helpless despair his husband had depicted.

The cello wept, and suddenly Nico cried out.

Diago tasted the other nefil's sorrow and fear. The pleasurable warmth he usually denied himself flooded his chest and left him light-headed.

Looking down into the theater, he noted the contentment on Alvaro's face as his father inhaled Nico's grief. Beside him, Alessandro tilted back his head, his gaze rapt with pleasure.

Diago finished the last notes and let the bow fall from the strings.

Behind him, the dark sounds of the painting cracked like thunder. He whirled and glimpsed the colors billowing toward him. *What the hell is happening?*

Ashes soured on his tongue. The bitter-almond scent of

cyanide coupled with the stench of charred flesh. A million voices keened a litany of terror, falling sharp like chords from bitter strings . . .

. . . *I'm better off dead than on the road* . . .

. . . *my brother* . . . *no not my brother* . . .

. . . *is there water do you have water please* . . . *a gold watch for water* . . .

. . . *leave it Mother leave it you must come away* . . .

. . . *my child my child my child* . . .

. . . *goddamn you Nazi pigs* . . .

And the dark sounds of their dying rolled on, growing louder, rising to become a crescendo, measured by the tempo of gunshots, and the faint whisper of gas hissing through pipes.

From somewhere behind him, the vibrations of footsteps thundered across the stage. Then something hard struck the back of Diago's head and the world went black.

It was a mercy.

[20]

THE THEATER OF DREAMS

Diago came to in painful stages. He shifted his position and realized he sat in the same seat Alvaro had recently occupied. His head ached. A sour smell told him he'd vomited on himself; although someone had gone to the effort to clean him up.

The memory of the portrait's dark sounds clung to the edge of his senses. He wanted to rush the stage and release those poor mortals from their torment.

An attempt to stand failed. Something held him against the seat. He tried to move his arms, but his hands were lashed to the chair's struts. A rope stretched across his chest, binding him to the backrest. Panic infiltrated the fuzziness in his brain. *What the hell?*

The steady click of heels against the stage echoed throughout the auditorium. It was Christina. His anxiety receded somewhat. At least it wasn't Alessandro.

She descended the stage stairs and came to sit beside him. "How do you feel?"

"Sick. What happened?"

"Edur had to knock you out."

"I bet he enjoyed that."

"Somewhat." She touched the bump on the back of his head and withdrew her hand when he winced.

"Why did he hit me?"

"To save your life."

"I don't understand."

"You were about to see something that you're not ready to see. Anyway, you're safe now. Alessandro reinforced the sigils that hold the sounds against the canvas. You won't break through again."

Alessandro only could have performed that act if the painting was his. *He is Teufel.* But as one question was answered, another popped up in its place. *What are they hiding?*

Diago's gaze flickered to the stage. *The psalm?* It had to be. Documents had been concealed within canvases in the past.

Just to see what she would do, he deliberately referred to Teufel as Alessandro in his next question. "Something I've wondered . . . why did Alessandro ship the painting to you?"

She didn't appear to notice, or she didn't care that he'd made the connection between Teufel and Alessandro. "The Allies are bombing railway lines throughout Poland and Germany. Everything was a risk, but the route through Italy didn't carry quite the same hazards, and he was determined that it should arrive safely."

"Because . . . ?"

"That is on a need-to-know basis and you don't need to know. Let's call it classified information and leave it there."

The theater felt empty but for the two of them. "Where is everyone?"

"Sated and sleepy. They've gone to dream Nico's dream."

And Nico? Diago's gaze automatically went to the orchestra pit where the other nefil had stood. *Probably with Alessandro. Miquel said he was Teufel's servant.*

"Why am I tied up?"

"Because no one trusts you enough to let you run loose while they sleep." She lifted her black cigarette holder and inserted a cigarette. "Including me."

"Then why are you here?"

"You and I must come to an accord." She lit the cigarette and exhaled a cloud of blue smoke over the orchestra pit. "Do you know what happened at Houska Castle?"

"No." *Not the pertinent details.*

"Alessandro went to the chapel."

Diago doubted he was there to pray. The castle's chapel had been erected over an abyss, which the mortals swore was a pit to hell. *If only they really knew.* "Did he find God there?"

"In a manner of speaking."

That didn't bode well.

Christina tapped her cigarette's ashes to the floor. "Early in the war, Alvaro ordered Alessandro to take a platoon of daimon-born nefilim to secure the Houska gate. He wanted to beat the Nazis to the area. Alessandro used the opportunity to enter the chapel. Instead of positioning his troops and patrolling the area, he had his nefilim lower him into the abyss.

"While Alessandro disobeyed his orders and neglected the perimeter, a troop of Die Nephilim pushed back the daimon-born platoon and took over the entire area. Alessandro barely escaped with his life. He tells a very exciting version of the story whereby he is the hero." She took a long, angry draw from her cigarette and huffed the smoke through her nose.

From behind them, distant laughter echoed from the direction of the lobby. A door opened and shut and then silence reigned again.

Christina touched Diago's knee, and then she stood and strolled to the auditorium door. Diago heard her open it to check the lobby. She returned to him, apparently satisfied they were alone again.

Resuming her seat, she continued her tale. "One of the troops from Alessandro's platoon made it to Perpignan before we left. He said that Alessandro descended into the pit for three days. While he was there, he made a deal with a devil, and when he came out, he was sharing his body with Beleth."

Beleth? Diago had been prepared for bad news, but not for anything this terrible. Beleth was one of the most ferocious daimonic kings, a god of war. With eighty-five legions of daimons under his command, he'd smash through the Inner Guard's broken divisions with the efficiency of a panzer unit crushing infantry.

"Are you sure?"

"Based on the signs I've witnessed, yes."

He couldn't accept that, though—it was too scary. *Christina is wrong. She has to be wrong.* "What kind of signs?"

"Some of the daimon-born claim that at times he appears

to have no face. Others have noticed a thin tail that curls around his ankles."

The descriptions matched Miquel's account of his dream-meeting with Nico. Diago said nothing.

Christina talked faster, breathlessly outlining both her deductions and her plan. "Alessandro and Beleth have been trying for weeks to get an audience with Jordi Abelló. Beleth intends to possess Abelló's body, as he has taken Alessandro's, in order to command Die Nephilim. Beleth wants to use the angel-born nefilim to shatter the wards at Houska and open the gateway." Christina put out her cigarette. "We must stop him."

"What?" The statement made no sense. Moloch wanted nothing more than for the daimons to regain the mortal realm.

"We must stop Beleth."

Everything was moving too fast, but it didn't take him long to work out why she wanted Alessandro out of the way. Christina intended to become Moloch's high priestess. *And she doesn't want competition for the mortals' affections.*

Diago glanced at the stage. "Is this some sort of test?"

"Shut up and listen." Christina squeezed his shoulder and quickly confirmed his suspicions. "Once Beleth opens the gateway and floods the mortal realm with daimons, they'll enslave both the nefilim and the mortals, demanding our adulation and sacrifice, just as they did in the old days. I say good riddance to them."

"Do you really think you can murder a daimon?"

"Everything dies, Diago, even the daimons."

The angel Prieto had once expressed a similar sentiment to him. *Everything dies, Diago . . . even the angels.* And while the statement held true, Christina's plans were ambitious beyond imagination.

She lowered her voice to a harsh whisper. "Beleth chose his host wisely. As an elder of the Council of Nine, we can't openly assassinate Alessandro without being seen as traitors to our own court. But he needs to disappear. Forever and discreetly. His demise cannot be traced back to us."

Us? Was she already implicating him in her plot?

Diago tried to twist in the seat to see if anyone else was in the theater. *Had she let someone in when she went to check the door?* The ropes held him firmly in place. "You're testing me and my allegiance to Alvaro, aren't you? It's got to be a test, because Alvaro seemed fine with Alessandro."

"That's because Moloch wants to open the gateway, and what Moloch wants, Alvaro wants." When he didn't immediately respond, her glare darkened. "Let me make this personal. Alvaro can't take you back into the ranks of the daimon-born without bringing it before the Nine." She leaned close until she was almost in his lap. "The same council that listened to Alessandro at your Gloaming."

"I told you before: I didn't have a Gloaming." Or had he? What had Alvaro said earlier? *No, this time we do things my way.* This time.

"Stop lying to yourself, Diago. You had a Gloaming. You just don't want to remember it." Her words snapped through his brain. "I was there, I saw it. All of six years old, and you performed like a maestro. You were so proud of yourself. They tested your knowledge of instruments and tone. You didn't forget a single lyric of the old ballads."

Because I wanted my father to love me. Diago wrenched

his gaze from hers and stared into the darkness of the orchestra pit.

Her voice dropped to a sibilant hiss. "They should have accepted you, but Alessandro called you an angelic abomination. He said you could never be one of the daimon-born, and went so far as to intimate that you be given the second death."

If he could have leapt from the chair and fled his cousin's words, he would have.

She's doing this to upset me, and I won't give her the goddamn satisfaction. He closed his eyes and counted backward. *489, 488, 487 . . .*

Her voice shattered his concentration. "Moloch refused to entertain the idea of giving you the second death, but he wanted peace with his nobles. He acceded to their demands to expel you from the court and decreed you'd be enslaved with a minor family. Alvaro bowed to them then, because Moloch hadn't chosen him at that time. He was only a nefil, and a lower member of the court, at that. He didn't even speak in your defense. He left you, because he is a coward. You did nothing wrong. Do you hear me?"

Diago's breath came in short bursts.

Christina brushed a tear from his cheek and licked it from her finger. "You did nothing wrong."

That wasn't what he had thought at the time. Certain he'd made some critical error, some faux pas he couldn't fathom, he'd run after his father, begging him not to leave . . . *I'll be good, I'll be good, I'll be good . . .*

Except his father didn't return. He left Diago with some woman who claimed to be an aunt. *And maybe she was a distant relative.* But her family didn't want him in their house, so they sold him to a brothel. *Do what they say and you will eat.*

That, too, was a lie. He was forced to fight the other boys for his bread, and though he was small, he discovered viciousness trumped size. And when the strangers who visited the brothel touched him, he learned not to cry. He taught himself to smile with his mouth, and never let them see the hate he buried in his heart.

Now he remembered.

His cousin kissed his tears and drank his grief. "Hear me, Diago, once you've served your purpose for them and encouraged the Ramírez girl to remove her father's wards, Beleth will destroy you. They will give you the second death and then they will hunt Rafael. I'm your only friend here."

And this is what my family does . . . they drive nails of grief into my heart and then claim that no one loves me like they do. All to force me to perform whatever acts they're too craven to commit themselves.

Except Christina's scenario wasn't entirely contrived. Especially if Beleth possessed Alessandro in the same manner that Moloch shared a body with Alvaro. *What Moloch wants, Alvaro wants.* Wouldn't it be the same for Beleth and Alessandro?

Diago didn't have to consider the issue for long. *No sooner had I arrived than Alessandro ordered Alvaro to kill me.*

The threat to him and Rafael was real, especially if something happened to Alvaro.

An ember of rage touched his heart, but Diago didn't give it oxygen to grow. He shoved his anger deep. This wasn't the time. "Why do you need me?"

"A king or queen of the Inner Guard possesses the power

to kill a daimon. I want you to be present when Alessandro meets with Abelló. Beleth will attempt to possess the angel-born nefil. We'll let Beleth's arrogance be his downfall, because I doubt he'll be successful.

"You and I both know that Abelló will call down the power of the Thrones and either destroy Beleth, or force him back into the daimonic realms. Still, the distraction works in our favor. While Abelló deals with Beleth, you can shoot Alessandro, and once Beleth is subdued, shoot Abelló. That will eliminate all three threats and give me dominion over Spain and France when Alvaro makes me his high priestess."

He noticed her grand plan incorporated no escape strategy for him. *Don't bog her down with details.* Because it didn't matter. He had no intention of murdering a king of the Inner Guard for his daimonic kin.

"But that leaves other divisions of the Inner Guard to be dealt with."

"The Inner Guard is almost shattered from infighting. It'll be centuries before they regain what they've lost. By then, my territories will be secure. Are you with me?"

"Yes." *Because if I can take down Alessandro and pin his murder on the Nazis, then I'm all for that plan.*

"I knew I could count on you." She gave his shoulder another squeeze.

"Good. Untie me."

"I can't." She ran her finger between the rope and his chest. "If I do, they'll suspect I did it, because I spoke for you." She kissed his cheek. "Don't worry. We won't forget you." She stood and walked away, humming "J'attendrai."

Diago smiled at her back. And there it was: a full confession. Christina had implicated herself. Guillermo could move on that information alone to raid the theater.

Except for one small problem—Diago had no way to tell him. Twisting his wrists against the heavy ropes, he began the difficult task of working himself free. He needed to get out of the theater and to the café.

The time had come to set fire to the Scorpion Court, and Diago had no problem striking the match.

[21]

CHÂTEAU DE L'ENTREPRENANTE
FONTAINEBLEAU

Ysabel curled on her side and blinked at the clock across the room. The dial blurred and wouldn't swim into focus.

Another of Jimenez's endless shots had stolen her morning. She remembered calling her father, and then breakfast with Jordi . . . *and then back to my room for another shot.*

Jimenez was giving her morphine. Of that she was certain. She guessed he diluted her doses with saline, because while the drug slurred her thoughts, it wasn't always enough to knock her out.

Until today. "Fuck this." She needed her brain moving on all cylinders. Forcing herself out of bed, she crossed the room and checked the clock.

She'd missed lunch. Esser had probably come to rouse her, found her sleeping soundly, and then crept back out. They knew she'd ring for food if she grew hungry. *Obviously, Uncle Jordi is busy today.*

Next to the clock, the Virginia Woolf book lay open to "A Haunted House." The words *doors go shutting* were underlined until they were almost blacked out.

Did I do that? Touching the page, she vaguely recalled taking a pen to the book. It had been late last night when the morphine wore off and left her anxious and afraid.

Outside her room a door slammed. Ysa's skin crawled. She resisted the urge to drag her fingernails over her flesh.

Concentrate. For the love of the Thrones, concentrate before the bastards kill me. Taking slow, deep breaths, she considered the problem.

Jimenez retained the bulk of the morphine for Jordi. Ysa had noticed that the vials he used for her were clearly labeled with a red dot. If she could find some empty vials and fill them with saline, then she could switch them out when Jimenez wasn't looking.

Put a red dot on the label and he'll never know. But that meant she needed vials. She would never get past the guards at Jimenez's clinic door. Not that she needed to. His bedroom was in the next wing.

She recalled the day Strzyga brought Jimenez the morphine. Jimenez had moved the vials into his bedroom, and Ysa doubted he'd relocated it. Why would he?

His room was close to Jordi's third-floor suites. *And right down the hall from me.* That way, if either of them required a shot, he had their medication at hand.

She looked at the shoes beside her wardrobe and left them there. Now was the time for stealth.

She padded barefoot to the door and peeked outside. The corridor was empty. Sergeant Esser wasn't visible. Everyone seemed to be downstairs going about their day.

Of course they are. I'm supposed to be asleep. Slipping outside, she eased her door shut and walked down the hall, staying away from the balcony.

At the landing, she checked both ways, making sure she didn't stumble over a servant. A quick glance assured her the library was empty. She paused at Jimenez's door and listened. No one moved on the other side.

It's now or never. She reached into her hair and removed a couple of hairpins, bending them into shape as she knelt before the lock. No sigils protected the door. With a quickness that would have drawn approval from her father, she picked the lock and stepped inside, shutting the door softly.

She wasn't sure what she'd expected, but the disarray of the room surprised her. A jacket was thrown carelessly over the back of a chair. The bed remained unmade. Vials, both empty and full, were clustered on a table against the back wall. The space was shared with a Bunsen burner and Erlenmeyer flasks of various sizes. Piles of notes were stacked in no particular order and written on everything from notepads to napkins.

Christ, he's a pig. Ysa ignored the rest of the debris and pocketed four empty vials. As she did, a stack of notes cascaded to the floor. Kneeling, she gathered the pages, reaching deep under the table for one errant sheet.

Her fingernail snagged a wire. She moved a grimy undershirt and found a homemade radio. Another cord led her to the headset, which was squirreled behind a set of medical texts.

What is our good doctor listening to? Careful not to jostle the dial, Ysa moved the radio closer and lifted the headset. She noodled the switch. A British announcer read the news. As much as she wanted to listen, she snapped the unit off and returned it to its hiding place, hopefully undisturbed.

The radio itself wouldn't get Jimenez in trouble, but if Jordi knew Jimenez was listening to Radio London, Jimenez's life might get complicated quickly.

He wasn't in the French Resistance. Of that she was certain. A nefil so close to Jordi wouldn't have escaped Los Nefilim's attention.

Then what is he doing? Ysa stood and waited for a wave of dizziness to pass before placing the notes back on the desk in a rough semblance of their earlier arrangement.

Curious, she read the top page. It was an arcane mixture of astrology and biology, none of which made sense to her. From what she could cobble together, Jimenez wasn't working on newer or better drugs to further Jordi's Reich. Rather, he was trying to predict the future, and not for Die Nephilim, but for himself.

He's trying to figure out how to align himself. Jimenez was busy looking out for number one.

The door opened. Ysa whirled.

Jimenez stood there with his mouth open. "What the hell are you doing in my room?"

Well. If nothing else, she'd managed to knock that oily smile off his face. She smoothed her dress and cleared her throat. "I . . . um . . . wasn't feeling well, so I thought I would come and find you."

"I was in the clinic."

"Every time I leave the floor, someone escorts me back

to my room." But now that Jimenez was here, another idea struck her. Switching out the vials entertained a certain amount of risk. *But if I can blackmail him into willingly giving me a saline shot, then Jordi will never be the wiser.* And given Jimenez's tendency toward self-preservation, Ysa had the chance to make him an offer he couldn't refuse.

If extortion fails, I've got the vials as a backup plan. With a grimace, she put her hand on her stomach. "I need to speak with you alone, Herr Doctor." Leaning forward, she stage-whispered, "It's a lady's troubles, if you take my meaning."

Jimenez blinked. "So you broke into my room?"

"The door was unlocked, so I knocked and came inside. I thought you'd just stepped out for a moment."

Jimenez entered the room, his eye darting to the medical texts hiding the radio. "I must ask you to leave. If you will go to your room and wait, I'll be there in a few minutes."

Ysa clutched her stomach and doubled over. "Oh, it hurts! Into my thighs!" Staggering to the bed, she swallowed her revulsion and collapsed on the mattress. "I think I'm bleeding."

"Not there!" Eyes wide with panic, Jimenez rushed to her side.

Ysabel grabbed his collar and yanked his face close to hers. She hissed in his ear, "You'll want to shut that door, Herr Doctor. You and I need to discuss your radio preferences."

Jimenez blanched white. "What?"

"Do you want me to say it louder?"

His jowls trembled as he shook his head.

"Then shut the fucking door." She released him.

Jimenez reeled backward and closed the bedroom door. While his back was to her, Ysa stood and quickly checked to make sure the vials were still in her pocket. "Tell me, Herr Doctor, do you think my uncle would be comfortable with your astrological predictions?"

Bright patches of red flowered across his cheeks. He walked past her and scooped the papers from the desk. "You'll have a hard time proving it. And who do you think your uncle intends to believe? You?" He put the papers in the hearth and struck a match. "Or his trusted doctor? Hmm?" He lit the papers and rose, warming his hands at his little fire.

She merely raised her eyebrows. *This is a game where I hold all the cards.* "He must trust you, because you've been perfectly candid with him as to where you're buying his morphine supply. Haven't you?"

The red splotches on Jimenez's face deepened. "I acquire his morphine from perfectly legitimate channels."

"Who do you mean? Dr. Strzyga?" She pointed toward the corridor. "I was in the library when he came. He is daimon-born. And we know the daimon-born can't be trusted."

"Strzyga can."

"With the life of a king of the Inner Guard? Are you sure about that, *Herr Doctor* Jimenez? It's possible the daimon-born are using you to poison my uncle. As a matter of fact"—she left the bedside and took two steps toward him— "it's probable that you're aiding a daimonic takeover of Die Nephilim that will leave you as king."

Jimenez went pale. "You horrid bitch."

"Don't be vulgar." She advanced again and was gratified to see him back away from her. "Listen to reason. I can keep your secrets, but in order to do that, I need clarity of mind. Your shots are disrupting my thought process. I could slip anytime and tell my uncle what I've witnessed." She pointed in the direction of her bedroom. "Poor Greta fell asleep on duty.

"What do you think my uncle will do to an actual traitor?"

Jimenez turned ashen. "I'm not a traitor."

"It doesn't matter if you are or aren't. I can make my uncle suspect that you are." She gave him her most winning smile. "You asked who he'd believe? I'm betting he'll believe me."

He flinched as if she'd struck him. "If I don't give you the shots, he'll know."

"Not if I continue to sleep and lurch like a drunken sailor."

He stared at her. "You would do that to protect me?"

She couldn't care less about him, but she didn't need to say so. "To protect us both, my dear doctor."

"You're asking me to betray your uncle." He glanced down at the needle marks on her arm.

"That sounds so ugly when you say it." When he didn't answer, she lowered her voice even more. *Time to drive the point home and sweeten the pot.* "I'm sure I don't have to tell a man of your expertise that wars are all about strategy, weapons, and luck. Today's winners might be tomorrow's losers. But that's all merely speculation."

"The Reich is—"

"Losing," she hissed. "And you know it." She jabbed her finger at the radio beneath his desk. "The Germans have lost Russia, whether they admit it or not. The Allies have taken North Africa and much of Italy. This war is drawing to a tedious, bloody close, Herr Doctor. You never know when you will need a friend in high places.

"Withhold the shots, keep my secret, and I'll keep yours. And in return, if you find yourself on the losing side, I'll stand ready to speak well of your actions. For this, I give you my oath in the name of my father, Guillermo Ramírez, King of Los Nefilim."

Vows were sacred to the nefilim—she didn't need to explain that to Jimenez. Just when she thought he would call the guards, he nodded. "I accept your oath."

Someone knocked on the door.

They both jumped.

"A moment!" Jimenez called out. He gestured toward the wardrobe.

Jordi turned the latch and entered the room.

How long has he been in the hall? How much has he heard? Ysa's heart rattled in her chest. *Steady. Hold steady.*

Jimenez appeared ready to faint. He flung his arm up a fraction of a second too late and squealed his Sieg Heil at the ceiling.

Jordi ignored him and directed his question to Ysa. "Why aren't you in your room?"

"I wasn't feeling well, so I came to find the doctor."

He glanced at her feet. "Then where are your shoes?"

"I felt unsteady after I woke and didn't want to break an ankle staggering around in heels."

A corner of Jordi's lips quirked upward before he glanced at Jimenez and readjusted his scowl. "I understand you met with Field Marshal Heines this morning."

Jimenez fidgeted. "He had a few medical questions about Queen Jaeger's death, but I was able to put his mind at ease."

Put his mind at ease about what? And why is Heines questioning Jimenez about her death? Unless he suspected foul play. From what Ysa had seen during her interrogation, Heines was methodical. He didn't appear to be the sort that jumped to conclusions. *No, he's like Miquel; he waits for the dust to settle so he can see clearly, then he builds his case.*

Jimenez's explanation didn't seem to reassure Jordi. "And where is Field Marshal Heines?"

The doctor relaxed. "He left for Paris about an hour ago."

Jordi drew his pistol and shot Jimenez—once through the throat and twice in the chest. The doctor stood in place, and for a wild moment Ysa thought he might continue speaking. Then he tilted backward, falling against the wardrobe.

Jordi didn't holster his pistol. "It appears I'm in need of a new doctor."

Ysa drew a short, ragged breath into her body. It wasn't the murder so much as Jordi's lack of expression. *I never saw it coming. His face belied nothing.*

Jordi pointed his pistol at her chest. He smiled. She found she liked him better when he didn't. "How are you feeling now, Ysabel?"

"A little faint."

"Why are you really in his room?"

Walk the truth close to the lie. "I thought I heard a radio program last night. It sounded like it was coming from here, so I came to see, and I found this." She retrieved the hidden radio and showed Jordi the dial. "He's been listening to Radio London. He's a traitor."

Jordi examined her for another moment, and then he holstered his pistol. Whether he believed her or not, she couldn't tell. "Go to your room. Sergeant Esser is bringing you a uniform for tomorrow's meeting with your father."

A Nazi uniform, no doubt, because that will break my father's heart, and Jordi knows it. Ysa lowered her eyes so he wouldn't see her anger.

Jordi didn't seem to notice. "Once you've changed, come upstairs, and bring Jimenez's bag with you."

"I'll be there as soon as I can." She followed him into the hall and watched him ascend the stairs to his suite. *What is he planning?*

She was almost sorry Jimenez was dead; he was a known factor. At least she'd gotten her wish: the drugs were gone from her system, and with them, any limitations on her song.

In her room, she waited impatiently for Sergeant Esser. She glanced at the mantel and realized the Woolf book was still there.

Probably a good idea to hide that. When she retrieved the book, a slip of paper fell to the floor.

It was a page from Dumas's *The Three Musketeers.*

That was odd. She was sure all the French books had been pulled from the library. *So where did it come from?*

She flipped the page over and saw that someone had underlined the phrase *Un pour tous, tous pour un* in Dumas's work. *One for all, and all for one.*

Only two other people understood what that phrase meant to her: Violeta and Rafael. But Rafael couldn't possibly be here. Jordi would recognize him in an instant.

But not Violeta.

A surge of hope made her heart beat faster. Maybe her

father wasn't walking into a trap, after all. Maybe he was in the process of setting a snare of his own.

Then don't get caught between them.

An hour later, Ysa climbed the stairs to the third floor, gripping Jimenez's black case in her hand. Stultz met her at the landing and escorted her to Jordi's suite.

Shadows fluttered along the walls—ill angels guarding a sick nefil.

Jordi's door was open.

Stultz went ahead to announce her. He gave Jordi a sharp salute. "Fräulein Ramírez, my Führer!" He snapped his heels and stepped back.

Ysa crossed the threshold to find her uncle behind his desk, patiently signing forms. "You may go, Stultz."

Stultz fired off another salute and shut the door on his way out.

Jordi barely noticed him. His hand trembled slightly as he lifted the page from the blotter and placed it on the stack. A thin sheen of sweat covered his brow.

Withdrawal. She placed the bag on his desk. Counting the days, she tried to assess how much of the drug Jimenez had given her. *Not nearly enough to cause the severe withdrawal symptoms Jordi is experiencing.*

She might feel some discomfort over the next few hours, but she doubted she would be debilitated. "Can I get you anything?"

He set aside his pen and opened the bag. "You already have."

She noticed that he wore Miquel's wedding band on his left hand. *As if they're married. How odd.*

Withdrawing the syringe and a vial of morphine, Jordi rolled up his sleeve. She helped him tie the rubber tube around his biceps. With a shaking hand, he lifted the syringe and attempted to insert the needle into the vial.

Ysa watched him until she could stand it no more. She gently extracted the syringe and vial from his hands. "Allow me."

His resistance was token at best. "I can do it."

"I know." Certain men must feel in control at all times. Jordi was one. She'd play into his vanities as long as it worked in her favor.

Ysa lowered his arm and swabbed alcohol over the vein. Before he could protest again, she drew the dose and gave him the shot.

He closed his eyes in relief. "Thank you."

"When is your next shot due?"

"In two hours."

Now she understood why Jimenez had such a problem with supplies. *There is enough for today and tomorrow.* That was all that mattered.

While Jordi stretched out and relaxed, she snatched glances at the letter he'd just signed. It was addressed to the field marshals at the Russian front and typed in hard bold letters:

> If we are not strong enough to hold our lines, then we are surely too weak to command Die Nephilim and the Inner Guard. We are fit only for destruction.
>
> Therefore, any mention of retreat by the General Staff will be considered defeatism, and the offending party will be shot without trial. If we cannot conquer,

then we shall leave no other division of the Inner Guard to triumph over Die Nephilim. This will not be another 1918.

We shall not capitulate.

Another quick look assured her that the stack of papers on his desk was identical to the one she'd just read. *Nothing matters to him but victory.*

Holding up his hand, Jordi examined Miquel's ring. "Do you know who used to own this ring?"

She saw no reason to be coy. "Miquel."

"He and Diago placed sigils on their wedding bands— glyphs about love, honesty, and trust." Jordi's lip twisted with derision. "How can a liar like Diago know anything about those things? Hmm?"

Her hands slowed as she arranged items in the bag. Guarding her face had become almost second nature over these last few days. She met his gaze with a mildly attentive expression. "It's an interesting question. One I haven't thought about."

He waved her comment aside with an absent flick of his wrist. "I'll tell you the answer: Diago can't. He's been using Miquel. It's a shame that I have to save one of your father's own nefilim from the daimon-born."

Tell him what he wants to hear. She seized the opportunity to reinforce Jordi's prejudices. "Now that you mention it . . . all this could indicate that Papá's slide into senility has been going on longer than we think."

Jordi's mouth quirked into a tight smile. "I have spent the last few years erasing those wards from Miquel's ring."

Praise him. Give him credit for doing an honorable thing. "You're trying to save Miquel," she murmured, though she doubted his motives were that pure. *No, he wants to drive a wedge between them, deprive them of the happiness he can't find for himself.*

"Indeed." He seemed amused by her naivete. A wicked light sparked in the darkness of his pupils.

Ysa closed the bag.

"No, no, my dear." He reached over to reopen the case. "You haven't had your dose."

She placed her hand over his. "No. Our supply is low, and morphine is becoming more difficult to acquire. When my father gets here, both of us will have to work hard to convince him to step down as a king of the Inner Guard. We'll need all our faculties to motivate him to do so peacefully. Splitting the morphine rations will leave us barely able to function."

He hesitated, and for a moment she feared he was going to force her to use the drug regardless.

Time to reinforce the argument. "Besides, it's more important that you receive the medicine. *You* are the king of Die Nephilim. They need you."

His fingers relaxed beneath hers. "You're right, of course. Once we've helped your father, we have another matter to attend."

We. That was a good sign. "Regarding what?"

"The daimon-born have contacted me. One of the elders from the Scorpion Court has requested an audience. He feels Die Nephilim's interests might be aligned with those of the daimon-born."

For once, she didn't have to fake her concern. "How could that possibly be?"

"I don't know, but I've decided to hear him. He has offered to bring Diago Alvarez with him."

What the hell was going on? Without missing a beat, she played her role. "Then it's true. Diago has rejoined the daimon-born."

"If he has, they don't want him. This Alessandro Strzyga is turning Diago over to us as a prisoner. He is petitioning that the Inner Guard give Diago the second death."

She inhaled sharply. *Something has gone very wrong.*

"You seem distressed."

She struggled to regain her composure. "The second death is so . . . extreme."

"Only because your father taught you to believe so. The fact is that some nefilim simply need to be eradicated for the good of the mortal realm. I want you to witness my judgment of him, and then help me administer the sentence."

"You're going to do it?"

"Of course. Diago Alvarez should never have been born. He is an affront to the natural order of life."

And Rafael? What does he intend to do to Rafael? Ysa didn't ask. She didn't want to know.

The phone on Jordi's desk rang. He answered and then told the other party to hold on. Turning to her, he whispered, "I have to take this. Let Esser and Stultz know where you are in case I need you."

"I'll see you in a couple of hours." When Jordi turned back to his call, Ysa took the biack bag with her.

As she slipped out of his room, an idea formed. The morphine kept Jordi from going into withdrawal and somehow enhanced his song. If she diluted the drug's strength, the withdrawal symptoms might distract him. *Keep him off balance.*

But she would have to start with his next dose. Her father would arrive sometime tomorrow, along with Diago and Strzyga. She had less than twenty-four hours to disable him.

It was ten minutes past three.

Time to get to work.

[22]

THE THEATER OF DREAMS

Diago worked his right wrist against his bonds and winced at the rope burn scoring his flesh. *It'll heal . . . keep going.*

The cord felt looser, and if he could gain just a little more play, he might be able to slide his right hand free. *Times when that missing pinkie works in my favor.*

A soft click froze him in place. The sound originated behind him. *That is the door.* He couldn't turn to see whose footsteps echoed in the quiet auditorium, but the tread was heavy.

He didn't have to wait long for Francisco's pin-striped bulk to drift into view. The ugly nefil grinned. "Look what I found."

Diago didn't give him the satisfaction of either a retort or fear. Instead, he twisted his right arm. His skin finally broke and blood seeped beneath the rope.

Francisco leaned forward and grabbed a handful of Diago's hair to jerk his head backward. Diago found himself looking at the ceiling. Francisco was so close, their legs touched.

The wicked gleam of a blade drifted into view—Francisco's knife.

Diago shifted his position, pretending to slink away in fear. If he kicked upward, he had a good shot at Francisco's balls. Even if he missed, the movement would startle the bigger nefil into jumping backward. *I hope.*

"Francisco." He tsked and designed his insult to make the other nefil rethink his line of attack. "You disappoint me. Using mortal means to extract retribution. That's how the firstborn deal with slights."

Francisco scowled at the slur. The blade wavered.

It's now or never. Diago kicked. Even from his awkward position, he felt the satisfying impact of his shin making solid contact with the bigger nefil's crotch.

Francisco dropped the knife and roared. He staggered backward, gripping his wounded testicles as he dropped to his knees.

Throwing his body hard to the left, Diago jerked his right hand upward. The rope slipped to his knuckles. Another pull freed his arm. His left wrist was still lashed to the seat's support. Slipping under the rope around his chest, he reached for Francisco's fallen knife. The blade remained just outside his reach.

Red-faced and puffing, Francisco lunged. He slammed his fist on the back of Diago's hand and easily grasped the knife's hilt with the other. "I'll fucking kill you."

Alvaro's voice startled them both. "Stand down, Francisco."

I never thought I'd be happy to see my father. Neither of them moved. For eight beats of his heart, Diago thought the ugly nefil would disobey him.

Then Francisco shoved Diago against the row as he stood. He saluted Alvaro and backed away.

Alvaro indicated the door. "Go back to your post. I'll deal with your punishment later."

Francisco's mouth dropped open. "He assaulted—"

Alvaro rapped his walking stick against the floor. White-hot derision accompanied the words falling past his sneer. "And you abandoned your post in order to attack a defense-less nefil. That means you're afraid of facing him as an equal. You're weak, Francisco. I question Christina's judgment in bringing you into the Scorpion Court."

There he is—that's the Alvaro I know. His tongue was the sharpest weapon he owned.

Diago remained kneeling beside the chair. He knew from experience that drawing his father's eye risked the same round of verbal abuse directed at him. *And he can recount my failings to his heart's desire. Just not in front of a slag like Francisco.*

The ugly nefil's mouth worked, but his brain couldn't seem to catch up.

Alvaro pointed his stick toward the door. Francisco's sense of self-preservation finally kicked in, and he left without another word.

Diago waited to see what his father would do next. To his surprise, Alvaro formed a sigil and screeched a high, sharp note. A glittering ward dodged between the seats and sliced through the rope binding Diago's left wrist to the chair's strut.

Alvaro came close and held out his hand. "Come here, son."

Careful, Diago warned himself as he allowed Alvaro to help him to his feet. His father was the most dangerous when he became solicitous, charming. *He wants something.*

"You're hurt." He lifted Diago's wrist to his lips.

Diago gently worked his hand free before Alvaro's tongue touched his skin. "It's fine." He straightened his coat and ran his palms through his hair, using the movements to put an arm's length of distance between them.

Swallowing hard, Diago glanced up at the painting. Christina's accusation sailed through his thoughts. *He didn't even argue for you.* "I'm fine."

Alvaro followed his gaze. "Do you remember your Gloaming?"

I do now. But Diago found the acknowledgment locked in his throat. He was afraid that if he opened his mouth, all that would emerge would be centuries of pain in one long howl.

Had anyone asked, he couldn't have articulated why he cared so much. It was like he'd told his own son—emotions were inexplicable, especially when it came to family. Had Alvaro returned for him when he was a child, Diago would have willingly followed him. In the end, he might have basked in his father's abuse and called it love simply because he knew no better.

But no more. *I see him plainly now, and regardless of what my heart wants, my mind knows the truth—he does not love me.*

Alvaro motioned at the portrait with his walking stick. "Why do you think Alessandro chose to replicate that particular event with those dark sounds?"

Still not trusting his voice, Diago shrugged. *I've got to get a grip on myself. I'm going to have to speak eventually.* He began the erection of his wall, and brick by brick, he sheltered his heart. Except now there were cracks in the mortar and he couldn't fill them in with numbers, or chords, or false dreams of comfort.

"All art has a purpose." Alvaro cocked his head as he examined the painting. "He used dark sounds—grief and fear and death."

And prayers . . . there were prayers entwined in that suffering. Sounds of hope . . . Diago held those thoughts close. His father didn't like his lectures interrupted.

Alvaro continued. "The very medium speaks to a sense of loss. And the subjects of the painting: you and me, when the world broke us apart."

"Did you speak for me?" The question escaped before Diago could stop it. He wasn't even sure why it mattered to him, but he wanted to hear the truth from his father's lips. *Just once, tell me the fucking truth.*

Alvaro skirted the issue. "Alessandro was always jealous that my line produced a child who is half-angel. Neither he nor any of his progeny were able to do it. You are as rare as you are beautiful."

"You're didn't answer the question."

"Frankly, Diago, you did yourself no favors in your first-born life. I'd hoped that by this incarnation, the elders' memories might be tempered by time, but Alessandro's envy won the day. He spoke against you in this incarnation."

Translation: it's all my fault. And maybe he's right. The house lights blurred and he rubbed his eyes. He didn't ask again. He didn't need to.

Alvaro's answer was obvious by his evasions. He hadn't spoken for his son. To do so would have jeopardized his own standing with both Moloch and the elders, and Alvaro wasn't going to hurt his chances for advancement.

Because that was how the Scorpion Court worked. It was every nefil for themselves.

Remember why I'm here . . . to protect my real family. The thought of Miquel and Rafael grounded him. *Play the game . . . see how the pieces move.* "What can I do to help you?"

Alvaro composed his expression to reflect the very image of benevolent forgiveness. "Alessandro has arranged to meet with Abelló tomorrow."

Diago's heart skipped. That was when Guillermo was supposed to arrive at Fontainebleau. What the hell kind of game was Jordi playing?

"You seem surprised."

"Stunned, actually. I can't imagine why Abelló would meet with the daimon-born."

"Because Alessandro has told him that he is bringing you."

"Me?"

"As a gift."

A cold knot of fear twisted in Diago's gut. "Did anyone think to run this by me?"

"While you were down here having fun with Francisco—"

"That wasn't fun."

"—Alessandro tried one last time to arrange a meeting with Abelló. It was only when he dangled bringing you as a prisoner that Abelló agreed to the visit."

Curious how his father might answer the question, Diago asked, "Why does Alessandro want to meet with him?"

"To possess him. Alessandro is now the vessel for Beleth. With Abelló's physical body, we can command Die Nephilim."

And the road to the Houska gate is cleared. Christina's confession had been valuable, but hearing the plan straight from Alvaro's mouth was gold.

Diago nodded solemnly. "I see. So while Beleth is busy possessing Abelló, what is my job?"

Alvaro took Diago's arm and led him up the aisle. "Find Ysabel. You know her. Make her want to come and help us. We need her to decipher Guillermo's psalm."

"I can do that for you, Father."

"And there is one more thing." Alvaro paused. "I want you to watch Christina."

"Christina?"

"She has her heart set on becoming my high priestess. I need to make certain that her intentions are pure."

Diago tried to imagine the word *pure* associated with his cousin and utterly failed. *Is this a test? Are they working together, trying to trip me through my own actions?* Rather than voice his confusion, he gave his father an expression of polite interest. "I see."

"Report any encounters you might have with her to me. I want to know everything she tells you. She has a tendency to overstep her bounds. If she does so again, I'll be forced to expel her from the court."

Jesus. I'm standing in the center of a veritable ouroboros of deceit. "You can depend on me."

"Good. Come upstairs. Have something to eat. We can discuss tomorrow's plan. My son."

Diago wasn't sure what frightened him more: the danger to Ysabel, or the ease with which he found himself sliding back into his old deceptive ways.

[23]

Twilight settled over the city as Rafael guided the car through the Place de l'Étoile. From where he sat in the backseat, Miquel lit a cigarette.

"You're smoking an awful lot back there." Rafael switched lanes to reach the avenue Mac-Mahon.

"Driving in Paris always makes me nervous."

"You're not driving. I am."

"Which is why I'm nervous."

Rafael glanced into the rearview mirror.

Miquel pointed. "Eyes on the road." But he saw his son's smile. He had to admit, Rafael had done an excellent job so far, but Miquel didn't say so yet. He didn't want him to get cocky. *He gets full of himself and forgets he's not immortal.*

Miquel had almost finished the cigarette by the time they reached the hotel. He lowered the window and pushed out the butt as Rafael wheeled the car close to the curb.

Miquel adjusted his cap. "It's showtime."

Before the doorman reached the car, Rafael exited and had Miquel's door open. He snapped to attention as Miquel stood.

Ignoring both his son and the doorman, Miquel entered the building. A careful look told him the guests lounging around the lobby appeared to be mortal.

A few German soldiers eyed his uniform. The rank on their sleeves put them beneath his notice.

By the time he checked in under his assumed name, Rafael was behind him with their bags. They took the elevator to the fifth floor and entered their suite.

Miquel tossed his hat to the bed. "Any nefilim?"

Rafael loosened his tie and shook his head. "All mortal."

"So far, so good." Miquel went to the window and checked the street. Seeing no unusual activity, he closed the curtains. He couldn't kick the bad feeling he had about this trip. *Everything is going far too smoothly.*

Rafael opened his suitcase and changed from his uniform to street clothes. He dropped his pistol and three magazines to the bed. From his breast pocket, he withdrew the jewelry box that contained the etching of his mother wrapped in velvet.

Miquel checked the magazine rounds. "Call me at dawn. Ask for Juan if you've managed to clear all the wards, Mariette if you fail. That way I'll know if it's safe to send our people in."

Nodding, Rafael tucked his holster and pistol under his bulky sweater. "Can you tell I'm carrying a gun?"

"No." Miquel adjusted the tail of the sweater. "Good job."

After Rafael returned the velvet box to his breast pocket,

he withdrew a small pack from his suitcase. An electric torch and a coil of rope were inside. He placed the extra magazines in the bag. "I'll take the hotel stairs and then head to the metro. Monique and Louis are meeting me in the Saint-Martin station in"—he checked his watch—"two hours."

Monique and Louis Benoist were both lieutenants in Les Néphilim. They'd moved ammunition and portions of their resistance activities into Paris's closed metro stations.

Rafael pulled his cap on and turned. For a split second, he looked so much like a young Diago, Miquel almost called him by his father's name.

"What's the matter?" Rafael asked.

"What?"

"You're looking at me funny."

Miquel shrugged. "Nothing. You just resembled your papá for a minute there. That's all. Which reminds me: he told me to make sure you—"

Rafael lifted his hand. "I know, I know. Stay away from my grandfather."

"Don't make this another 1939."

He put his hand over his heart. "I promise. I'm following orders to the letter. What are you taking for your meeting with Heines?"

"Booze and my incredible charm."

"You might need more booze," Rafael teased.

Miquel cuffed him playfully and knocked his hat askew. "Get out of here and be sure to come back safe. I don't want to have to answer to your father if something goes bad. Got it?"

Rafael's countenance grew serious. "Do you think he's okay?"

"Your papá is a smart guy. He knew what he was walking into."

"That doesn't answer my question."

Fair enough. Miquel knew better than to downplay the risks. "I think he's taken some hard knocks by now. We need to be ready to help him when he gets out of there."

"Like he helped us in '39."

"Hopefully, it won't be that bad." Miquel gripped his son's shoulders and looked him in the eye. "We'll deal with all that when the time comes, but for right now, you're in the moment, Rafael. Don't think about Papá, Don Guillermo, or Ysabel. You've got a job to do. Put your whole mind and your whole heart into your task, and we'll see each other on the other side."

Rafael hugged Miquel. The move was so sudden, Miquel was taken aback.

He embraced his son. "What's the matter?"

"I'm scared."

"It's okay. I am, too. I'm terrified. But we do what we have to do." Miquel gave him a hard squeeze and then pulled back so he could look Rafael in the eye. "You survived an encounter with a Grigori, and you did that because you remembered your training. You're smart and resourceful. I'm proud you're my son." He patted Rafael's cheek. "You're going to be fine."

Rafael wiped his eyes. "If you say so."

"I say so."

Rafael gave him a closefisted salute. "Sí, Señor General."

Miquel said quietly, "I will watch for you, my son."

"And I for you, Papá." Rafael opened the door and checked the hallway before he left.

Miquel went to the mirror and combed his hair. When he settled his hat back on his head, he gave it a jaunty angle. It was time to hunt.

Starting with the cabarets on the list Guillermo had given him, Miquel spent the better part of the evening visiting one establishment after another. He turned up no sign of Heines.

Standing outside the Moulin Rouge, he scanned the crowds and thought about his colleague. Either Heines had decided to stay in this evening, or he pursued other delights among the mortals.

Miquel smoked and recalled how they had torn through Paris during the heady days after the armistice. For two glorious nights, they trawled the city in an alcoholic daze; Heines had introduced Miquel to all his favorite brothels.

And Heines is one nefil with exquisite taste. Miquel crushed his cigarette and hailed a cab. As he got in, he barked at the driver, "Le Sphinx."

Although Le Sphinx hadn't been around in 1918, it was precisely the kind of maison close that Heines preferred—the women weren't forced to have sex with the patrons; some even served only as hostesses. The brothel was requisitioned solely for the use of German officers and French collaborators, which kept out the riffraff.

Although Le Sphinx was far from the only such brothel operating in Paris, Miquel chose it as his starting place, because of the building's close proximity to the literary cafés La Coupole and Café du Dôme. Heines sought out the company of artists almost as intently as he chased music and mortal women.

Twenty minutes later, Miquel found himself on the left

bank of the Seine at the boulevard Edgar-Quinet. While no sign hung over Le Sphinx's door, the establishment was easily identified by the gypsum mask of the Sphinx that decorated the façade.

Miquel left the taxi and went to the entrance. A large mortal blocked the door. "I'm sorry, monsieur, only German officers."

Normally Miquel would talk his way past the mortal, but the night was wearing thin. He formed a small sigil of light to momentarily blind the doorman. "It's a German uniform," he sang softly.

The mortal blinked and smiled. "I apologize." He opened the door and Miquel stepped inside.

If only everything were that easy. Miquel found his way to the crowded dance floor. A band played and several couples danced to a slow song.

He allowed his gaze to drift over the group but saw no one that resembled Heines. Drifting deeper into the establishment, he went to the restaurant, where he finally located Heines enjoying a quiet drink with a beautiful mortal.

The other nefil noted Miquel's presence almost immediately. His gaze flickered to him and then back to the lady.

Fortunately, stealth wasn't in Miquel's plan. He walked up to the table. "Heines? Erich Heines? Is that you, my friend?" He turned to the lady and bowed, taking her hand and brushing his lips across her knuckles by way of greeting. "I thought it had to be him, because he is always in the company of a beautiful woman."

Her gaze appraised him and it was clear she liked what she saw. "Monsieur. Have the Spanish come to invade?"

"In a manner of speaking." He winked at her.

She gave him an obligatory titter.

Only Heines didn't seem to be amused by their banter. "Would you pardon us for a few moments, Édith? I'd like to reminisce a bit with my . . . old friend."

"Of course." She excused herself and, with a final head-to-toe review of Miquel's body, she left them to return to the dance floor.

"De Torrellas." Heines was obviously deep in his cups, far from his first drink. "I should have heard you come through the door, because you've got balls that clang to be walking around Paris right now."

"I'm not sure if you've just complimented me or insulted me."

A moment of clarity broke the alcoholic haze in Heines's eyes. "I should have you arrested."

"But you won't. At least not until you've heard what I have to say."

"Really, and why is that?"

"Because I've been known to take risks, but nothing in my behavior ever indicated that I'm suicidal. And you know that if I'm here, it's because of trouble that goes over and beyond divisional squabbles."

"Is that what you call this war, a squabble?"

Miquel refused to be baited. "We have intelligence of a possible daimonic uprising in Paris."

A change washed over Heines's countenance. Whereas before he was drunk and irritated, he now seemed less drunk and more attentive, although far from convinced. "And who told you? That little daimonic bitch that you're fucking?"

He's still using his pet slur for Diago. Miquel ignored the insult—this time. "Alvaro is in Paris to choose Moloch's high priest. The Scorpion Court is gathering. We suspect they plan to attack the Houska gate."

Heines stared at him for almost a full minute. "Suspicions. But no proof."

"Yet. Guillermo is taking it seriously." Miquel lit a cigarette. "It seems that the mortals' hatred and thirst for killing have generated the very situation we were created to repress. We might as well march into Alvaro's court and hand him the keys to the mortal realm."

Heines signaled the bartender and raised his glass. He held up two fingers and indicated Miquel.

Either that's the signal to have me arrested, or he's buying me a drink. Neither of them spoke until the waiter arrived with two tumblers.

Miquel felt a headache creep up from his neck and into his scalp. He didn't allow his tension to echo through his voice. "This is a matter for the Inner Guard. Guillermo himself is coming tomorrow to speak with Abelló about it."

"Ramírez is coming to save his daughter. Now, isn't that true?"

"No one can fault him that, now, can they? And while he is here, he will speak to Abelló about the daimons."

Heines sniffed and shrugged. "Ramírez will find his brother in the Scorpion Court's debt."

"How so?"

"What do you know about the Strzyga family?"

Miquel swirled the liquor in his glass. "They're one of the more prominent branches of the Scorpion Court. Not low-level dealers by any stretch of the imagination—they're coordinated and connected. Why?"

"Abelló's doctor, Jimenez, has been dealing with a *Doctor*

Strzyga to procure Abelló's morphine." Heines turned his head as if he wanted to spit. "Ilsa never wanted this."

Not Jaeger, but Ilsa. At some point in this ugly mess, something had shifted in Heines's relationship with Die Nephilim's queen, Ilsa Jaeger.

Heines didn't seem to notice his slip. "She never wanted the camps; and she would never throw troops at losing battles to placate a madman."

Miquel wasn't sure if the reference to a madman was directed at Abelló or at Hitler. *Doesn't matter—they've somehow become one and the same in terms of philosophies.* "Then why did she go along with it for so long?"

He fortified himself with the liquor before speaking. "At first she thought she could control Hitler through Abelló. When she realized their goals were opposite hers, she spent the last two years trying to change course."

Miquel wondered if that new direction included involvement with the German resistance.

"Things came to a head last year. Abelló wanted a scorched-earth policy; Ilsa was adamantly opposed."

"How did she die?"

Heines drained his glass and curled his fingers into a fist. "Ilsa and I had become lovers. Shortly after Ulrich's death, she grew depressed . . . they'd been together for so long . . . she said it felt like an amputation within her mind, as if someone had lopped off part of her soul.

"Around this time, I began to notice needle marks on her arms. Jimenez gave her shots—vitamins, she said, to give her energy. Then she began having seizures. Violent ones. Within days, she was dead.

"This morning, I threatened Jimenez. He revealed that

in exchange for certain protections, he'd testify regarding Abelló's involvement in Ilsa's treatment." Heines's lip curled around the word *treatment* as if it left a bad taste in his mouth.

Probably because it does. "I'm sorry. I can't imagine your loss. If Abelló orchestrated Queen Jaeger's death, he should be brought to justice through the Guard's tribunals."

Miquel savored the whiskey's sweetness, letting it linger on his tongue. *Honey this next part . . .* "You said yourself she wanted to change course. So here's your chance. Let's work together, come up with a way to stop the daimon-born. Then maybe we can negotiate an end to the war before our divisions are completely destroyed. Will you come with me tomorrow to meet with Guillermo?"

"We'll meet at Fontainebleau."

"We need to meet with Guillermo *before* he arrives at Fontainebleau."

Heines stared into his drink, but his answer wasn't long in coming. He grabbed a cocktail napkin and jotted down his number. "Call me in the morning. I'll send my car to pick you up. I'll make you no promises other than to listen."

"How do I know this car won't take me to Fresnes?"

Heines's mouth twitched. "Because you have my vow." He gestured to the door. "Now get out of here before one of my nefilim shows up and notices us together."

Miquel knocked back his drink and left. *Either he's playing me so he can summon the Gestapo, or he'll sober up in the morning and realize he made a terrible mistake.*

It was going to be a very long night.

[24]

23 January 1944

DARK SOUNDS

Hotels were like subways, a maze of corridors and doors, differing only in size and scope. Rafael took the stairs to the first floor, but rather than turn toward the lobby, he used his instinctive sense of direction to exit the building through the servants' corridors.

The alley outside was deserted. He hurried to the street and headed for the Argentine station. With the memory of Miquel's hug fading, his fear returned, but he didn't feed it. *Keep your focus. Do like Papá says: complete one objective, take a deep breath, then move to the next. Get to the subway station.*

Pulling his cap low over his eyes, he watched for soldiers as he walked. That was his biggest obstacle to getting underground—arriving without encountering the police. It was all he could do to restrain his pace.

But he did, because he had to. As dangerous as the mortal

soldiers were, a nefil would quickly spot him if he forgot himself.

Move like a mortal. He measured his pace to reflect those of the people around him, careful not to step too fast or too slow. Mingling close to groups was another way of avoiding an alert nefil's eye, and Rafael took advantage of the street's congestion whenever he could.

He managed to get to the station without encountering an obstacle. The maintenance entrance wasn't guarded. He opened the door and went inside as if he had every right to be there.

Stopping in the semidarkness, he listened. He wasn't safe here. The Nazis, as well as resistance fighters, used the underground passages. He'd be just as likely to encounter an enemy as a friend.

Then move with care. Walking quietly, he started down the corridor.

Although it had been years since he'd used the Paris metro for clandestine operations, little had changed. The smell of the trains and dust gave him a nostalgic rush and made him long for his home in Barcelona. That was where he'd learned to use the subways and sewers to carry messages between the fighters.

But Barcelona was a long way away. Like his fear, he silenced his longing for home. *Stay focused.*

He stepped into a service tunnel and got his bearings. The passageways were strangely quiet, nothing like the days before the war when the trains rumbled almost constantly.

Creeping along the tracks, he stayed close to the wall. Only a few electric lights illuminated the rails, but like his father, Rafael's daimonic vision enabled him to see in all but complete darkness, and this was far from complete.

In the process of avoiding metro workers and the busier stations, it took him almost the full two hours to reach the Saint-Martin station. As he approached the platform, a woman stepped from the shadows.

Tall and thin, she had a face like a chisel, all angles and sharp edges. Wisps of her long red hair escaped the scarf she wore.

Rafael supposed that before the war the wrinkles around her eyes might have been laugh lines, but no more. *Like us all, she is weary.*

"Halt." She pointed a pistol at his chest.

"Ay, ay, ay, Monique. It's me, Rafael." He took off his hat so she could see his eyes.

She visibly relaxed. Quickly holstering the gun, she nodded to the platform. "Louis is over there."

Papá would say breathe. Rafael allowed himself a small smile as he followed her. They passed the grille that blocked the stairs going to the surface. Rafael noticed the lock was missing. *Probably in Monique's or Louis's pocket.*

A couple of broken chairs sat side by side. Several cigarette butts littered the ground.

Louis stepped from a booth and holstered his own gun. He was a small man with soft features and a receding chin. His nose seemed to be the largest part of him.

Disappointed with his prowess, Rafael whispered, "I must have made a lot of noise."

Louis offered him a smile. "Not much gets by Monique. She's got the hearing of a bat."

"And we've been watching for you." Monique retrieved a pack. "Have you eaten?"

Rafael shook his head. "Has anyone heard from my papá?"

She produced a bit of bread, some cheese, and a dried pear. "We know he arrived and went in. But he hasn't emerged yet."

Rafael's stomach lurched with fear. In his anxiety, he touched the jewelry box in his pocket. Even though he knew she couldn't hear him, he called his mother's name and asked her to watch over Papá. To Monique he said, "Then we don't know what's going on in there."

Monique didn't appear concerned. "Guillermo wants us to prepare for a raid as if we have evidence. Then, if he gets confirmation from Diago, we're ready to take them down."

That sounded like Don Guillermo. He never made a move unless all his pieces were in place for success. "It's easier to disperse an army than to gather one."

"Smart boy," Louis muttered. "Go on and eat, then. I'll show you the maps." Under the nearest light, he spread the papers on the floor. The illustrations disclosed the sewer lines that led to the Theater of Dreams and the adjacent hotel.

Louis pointed at the map with a dirty fingernail. "We believe the daimons have traps set along this line, and here."

A match flared and was soon followed by the scent of cigarette smoke. Even sitting, Monique seemed tall.

Louis nodded at the grille blocking the stairs. "Go back out to the street. Half a block on the left, you'll find the entrance to the sewers. Follow this tunnel. It will bring you to a door. We've not been able to get close enough to break the sigils around it, but we believe it leads to the basement of the old hotel beside the theater."

Louis laid a different map over the first. He ran his finger down a narrow corridor. "This hallway is the only connection between the hotel and the theater. We suspect the daimon-born are using the basement exit for an escape route."

Rafael wolfed down his food as he memorized the lines. "And this door?"

"Leads to the theater lobby. Don't go in if you can avoid it, but if you're caught out, there are a few exits. Through the front, of course, or the way you came in. Backstage, stage right, is another door. It opens on the alley behind the café."

"How crowded are the streets there?" Rafael didn't mention mortals, but they knew what he meant.

Monique answered, "Not very. The café closes at nine and reopens at seven. If you get the sigils cleared, go to the café and order coffee with milk. If you don't think it's safe for the angel-born, order black coffee and a roll."

"Do we have nefilim working there?"

"We do. They'll know what to do with the information." She exhaled twin streams of smoke from her nostrils, looking for all the world like an ancient and weary dragon. "Once Louis gets you to street level, we're leaving to take our positions near the theater."

"Thank you, Monique." He touched the brim of his hat. "Watch for me."

"We will." She nodded to Louis.

He opened the grille and took Rafael to the street, looking both ways before giving him the all-clear. Back in the open, Rafael followed Louis's directions and found the sewer entrance.

Once inside, he consulted the map and then followed the

narrow tunnel. *Now for the next phase.* But this would be the hardest part.

Bricks and bits of broken concrete littered the path. Rolling the soles of his boots toe to heel along the uneven surface made his going tedious but prevented him from turning an ankle in the rubble. He moved with the grace of a ballet dancer, a master thief, one who was as at home beneath the ground as above.

The skills learned as a child of soldiers always at war.

He watched for the first intersection, hoping he wouldn't come across any collapsed portions. What he didn't have time for were multiple detours.

Rafael reached the other side of the street in less than an hour. He stopped and considered his next move.

After their adventure beneath the Pyrenees during those last days of the Spanish Civil War, his father had taught Rafael how to wield his daimonic song. Whereas angelic sigils relied on the manipulation of light and sound, daimonic spells combined emotion with pitch to achieve the same effect. The more negative the emotion, the more powerful the ward.

Maybe it was because of his past, but Rafael's papá was exceptionally skilled in creating deadly daimonic sigils. *Because that pain never leaves him.*

The problem was that Rafael's experiences didn't quite have the same intensity. *But this spell requires darkness.* The light of his angelic song might trigger any daimonic traps within the tunnels. In order to pass unheeded, he needed to draw on his negative emotions.

So terror and rage it is. He'd spent the long drive to Paris thinking about which memory to use, because the success of the spell rested in the interpretation of the chords. That meant he had to rouse the feelings and experience them in his heart before channeling them into his song.

Closing his eyes, he summoned the memory of his captivity in Jordi's pocket realm. He remembered sitting on a hard chair in a cold concrete room. Carlos Vela was there. Sly-eyed and arrogant, he'd tried to scare Rafael and keep him off-balance. *How'd that work out for you, Carlos?*

But that thought brought him bitter elation. *Not the emotion I need.* He concentrated harder.

He reimagined the pain of the Grigori's sigils gnawing into his wrists. With forefinger and thumb, he traced the scars that had yet to disappear.

In that memory, Rafael found his fear.

Almost immediately, the image of Miquel hit his mind's eye. Too thin and ashen, his father had barely been alive. *He'd lifted his head. His eyes were so unfocused. A string of bloody drool escaped the corner of his mouth.*

And in that memory, Rafael found his rage.

He coughed a harsh note into his palm. A black scorpion wiggled to life and flicked a drop of gold from its tail.

Mamá's tear. Looking down at his signet, he saw the stone glow softly. *Oh shit, if the daimon-born sense me before I even start, I'm lost.*

His new fear fed the scorpion, turning it black against his palm. The gold faded but didn't quite disappear. Rafael calmed somewhat. Papá had once assured him that as long as the negative emotions composed the dominant chords, the daimons wouldn't notice the minor angelic notes.

Rafael lowered himself to one knee and hummed. The scorpion rolled off his palm and scuttled forward. It had gone no more than two meters before it stopped and shivered, pointing upward with its tail.

A thin line of shadows, which were a shade darker than the blackness surrounding him, were interlinked at ankle-level—a line that most people would have walked through without seeing. Within the blue-black hues, Rafael detected the faint outlines of interwoven sounds.

Dark sounds. The souls of dead mortals vibrated around one another, bound together by a nefil's wards. Had Rafael touched the trip wire with his ankle, the howls of a thousand voices would have filled the sewer and warned the daimon-born of his presence.

Creeping closer, he knelt in front of the daimonic trap and examined it. Teasing apart the chords of an angelic song required snipping the intricate lines of light that formed clefs, quavers, ghost notes, caesuras, glissandi, portamenti . . . a veritable catalogue of symbols and sound.

Extricating dark sounds relied on distinguishing one voice from another, separating it from the chorus, and releasing the tormented souls. More than technical skill, working with dark sounds necessitated compassion.

The first step was simply to call out and then listen. Rafael hummed a soothing note and touched a strand.

He heard a youth crying. *I'm not ready to die. I'm not ready—* A gunshot silenced his sobs.

Rafael located the beginning and the end of the sound. Delicately, as if plucking a string for the softest of chords, he untangled the youth's pleas from those of the others.

The boy was mortal, but that didn't matter. *Even the nefilim are mortal, too.* Opening his palm, he set the dark sound free. *Peace, brother.*

The next one was a woman's voice. She screamed in a mix of terror and rage. *Let me go, damn you! Let go! Let go—* The wet sluice of a knife plunging into flesh stopped her cries.

As he had with the gunshot victim, Rafael separated the woman from the others and released her spirit into the night. *Peace, sister.*

More awaited him: a homeless woman, disoriented in the tunnels, who died weeping for the daughter she lost; a soldier full of anger and regret, who'd held his service revolver to his temple and pulled the trigger one last time; a child, wandering away from a broken home; the sounds multiplied and wove together to form a lament for innocence lost.

By the time Rafael finished, their grief became a part of him, and for the first time in his life, he realized why his papá's daimonic magic was so strong. It wasn't because of self-pity, or the terrible things the daimons did to him when he was a child.

It's his empathy for others. He feels their pain as his own and translates it into song. A tear slid from his eye and trailed down his cheek.

It's okay to cry, he heard his papá say. *It's okay.*

Then Miquel's voice rang through his head: *You're in the moment . . . put your whole mind and your whole heart into your task.*

Except he didn't say what to do when Rafael's heart was breaking.

No. It was Papá who knew that solution. He never said it out loud, but his actions spoke volumes. *Just keep going, putting one foot in front of the other.*

Exhaling softly, Rafael collected himself, and then released his scorpion again. Five meters later, he came across another trap, this one more complex. Settling down, he reached out and touched the first dark sound. An infant's terrified wails filled his head, the cries already weakening from hunger and the cold.

Three hours later, Rafael released the last dark sound and rubbed his eyes. Looking back the way he'd come, he realized he cleared thirty meters of daimonic traps.

At least the dark sounds are no longer bound to the mortal realm. Freed of the daimon-born's spells, they would eventually fade and become silence. As for their pain, Rafael now carried it in his song. *And they won't be forgotten.*

Wiping his nose with the sleeve of his coat, he turned back to his goal. The theater's metal door lay just ahead.

A single bulb hung from a cord. The filaments flickered and buzzed as if they were almost ready to blow. The tunnel dead-ended just beyond the light. *Not a good place to get caught.*

Streaks of rust and mold darkened the door's veneer. The dented doorknob threw a long shadow against the floor.

That's the perfect spot for a trip wire. Rafael sent his scorpion to check the floor, the walls, and the ceiling for any traps. The arachnid scuttled forward, feeling the bricks with its chela.

Rafael glanced over his shoulder again. The wait became excruciating.

His imagination turned each ping of water into a footstep—every echo became a voice. Shivering in the cold and damp, he forced himself to focus on his scorpion, watch-

ing for the telltale shiver that indicated the arachnid had
found another booby trap laid by the daimon-born.

His patience was rewarded. The scorpion found a trip
wire in the spot he'd suspected.

Unlike the dark sounds in the tunnel, these sigils were
crafted entirely from a nefil's song and were fashioned to kill
with electrical shocks. He knelt beside it, searching for the
telltale loop that indicated the beginning of the ward.

This process was similar to finding the wire that activated
a bomb. For the better part of an hour he studied the glyph,
before he found the line he needed. At least, it looked like it
might be the right one.

If I'm wrong . . . In spite of the cold, a bead of sweat trickled down the side of his face. Before he could second-guess
himself, he hummed a high note and sent it at the thread.

The sigil popped. Then it sizzled, leaving a scorched scent
in the air.

Rafael stood and looked at the door. What he'd initially
taken for rust and mold were actually sigils. Viridian lines that
were more black than green teemed and slithered over the
metal, cascading downward and then back up in a continual
loop.

Something familiar in those lines . . . It took him another
moment before he saw the similarity between these wards
and those made by his father . . . *and me.*

A splash of water startled him. He looked back the way
he had come. When nothing moved after a count to sixty,
Rafael returned to his examination of the half-familiar patterns. *These weren't made by just any nefil . . . these glyphs
were fashioned by Alvaro.*

The click of a heel striking the floor caused Rafael's heart to stutter. He whirled.

For the first time in years, Rafael froze. Both mind and limbs refused to move. All he saw was his nightmare come to life.

He grabbed me by my throat . . .

Alvaro's grin revealed yellowed teeth filed to points. The daimon widened his white eyes dramatically. "Boo!"

Before Rafael could form a glyph, Alvaro's ward struck his forehead . . . and he felt himself falling against the wall . . . then the world went black.

[25]

24 January 1944

THE THEATER OF DREAMS

Diago awoke to someone pounding on his door. He blinked at the unfamiliar surroundings. Two seconds passed before he remembered where he was . . . and why. *Paris . . . the Theater of Dreams . . .*

They'd given him a bedroom on a heavily guarded floor. He had no chance to slip away. His every move was being watched. Whether his guards were acting on Christina's instructions or Alvaro's, he had no way of knowing.

Last night he'd pushed the bureau in front of the door so he could sleep with both eyes shut. He'd been more tired than he thought and had fallen into a deep sleep.

The knocking continued unbated. Diago rolled out of bed and bumped against the nightstand, upsetting a glass of water. The glass hit the floor and shattered.

Ignoring it, he straightened the rumpled clothing he'd worn to bed. "Coming," he muttered at the incessant knocking.

At the basin, he poured water into the bowl and splashed his face and hair. Finally, in some semblance of order, he shoved the dresser away from the door and opened it.

It was Nico. The nefil appeared relieved. "They want you to come."

Diago glanced outside the door. The corridor was empty. *Should I make a run for it?* He could take Nico with him, get to a safe house, and then send a message to the café.

Nico must have read his mind. "Don't even think about it," he whispered. "If you ring for the elevator, it'll arrive with two nefilim in the car. Two more are guarding the stairwell." He winced as if in pain. "They're hoping you'll try to escape. Alessandro has ordered them to shoot to kill."

Fine. Although it wasn't. He pulled Nico into the room and shut the door.

The terrified nefil chanted, "Don't. Please don't. I've already said more than I should have."

"Shh, shh, Nico, listen to me." He cradled the other man's face between his palms and forced him to meet his gaze. "Listen. Will you listen?"

"No. You can't say anything to me." He unbuttoned his shirt and jerked it open.

On his chest, just over his heart, his skin bulged in the shape of a scorpion. The arachnid took the form of a purplish bruise. The chela and walking legs squirmed beneath the skin's dermis. The tail wasn't visible.

Because the stinger is buried in his heart. Diago immediately recognized the spell. Whenever one of the daimon-born commanded a slave, they made a cut in the nefil's flesh and sent a note of their song into the wound. The chord then turned into a scorpion that wrapped itself around the victim's heart. If Nico defied Alessandro's orders, the scorpion released its venom.

That explained why Nico hadn't tried to escape. To do so meant an agonizing death.

"Forget me. I am dead." Nico struggled for composure.

"No." Diago took Nico's arms. *He's so thin. How does he even keep standing?* The image of Petre lying in Juanita's infirmary haunted Diago. "You're not dead. Not yet. The spell can be broken."

"Don't lie to me."

"I'm not lying to you. Rafael did."

"Rafael is part daimon, too. This is different." Nico buttoned his shirt. "It doesn't matter. They want you to come upstairs."

Diago wasn't done, though. "We've been searching for you since July. By the time we found out you'd been sent to Mauthausen, you managed to contact Miquel through his dreams. We haven't given up, and you shouldn't, either. I'm going to get you out of here."

"Alessandro intends to murder you." Nico tightened his lips and shuddered beneath a fresh round of agony.

He shouldn't have said that. "Don't endanger yourself. I know what I'm dealing with here. I can trust no one—no one but you."

Calmer now, Nico wiped his eyes.

"I'll be back for you."

"What do you need me to do?"

He placed his palm over Nico's heart. "Keep yourself safe."

"Then please come upstairs. They want to leave."

Diago opened the door. "Lead the way."

Nico took him to Alvaro's suite on the fourth floor. Alessandro and Alvaro were having coffee.

Nico immediately went to one corner of the room. He stood far enough away from Alessandro that the daimon-born nefil didn't have to see him, but close enough to respond if he was needed.

Alessandro watched Nico with a raised eyebrow. "He's upset. Were you feeding on my nefil?"

Knowing that Beleth now possessed Alessandro made his abuse of the angel-born nefil even more perverse. *And I'll find a way to make him pay for that.* But first this morning's job had to be done.

Smiling with his mouth to hide the hate in his heart, Diago said, "After yesterday, I thought he was community property."

Alvaro glanced at him. "You look like shit."

"Well, I'm supposed to be a prisoner, aren't I?"

Alessandro placed his cup on the table. "Remember our story: we captured you and are giving you to Abelló as a token of our goodwill."

Diago didn't wait to be invited. He poured himself a cup of coffee. *Real coffee.* Since it might very well be his last meal, he savored it. "And what is my role?"

Alvaro watched him carefully. "Just do as you're told and keep your mouth shut."

Alessandro snapped his fingers. "We should gag him."

If they gagged him, they'd take away his ability to sing a glyph to life. "No gag."

Nico came forward and snapped to attention beside Alessandro. "Inmate 35222 is obediently present."

It was a humiliating routine. Diago's gut clenched with anger, but his rage didn't show on his face.

Alessandro gestured at Diago. "Cuff him."

Diago balked. "No cuffs. No. No one said anything about gags or cuffs last night. We go in, take down Abelló, and get out. How can I help if I'm restrained?"

"We've got to get them to drop their guard." Alvaro tapped one restless finger against his thigh. "No gag, but you'll wear the cuffs."

"Deal's off." Diago set the coffee cup on the tray and turned to leave.

Alvaro struck the floor with his walking stick. "Stop!"

Diago froze. When he turned, he let them see the cunning in his eyes. "How about this for a story, since the whole affair is something of a farce? Rather than subdue me, you lied to me and made me a part of Alessandro's escort."

Alvaro considered the idea.

Alessandro immediately discounted it. "No. He wears cuffs."

"No," Alvaro said. "We do it his way."

Is he just being contrary to piss off Alessandro? Or does he suspect Alessandro means to kill me?

Alessandro's lip curled. "If you say so. But he carries no gun."

"Fine." Diago adjusted his tie. "I don't need a gun to be scary."

Alessandro flicked his wrist at Nico.

The nefil returned to his corner.

Alessandro stood and stretched. "Francisco will drive us." He gestured absently at Nico and spoke to Alvaro. "Feel free to amuse yourself with him while I'm gone."

Nico made no sign that he heard. Diago wondered how high the wall around the other nefil's heart had grown. *And whether we'll break him free again.*

But that concern was contingent on all of them staying alive.

As Diago followed Alessandro out the door and down the hall, he wondered if Guillermo had arrived at l'Entreprenante. *Because if anything goes wrong, or if anyone is late, I'm dead.*

[26]

PARIS

Miquel glared at the silent phone as if he could force it to ring by sheer will-power alone. He checked his watch again in what was becoming a nervous ritual. Phone, watch, and then a walk to the window, where the dawn had become the day.

And still no word from Rafael.

"Come on, osito," he whispered. Though they called Rafael little bear less and less as he grew older, the pet name still slipped through Miquel's lips when he was stressed. "Call me. Tell me you're all right."

The phone mocked him with its silence.

And I can wait no longer. It was time to follow his own rules. *Keep your eyes on the job. He'll be all right. He's been through worse than this.*

Miquel picked up the receiver and dialed the number Heines had given him. Five rings later, he heard Heines's voice in his ear. "Hello?"

The other nefil sounded as chipper as if he hadn't been slightly drunk the night before. *Something else I'd forgotten—he has an amazing tolerance for alcohol.* "Heines? It's General Rosales." He hadn't given Heines his alias last night, but the name wasn't important. Heines would recognize Miquel's voice.

"Are you ready to go?"

No, not until I hear from my son. "Absolutely." He gave Heines the hotel's address.

"My car will be there in twenty minutes."

"I'll watch for you." Miquel hung up and checked the time. He'd wait fifteen more minutes before he went downstairs. *Come on, Rafael. Call me.*

[27]

UNDISCLOSED LOCATION

Everything was going wrong.

Guillermo paced on the roadside while Bernardo changed the car's tire.

"How much longer?" Guillermo checked his watch.

"A few more minutes," Bernardo drawled, as sanguine as if they had all day.

"Christ, you said that an hour ago."

Bernardo shrugged with casual disregard for Guillermo's impatience. "It was a long walk to the service station and back."

Guillermo knew a rebuke when he heard one. "I could help you. I've changed a few tires in my day."

"I can see you impressing Abelló with tire black on your hands." Bernardo's eye went to Guillermo's Nationalist uniform with the stars of a capitán general on his epaulets and hat. "Stay put. I'm almost done."

Without another word, he went back to work and fifteen minutes later, he gave the lug wrench one final twist. "There. Finished." He returned the tools and luggage to the trunk. Taking his uniform jacket from the front seat, he buttoned his coat and settled his hat on his head. With a flourish, he opened the back door.

Guillermo settled himself in the backseat and toyed with his lighter. Bernardo took the driver's seat and got them back on the road. The Spanish flags on the front fenders snapped merrily in the wind as the car picked up speed.

Another half hour passed before they reached a dirt lane that ran between two hedges. Guillermo sat up and tried to discern whether another car had been here before them. He saw no indication that anyone had beaten them to the rendezvous point.

A kilometer later, they were parked in front of an abandoned farmhouse. It was the one Diago had often used as a stopping point on his way north. Bernardo unholstered his gun and went inside to make sure the building was empty.

Guillermo checked his watch. They were twenty minutes late. Had Heines gotten tired of waiting? No, he quickly discounted the idea. Even if Heines had left, Miquel would have stayed behind. The only other answer was that Miquel had failed his mission.

Guillermo flicked the lighter's lid four times. His stomach lurched when he considered that he might have killed his best friend's husband. That they'd all willingly gone to their assignments remained irrelevant. Their lives were in his hands.

"The house is clear," Bernardo announced as he walked toward the car. "And I saw a trail of dust from the upstairs window. Someone is coming." He pointed to the lane.

It was another four minutes before the Mercedes was visible.

Guillermo didn't relax. They still had tricky ground to cover.

Putting his hands behind his back, he straightened.

The Mercedes stopped behind their car, and the driver, a young Nazi, got out and opened the rear passenger door for Heines.

Miquel emerged from the other side. He still had his pistol and appeared unharmed.

Guillermo felt a fraction of his tension recede. Heines had at least listened to their proposal.

Miquel moved to stand just behind Guillermo's right shoulder. His features were inscrutable, but that was Miquel. He could be positively jubilant that Heines agreed to work with them, or devastated that they'd just tipped their hand to Jordi, and his face wouldn't belie his thoughts.

Sometimes Guillermo wished he wouldn't be quite so unreadable.

Heines stopped merely a few paces away.

Guillermo dispensed with both pleasantries and aliases. "Field Marshal Heines, I assume General de Torrellas has informed you of the daimonic uprising that we face?"

"He has."

"Your presence here indicates you remain true to the Inner Guard."

"I do. It is my understanding that if I help you, we have

the beginnings of a truce. One that will definitely save the lives of both mortals and nefilim; one that might filter up to the angels?"

Guillermo shrugged. "I can't make any promises about the angels. Insofar as the Inner Guard is concerned, I will speak well of your allegiance and make sure you lead the council to restructure Die Nephilim. Do I have your word?"

Heines extended his hand. "You have my oath that I will help you."

Guillermo didn't kid himself. He secured Heines's help only because Jordi was the bigger threat. Nonetheless, he took the other nefil's hand and shook. "I'm on my way to l'Entreprenante to meet with my brother now."

"So am I. Abelló called me in early. He wants me on the grounds when he meets with one of the daimon-born nefilim, Alessandro Strzyga."

One of the Council's Nine elders. That was interesting news. "Why is he meeting with him?"

"Strzyga has been pushing for a meeting with Abelló for a week now, and it seems he's finally found his ticket in. He petitioned Abelló to give Diago Alvarez the second death." His gaze flickered to Miquel. "Strzyga is bringing Alvarez to l'Entreprenante this morning."

Shit and bitter shit. Still, Guillermo didn't panic. They had time. Giving a nefil the second death was a complicated process, and he had no doubt Jordi intended to savor Diago's subjugation. *We're coming, my friend. Hold on.* "Alvarez is one of mine."

"And if we get there in time, you can keep him. But we've

got to hurry." Without waiting for Guillermo's answer, Heines returned to his car. "I know you have safe conduct, but follow me anyway. We can go in together." He got into the backseat, and his driver shut the door.

Guillermo and Miquel got into their car, and it wasn't long before Bernardo followed the Mercedes to the road.

Bernardo glanced in the rearview mirror. "What's the plan?"

Guillermo checked his pistol's magazine. "We're playing this song by ear. Follow orders, no questions." He glanced at Miquel. "Has Rafael cleared those sigils?"

Miquel stared out the window. "He was supposed to call at dawn and never did."

Guillermo winced. "We'll find him."

"He can take care of himself."

From Miquel's tone, Guillermo knew the discussion was over. Miquel was worried, but he never engaged in speculation. He had his eyes on the task ahead.

So put him to work. "When we get to l'Entreprenante, I'll go inside with Heines and take care of business. I want Bernardo to take you back into the city."

"What about Diago?"

"We've got people seeded inside l'Enreprenante. They'll take care of Diago while Ysabel and I handle Jordi. You find Rafael, coordinate that raid, and take the Scorpion Court down."

"What about requiring direct evidence of wrongdoing?"

"If Strzyga wants Diago dead, it's because he's seen too much and has evidence against them. That's my story and I'm sticking to it."

"What about you?"

"I'll be fine. But just in case everything goes sideways, I want you to know I've been honored to fight at your side. I will watch for you, my good friend."

"And I for you," Miquel whispered.

[28]

CHÂTEAU DE L'ENTREPRENANTE
FONTAINEBLEAU

The ride to l'Entreprenante was a silent affair. Francisco kept his one good eye on the road. Riding beside him in the front seat, Diago pretended not to notice the other nefil's white-knuckled grip on the steering wheel.

He's terrified. Whether he feared Alessandro, the Inner Guard, or if Christina had given some assignment outside the range of his abilities, Diago had no idea. He was only certain that scared nefilim made mistakes. *And Francisco is a veritable bomb waiting to explode.*

Alessandro rode in the backseat behind Francisco, which made Diago more comfortable. He never wanted the elder behind him and that was before Beleth was involved.

For his part, Alessandro sat ramrod-straight, the very image of nobility. *It's almost like he's forgotten both Francisco and me.*

Diago didn't kid himself. When the time came to act, the elder would do so with ruthless precision.

The gates of l'Entreprenante finally came into view. Francisco eased the car to a halt. "What do I say?"

Oh Jesus Christ. "Just roll down the window."

Francisco worked the crank and lowered it halfway.

The young Nazi bent low to examine them. "Your papers?"

They all passed their identification to the guard. He examined them and nodded. "Follow the drive. You'll be directed as to where to park."

Francisco nodded, his lips white.

The guards neutralized the wards and then opened the gates. Francisco drove through. He glanced in the rearview mirror.

"We're trapped," Francisco muttered.

Diago ignored him. Alessandro didn't even dignify the comment with a reply. His gaze was locked on the drive as the château came into view.

On the front steps, Erich Heines watched their approach. He rested his hand on his holster in a seemingly casual gesture.

Two staff cars were parked in the circular drive. The second vehicle had Spanish flags on the front fenders.

Bernardo opened the rear passenger door, and Guillermo got out. Another figure remained inside. Diago recognized his husband's profile.

Francisco parked and got out to open the door for Alessandro.

Diago emerged from the vehicle. Now was the time to break his cover. He stepped toward Guillermo.

A hand landed on his shoulder and whirled him around. "You fucking traitor!"

Diago found himself facing Bernardo's broad chest. He looked up and whispered. "Not now. We've got to—"

"What is this?" Alessandro demanded. "Release him."

Through gritted teeth, Diago hissed, "Do it."

Bernardo's fingers relaxed slightly as he looked toward Guillermo.

Diago twisted toward his old friend, who shook his head.

Guillermo scowled. "He is a traitor to Los Nefilim. We've been hunting him, and he is *ours* to deal with. Get him out of here." The order seemed to be aimed at both Bernardo and Diago.

But why? What the hell was going on? "Wait—"

Alessandro motioned for Francisco to intervene while he attempted to distract Guillermo. "He is a gift for Herr Abelló. He stays with me. Francisco, bring him with us."

Francisco gauged Bernardo's height and girth—any match between them would be even. Already jittery from the number of angel-born surrounding them, Francisco took one hesitant step forward, and then halted in the face of Bernardo's glare.

Guillermo didn't back down. "He's our prisoner."

Heines motioned to two young Nazis. "If that one moves"—he pointed at Francisco—"shoot him."

They lifted their guns and aimed them at Francisco. The huge nefil raised his hands in the air.

Shit, this is all going wrong. "Guillermo, please, a moment. Just one word and then I'll go."

Guillermo nodded at Bernardo. "Get him out of here now."

Diago jerked away from Bernardo and took two steps toward the stairs. "You've got to listen—"

Bernardo's hand landed on his shoulder again. This time when he spun Diago around, the huge nefil's fist caught the side of Diago's face.

A blast of white light burst across his vision and then he was falling. The next thing he knew, he was in the backseat of a car. He smelled his husband's aftershave.

From a distance, he heard Miquel's voice. "You don't know your own fucking strength, Bernardo."

From the front came a grumble that sounded similar to an apology. Then the car was moving. The last thing Diago remembered seeing was Guillermo, following Heines into the building.

By the time he woke, they were almost in Paris. Diago stared upward and out the window, where streetlamps had replaced the branches of trees. He felt Miquel's palm, warm on the side of his face.

"We've got to go back," he mumbled. "Strzyga is possessed by a daimon."

Miquel looked down at him. "And Guillermo is a king of the Inner Guard. He destroyed a Grigori—an angel—with the power of the Thrones. Do you think he's afraid of a daimon?"

"I know its name."

Miquel placed his thumb over Diago's lips. "Guillermo knows the daimons and their names. He can take care of himself."

"But—"

"Rafael left last night to clear the daimonic wards around the Theater of Dreams. He was supposed to check in with me this morning. He didn't call."

Diago struggled to sit up. He remembered walking with his son while Rafael told him about his dream:

Except in my nightmare, the snakes didn't tear into Moloch's body. In my nightmare, he brushed them aside and laughed at me. He grabbed my throat, and when I screamed, he turned into mist and rushed into my mouth and suddenly he was me.

Miquel was talking again, but Diago couldn't make sense of his words. The car was moving too fast and not fast enough and he felt sick, but there was nothing in his stomach. He rolled down the window and let the cold air clear his head.

The car was suddenly quiet. Miquel reached around Diago and cranked the window up. He spoke slowly and Diago held on to every word.

"Guillermo has ordered me to raid the Theater of Dreams. He believes we can take the Scorpion Court down based on the fact that Alessandro petitioned Jordi to give you the second death. Guillermo said that was proof you found something."

Diago's mind lurched into gear again. *So that's how Alessandro finally got his meeting with Jordi. And my father was just fine with the trade-off.* He didn't allow himself to dwell on his father's betrayal. "Guillermo's reasoning is too thin. I have the proof he needs." Then he proceeded to tell his husband everything he'd learned while he was with his family.

When he finished, Miquel tapped Bernardo's shoulder. "Step on it."

The streets flew by one by one. Once, he'd shunned the idea of patricide, but if a decision came between saving his father or saving his son, Diago didn't have to think twice which it would be. *But only if we're there in time.*

[29]

CHÂTEAU DE L'ENTREPRENANTE

FONTAINEBLEAU

Ysabel carefully added saline solution to the vial of morphine for Jordi's late morning dose. A knock at her door almost caused her to drop both the syringe and the medicine to the floor. *Shit.*

"Yes?" she called out cheerfully. "Who is it?"

"Stultz, fräulein."

Of course it's Stultz. Stultz knocking on doors, pulsing like a heart, lurking in the shadows, always following her. Stultz and Esser were her constant companions and only visitors. Of the two, she preferred Esser. Everything about Stultz gave her the willies; from his constant fawning to the way he always turned up unannounced at her door.

"Herr Abelló requires your presence in the conference room. Now, please."

Has Jordi figured out that I'm tinkering with his medication? She checked her watch. Or had her father arrived?

Heart beating faster, Ysa cleaned the syringe and capped it. No one had thought to search Jimenez's bag before giving it to Ysa, not even the formidable Sergeant Esser.

To her delight, she'd found a scalpel and a small pair of scissors. Ysa slipped the scalpel in one pocket and the scissors in another. She checked her image in the mirror to make sure that neither object bulged, and then hurried to the door.

Stultz's normal air of smug confidence had been knocked askew. He fidgeted and seemed disconcerted.

Something was definitely going on. "What's wrong?"

"Please follow me." He didn't wait but immediately set off toward the stairs.

Ysa hurried after him. In the entry hall, she noted Strzyga had arrived. He was agitated, pacing before the entrance and scowling. When he saw her, he froze. His gaze locked on her face before she turned her back on him and followed Stultz to the conference rooms.

She didn't see Diago. Had Jordi's nefilim already arrested him? She had no way to know and no time to find out. *I need to play the hand I'm dealt. Wherever he is, Diago can take care of himself until Jordi is under control.*

Stultz opened the door and snapped to attention. "Fräulein Ramírez."

Composing herself, she entered the chamber and found Jordi standing before the large table. A thin sheen of sweat covered his forehead. He patted it dry with a handkerchief. She didn't fail to notice the pistol on his hip. He was never without it.

She remembered how quickly he'd shot Jimenez. *Be ready for anything.*

"Uncle Jordi." She went to him. "Are you all right?"

"Your father has come. He is being searched and then Field Marshal Heines will bring him here."

Ysa knew better than to let her relief show on her face. *Jordi has to believe I'm on his side.* "You don't look well. Let me go back and get my bag."

"No time." He gripped her arm and pushed her onto the chair farthest from the door. "Sit."

The scalpel poked her hip. She bit her lip and hoped it didn't break the skin. A spot of blood on her uniform might give away the weapon's presence.

Jordi didn't take his seat. He stood behind her, his hand on her shoulder.

It felt heavy, that hand.

And possessive. She made no sign she noticed.

Another knock came to the door. Heines entered and saluted Jordi. "Herr Guillermo Ramírez, Capitán General, Los Nefilim."

While Jordi was distracted by Heines, she reached into her pocket and withdrew the scalpel, concealing it on her lap beneath her palm.

Her father entered the dining room alone. He wasn't armed.

The hand on Ysa's shoulder pressed harder, holding her in her seat. Had she made some attempt to rise? Possibly. It was an ingrained gesture. She always ran to her papá.

A quick glance at Jordi's free hand assured her that he still clutched his handkerchief. A spasm seemed to shudder through him.

The withdrawal. He's in pain. My dosage and timing . . .

The fact that it worked gave her some hope.

Her father's gaze snapped to the remnants of the bruises

on her face and then to Jordi. She couldn't read him. That frightened her. She was always able to read her father.

Guillermo stood at ease. "Jordi."

Jordi's fingers dug into her shoulder. "Guillermo. Please join us." He gestured to the chair at the far end of the table.

Guillermo ignored him. He looked at Ysabel. "Are you hurt?"

"No, Papá. I hope you are well and not having one of your bad days."

She glimpsed a flicker of his usual amusement in the turn of his lips before his expression closed again. "I took my medicine today. I'm fine."

Jordi spoke from behind her. "What kind of medication, Guillermo?"

He shrugged and batted the question aside. "Something my Juanita gives me. It helps me remember."

"Good. Good. Do you remember asking for my forgiveness for the sins of your firstborn life?"

"I do, I do. As a matter of fact, I asked your forgiveness right before I blew your fingers off. In that tunnel. In '39. I remember that." He tapped his temple with one finger and winked. "It's all still there."

"Papá, you're rambling."

Jordi's fingers tensed on her shoulder. "It's all right, Ysa. Let your papá talk." He turned his attention back to her father. "Didn't you admit you were wrong for how you treated me in our firstborn lives?"

"I think the discussion was more nuanced than that."

Jordi's grip tightened. "Nuanced in that you lied. You didn't mean it. And so now we stand as kings opposed."

"We can't." Guillermo inched closer. "Jordi, we must work together."

Jordi lowered his free hand closer to the flap of his holster. He didn't release the handkerchief.

Yet. Ysa tried to catch her father's eye. But he was focused entirely on his brother.

Guillermo halted and laid out his case. "The Scorpion Court is gathering in Paris, and we have reason to believe they are preparing to stage a daimonic uprising. Dissension within the Inner Guard has caused millions of innocents to die. We've fed the daimon-born nefilim until they have grown in power, and now they're ready to seize the mortal realms. We allowed this to happen."

"Are you blaming me?"

"We're all at fault! Don't you see? We've become like mortals, bickering over territorial lines and forcing our ideologies on those weaker than us."

Ysa wanted to cry. Her father was attempting to do what he did best, rally the nefilim around a common cause, but she could have warned him that Jordi was immune to this approach. She recalled his speech to her shortly after she arrived. *He believes we are gods.*

Jordi interrupted Guillermo with an abrupt gesture. "That is our purpose, Guillermo. We were born to rule the mortals. It's the weaker nefilim like you who are holding us back."

Her father's cheeks reddened with his anger. "No! We were created to protect the mortals from the daimonic realms. But all we've done is instigate wars that feed the very enemy we've been commanded to restrain."

Jordi's grip tightened on her shoulder with his rage.

"Gentlemen, please. Papá, calm down before you have one of your episodes." Her father's glare narrowed at her, but she didn't back down. These two would never come to an understanding of any kind. She flinched and tried to move away from Jordi's hand. "Uncle Jordi, you're going to break my collarbone."

He eased his hold on her but didn't let go.

She sighed with relief. "Neither of you are willing to budge an inch, and that's the problem."

Jordi's voice grew cold. "Be quiet, Ysa."

His tone quite clearly implied that the grown-ups were talking and she should be still. Rage darkened the edges of her vision.

Guillermo defended her. "She has a point, Jordi. Meet me halfway. Let's put down this uprising together—Die Nephilim and Los Nefilim side by side. We can set the example for the others. Together. As brothers."

The conference room door opened and Strzyga entered.

Stultz came huffing in behind the daimon-born nefil. "Apologies, Herr Abelló! He pushed right past me!"

Jordi snapped, "Find Heines and bring him here."

Stultz nodded and shot from the room.

Strzyga turned and closed the door, twisting the lock as he did.

Why is he locking the door? Ysa wondered. She glanced at her father. He focused on Strzyga's progress into the room.

"Excuse me, Herr Ramírez." The daimon-born nefil bowed to Guillermo. He acknowledged Ysa with a tilt of his head. "Fräulein." He reserved his deepest bow for Jordi.

"Herr Abelló, I was told to return another day, but I have waited far too long for this interview."

"Strzyga," Jordi acknowledged him after a glance toward Guillermo. "Did you bring Alvarez?"

"I did." Strzyga made an apologetic noise in the back of his throat. "But unfortunately, he was abducted by your brother's men."

Guillermo lifted his chin. "Alvarez is a traitor to my nefilim. He's mine to judge."

Jordi clicked his tongue. "I told you that snake would eventually bite."

Guillermo bowed his head to Jordi. "And you were right. I should have listened to you."

Ysa relaxed somewhat. *Papá is getting the hang of working him.*

Strzyga lifted his hands. "Alvarez is of no consequence right now. I have a proposal, Herr Abelló. One for your ears only."

Jordi didn't appear interested. "My brother says he has evidence of a daimonic uprising in Paris. You're a member of the Scorpion Court. What do you have to say about these allegations?"

"I say they are lies. The daimon-born are engaged in nothing more than a peaceful gathering. Please, Herr Abelló, an hour of your time, that is all I require."

Require for what? Ysa wondered.

Jordi kept a civil tone. "Not today, Herr Strzyga. It seems my brother has tried to entrap me into making false accusations against the Scorpion Court. That is a violation of his responsibilities as king."

Ysa glanced at her father. *Uh-oh.* She knew that look—
the tightening of his lips and the narrowing of his eyes.

He wasn't pretending. He was furious. "You'll believe a
daimon-born nefil over me? A king of the Inner Guard?"

To her surprise, Jordi laughed at him. "You're angry,
Guillermo, unbalanced. Your own daughter says so. How
can I be sure what you're saying is true and not part of some
delusion?"

Ysa barely kept her mouth from dropping open. She'd
only meant for Jordi to underestimate her father, not be
convinced Guillermo was completely unreliable. *I overplayed
it and he bought it.*

The question now was how to undo the damage so that
Jordi would believe her father.

As he had so often done when she was young, her father
saved her. "Check with Heines, Jordi. Because of my"—he
switched his glare to Ysa—"infirmities, I make sure to cor-
roborate my evidence with reliable sources."

Jordi didn't appear convinced. "I don't know what to believe when it comes to you, brother. You'll say whatever you
need to get what you want. You and Alvarez were meant for
each other—you're both liars."

Ysa stiffened at the insult.

Jordi's aura flamed around him. It was the same kind
of warning flare of power that he'd shown her in Sainte-
Geneviève.

So far, her father kept his own aura close to his body. But
she registered the dangerous glitter in his eyes and knew his
fuse grew shorter by the minute.

Meanwhile, she noticed Strzyga moving on the periphery

of her vision. The daimon-born nefil fed on their rage, uncertainty, and fear. He walked to the foot of the table and dragged darkness in his wake. A black shadow trailed from the hem of his jacket, like a tail. Something twitched from the corner of his lips—a second tongue . . . or a tentacle.

With a too-wide smile, Strzyga said, "I can't wait any longer, Abelló. An hour. No more."

Jordi's hand hovered over his pistol. "Get out, Strzyga. Come another day."

"No." The room's temperature noticeably decreased. A thin line of blood squirted from Strzyga's jawline. Another tentacle squirmed just beneath his flesh.

Her father's eyes widened. "Jordi—look! The evidence is in the room before us. That is no nefil. It's a daimon, and it's shedding its mortal form."

The panic in Guillermo's voice jettisoned Ysa from the chair. She no longer tried to hide the scalpel. This time, Jordi didn't stop her. *Fuck, fuck, fucker, it's* becoming *right in front of us.*

Jordi drew his pistol and fired three shots at Strzyga. In the midst of withdrawal or not, he was still an expert marksman. The bullets tore neatly through Strzyga's chest. The nefil staggered backward with each impact. He hit the wall and slid down to sit against the wainscoting. The tentacles emerging from Strzyga's wounds wriggled frantically.

"Let that be a lesson to you, Ysa. Kill the host before the daimon fully emerges and you can stop it from manifesting."

That is ridiculous. She'd never heard of such a tactic. A quick glance at her father's scowl told her he didn't buy the explanation, either.

More, the mass of thin organs showed no sign of dying. In fact, they seemed to be growing stronger. She turned to say so and saw that Jordi aimed his pistol at Guillermo.

"And now you, my brother."

Guillermo lifted his hands. "What the hell are you doing?"

"Eliminating a problem. Why do you think I allowed Strzyga to arrive here at the same time as you? So I would be able to rid myself of both a daimon-born nefil and my traitorous brother."

"Uncle Jordi, no." Ysa stepped forward but halted when she saw his finger tighten on the trigger. "Please. The Inner Guard will try you for murder."

"How can they, when it's so simple? Strzyga shot Guillermo, and then I killed Strzyga."

Christ, did he really believe she would go along with that? *Or does he intend to eliminate me, too?* She could barely find enough of her voice to whisper, "Jordi, no. Please."

Guillermo said softly, "So you kill me. Tell me, then, Jordi, how do you explain poisoning Jaeger?"

Jordi shook his head. "That is a lie Heines is spreading."

But it wasn't. Now she understood why Jordi was so upset that Jimenez had talked to Heines—not because of a lie. If anyone poisoned Queen Jaeger, it was Jimenez, and he did the deed on Jordi's orders. *And Jordi shot Jimenez, because two men can keep a secret when one is dead.*

Ysabel didn't let herself think. She charged her uncle. *Hit him low—at the waist.*

Jordi whirled, aiming the pistol at her, but he was too late. Her shoulder took him in the abdomen. The pistol fired, the shot loud and close, just over her head.

Jordi's back hit the wall. Remembering the scalpel, Ysa

slashed wildly. The thick wool of Jordi's uniform saved him from a deeper cut, but the blade sliced into his hip. Ysa gouged another furrow on his thigh.

Jordi cried out, more in shock than pain. He brought his fist down on her back.

The blow stunned her but she didn't let go. *The gun! Where's the gun?* Then she saw where it had hit the floor, less than a meter away.

Suddenly her father was there. He kicked the pistol out of Jordi's reach. With one huge hand, he grabbed Ysa's collar and yanked her free of Jordi's grip.

He shoved her backward, toward the door. "Go!"

Ysa's momentum carried her into a chair. She tripped, falling to the floor. Behind her, she heard the meaty thump of a fist striking flesh.

Outside the room, someone pounded on the door. *Heines? Is it Heines who keeps yelling?*

A muffled voice shouted, "It's locked! Get an ax! I want nefilim here now!"

The shutters slammed across the windows. The electric lights dimmed until the room was cloaked in shadows.

From her position, she glimpsed movement on the floor. Something thin wriggled like a snake. *No. Not a snake . . . a tentacle.* She looked back toward Strzyga's body. More of the limbs were bursting through his flesh, like a fungus blooming from a rotten flower. Jordi's bullets might have killed the host, but the daimon was alive and well. *And it's still becoming.* "Papá! The daimon!"

Guillermo whirled. "Oh shit."

Jordi saw the threat coming for them at the same time. His eyes went wide. "Ysa! The gun!"

Has he forgotten he is nefil? She scrambled to her feet and gave a shout. Using the scalpel, she sliced the red-gold vibrations of her song and formed a sigil shaped like an ax. She sent it against the tentacle, slicing the organ in half. Two more slivers of flesh emerged from the wound to create another set of slender arms. *Fuck.*

"Ysa! To me!" Her father got to his feet.

A thick black tentacle sped past Guillermo's foot and latched onto Jordi's leg. An acidic odor filled the room. His trousers smoked and melted against his flesh. Her uncle screamed.

The tentacle aimed its tip for the gash Ysa had gouged in his side. *But why?*

Guillermo formed a glyph for fire. It was obvious he couldn't strike the appendage wrapped around Jordi's leg without further injuring Jordi. He aimed the sigil to hit the tentacle halfway between him and Strzyga's body.

Sparks flew from the ward as it consumed the limb in a blaze. Strzyga's body jittered on the floor, as if an electrical current ran through him.

Jordi screamed. The tentacle released him. Whatever acid the daimon had released on his thigh continued to burn. Half-mad from the agony, Jordi pushed himself backward as if he might somehow escape his own leg.

Guillermo turned to his brother. "It's seeking a way into your body. It wants to possess you."

Ysa came to her uncle's side. "But how?"

"The tentacles. The daimon enters through a wound. Once inside Jordi's body, it'll wrap itself around his brain. Using his memories, it'll pass itself off as him, controlling his every thought, his every move." Guillermo knelt next to his brother so that Jordi was between them. Placing his palm over the knife wound with his right hand, her father called on the power of the Thrones. Coals of red-gold light smoldered from the stone in Guillermo's signet to seal the gash on Jordi's side and thigh.

Sweat fell into Jordi's eyes. "We're kings of the Inner Guard! We can kill it."

Guillermo agreed. "Kill it or send it back to the daimonic realm."

"Kill it." Jordi growled through gritted teeth.

Ysa barely heard them. Across the room, Strzyga's body continued to writhe on the floor. Black tendrils snaked from his mouth—first three, then four, then five, then too many to count—headless snakes that swayed hypnotically, seeking prey. Strzyga's jaw cracked with a sickening crunch.

Guillermo glanced at the horror show across the room. "We must sing together to destroy it. Jordi, use the power of your signet."

Jordi lifted his right hand. A glimmer of panic shadowed his eyes. The Thrones' tear in his ring didn't glow as Guillermo's did.

Ysa stared at it. *Something is wrong with the stone.*

Jordi's nostrils flared. His lips were white. "I'll join my song with yours when it's time!"

Guillermo formed a ward. "It's time!"

"Come on, Uncle Jordi, you can do this." She took his hand and touched the cold stone within the ring's setting. Jordi tried to pull free, but Ysa gripped his wrist and wouldn't let go. "What the hell is wrong?"

Jordi's fingers curled into a fist. "It's Jaeger! She was corrupt and damaged the stone. I have to work through her sabotage. Begin, Guillermo! I'll join you in a moment."

Before Guillermo could answer, a wet ripping noise drew their attention back to the daimon. The tentacles tore the last of Strzyga's flesh away from its triangular head. Jaws filled with multiple rows of needle-sharp teeth snapped at the air.

"Oh shit," Ysa breathed.

"Recognize him?" Guillermo pointed to the daimon's six red eyes. "See the brow ridges, how they angle upward?"

She gaped at her father. "I can't believe you're giving me a lesson on daimons right now."

"You have to know his name so you know which sigil banishes him."

The heavy head turned to face them and she instantly recognized him from her father's drawing in *Ars Goetia*. "Beleth." She whispered the daimon's name through numb lips.

A daimon of war. Beleth coupled with a mad scientist like Moloch, who exulted in the creation of weapons of mass destruction, meant the Scorpion Court would burn the mortal realm and everyone in it. *Including us.*

Ysa glared at Jordi. "Fucking Beleth, and you invited it here for your own selfish ends."

He didn't flinch from her accusation but met her glare boldly with one of his own. "I don't have to justify myself to you."

"Because you can't!" she screamed in his face.

The warning in her father's voice barely penetrated her rage and fear. "Ysa. Focus on the task at hand."

He was right. *As usual.* She'd take care of Jordi later. Right now, Beleth was their common enemy, and even though they outnumbered him, they didn't hold the advantage in this fight.

Beleth was a king himself, newly reborn after centuries of rest. She had only to gauge the lines of her father's face to know he hadn't slept. A tired nefil against a fully powered daimon.

In normal circumstances, it took two bearers of the Thrones' tears to engage a daimon such as Beleth—one to form the killing sigil and the other to distract the daimon with constant attacks.

"Papá?"

"You stay where you are." Guillermo bravely stood and faced the daimon alone. He spoke to his brother. "Jordi, even without the ring, you're still powerful. Lend us your voice." Guillermo gave them the opening note and established the song's key. He gestured for Jordi and Ysa to join their voices with his.

Ysa parted her lips and harmonized with him, adding the colors of her song to those of her father. After a moment's hesitation, Jordi joined them, but Ysa sensed he held back, in essence giving them sotto voce.

She couldn't decide if it was because he was ashamed and didn't want his brother to see the Grigori's essence, or if he truly wanted them all to burn. Nor did it matter. A partial effort was better than none.

At least for now.

Guillermo formed the first lines of his sigil, guiding the vibrations of sound with care. His brow furrowed and sweat trickled down his temples.

Across the room, Beleth finally succeeded in freeing itself of Strzyga's body. Wrapped in the nefil's viscera, the daimon stood on two legs. Four thick tentacles extended from its torso. Smaller limbs shot from its head.

Now Ysa knew what inspired the legends of Medusa. The image was so horrifying, she felt as if her body had turned to stone.

But her father's hands never wavered. His baritone remained consistent as he formed each curl of the ward's design.

Beleth struck without warning. A tentacle carried a band of darkness that sliced through Guillermo's ward, shattering it. A bruise spread across her father's face and he was thrown against the wall with enough force to crack the plaster.

Another of Beleth's limbs shot toward Jordi, scoring the floor with its acidic touch, while a third slithered toward Guillermo. The big nefil groaned and rolled to his knees.

But he's not moving fast enough.

Jordi yanked his hand free of Ysa's grip and frantically designed a protective ward. The light struck the gold of the signet's band as his hands moved.

But not the stone. The Thrones' tear remains dark. Without considering the ramifications of her actions, Ysa grabbed Jordi's wrist again, and this time she wrenched the ring from his finger.

"No!" Jordi screamed. He tried to rise, but his wounded leg wouldn't support him.

Ysa clasped the ring in her hand and stepped over him. His fingers snatched at the hem of her skirt, but she easily pulled free to position herself between the brothers. With her proud song, she created sigils of fire that flew upward between them and Beleth.

It was a distraction, one that wouldn't last, but she'd bought them a little time. The signet burned hot against her palm. She didn't put it on. To do so meant she accepted the responsibility to rule Die Nephilim.

And I'm destined for Los Nefilim. She had no desire to reign cold Germany. *Spain is my home.*

Beleth's tentacles scraped against her wards, extinguishing the flames with claws of darkness. Icy fingers raked her flesh and left behind welts of frostbite on her forearms.

Her wards were failing beneath the daimon's onslaught.

"Papá?" She risked a glance over her shoulder.

Her father groaned. He'd gotten one foot under himself. He pressed his palm against the wall. Plaster crumbled beneath his fingers and his hand slipped. He crashed back to his knees.

To her right, Jordi crawled toward her, his tormented gaze locked on her fist. If he reached her and she was forced to struggle for the signet, Beleth would kill them all.

"I'm so sorry, Papá," she whispered. She jammed the signet onto her finger.

A bolt of agony rushed up her arm. The metal chewed into her skin as if the band had teeth. Tendrils of light burst into the gashes and left electric tremors coursing through her veins. The hair on her body rose in response to the shocks. Ethereal chords exploded in her mind. She felt her body rising as if carried upward on the current of the song. Her toes left the floor.

The music poured straight into her soul. *The Thrones.* They examined her, probed her aura with the vibrations of their strange voices . . . and she saw the firmaments spread before her in a brilliant display of color and sound . . . a river of fire . . . boundless space flowing into . . . time without end . . . infinity rising, engulfing her existence . . . *and I am nothing but a speck of dust in this wide expanse* . . .

Terrified by the visions bursting through her brain, she realized she'd made a mistake. A horrible mistake. She tried to remove the ring but found she couldn't. The signet had become one with her flesh.

Then why was I able to take it from Jordi so easily? She twisted it again, but short of cutting off her finger, she couldn't remove the ring. And then she realized the answer to her own question.

She was able to take the ring from Jordi because he wasn't a true king of the Inner Guard. *The remnants of the Grigori's song.* She'd seen it wrapped around her uncle's heart. The Thrones had searched Jordi's song and found him corrupt.

Jordi might have worn the signet, but he would never command the angels' fire in this incarnation. Like Miquel's wedding band, Jaeger's ring was nothing but a trophy.

As if this revelation was what the Thrones needed to hear, their voices diminished to murmurs. On her finger, the tear embedded in the signet's setting flared to life.

A sudden rush of power surged up through her arms and into her brain. The welts on her arms healed. Her feet settled back to the floor.

This is the feeling Jordi strives to re-create through the drugs. But no narcotic could ever come close to replicating the sensation she experienced. As the room gradually swam back into focus, she now understood why her uncle so desperately craved the signet.

Her wall of fire flickered and died. In the shadows, she made out the figure of Beleth. The daimon king had crawled into the opposite corner, shielding his multiple eyes from the rays of light snapping around Ysa's body.

And somehow the daimon-born discovered Jordi's weakness. That explained Beleth's dangerous gamble to possess an angel-born nefil. He'd known Jordi wouldn't be able to defend himself from a daimonic attack. *But he hadn't counted on us being here, too.*

The sounds within the mortal realm flowed back around her. The crackle of dying glyphs rushed along the baseboards. The pounding on the door had taken the rhythmic measure of an ax's blows. The chant of several nefilim seeped through splinters as they tried to break into the conference room.

Ysa listened for members of Los Nefilim, but instead she heard Stultz, Esser, and Heines . . . *and others, so many others* . . . but none were the voices most dear to her heart.

Jordi had abandoned his attempt to accost her. Shifting his course, he crawled toward the pistol.

A hand landed on her shoulder. She whirled. Her father stood beside her. The bruise on the side of his face pulsed in spectacular shades of black and blue and yellow. He'd smeared a line of blood beneath his nose to his cheek.

Yet in spite of his injuries, his voice thundered through the room. ". . . with me! I need you with me, Ysa!"

She blinked at him. "Here! I'm here!"

Beleth likewise came to himself. With no obstacles between him and his prey, he shot another tentacle at Jordi's ankle.

Jordi stretched his arm. His fingertips brushed the pistol's grip. Then the daimon's organ wrapped around his shin, yanking him backward and away from the gun.

Jordi shrieked and grabbed the table's leg, holding on while the daimon's acid ate down to the bone.

Ysabel started when her father grabbed her wrist. His hoarse whisper was barely audible beneath Jordi's howls. "The strongest nefil leads the attack. I'll distract Beleth. You create the banishing sigil. Send him back to the daimonic realm."

And then he was gone, moving quickly to get between Jordi and Beleth.

The banishing sigil . . . Jordi had wanted Beleth dead. Guillermo rarely killed unless it was a necessary act.

Facing Beleth, she swallowed hard and focused her mind. *I can do this.* Her father had schooled her until she could form the glyphs in her sleep. She sang a note and the fire that accompanied her song blazed in the dim room.

As she drew her finger through the vibrations, she noticed other colors moving through the threads of her song. *It's the auras of the members of Die Nephilim.*

Because they chanted in the nearby hallway, their voices flowed into the Thrones' tear and became entwined with hers. It was as if she'd become an amplifier for their magic. The icy blue threads of Heines's aura blended with Esser's deeper azure and augmented Stultz's cerulean tones. Ysa melded them into one band of clear cobalt light and interspersed the notes throughout her banishing sigil.

She drew the lines together, concentrating on her task.

From the corner of her eye, she saw her father shape a spear of light from the dying bulbs overhead. He hefted the shaft and used it to sever the tentacle wrapped around Jordi's ankle.

Jordi drew his injured leg away from the daimon's organ. His foot hung at a strange angle. All that held it to his leg were white bits of bone and the few remaining tendons. Her uncle sobbed from the pain.

She shut the sound out of her mind.

Beleth sent a blast of frigid air at Guillermo, knocking him backward again. But it was a glancing blow. This time, her father rolled to his feet and twirled the spear, throwing it at Beleth's head.

The daimon ducked and the spear shattered the window behind him, forcing the shutters open. Daylight flooded the room as Ysa finished the last line of her sigil.

"To my song!" she cried loud enough for the nefilim in the hall to hear. The stone on her signet flared with blinding light.

From across the room, her father joined her. The beams within his signet reached out to hers.

They channeled their light into the glyph. The ward burst across the room and engulfed Beleth. The daimon roared. Its tentacles formed a glyph of its own. Beleth brought the full weight of its force against them.

The blow sent her reeling, but she quickly caught her balance and began again. Beleth fought his bonds as Ysa and Guillermo created the next ward together. This time, Guillermo sent the glyph forward with his baritone.

The sigil struck the daimon. Beleth's body disappeared and then reappeared. Bands of light rippled across its flesh.

It looks like a bulb shorting out. But the daimon wasn't gone. Not yet.

Ysa created a third sigil, and this time her father allowed her to lead. Shoving the glyph with all her might, she channeled every ounce of her newfound power into the ward. The glyph struck Beleth and the daimon finally disappeared.

The silence was so sudden, Ysabel thought she'd gone deaf. She looked down. The stone in her signet glowed softly.

"Well." A shaky smile touched her father's mouth as he retrieved Jordi's pistol. "You got the hang of it."

She made a noise somewhere between a laugh and a sob.

The door burst open and Heines stumbled in. He surveyed the damage and then his eye fell on Ysa. "What the hell?"

She wasn't sure if he wanted her to explain Jordi's condition, or the destruction of the room and its furniture, or the daimonic body parts littering the floor, or the ring on her finger.

Her father went to Jordi's side, shielding his body from the curious nefilim crowding behind Heines.

Jordi twisted and tried to see around Guillermo. "Heines! They attacked me! Arrest them!"

Heines didn't acknowledge Jordi's cries. His gaze swept to Ysa's hand, where the Thrones' tear still pulsed, and then up to her face.

Ysa moved toward her uncle and father. "Herr Abelló is injured. We need a stretcher."

Heines didn't immediately move.

"Now, please."

He turned and passed the order along to someone behind him, but he didn't leave.

And maybe having a witness is a good idea. She went to Jordi's side.

The hate in her uncle's eyes prevented her from reaching out to him. "You little bitch. This was your plan all along. Wasn't it?"

"No," she said with pity.

Her father knelt beside his brother. "Could you give us

a minute, Ysa? Don't leave . . . just . . ." He nodded toward Heines, and she got the message loud and clear. Joining Heines at the door, she shooed the other onlookers away. "Everything is under control. Go back to your posts."

She almost didn't recognize Violeta, because of the Nazi uniform she wore. Her friend pushed to the front and glanced at the signet on her hand. "Ysa?"

Ysa took Violeta's hand and squeezed her fingers, all the while avoiding the betrayal in her friend's eyes. *I didn't want to be queen . . . not like this.* But it was all too much to explain, and other members of Die Nephilim clustered together, whispering among themselves while giving Ysa furtive glances.

"My Musketeer," Ysa murmured. "Please trust me. I'll explain later." Then, without waiting for an answer, she returned to the conference room.

Heines remained at the door while Ysa edged deeper into the room. Positioning herself so she could see both her father and her uncle, she waited by the wall.

Guillermo held his brother. "You don't have to die alone this time, Jordi. I'll stay with you."

"What are you talking about?" He indicated his injured foot. "The surgeons can fix me. I'm not dying."

"Then you'll go on trial. The Inner Guard will convict you of Jaeger's murder, and when they do, they'll see the remains of the Grigori's song in your aura. You know our laws as well as I do. At that point, the judges will recommend the second death. You are my brother. I can forgive you, because I understand what you're going through. They will not."

From where she stood, Ysa watched Jordi's face as the truth of her father's words penetrated his rage and the twin fogs of pain and the withdrawal. He swallowed hard and stared at the ceiling. For several minutes, he said nothing. Guillermo gave him all the time he needed.

Jordi shifted his weight. "So. You win." His tongue moved in his mouth. "This time." He bit down.

Ysa heard something crunch between his teeth. His body spasmed. She hurried forward and tried to pry Jordi's teeth apart, but the bitter smell of almonds wafted from between his lips. A seizure rattled his body, and then his breathing stopped.

"Cyanide," she murmured.

Guillermo didn't answer. He gently rocked his brother as he died.

[30]

THE THEATER OF DREAMS

Rafael awoke on a bed. His arm had fallen asleep; the nerves sent a painful buzzing sensation into his hand. In an attempt to stretch, he found he could barely move.

What the hell? His hands were cuffed behind his back, and his ankles were lashed together. He groaned, his voice muffled behind a gag.

In gradual stages, the night's events came back to him: he'd sabotaged ward after ward of dark sounds until he reached the theater's basement door. That was where he'd been caught. The last thing he remembered was seeing Alvaro's face.

The memory was like waking from a nightmare. His heart suddenly punched his chest, his limbs were paralyzed with fear.

Easy, easy, no one is hurting me now. Figure out what is going on. His adrenaline slowed and he took stock of his physical condition. He was exhausted. Whatever spell

Alvaro had used left him unrested and on edge. His head ached, and he felt a bruise on the side of his face, but that could have happened when Alvaro's ward hit him.

Calming, he turned his head to the right and found himself staring at a nondescript wall. A cheap nightstand was beside the bed.

It's the hotel. Alvaro must have brought him here.

Fine.

Not that it was. He wondered how long he'd been out.

Long enough for someone to search him. His gun was gone, but he realized no one had taken his signet ring, or the jewelry box from his breast pocket. He didn't question why the daimon-born avoided touching the signet. The angel's tear would be worthless to most of them, painful to others.

Likewise, they probably deemed the etching as worthless, and that was okay. Having his mother's image close to his heart gave him a bit more courage.

He wondered if his father was somewhere nearby. Monique said they hadn't seen Diago leave the hotel, but that was last night. *Surely if he knew I was here, he'd come. Or has something happened to him, too?* Rafael didn't want to think that thought. *He's okay. He's got to be okay.*

Twisting on the naked mattress, he saw he wasn't alone. A skeleton sat on a chair beside the door.

Don't be an idiot. He closed his eyes and opened them again.

The man wore a striped uniform with a pink triangular badge on the chest. Like Miquel, Rafael knew the colored badges and what they represented. *He's a camp inmate. Homosexual. Is that where they're taking me? To a camp?*

He heard Miquel's voice inside his head: *Keep your eye on the task—mortal or nefil?*

The man was nefil and angel-born. It was his eyes that finally gave away his identity. *Nico.*

Stunned to see the other nefil here, Rafael grunted to let Nico know he was awake. *Come on, Nico, find the key to these cuffs.*

Then Rafael saw the pistol in the other nefil's hand. *My gun.* He couldn't tell if the magazine was the same, but he saw no reason why they would have checked the rounds. If they hadn't, then the silver-tipped bullets would still be loaded.

And I'm not immune to the pain those rounds can produce. Rafael lifted his wrists, hoping Nico would get the implication. *Unlock the cuffs.*

The Italian bit his lower lip and shook his head. Unbuttoning his shirt, he showed Rafael the scorpion buried beneath his skin. A tear slid down his cheek.

Oh, Nico, no. Rafael nodded to signify he understood. *If he's been told to guard me, then that is what he must do.*

Someone walked down the hall, the shadow of their footsteps darkening the threshold of Rafael's room before moving on. Silence descended over the floor again. A few more minutes passed.

Rafael looked for a clock, anything to tell him what time of day it was. He wondered if Miquel had been successful in persuading Heines to join Los Nefilim's move against the daimon-born. They could be on their way right now. He wanted so desperately to hope they would stage an eleventh-hour rescue.

Nico shifted his position on the chair. Three seconds later, he rocked his torso gently, tapping one foot against the floor.

Rafael was trying to figure out how to ask him what was wrong when Nico grimaced. A sheen of sweat burst across his forehead. He bent forward; his mouth opened in a perfect O. The blood drained from his face.

Nico? Rafael chewed the rag and wished he could spit it out. He wanted to tell his comrade to follow the daimon-born's command. Helpless, he could only watch in horror as the other nefil dry-heaved for almost a full minute.

With one hand against his throat, Nico placed the pistol on the floor. Rafael shook his head, hoping Nico would see and understand. *Please don't die for me . . . not like this.*

A dribble of black blood oozed from the corner of Nico's mouth. He wiped it with the back of his hand. "What is happening—"

The question ended abruptly. He coughed and immediately cupped his hand under his chin. Rushing into the small bathroom, he spat a mouthful of blood into the toilet. His entire body spasmed and he went to his knees.

Rafael tasted the other nefil's terror and pain, a rancid flavor that coated his tongue. Unlike his father, Rafael's angelic qualities were stronger. Though he was aware of Nico's overpowering emotions, he easily brushed aside any desire to feed on his pain. Craning his neck, he simply wished he could offer the other nefil some word of comfort.

In the lavatory, a convulsion rippled through Nico's body. Black blood poured from his mouth and nose.

Nico couldn't possibly lose that much blood and still be breathing. *What, then?*

The nefil raised his head just enough for Rafael to glimpse

the shadow of a sigil in the dark mass pouring from his mouth. *It's not blood, but a song! The scorpion . . . it's dying!*

Another minute passed and the gray shadow of a scorpion finally slithered through Nico's lips. The dead arachnid fell into the porcelain bowl. Nico wiped his mouth with one shaking hand and immediately pulled the chain to flush the toilet.

For a long time, he knelt, his head resting on the seat. Had it not been for the rise and fall of his chest, Rafael would have thought him dead. Unable to take the silence any longer, Rafael made a questioning sound in the back of his throat.

Nico lifted his head. "I'm okay," he croaked. "I think."

He used the sink to pull himself up. Then he unbuttoned his shirt and touched his chest, staring at his image. "It's gone," he whispered.

Rafael made another questioning sound.

Nico seemed to come back to himself. He hurried to Rafael's side and loosened the gag. "What is this?" He pointed to his chest. "What does it mean?"

"The daimon-born nefil that sang the spell is dead. You're free."

Nico stared at him in obvious shock, as if he dared not believe. "But Strzyga wasn't just a nefil. He was possessed by an actual daimon."

"Who?"

"Alessandro Strzyga. I didn't find out his true name—"

"No, which daim—"

But Nico talked right over Rafael's interruption. "—until after we arrived in Paris. You probably know him as Herr Teufel. He was like Moloch and Alvaro. Strzyga was possessed by the daimon Beleth."

Beleth? The daimon of war? "I doubt anyone killed Beleth, but his host, Strzyga, is definitely dead. Where are they?"

"Strzyga and your father went to l'Entreprenante. When they left, Alvaro had the others bring me here to guard you."

Damn it. He'd hoped his papá was somewhere close. At least now he knew not to expect a last-minute rescue. "Strzyga willingly went to face a king of the Inner Guard?"

"Yes. He says Jordi is weak. That he isn't a true king of the Inner Guard. Beleth was supposed to take over Jordi's body."

Rafael glanced at Nico's chest. "I'd say Beleth and Strzyga miscalculated." *Or Don Guillermo arrived in time to handle the situation.* He hoped it was the latter. "Can you unlock me now?"

Nico's gaze grew distant. "I should feel something . . . shouldn't I? Relief, maybe? I'm just numb."

A common reaction for some survivors. Unfortunately, Rafael didn't have time to empathize. "We're going to be dead if we don't get out of here. Can you unlock the cuffs?"

Nico snapped back to himself. "If I do, we'll never make it to the first floor. All the exits are heavily guarded." He reached into his pocket and withdrew a key. Leaning over Rafael's body, he pressed it against his palm. "The daimon-born are preparing for a great ceremony. I think most of them have gone downstairs. Alvaro is naming his high priest as soon as Strzyga returns and he wants you in the theater with the rest of the court."

"Of course he does. He has always wanted to make me part of the Scorpion Court." Rafael curled his fingers around the key. "At least Strzyga isn't coming back. That's one less elder to deal with." *Thank the Thrones for that small favor.* "How long have I been out?"

"A few hours. I'm not sure how much longer they'll wait. I heard one nefil remark in passing that Alvaro is becoming agitated and intends to proceed without Strzyga."

"How are we going to get out of here?"

"We'll play along. I'll loosen the gag and retie it. Keep it in your mouth. We'll let them get us as far as the main lobby. Then I'll provide a distraction, and you run for it. Find more nefilim and return if you can."

Rafael scrutinized the other nefil. Nico didn't appear to be fit enough to fight his way out of a roomful of mortals, much less the daimon-born. "I'm not leaving you."

From down the hall, they heard the elevator's gears hum and then halt.

Nico whispered, "I won't just slow you down, I'll get us both killed. You run. Desperation will lend me the strength to do what I need to do." He retied the gag before Rafael could protest again.

Nico buttoned his shirt, and then resumed his seat. He retrieved the gun and pointed it at Rafael.

Someone else walked down the hall . . . no, two or three people together. Rafael's heart kicked up a notch as the doorknob turned.

Edur entered the room with two other nefilim in tow. They were all dressed in new suits, their hair immaculately styled and oiled. A pair of ruby cuff links glittered on Edur's sleeves, and Rafael recalled the stud pulled from Carlos's throat.

Most nefilim had a signature, not just the one in their

songs. When they killed, they left a memento, some trinket most associated with them and known only to other nefilim.

Edur noticed the direction of Rafael's gaze. He flicked an imaginary piece of lint from his sleeve. "Alvaro's ceremony will begin soon. It's going to be a grand affair. Pity you won't be attired for the occasion."

He spoke to the other two nefilim. "Untie his legs. I'll be damned if we're carrying him as if he's already the high priest."

The resentment in Edur's statement went like a nail through Rafael. *Me? Is that who Moloch has chosen to be his next vessel?*

His heart stammered at the thought. On the heels of that came another: *Christina is ambitious. She wants to be high priestess, and Edur is her hand.*

Rafael quickly realized that Edur intended to send him into his next incarnation before they reached the theater. Whatever he planned would have to look like an accident; otherwise, he'd incur Moloch's wrath and destroy Christina's chances of becoming high priestess.

Rafael wasn't sure whether he should be relieved or frightened. Death saved him from his grandfather but also meant his father's grief.

Not that he was ready to give up. Nico's plan was their best move. *Wait and see what Edur does.*

Christina's lover seemed to finally register Nico's presence. "You follow us. If he tries to escape, shoot him."

Nico winced, the pantomime of pain not quite reaching his eyes. His hand fluttered at his side as if he might lift it to his chest, where the scorpion had been burrowed beneath his flesh. He muttered a reluctant acknowledgment of the order through gritted teeth. "Yes, sir."

One of the nefilim untied Rafael's legs. The other dragged him to his feet.

Rafael didn't have to pretend to be wobbly. The circulation returned to his legs with a vengeance. His feet felt like sponges.

Edur grabbed his arm and dragged him into the hall. He motioned to a door near the elevator. "You two take the stairs."

One of the nefilim was smart enough to question the plan. "Why us? Make the queer take the stairs."

Edur formed a quick sigil. The spark flashed from his fingertips. He snapped it at the nefil. A hole in the shape of a scorpion appeared in the wall beside the man's head.

The nefil flinched a second too late and then seemed to realize that Edur had simply fired a warning glyph. Closing his mouth, he hustled his companion toward the stairs.

Edur took Rafael's arm again. He motioned at the elevator. "You first," he said to Nico.

The angel-born nefil opened the gate and got inside. Edur shoved Rafael in next. Then he entered and selected the lobby. While they were between floors, Edur pulled the emergency crank.

The elevator's gears grinded to a halt. Rafael used the noise as cover to spring the lock on the cuffs. He kept his hands behind his back and gripped the metal bracelets in his fist. They were heavy enough to make a decent weapon.

The daimon-born nefil didn't turn. "Shoot him," he commanded.

"What?" Nico's confusion was real.

"Shoot him in the back of his head. He's trying to escape."

Rafael ducked his chin and spit out the gag. "I expected a more elaborate plan from you."

As the other nefil turned to gape at him, Rafael punched him. The cuffs worked like brass knuckles and pushed more weight behind the blow. Edur went down. Rafael knelt over him and gave him two more quick jabs to the temple.

Nico stared at the blood pooling beneath Edur's head. "Did you kill him?

"I don't know." *And right now, I don't care.* His regret was always a delayed reaction. He put it down to the adrenaline pumping through his body.

All Rafael knew for certain was their chances of escape had marginally improved. They might be able to make a run for it, depending on how many people were in the lobby. Another glance at Nico's emaciated form told Rafael his comrade wouldn't make it far.

An idea suddenly formed. The angel-born might still be coming to raid the theater. *And if they do, they need to know I failed to clear the wards from the door.* He turned to Nico. "Listen carefully, go to the Backstage Café. Order black coffee and a roll. They'll know what it means. It's imperative they get the message. They'll be able to hide you."

"What about you?"

"I'll draw the more dangerous nefilim after me. I'm fast, and I know the city. I can lose them. Ready?"

Nico's lips were tight with fear. "As ready as I'll ever be."

"Desperation," Rafael whispered and winked.

Nico rewarded him with the shadow of a smile.

Turning back to the emergency crank, Rafael released it.

As the car began to descend again, he formed a concussive sigil. The ward seemed too thin at the center.

"You're tired," Nico murmured.

"We've got surprise on our side. When the door opens, I'm hitting whoever is standing there with this glyph. Be ready to run."

Nico stepped beside him. "On your mark."

Feeling somewhat in control again, Rafael watched the dial as it indicated the floors. Two . . . one . . .

The car stopped. He threw open the gate. The two nefilim who'd been forced to take the stairs were waiting for them.

One of the men stared at Edur's inert form even as the other one snarled at Nico, "What the fuck took you so long?"

Rafael stamped his foot and sang out, charging his sigil with his voice. The men barely had to time to register that their captive was free before the ward hit them. They were thrown backward and slammed against the far wall. One nefil groaned and tried to rise, groping at his jacket, probably for a gun. The other man lay still, blood trickling from his nose and ears.

Rafael quickly assessed the area. The only other nefil was the woman at the registration desk. *The others must already be in the theater.*

The woman wasted no time. She ducked beneath the counter before returning with a tommy gun in her hands. "Don't move!"

Nico stepped around Rafael and shot her in the chest. As she fell backward, she loosed a spray of bullets across the ceiling.

The nefil by the wall tugged his pistol free. Nico wasted no time putting a bullet in him, too.

That will bring them running. Rafael shoved Nico toward the street doors. "Go!"

A second elevator descended next to theirs. Four pairs of feet were already visible through the gate.

From the other car, a voice shouted, "What the hell is going on down there?"

Rafael recognized his grandfather's voice. He froze, his heart slamming against his chest.

The people in the elevator shuffled as Alvaro's bodyguards moved to stand in front of him. An authoritative voice led the nefilim in the creation of a ward.

Rafael didn't wait around to see what form that sigil might take. He jogged after Nico, who was already at the glass doors. The Italian paused.

"Go!" Rafael picked up speed.

Nico turned left and ran. Frightened mortals scattered around him. Whether they were alarmed by his gun or his prison uniform, Rafael neither knew nor cared. Nico didn't have far to go.

"Rafael?" Alvaro's voice rolled through the lobby like thunder. "Is that you?"

Rafael didn't answer. He hit the door at a run, shoving it open with his shoulder. *Don't look back, don't look back, Papá always says don't look back.*

The mortals on the street hurried out of his way. They inadvertently cleared a path for his escape.

As he turned right, he glimpsed his grandfather's rage manifest as a vindictive glyph. The concussive mass roiled across the lobby in the form of green sounds so dark they appeared to be black.

Rafael stumbled and then got his feet under him, sprinting away from the entrance. Behind him, the glass doors shattered, bursting outward in a thousand daggers of crystalline light. He instinctively ducked even though he was no longer in danger of being hit.

Several mortals weren't so lucky. Screams and moans of pain suddenly filled the street.

At the next block, the curious began to gather. Rafael burst through a cluster of people and turned left. The only thought in his mind was to get to the metro. *I can lose them in the tunnels.*

He went one block and executed a hard right into an alley. The click of claws against the pavement caused him to turn. A black wave of scorpions flowed over the bricks.

With a cry of horror, Rafael increased his speed. *Don't look back!* he chastised himself. But at the same time, he was glad he did—he couldn't lead that pestilence onto a metro platform filled with mortals. Those who didn't die from the sight of his grandfather's song would be driven insane.

Saint-Martin. The station was empty and he could access it from the street. *From there I can get into the other tunnels without risking the mortals' lives.*

Rafael got his bearings and aimed himself for the maintenance entrance Louis had used last night. He ran so fast, he almost passed the metal door. Skidding in the alley's refuse, he grabbed the latch and swung it open, launching himself down the stairs.

At the deserted platform, three lights still functioned, but the station remained shrouded in gloom. The door to the empty ticket box stood open. Monique's rolling chair was parked beside it.

Rafael was on the fourth stair from the platform when

something hard struck his ankles. It was Alvaro's walking stick.

He lost his footing and crashed to the concrete floor. The jewelry box burst from his pocket and slewed against the wheel of the chair. The lid popped open. Crawling on his hands and knees, Rafael snatched the velvet that wrapped the glass shard of his mother's etching.

Clenching it in his fist, he got his feet under him and stumbled toward the platform's edge. He wasn't moving fast enough.

A cyclone of scorpions surged past him. The arachnids flowed upward to build a wall between him and the tracks, cutting off his escape.

Fine. This is fucking fine. If he wants a fight, I'll give him one. Doubled over by the stitch in his side, Rafael gasped and backed away from the grille that led to the stairs. He needed his wind in order to sing, but his throat was tight with fear. *Relax, relax, try and relax.*

Alvaro descended to the platform and retrieved his cane. His black jackboots were polished to a high sheen. He wore an officer's uniform with a pistol and a knife at his belt. Golden epaulets adorned his shoulders and the Scorpion Court's device—Moloch's sigil nestled within a double circle—rested on his breast. He removed the dark glasses he wore among the mortals and tucked them into a pocket. His eyes shone whitely in the station's gloom.

"There you are, my pretty child." Alvaro's mellifluous tones echoed against the tiles.

Miquel had taught Rafael to watch the daimon-born for tricks. *They use a verbal sleight of hand and deflect with words . . . listen for their tone of voice. That's your clue.*

The scorpions composing the wall buzzed like a high-tension wire. Alvaro soothed them with a motion of his hand.

The gesture came a moment too late. *Alvaro is nervous.*

That knowledge changed the dynamics of their encounter. The pain in Rafael's side began to ease. He straightened. *Focus. Whole mind. Whole heart.*

Alvaro stopped beside Monique's chair. "This is, perhaps, good that we meet together in private before the ceremony. I would much prefer that you accept your new vocation willingly."

"What vocation?" Rafael clutched the velvet so tightly, the glass shard wrapped within punctured his palm and drew a pearl of blood. He loosened his grip. "To be your high priest?"

"It's what you were bred for. I negotiated with the angels for an infant—one whose aura contained their ethereal tones. Your father's line ties you to my court. When Moloch joins his soul with yours, you will be a god, Rafael."

"I don't want to be a god. I want my family."

"We—the Scorpion Court—*are* your family. Your real family, Rafael. Even Diago has seen the error of his ways. Los Nefilim turned on him, just as I knew they would. He has rejoined the court, my dear child. He is here, with us. Nothing would make him happier than to have his son at his side."

The wall of scorpions rattled, a swirling mass of bodies rasping over one another. Alvaro lifted a finger and they quieted.

He's lying. Rafael decided to call him on it. "Then why didn't he ask me to come with him? Why did he leave me with Los Nefilim if he's so happy to have me at his side?"

Alvaro brushed the concern aside. "Your father always looks after himself first. He's been selfish like that since his firstborn incarnation."

The rationale made no sense. *He can't describe how one person cares for another, because he doesn't understand love.*

Behind Alvaro, a shadow moved at the top of the stairs. His grandfather's goons had obviously followed him.

Then I've got nothing to lose. "You're lying." He glared defiantly at his grandfather. "My papá loves me, and he has always put my welfare first. You don't know what love is."

His attitude piqued Alvaro's anger. The scorpion wall whirred with the intensity of a band saw.

Alvaro made no effort to quiet the arachnids. He eased forward, closing the distance between them.

A nasty edge seeped into his voice. "Your papá is incapable of loving anyone but himself. I know, because I worked to stamp the emotion from his soul. I personally saw to his upbringing. Everything that happened to him—from his birth to his Gloaming to his placement within the court—happened with my approval."

The figure at the top of the stairs descended to the platform. Rafael's eyes widened. It was his father. "Papá?" A spark of hope ignited in his chest.

"That explains why you didn't speak for me, Alvaro. When Alessandro called me an abomination and demanded the court give me the second death, that was all part of your master plan, too. Is that so?"

Alvaro positioned himself so he could see both son and grandson. "You misunderstand."

"No, no . . . it's all crystal clear now. You wanted to punish me for the infractions of my firstborn life. So you groomed me to love you, and then you cast me aside, know-ing it would break me. You turned me over to . . ."

Rafael waited, but his father didn't complete the sentence. He seemed to choke on his words. *He's trying not to cry.*

Diago snapped his fingers and quickly regained control of his voice. "And then you sent me to l'Entreprenante with Alessandro, knowing he petitioned Jordi to give me the sec-ond death. No. I understand everything, *Father*."

With a shout, Diago directed his rage to become a rush of green fire that enveloped the scorpion wall. The scorched arachnids burst, their bodies popping and sizzling as they died. The flames receded; Alvaro's wall was gone.

Diago indicated the tunnel. "Go, Rafael, run. I'll find you."

Rafael kicked the debris out of his way. "I'm not leaving you. You never left me. I'm not leaving you." At his father's severe look, Rafael shook his head. "I'm not."

Alvaro placed his palm over his heart. "This is so touching."

"Oh fuck off," Rafael muttered.

Diago's glare should have reduced Alvaro to a pile of ash. "So what now, Alvaro? What is the next step in your master plan?"

Undisturbed by Diago's anger, Alvaro smiled. "My grand-son is going to become my high priest, and my son is going to pay for his crimes against the Scorpion Court." He sang a high note and formed a glyph as he drew his knife.

Without warning, he flung himself at Rafael.

Rafael ducked and spun. As he did, he felt something scrape the back of his hand; whether it was the ward or Al-varo's knife, he didn't know. He just kept moving and ran past Alvaro to reach Diago's side.

His father took Rafael's wrist and examined the back of his hand. "It's just a cut."

Alvaro shouted and flung a ward over their heads. Before either of them could respond, the gate slammed shut, cutting off their exit to the street.

Turning his open palm downward, Alvaro smiled. Scorpions flowed from his hand to the floor. Millions of the arachnids scuttled across the platform.

With the knife, Alvaro pointed to the cut on Rafael's hand and then to the scrapes on Diago's cheek. "If one gets in, it'll wrap around your hearts."

Hearts. Alvaro meant to enslave them both. "Papá?"

Diago formed a protective ward and charged it with his voice. Rafael moved in tandem with his father, designing a glyph of his own. They joined their shields to establish a single barrier of crackling energy between them and Alvaro.

With a snarl, Diago growled, "Send them."

It was a challenge. It was a command.

To Rafael, he murmured, "Hold the shield."

Rafael didn't answer. He didn't need to, because his father trusted him. This wasn't the first time they'd fought side by side. He concentrated on the shimmering wards.

Unbothered by their defenses, Alvaro shouted a command of his own. The scorpions surged forward.

Beside Rafael, his father sang a different song—this one an attack. He lifted his hands. Viridian fire shimmered over the first wave of arachnids, leaving them to smolder and die. The survivors climbed the backs of the dead.

Rafael held their shield and watched the coming tsunami. Sweat trickled across his scalp.

The first scorpions touched the edge of the shield. They crackled as they died.

Rafael caught movement near the tracks. Another wave of scorpions rushed over the platform to attack their exposed flank.

"Shit!" Rafael whirled and hastily erected another ward. Three lines within the glyph glimmered weakly. The scorpions clambered into the cracks, forcing the threads of light apart with their claws. "It's not going to hold."

A single scorpion broke through. With a curse, Rafael crushed it beneath his heel and repaired the ward. But as soon as he fixed one line, another broke. It was like plugging the cracks of a dam—soon it would explode.

Behind him, Diago began to sing, his voice gaining strength with every lyric. The sound became a hymn, a lament, a dirge, sang in a key so sharp, Rafael wondered why his father's tongue didn't bleed.

Diago sang for the child he was; he sang for the broken man he became; he sang for a hundred years of loneliness and pain; for the dark nights that left him walking . . . walking . . . walking . . . placing sigils on the doors and windows, one for the father, one for the son, and one to drive away the ghosts.

Throughout it all, Alvaro stood immobile, unmoved by the anguish in his son's song.

He's not feeding on it, Rafael suddenly realized as he repaired another line in his protective ward. Because if Alvaro drank his son's heartache, then he'd have to admit it was real. *He's gaslighting him*. Just one more cruel blow to add to all the others.

Diago reached into the gloom and drew out a black shadow, forming a jagged sigil. The fire from his signet sent glittering silver edges along the borders. It was a circular saw of mourning, designed to cut to the bone. Lunging forward, he threw the blade at Alvaro's heart.

On the other side of the platform, Alvaro twirled his cane and spun a wave of darkness into a shield. Diago's glyph smashed against it, driving Alvaro three meters backward before his grief evaporated, bleeding into the tunnel's darkness.

Then Diago whirled again and kicked the floor. A final wave of fire shot from his heel and encircled them, blazing through Alvaro's scorpions, killing all but a few.

Rafael couldn't hold the protective barriers any longer. He allowed his song to fade as he stamped on the remaining arachnids squirming at his feet. When he finished, he turned to his father.

"Are you ready?" Diago croaked the question, his voice almost spent.

"Yes." The word slipped through Rafael's lips with the ease of a thousand childhood lies. He tried not to let his fear show as he faced his furious grandfather.

With a shriek of rage, Alvaro straightened and flung his cane. The stick flashed through the air and became a spear aimed at Diago's heart.

Rafael snatched a beam of electric light and shaped it into a new protective ward. Placing himself in front of his father, he crossed his arms behind the shield and stood firm.

Alvaro's spear struck the glyph. It was like being hit by a truck.

Gritting his teeth, Rafael felt himself pushed backward.

He bent his knees and dug in, but his efforts were useless. The toes of his shoes slid over the floor. Pinpoints of light skittered over the ward until cracks appeared.

I'm losing my hold on it. At least it will take me and not Papá. That is, until his father shoved him aside.

Alvaro's spear punctured the shield and rushed forward. Diago threw himself to the left. He wasn't fast enough. The spear went sideways and caught him across his chest, driving him back against the grille. His head struck the metal bars. He slumped to the foot of the stairs.

With a groan, Diago tried to stand. His hand slipped and he went down again.

Rafael exhaled with relief. *At least he's alive. He'll be okay. He's got to be okay.* He stumbled to his feet and faced his grandfather. *I just need to buy us some time.*

Alvaro lifted his hand and barked a harsh note. A glyph burst from his fingertips.

Christ, it's fast, it's coming too fast. Rafael moved his hands, but Alvaro's ward smashed against him before he could establish another barrier.

The force of the blow lifted him off his feet. His body flew backward. His back struck the tiles. For two seconds, he couldn't breathe. He gasped and air suddenly rushed into his lungs.

His hand was empty. *The shard!* As he scrambled to his knees, he searched the filthy floor. *Please don't let it be broken, please, please, please . . .*

Alvaro found it first. His lip curled into a sneer.

"That's mine!" Rafael bit his tongue before he could say more.

Alvaro brought his heel down on the glass.

Rafael didn't try to stop the anguished cry that tore from his throat. Twice now, he had lost his mother, first to the angels and now to the daimons. Tears blurred the image of Alvaro grinding the glass to dust.

"No! Stop! Stop it! Please!" He filled the station with the dark sound of his grief.

Alvaro whirled and closed the distance between them. He grabbed Rafael and slammed him against the tiles.

Grasping Rafael's neck, Alvaro lifted him until his toes barely brushed the floor. Shadows drifted over his grandfather's countenance. Shades of puce and gray leaked from the corners of his eyes. Moloch's wizened features superimposed themselves over Alvaro's face.

My grandfather isn't here anymore. Rafael fought to breathe. *This is Moloch.*

"Come back with me and willingly take your vows to become my high priest, and I'll let your father live." Moloch pressed his lips against Rafael's ear. "Or I can take you right here. Right now. The choice is yours."

Rafael could barely inhale. He pried at Moloch's fingers and kicked out. His foot found only air.

"Fine," Moloch whispered. "Open your mouth."

Rafael heard footsteps. Just as he turned his head, Diago hit them, hard. His forward motion split them apart. Rafael tumbled across the concrete and landed on his side.

Diago shoved Moloch against the wall. The daimon squirmed free.

He slammed his fist against Diago's chin, knocking him to the floor. "You're useless."

Diago struggled to his knees.

Moloch kicked him in the stomach hard enough to lift his body from the floor. "Crying, whining wretch!" With every word he delivered another blow.

He's going to kill him. Glancing in the direction of the crushed shard, Rafael caught the glimmer of light against glass.

Mamá. She's still there. A piece of her is still there. He recalled the warmth of her touch. *We've been doing this wrong.*

Papá had given him the secret. *Don't turn your heart to hate.*

They'd never defeat Moloch with their grief and fury. That was what the daimon *wanted* them to feel. He knew how to meet their angst and turn it against them.

It's love that he doesn't understand. And because of that, Moloch would be defenseless against the tenderness they felt for one another.

Carefully, so as not to attract the daimon's attention, Rafael eased himself to his knees. He closed his eyes and reached past his rage and frustration to touch his first memories.

Moloch's shouts faded until Rafael resurrected the scratch of a needle against vinyl. He remembered his mamá playing records and teaching him his first flamenco steps when he was barely able to walk. He'd stamped after her, reaching for her skirts, and she'd swept him into her arms, swinging him high to hear his delighted squeals.

And later, his father tucking him into bed at night, never objecting to Rafael praying over his mother's tear; Miquel guiding his fingers through the letters as he taught Rafael to read.

In his mind's eye, he saw Juanita patiently leading him through the design of an angelic ward; Guillermo showing him how to measure the heat of a fire in a forge; and Ysabel—who pronounced herself his big sister—giving him her toys and championing him at every turn.

Rafael drew the breath of their love up from his diaphragm and through his throat. As he did, he realized his mother's magic didn't reside in a piece of glass. *She's here, with me,* within *me—all I have to do is remember.*

He exhaled and released the love from his soul. Mist traveled through his lips and turned into a mighty golden serpent. The light within the angel's tear of his signet merged with the snake's vibrant scales. He guided the serpent into the splinter of glass.

Moloch's voice roared through the station. "We should have strangled you at birth."

Rafael swallowed hard. His throat was raw. *What if I can't reach the right pitch?*

His father's lessons came back to him in a flash. Sometimes the interpretation of the song was more important than hitting perfect notes. *It's the feeling that gives a song power.*

Rafael staggered to his feet. He hummed a broken chord. The strands of his ward responded with a shimmer of golden light.

Moloch kicked Diago again. "Don't you die, don't you dare die, because I'm dragging you back, and we're giving you the second death." Leaning forward, he spit on Diago's face.

A tear slid from Rafael's eye as he watched his father curl

into a fetal position on the filthy floor. *Oh, Papá, they don't deserve you.*

Rafael gave a wild cry. In his heart, the stars sang their lonesome song, and he caught the notes one by one. Striking his heel against the floor, he forced his love for his father into his song and found the hope that sustained him through his grief.

He channeled his will into the snake. A million glittering serpents rose from the broken mirror.

They flew like bullets at Moloch, who turned just in time to take the brunt of the spell right in the face. Wisps of smoke rose from the holes in his cheeks.

The daimon opened his mouth and shrieked.

Rafael directed the largest snake directly into Moloch's maw. The daimon's white eyes went wide. Clawing at his lips, he tried to dislodge the spell, but the serpent worked its way into his throat and ate his voice.

Golden light infiltrated the daimon's body and shot from his pores. Bright scales ripped the flesh from his hooked black bones.

Only this time, Miquel wasn't there to sweep Rafael out of danger and carry him away before his song was done. Now he had all the time he needed. He brought the full power of his aura against Alvaro and Moloch. In doing so, he sang their death.

Alvaro's body jittered to the edge of the platform and fell, breaking the link to Rafael's song.

The quiet descended hard and fast.

Too quick. Is it a trick? Rafael cautiously advanced to the ledge and looked down.

Alvaro's aura seeped through his lips in shades of green and entwined with Moloch's hues of puce and gray. The vibrations of daimon and nefil ultimately evaporated in the dank air.

"I will watch for you," Rafael rasped.

It was a promise. It was a warning.

Turning from the tracks, he staggered to his father.

Diago groaned and rolled to his back. He looked up at the ceiling. A trickle of blood oozed from the corner of his mouth.

"Papá?" Rafael knelt beside him.

"It's okay," he gasped. "I think I'm okay."

He didn't look okay. Rafael daubed at the blood. "I don't like this. You could have an internal injury."

His father rubbed his jaw. "It's all right. I lost a tooth. Maybe two. That's where the blood is coming from. Help me." He held out his hand and Rafael hauled him to his feet. Diago paused and leaned against the wall. "That might have been too fast." He scanned the platform. "Where's Alvaro?"

Rafael licked his lips. *How am I going to tell him I killed his father?* "He fell."

"Is he unconscious?"

"He's not going to bother us anymore."

Diago gave the platform a confused look. "What?"

Rafael guided him to the ledge and showed him the body. "I'm sorry, Papá." But in his heart, he wasn't sorry—he would never be sorry that Alvaro was gone.

Diago said nothing. He stared at his father's body and leaned on his son.

The moment stretched out for what seemed like forever.

Then Diago's arm tightened around Rafael's shoulders. "I loved him when I was young."

"And now?"

"Regret. But no grief." He sighed. "He killed my love for him so long ago . . ." He took another moment to gather himself. "You're not to feel guilty. He gave you no choice. Do you understand?"

Rafael exhaled with relief, not realizing until then how much he craved his father's absolution. "I thought only a king or queen of the Inner Guard could kill a daimon."

"Alvaro wasn't daimon. He was a nefil possessed by the spirit of a daimon. When your song shredded Moloch's flesh in that sewer in Barcelona, you left his spirit . . . homeless, and Alvaro let him in."

His father swallowed hard and nodded at the corpse. "I don't think I can get down there and come back up. On his finger is a ring. Can you get it?"

"Sure." He descended to the tracks and retrieved Alvaro's signet. The stone had turned a milky white.

Rafael climbed back to the platform. "What are you going to do with it?"

"Nothing. *You're* going to give it to Guillermo as proof of Alvaro's death." He squeezed Rafael's shoulder. "Let's get out of here."

They walked back to the grille. Alvaro's spell barring the gate had disappeared at his death. His walking stick lay on the steps. Diago kicked it out of their way.

As they climbed back to the street, Rafael asked, "How did you know I was down here with him?"

"Your grandfather left a trail of scorpions for his nefilim to follow."

Rafael took the brunt of his father's weight. "Why didn't they come?"

"They had other worries." A weary smile creased his lips. "Let's go back to the café. I'm hungry."

Rafael didn't bother to ask if it was safe. His father never willingly led him into danger. Besides, he wanted to see if Nico had made it. And Miquel.

He wanted his family.

His real family.

[31]

THE THEATER OF DREAMS

Diago's body began to mend as they walked back to the Theater of Dreams. Though he was sore and exhausted, he didn't think anything was broken. With time, he would heal; he might begin to feel more like himself. *Physically, anyway.*

Emotionally, he wasn't so sure. None of this had turned out like he'd planned. Rafael was supposed to grow up safe in Santuari, not be forced to commit parricide. He'd wanted his son to learn the art of dance, not the art of war.

Though he seems to be suited to it. While it wasn't a thought that made him happy, Diago was determined to support his son however he could.

They left the alley and Rafael finally spoke. "I don't understand something."

"Just one thing? And so young . . ."

"Papá . . ."

"What don't you understand?"

"How—with him as a parent—did you become such a good father?"

"Well." Diago swallowed past the lump in his throat. "In every situation, I always tried to think of what my father would do, and then I did the exact opposite."

Rafael chuckled. "That's a good philosophy."

"I think so."

It took them a half hour to return to the rue de la Ville Neuve. By the time they arrived, uniformed members of Los Nefilim and Les Néphilim had established cordons around the theater.

Three staff cars were parked on the street. Diago searched the nefilim for Ysabel but didn't see her. *Please let her be safe.*

Miquel squatted beside the rear passenger door of one of the cars, speaking earnestly to the occupant. As Diago drew closer, he saw it was Nico in the backseat.

The Italian sat quietly, picking at the metal bracelet he wore on his wrist. Someone had found a heavy coat and decent shoes for him.

Miquel reassured Nico. "Bernardo is going to take you to l'Entreprenante. Right now I want you to rest. I know it's hard, but try and relax. Okay?"

"Sure."

"You did a good job, Nico. We're going to take care of you." Miquel closed the door and patted the roof.

Bernardo pulled away and Miquel finally saw them. "Hey, what the hell happened?"

Diago answered the question with a question. "That's Guillermo's car. Where's Ysabel?"

He treated Diago to a grin. "Right behind you."

Diago and Rafael whirled together.

Ysabel strode just ahead of her father and Heines. Like them, she'd taken a few knocks, but otherwise she seemed fine. Her eyes lit up and she managed to embrace them both simultaneously. "We were so worried." Pulling back, she examined their faces. "Are you all right?"

"We're fine," Rafael answered. "How about you?"

"We're okay."

Guillermo reached them. "We have a problem. Nico says the psalm is hidden beneath the dark sounds of Strzyga's painting. Christina is on the stage with the portrait and Edur's body."

Rafael stared at Guillermo. "He's dead? I didn't mean to kill him."

Guillermo lifted his hand for silence. "No one is blaming you."

Except Christina. Diago held his tongue. He couldn't wrap his son in gauze and forever protect him from the daimonborn. *And given what I just witnessed, she is in more danger from him.*

Guillermo didn't notice Diago's distraction. "She is threatening to self-immolate and burn this whole block. We need that psalm. More importantly, we've got to get her out of there without setting the theater on fire. If this building goes, the mortals might not be able to contain the blaze. They're stretched thin, too. We're trying to clear the surrounding streets, but it's taking too much time. Diago? Can you talk her down?"

Diago held out his hand. "Give me Alvaro's ring."

Rafael placed the signet in his hand. "She's ambitious."

Diago made a low sound in the back of his throat that sounded like a growl. "Any other daimon-born nefilim in there with her?"

Guillermo shook his head. "We've accounted for all of them."

"Sigils?"

"None in the main auditorium. The balconies are warded."

"That means no sharpshooter."

"There's been enough killing."

Spoken like a king. Diago sighed, "Give me twenty minutes."

Guillermo clapped his shoulder. "I'm going in with you. I'll be out of sight in the lobby and so will Ysa."

Ysa? Why Ysa? When he raised his eyebrow, she lifted her hand so he could see Die Nephilim's signet on her finger.

Dumbfounded, Diago could only stammer. "How—?"

"Later." Guillermo cut off the question.

"I'm coming, too," Rafael said. "Out of sight. With them."

Guillermo pointed to Miquel and Heines. "See what you can do to clear the area in case we fail."

Miquel nodded and set off with Heines.

Diago didn't waste any time. He entered the theater and went straight to the auditorium, while the others fanned out behind him.

The doors were open. Christina sat at a grand piano, her hands in her lap. She wore a silk evening gown, looking like a concert pianist awaiting her opening cue.

Edur's body lay on the stage just in front of the portrait. His hands were folded neatly over his chest. Ruby cuff links glittered at his sleeves.

Diago rapped his knuckles against the door. "Christina. What are you doing?"

She turned her head in the direction of his voice. "If you're here, then Alvaro is dead."

"Probably not for long." He held up the signet. "And Moloch will eventually return, as well. He'll require a high priestess. That's why you need to take this. Now."

For the first time since he'd entered, she seemed to actually see him. Or maybe it was the glitter of the ring.

Her command was delivered with the imperiousness of a queen. "Approach."

Strolling toward the stage, he outlined his proposal. "By birthright, dominion over the Scorpion Court is mine, or my son's. I give it to you freely and unconditionally. If you're smart, and I know you are, you'll quickly consolidate your court."

She lifted her hands over the keyboard as if she intended to play the chord that would send her into her next incarnation. "This is a trick."

"No trick. Or it is, but not against you. It's entirely from self-interest. Take the ring, keep it from my father's hand for this incarnation and all others. Break his hold over the Scorpion Court and lead the daimon-born into a new century." He reached the foot of the stage and offered her the signet. "The old ways are dying. Let them go. When I look to the future, I see you, Christina."

Still in midair, her fingers twitched over the keys. "My Edur is dead."

"He died trying to help you achieve your dream. Would you have his sacrifice be in vain?" Diago turned the ring so that the stone gleamed beneath the house lights. "He will come again. Be ready to receive him, as high priestess of the Scorpion Court."

Her hands didn't move, but Diago sensed a shift in her demeanor. Her shoulders relaxed and the muscles in her neck seemed less tense.

Christina Banderas wanted many things, but Diago always knew she never wanted to die. Still, this was her grand finale, so he didn't rush the moment.

She met his gaze. "Freely and unconditionally?"

"Freely and unconditionally."

As her fingers hovered over the lower notes, she murmured, "I want to speak to Guillermo."

"I'm here." His baritone carried over the seats to reach them.

A knowing smile quirked at her lips. "I thought you'd be eavesdropping."

Guillermo spread his hands. "You know us too well."

"There are glyphs already embedded in the painting. All I have to do is strike the right chord to set it on fire. If I turn this psalm over to you, will that enable me to negotiate good terms for my nefilim?"

"It will."

Christina held out her hand. "Diago."

He glanced at Guillermo, who nodded.

Mounting the stage, he went to her and slipped the ring onto her finger.

She gripped his wrist, and her expression turned ugly. "I'll have Rafael's head on a platter for murdering my Edur."

Diago's countenance showed no emotion, but his heart

twisted. *Had I really expected her to do anything different?* Christina was daimon-born to her rotten soul.

Diago leaned close and whispered in her ear. "We will watch for you."

It was a promise.

It was a threat.

[32]

CHÂTEAU DE L'ENTREPRENANTE
FONTAINEBLEAU

The large conference room was full by the time Diago got there. Ysabel, Juanita, and Guillermo conferred with Miquel and Heines in one corner. Rafael and Violeta were engaged with a stern woman in a sergeant's uniform, who looked up when he crossed the threshold.

Esser . . . Sergeant Esser is her name. Diago nodded to her as he entered.

She returned his silent greeting with a bow of her head.

Ysabel noticed him and quickly wrapped up her conversation with the others. "Okay, we're ready to get started. Please take your places." She indicated the table. When they were seated, she turned to her right. "Field Marshal Heines, we'll begin with you. Progress report?"

"I have instructed our nefilim to begin disabling the protective sigils that line the beaches of the Atlantic Wall.

Unfortunately, it's a massive project, and we've lost an enormous number of nefilim to the war."

Guillermo spoke up. "Can the members of Los Nefilim help?

Heines shook his head. "The wards are keyed to the vocal ranges of specific nefilim, not all of whom are completely comfortable with the shift in leadership." He gave Ysa an uneasy glance.

Rather than be perturbed by the statement, Ysa elaborated. "We have members of Die Nephilim who question my legitimacy as queen. Some of them seem to have been quite in line with Jordi Abelló's vision for the Reich.

"Currently—because as Heines pointed out, we've lost so many nefilim—we're attempting to bring our more reluctant members on board; however, it's been difficult. Some will have to stand trial for war crimes. Others have promised allegiance only after the Thrones provide me with a Messenger." She exhaled and touched the heavy signet on her finger. "It's a delicate situation right now."

Heines agreed with her assessment. "So we need to prepare ourselves, and the Allies, for the reality that Die Nephilim's wards may not be entirely disabled by the time they begin their invasion. We're gathering coordinates on the locations of specific wards to pass along to the Allied nefilim."

Diago felt his breakfast lurch in his stomach. That wasn't the news he'd hoped to hear. Because if Heines couldn't disable all of Die Nephilim's wards, that meant Guillermo would still need the psalm.

As if she sensed his uneasiness, Ysa turned her attention to him next. "Diago, what do you have for us?"

"Nothing good, I'm afraid." He glanced at his son.

Rafael rose and distributed the photographs they'd taken of the damaged psalm. Due to their ability to manipulate the dark sounds, he and Rafael had been working to remove the psalm from Strzyga's painting. But it was painstaking—and, as with any restoration, there were gaps.

Diago cleared his throat. "Rafael and I managed to extract what was left of the psalm from the portrait. Unfortunately, Strzyga damaged portions of the page."

Guillermo chewed his cigar and muttered, "Damaged them how?"

"He used the dark sounds to tear the parchment into strips."

Rafael resumed his seat. "And then the strips into fragments. It was a continual process."

Diago clarified. "The dark sounds were essentially breaking the document apart, like dropping a piece of paper into water."

"Or chewing it," Rafael said. "Definitely like chewing it to bits."

Diago conceded the analogy with a tilt of his head. "That's a more accurate description of what we're dealing with. Guillermo's protective wards are the only reason fragments have survived at all."

Miquel lit a cigarette. "So we've still got Die Nephilim's protective wards to deal with and we've lost the psalm."

Diago tapped the glossy photo with one finger. "We haven't entirely lost the psalm. It's just a delicate process. But we can recover it. Over time."

Juanita pushed the photograph aside. "How much time?"

"With no distractions? A year? Maybe two?"

Violeta leaned forward. "But we have the other four pieces of the song. Surely we can rewrite the last part?"

Guillermo smiled sadly. "It wasn't the last part of the song; it was the most critical section of the spell. That's why it was in Sainte-Geneviève. The psalm outlined complex sigils and the coordinates necessary to make them work."

Miquel took an angry draw from his cigarette. "Christ, Alvaro and Jordi reach from the grave to throttle us."

Beneath the table, Diago touched his husband's thigh. "Will the Allies stop the invasion?"

"No." Guillermo shook his head. "We're getting those mortals across that channel if I have to ferry them on my back one by one."

Ysabel smiled wearily as if she had heard that vow before. "Let's hope it doesn't come to that." She nodded to Violeta, who stood and retrieved a map. Ysabel spread it on the table. "The Germans are convinced that the Allies will try to gain land at Pas-de-Calais. We're doing everything we can through Die Nephilim's resources to reinforce that idea. We've also spread additional disinformation that the attack will come via the Strait of Dover. And another round of deception indicates the Allies will proceed through Norway."

Guillermo glared at the map. "But the matter remains that we need to bring them around Die Nephilim's protective wards in Normandy."

Diago caught Rafael's eye and nodded.

His son took his cue. "Papá and I have been working on

the Key. We may have made a breakthrough that will allow us to utilize the song to disable Die Nephilim's wards and hide the armada from the mortals' eyes."

Guillermo stared at him. "What do you mean, *may have?*"

Diago answered. "We haven't been able test it, because the song will require many voices in order to be effective."

Juanita's eyes sparkled with angelic fires. "What was your breakthrough?"

Diago glanced around the table and decided to keep his explanation as simple as possible. "When I first arrived at the Theater of Dreams, a young cellist was attempting to play a song designed to evoke strong emotions in Nico. The cellist failed, not because he played badly, but because he couldn't feel the meaning behind the song."

Rafael grew more animated as he told of his contribution. "And in the metro, when I fought Alvaro, I realized the same thing. We've been trying to hammer out this song based on technique and style. In doing so, we neglected the most important part of music . . . our feelings. And in this particular piece we hear three primary emotions: the angels' anguish of leaving their home, which then segues to trust before the final and most important chords emerge to revolve around hope."

Diago touched his chest, leaving his finger to linger over his heart. "And we can empathize with all of those feelings. We know the sound of our own anguish, of being forced to leave our homes. We sang it in our hearts as we fled over the Pyrenees when the Nationalists drove us from Spain. But in that sorrow, we discovered the underlying harmony of trust.

We relied on one another. We held true to the principles we believed in and we unified our voices to sing as one.

"And the last part, the very final movement, is one of hope. In spite of the horrors this war has wrought, we still hope to bring peace to the mortals and to ourselves. That desire to make the world better is what drives us. And right now, what we hope is for the Allied invasion to succeed, right?

"So maybe we can divert the fleet around the worst of Die Nephilim's remaining wards while we shift the realms to hide the bulk of the ships from the mortals' view."

Guillermo studied the composition. "Like pulling a veil over the Germans' eyes."

"We're not angels, so we won't be able to sustain the illusion for long."

Juanita smiled. "Once we have the right notes, I can help sustain the ripple in time and space for a few hours."

Violeta whispered, "We just need to hold up for one night."

Guillermo flicked the lid of his lighter. "The Allies are shooting for a May invasion date. I'll give you until the end of April to make this work. That's your assignment. Pick your people."

Diago turned to Juanita. "Guillermo gave Nico the code name Nightingale because of the beauty of his voice. Do you think he'll be well enough to help soon?"

"He'll need another month. At least."

"Could we confer with him?"

"Just don't tire him out too much."

Diago gathered the photographs and nodded to Rafael. "We'll get started now."

Rafael collected his things. "Will you join us later, Doña Juanita?"

"I'd be honored," she said.

Diago left the room with his son at his side. A list of names rattled through his head. In their hearts, they carried the Key to the Allies' success.

[3 3]

4 June 1944

OVERLORD

Ysabel sat beside the radio with the headset on, listening to the white noise of static. The apartment she'd secured for them in Douvres placed her group of nefilim within range of the beachheads designated as Gold, Juno, and Sword by the Allies.

Her father commanded a unit stationed at Sainte-Marie-du-Mont with Rafael as their conductor. Their group was responsible for singing the Key from the beach the Allies had dubbed as Utah.

Juanita positioned herself in Saint-Laurent. From there, she would bring the nefilim's glyphs together over the Omaha beachhead.

Because Ysabel's force was the largest, Diago remained with her to conduct the nefilim when the time came. The balcony door opened and he entered.

"High seas and a heavy wind. They'll never make it

through this storm." He shook the rain from his coat and placed the binoculars on a side table.

Nico sat close to the heat and cradled a hot cup of tea. Although he'd gained some weight, he was still far from well. Even so, he'd insisted on remaining with Diago. "I'm amazed you can see anything out there."

"One of the nice things about being daimon is the excellent night vision." He turned to Ysa. "Any word?"

She shook her head. "Rousseau will give the signal when they're ready."

Nico nursed his tea. "It's the perfect time. Wehrmacht commanders are at the war games in Rennes, Rommel has gone to Hitler to beg for more tanks . . . the Nazis are ripe for the taking. I hope the Allies don't delay."

The radio clicked in her ear. Ysa hissed for quiet. She jotted down the message and looked up. "Not tomorrow. They're pulling out because of the storm. However, the weather is predicted to improve, and they've rescheduled the landing for six June." She took off the headset.

Diago made himself a cup of tea. "We've got the fifth column in place. The guns are in the church's cellar."

Ysabel rubbed her tired eyes. "Will you need to rehearse the chorus tomorrow?"

Diago had been relentless about training the nefilim to carry the right notes. With his ability to feed on their emotions, he instinctively knew if they faltered in their interpretation of the Key. That very skill was why he and Rafael were chosen to conduct the singers.

Diago didn't open his eyes. "Tomorrow we rest. We save our voices for the sixth."

Ysa held her notes over a trash can and set the paper on

fire. The flames curled the page, turning it to ashes. "I'm scared, Diago."

"Open your heart. The Thrones will lead you."

Releasing the last of the paper, she looked down at the ring on her hand and rubbed her finger over the stone. She hoped he was right.

At 2300, 5 June 1944, fifteen nefilim gathered in a chapel on the outskirts of Douvres. The low clouds carried the growls of approaching planes overland.

Diago held the choir silent for another forty minutes. At 2345, Ysabel gave him the sign to begin.

"Remember," he whispered to the nefilim, "follow Nico's lead. From the heart." Lifting his baton, he guided them into the first anguished notes of the Key.

Ysa formed the sigils and channeled the nefilim's voices into the wards she drew in the dust. The Thrones' tear on her ring flamed to life in the darkness, leaving no doubt that she was the rightful leader of Die Nephilim.

The soft golden vibrations poured through the church and out into a drain. Invisible to the mortals, the resonance of their song found its way into the sea.

The music of their voices fell with the hush of stars falling. Then the colors shifted. Diago was the first to notice. The world around them became clearer, more vibrant. Shades of gray lightened to white, and black to gray.

Everything grew still, like the world held its breath.

The city and the beaches all remained in the mortal realm, but a line of light stretched from the church into the gutter and then to the sea. And while the rest of the world remained in darkness, the realms shifted and the incoming ships rode from England to Normandy on celestial tides.

The nefilim sang all through the night while Ysa cast sigil after sigil into the sea. The nefilim's emotions washed over Diago as he conducted them toward hope, and when the song ended, they began again.

And again.

And again.

And again.

By 0800, the thunder of artillery provided the bass.

INNER GUARD DIVISION: DIE NEPHILIM
Ysabel Ramírez, Generalfeldmarschall
Abwehr Der Wehrmacht
9 May 1945
Abwehr Report No. 18201

To the Honorable Don Guillermo Ramírez,
Capitán General, Los Nefilim:

General Jodl and Admiral Dönitz capitulated
to General Eisenhower's terms at Reims on
7 May. Germany has officially surrendered.
Though the war is over, our biggest work
remains before us. I confer daily with
Madame Rousseau and our Allied counterparts
in an effort to bring healing to the
mortals. Unfortunately, the devastation is
immense.

But you know these things.

I understand that you intend to move Los
Nefilim's base of operations back into Spain.
To that end, we have intelligence that
indicates Jordi Abelló's lieutenant, Benito
Espina, has fled. We have agents who have
confirmed he is in Argentina. Whether he has
absconded with other nefilim tied to Abelló's
regime, we don't know.

Regardless, we will watch for them.

In another matter, Capitán Violeta Gebara
has requested to transfer to Die Nephilim.
If you can spare her, I would gratefully
take her into our ranks.

Kiss Mamá for me, and please convey my love
to Diago, Miquel, and Rafael. I miss them
all, but especially my dark rose.

At the first opportunity, I intend to visit
home.

                                   Watch for me.

[3 5]

7 July 1945

BARCELONA

Diago sat at the café's rear table, his back against the wall. Old habits died hard, which was probably a good thing. Franco's regime was everything Hitler had wanted. Unlike the Führer, Franco was firmly established here in Spain.

Sipping his hot chocolate, Diago opened the newspaper he'd purchased on the street. The headline sent a shiver through him. The United States had dropped an atomic bomb on Japan. As he read the article, he realized that both Nagasaki and Hiroshima had been attacked with the same weapon.

In what now felt like another lifetime, the angels had made a deal with the devil, and this was the destruction Moloch had wrought. He'd used his daimonic skills to create the blueprint for the Americans' atom bomb.

This is the death Moloch exchanged for the birth of my son. Diago closed the newspaper. He didn't want to read any more.

The café door opened and Guillermo entered. Diago lifted his hand, and his old friend joined him.

Guillermo glanced at the paper. "So you've seen."

"I remember the angel Prieto said the bomb would end the war. He was wrong."

"He was right. The Japanese refused to surrender. From the communiqués I had with the Americans, they felt they had no choice. The war was only going to end when one side or the other was beaten into submission."

Diago shuddered. "So many lives lost . . . and for what? Pride?"

Before Guillermo could answer, the waiter came to take his order.

Diago handed the newspaper to the man. "Get rid of that for me, would you?"

"Of course, sir."

Guillermo waited until the server returned with a cup of coffee before he spoke again. "Suero found the papers for our property at Santuari. He's getting them transferred into my name."

"We're going to rebuild?"

Guillermo drew a cigar from his pocket and lit it. "Damn right we are." He enjoyed his coffee and smoked. "I suppose you know, Miquel has asked Nico to be his secretary."

"Oh yes, that was discussed. What did Nico say?"

"Nico very graciously turned him down. He wants to be Los Nefilim's archivist."

"I think that would be a good job for him. Miquel needs someone who can put up with his more aggressive moods and bite back when necessary. Nico is still healing."

"Miquel is, too." Guillermo reached into his pocket

and placed Miquel's scarred wedding band on the table. "Jordi was wearing it when he died. Ysabel said he deliberately scarred the sigils, hoping to cause a rift between you. I didn't know what to do with it. I wanted to give it to Miquel, but I wasn't sure that was a good idea, so . . ." He shrugged.

Diago palmed the ring off the table and put it in his pocket. "You did right." Miquel didn't need the ring, or the pain of the memories. *Let some distance get between us and the war.*

Except Spain was still bleeding from its own wounds and probably would be for some time. He saw the fear in the mortals' eyes, the arrogance of Franco's police. To the outside world, the country might seem to be healing, but they didn't see the overflowing prisons, or hear the gunshots in the night.

Diago kept his voice low. "We're stuck with Franco, aren't we?"

"For a while," Guillermo admitted. "We're going to begin immediate infiltration. In two weeks, Miquel is joining the Barcelona police force as a new inspector from Madrid. Due to Franco's policies toward . . ."

It was apparent he didn't want to say *homosexuals* in the crowded café where a mortal might overhear, so Diago filled in the blank for him. "People like us."

"Precisely. Once we've rebuilt the main compound at Santuari, your family will be the first to move in along with Juanita and me. Until then, I hope you'll be okay staying in the city."

"The city is fine. We know how to keep a low profile. Miquel is posing as my brother-in-law, who is staying with us while he gets on his feet. Because of the war, people don't ask too many questions nowadays."

"He said it was in a nice place."

"After so many years of deprivation, I wanted us to have a few luxuries." For once, Diago had insisted on renting an apartment in one of the more expensive buildings. It wasn't La Pedrera, but his small family had all the modern conveniences along with an attic loft, which Rafael used as an art studio.

Guillermo withdrew a bankbook from his breast pocket. "Now for some good news. I received confirmation from the Inner Guard's main tribunal: your beautiful cousin and her Scorpion Court have been heavily fined and now they'll be exiled to Argentina. It was the only country that would take them."

"How marvelous. An entire ocean between us, and South America has a brand-new species of parasitoid wasp. She's probably already laying insidious little eggs in the populace."

Guillermo winced. "When you put it like that, I doubt the wisdom of the Inner Guard's tribunal."

"Don't. It doesn't matter where you send her, she'll create havoc. At least with Christina, we're dealing with a known factor."

"This is true." Guillermo placed his cigar on the ashtray. "The other part of the court's punishment included the forfeiture of their Spanish properties. These were liquidated. A cut of that money goes to get Los Nefilim back on its feet. The rest . . ." He pushed the bankbook across the table. "I know the money can't fully compensate you for what you've been through, but I think you should have it. It'll give you some breathing room."

Diago opened the booklet and looked at the figure. He gave a low whistle. "Guillermo, I . . ."

"It's okay. It's yours. Buy yourself something nice . . . like a mansion, or an island."

He could just about afford both, given the amount. Tucking the bankbook into his breast pocket, he bowed his head. "Thank you. So. What about me? What am I to do for Los Nefilim in this new Spain?"

"I'm glad you asked." Guillermo rescued his cigar from the ashtray and relit it. "Now that the dust has settled a bit, I'd like for you to go back to work on the psalm for me. See if we can reconstruct it. If, um, Rafael would like to stay around, then I'd love to have him on the project, too."

"We're riding out to Santuari this afternoon."

"You won't find anything but rubble."

"Still, he wants to visit it again." Whether to say hello, or goodbye, Diago didn't know. "I'll broach the subject with him and let you know what he says."

"Of course you know, as things come up, I'll eventually need you both back in the field, but for now"—he looked around the café—"let's just get acclimated."

"That sounds good. Real good." He lifted his cup and Guillermo raised his.

Two hours later, Diago drove Rafael to what was left of Santuari. Nothing but stone and the vague outlines of buildings remained. A crater occupied the area where Guillermo's great house once stood on the hill.

Diago found three of the walls of their own little house. The roof was gone and the kitchen obliterated. A rosebush struggled for life among the bricks.

Rafael walked through the debris until he stood in the area that used to be his room. He kicked aside a few stones. Kneeling, he dug through the debris to extract a tin that once held watercolors. He smiled and held it up for Diago to see. "I remember when you bought me this. It was when you came home from Germany, after you found your violin. Do you remember?"

Diago returned his son's smile and nodded. "I do."

Rafael dropped the tin and dusted his hands. "I remember I had a kitten. I named her Ghost." His smiled faded. "But we couldn't take her with us. And I cried and cried and hated myself because so many others had lost so much more."

Diago leaned against the wall that had once been their living room. "You were young. There is no shame in mourning a pet you loved."

"You gave me everything I wanted, and then we lost it all. And now I look at all this, and I realize the most precious things you've given me are those that I carry in my heart."

Diago bowed his head so that his son wouldn't see the tears in his eyes.

Rafael sighed and stood again, brushing his palms against his thighs. "Guillermo is going to rebuild it?"

Diago picked a blade of grass and spun it through his fingers. "He is. That's what I wanted to talk to you about. I, um, have some money now. Quite a bit. And if you would like to go to university somewhere . . ." He shrugged. "Anywhere. Tell me and we can send you."

"Do you want me to go away?"

Careful, now, and don't influence his decision. This has

to be his choice. "I want you to be happy. I mean, Ysabel is off on her own in Germany. I thought maybe you might like to travel, or . . ."

"Go to university?"

Diago smiled. "Whatever."

"What if I want to stay with Los Nefilim? Here in Spain?" A note of defiance seeped into his voice as if he thought Diago might argue against the decision. "What if I want to come back to Santuari with you and Miquel but in my own house? What if I wanted to do that?"

"Then I will support your decision."

"Would Guillermo have a job for me?"

"He's already asked me to see if you would like to continue reconstructing the psalm with me. I could certainly use your help. And, of course, as other assignments arise, we could both be called back into the field."

Rafael stared into the distance. "I'm not ready to leave."

"That's okay."

"Maybe someday I'll want to travel, but not today." He picked his way back to Diago. "Today, I want to be with my family. Let's go home."

Diago put his arm around his son and together they walked toward the car. They passed the foundation of the old barn, and as they did, they heard a kitten cry.

Father and son froze. Rafael was the first to move. He went to a pile of brush and moved it aside. The odd-eyed kitten was about six weeks old and almost starved. They saw no sign of the mother or any littermates.

Cleaned up, she would definitely be white.

Diago expected her to be feral, but she walked right up to

Rafael and brushed against his leg. She cried until he picked her up and cuddled her against his chest.

"Well," Diago murmured. "It looks like Ghost came back."

Rafael tucked the kitten into his shirt. "I'm not going to call her Ghost. I don't want her to disappear again."

"Neither do I." With a smile, Diago retrieved the keys to his car.

Later that night, Miquel was already in bed, reading a new romance novel. He looked up when Diago came into the bedroom. "I've got two weeks off." Closing the book, he placed it on his nightstand. "Where would you like to go?"

"I don't know." Diago took the bankbook from his pocket and tossed it on the bed. "Where do you want to go?"

"What's this?"

"My cut of Christina's properties."

Miquel looked at the figure and whistled. "Let's go someplace fancy."

Diago laughed. "Someplace with wine."

"Hell, let's buy a vineyard." Miquel closed the book and gave it back to Diago. "We'll sleep in tomorrow and then talk about it." He rolled out of bed and went to the bedroom door. "I'm getting a nightcap. Want one?"

"Sure." Diago waited until he was gone, and then he reached into his pocket and closed his fingers around Miquel's old wedding band. He considered giving it to his husband and almost immediately discounted the idea.

The past is dead. It's time to put it in its grave. They could visit the tomb anytime. *But not today.*

He opened a small box and placed the scarred ring inside.

Pushing it deep into a drawer, Diago moved his shirts to hide it away.

This wasn't the time to look back. They needed to look forward. The Inner Guard had work to do, and maybe, if they were persistent, they might bring healing to the world instead of pain.

He could only hope.

ACKNOWLEDGMENTS

Special thanks always go first and foremost to my family, especially to my husband, Dick, who does so many things to make sure I have time to write.

For my fabulous first readers: Rhi Hopkins, Glinda Harrison, and Karla Moon. To Ollivier Robert for helping me navigate the Paris metro and for sending me links to French resources I wouldn't otherwise have been able to locate on my own. Thanks also go to Ulff Lehmann for assistance with German translations.

I am exceptionally grateful to the United States Holocaust Memorial Museum for the information they maintain on their website and to the Auschwitz-Birkenau State Museum for their Twitter feed @AuschwitzMuseum. A very special thanks to the Mauthausen Memorial for answering my questions related to Spanish Republicans interned at Mauthausen during World War II.

If I made any mistakes in the facts, they are mine and certainly not theirs.

To the Extraordinary Fellows of Arcane Sorcery: You know who you are. You're a magnificent lot, and I'm proud to say I've been a part of your group.

To Lisa Rodgers, who always has my back and whose mad editing skills help me to be a better writer. And especially to David Pomerico and the team at Harper Voyager, who believed in this series and made it happen.

My deepest gratitude goes to my readers. This book couldn't have happened without you and your support. Thank you for giving this story your time. I hope you enjoyed it.

Watch for me . . .

GLOSSARY

ANGELS Creatures from another dimension that invaded the antediluvian earthly realm. They warred with the daimons for control of the mortals. The angels caused the Great Flood in order to force the daimons to capitulate to their demands. Rather than watch the mortals destroyed, the daimons surrendered. While no daimonic uprising has occurred in centuries, the angels sometimes engage in civil wars. These conflicts often bleed down into the mortal realm.

ANGEL-BORN NEFILIM (OFTEN SHORTENED TO ANGEL-BORN) Nefilim who can claim direct lineage to an angelic ancestor.

DAIMONS The old earth gods who resided in the mortal realm before the invasion of the angelic hordes. Most have retreated to homes deep beneath the earth and have removed themselves from mortal affairs. Others, like Diago's grandfather, Moloch, work toward reasserting themselves and their presence in the mortal world.

DAIMON-BORN NEFILIM (OFTEN SHORTENED TO DAIMON-BORN) Nefilim who claim direct lineage to a daimonic ancestor.

DIE NEPHILIM The German Inner Guard, led by Ilsa Jaeger. Her second-in-command is Erich Heines.

FALLEN The Fallen are angels who have been cast out of the angelic ranks and forced to live in the mortal realm.

GRIGORI Also known as the Watchers. A group of angels that committed vile crimes against the mortals. The Grigori were cast out of the angelic realms. Their wings were torn from their bodies and they were buried deep beneath the stones of the earth, where they live in eternal torment.

IL NEPHILIM The Italian Inner Guard, led by Matteo de Luca. His second-in-command is Chiara Ricci.

INNER GUARD The Inner Guard functions much like a central intelligence agency for the angels. The Inner Guard is comprised of angel-born nefilim that monitor daimonic activity for the angels. Each mortal country has a division of nefilim to serve in this capacity. During times of war, they often fight alongside mortals.

LES NÉPHILIM The French Inner Guard, led by Sabine Rousseau. Her second-in-command is Jean Marchand.

LOS NEFILIM The Spanish Inner Guard, led by Guillermo Ramírez. His second-in-command is Miquel de Torrellas.

MESSENGERS (ALSO KNOWN AS MALAKIM) These angels are the closest in form to the mortals, and because of this, they serve as messengers between the Thrones and the nefilim. They also mate with both the mortals and the nefilim in carefully orchestrated breeding plans designed to produce powerful nefilim.

NEFILIM/NEPHILIM The nefilim are often distinguished as either angel- or daimon-born. All nefilim reincarnate and retain memories of their past lives, with their firstborn and current lives being the most important.

OPHANIM An angelic species, the Ophanim have thousands of eyes and are the lords of fire that float just beyond the river of fire's shore. Shaped like blazing wheels, they spin in place and maintain the complex glyphs that are portals from one dimension to another.

PORTAL REALMS Unlike angelic realms, which create pathways to completely separate dimensions, portal realms remain just under the veneer of the mortal realm, like a body beneath a blanket. Such realms are often used by nefilim as bunkers or covert black sites, but they are extremely difficult to maintain.

PRINCIPALITIES Angels that rule over specific countries in the earthly realm. The kings and queens of the Inner Guard report to their respective Principality through the Messenger angel assigned to their division.

ROGUES Nefilim who do not join the Inner Guard are known as rogues. Rogues move independently among the mortals. While they lack the networks and structure that enable the Inner Guard to move freely during mortal wars, rogues have been known to organize to protect their own interests. They have their own set of arcane codes and rituals, which dictates their behavior among both the mortals and other nefilim.

THRONES Probably the closest thing that stands as a collective godhead to the nefilim. The Thrones are fiery angels that are never seen in the mortal realm.

SOURCEBOOKS AND INSPIRATIONS

Where Oblivion Lives

Andalusian Poems translated by Christopher Middleton and Leticia Garza-Falcon.

The Battle for Spain: The Spanish Civil War, 1936–1939 by Antony Beevor.

The Battlefields of the First World War: The Unseen Panoramas of the Western Front by Peter Barton.

The Dictionary of Homophobia: A Global History of Gay & Lesbian Experience edited by Louis-Georges Tin, translated by Marek Redburn.

The Evolution of Hitler's Germany by Horst von Maltitz.

Hitler: Ascent, 1889–1939 by Volker Ullrich.

The Legends of the Jews vols. 1–7 by Louis Ginzberg.

Los Invisibles: A History of Male Homosexuality in Spain, 1850–1939 by Richard Cleminson.

The Occult Roots of Nazism: Secret Aryan Cults and Their Influence on Nazi Ideology by Nicholas Goodrick-Clarke.

Shadow and Evil in Fairy Tales (rev. ed.) by Marie-Louise von Franz.

The Somme: Heroism and Horror in the First World War by Martin Gilbert.

The Spanish Labyrinth: An Account of the Social and Political Background of the Spanish Civil War by Gerald Brenan.

They Thought They Were Free: The Germans, 1933–45 by Milton Mayer.

Carved from Stone and Dream

The Battle for Spain: The Spanish Civil War, 1936–1939 by Antony Beevor.

Dark Mirrors: Azazel and Satanael in Early Jewish Demonology
by Andrei Orlov.

Blitzed: Drugs in the Third Reich by Norman Ohler.

The Legends of the Jews vols. 1–7 by Louis Ginzberg.

No Pasarán!: Writings from the Spanish Civil War edited by
Pete Ayrton.

*The Routes to Exile: France and the Spanish Civil War Refugees,
1939–2009* by Scott Soo.

*Sacred Space, Sacred Sound: The Acoustic Mysteries of Holy
Places* by Susan Elizabeth Hale.

The Spanish Civil War: Reaction, Revolution, Revenge by Paul
Preston.

*The Spanish Holocaust: Inquisition and Extermination in
Twentieth-Century Spain* by Paul Preston.

A Song with Teeth

*Code Name: Lise: The True Story of the Woman Who Became
WWII's Most Highly Decorated Spy* by Larry Loftis.

*D-Day Girls: The Spies Who Armed the Resistance, Sabotaged
the Nazis, and Helped Win World War II* by Sarah Rose.

D-Day: The First 24 Hours by Will Fowler.

D-Day, June 6, 1944: The Normandy Landings by Richard
Collier.

*The Holocaust: A History of the Jews of Europe During the
Second World War* by Martin Gilbert.

The Holocaust: A New History by Laurence Rees.

I, Pierre Seel, Deported Homosexual: A Memoir of Nazi Terror
by Pierre Seel.

An Iron Wind: Europe Under Hitler by Peter Fritzsche.

K. L. Reich by Joaquim Amat-Piniella, translated by Robert
Finley and Marta Marín-Dòmine.

The Last Days of Hitler by H. R. Trevor-Roper.

The Pink Triangle: The Nazi War Against Homosexuals by Richard Plant.

The Politics of Music in the Third Reich by Michael Meyer.

Spaniards in Mauthausen: Representations of a Nazi Concentration Camp, 1940–2015 by Sara J. Brenneis.

Spaniards in the Holocaust: Mauthausen, the Horror on the Danube by David Wingeate Pike.

They Fought Alone: The True Story of the Starr Brothers, British Secret Agents in Nazi-Occupied France by Charles Glass.

When Paris Went Dark: The City of Light Under German Occupation, 1940–1944 by Ronald Rosbottom.

ABOUT THE AUTHOR

T. Frohock has turned her love of dark fantasy and horror into tales of deliciously creepy fiction. She currently lives in North Carolina, where she has long been accused of telling stories, which is a Southern colloquialism for lying.

READ MORE FROM T. FROHOCK

Carved from Stone and Dream
In this sequel to *Where Oblivion Lives*, the first entry in the Los Nefilim series set during the Spanish Civil War, a coded notebook containing the identities of Los Nefilim's spies falls into enemy hands, and Diago is faced with an impossible choice: betray Los Nefilim or save his family.

Where Oblivion Lives
A dark, lyrical historical thriller, set in 1930s Spain and Germany, that brings to life the world of angels and demons from the novellas collected in *Los Nefilim*: Spanish Nephilim battling daimons in a supernatural war to save humankind.

Los Nefilim
Collected together for the first time, T. Frohock's three novellas—*In Midnight's Silence*, *Without Light or Guide*, and *The Second Death*—brings to life the world of Los Nefilim, Spanish Nephilim that possess the power to harness music and light in the supernatural war between the angels and daimons. In 1931, Los Nefilim's existence is shaken by the preternatural forces commanding them ... and a half-breed caught in-between.

The Second Death
The final chapter in T. Frohock's haunting and lyrical Los Nefilim novella trilogy—following *In Midnight's Silence* and *Without Light or Guide*—which bestselling author Mark Lawrence has called "a joy to read."

Without Light or Guide
The second novella in T. Frohock's Los Nefilim series—following *In Midnight's Silence*—*Without Light or Guide* continues Diago's journey through a world he was born into, yet doesn't quite understand.

In Midnight's Silence
A lyrical tale in a world of music and magic. The first novella in the Los Nefilim series — shows the lengths a man will go to save the people he loves, and the sides he'll choose when the sidelines are no longer an option.